UNEXPECTED BLESSINGS

Barbara Taylor Bradford was born in Leeds, and by the age of twenty was an editor and columnist on Fleet Street. Her first novel, *A Woman of Substance*, became an enduring bestseller and was followed by many others. *Unexpected Blessings* is her twentieth novel and another top ten bestseller. Her books have sold more than seventy million copies worldwide in more than ninety countries and forty languages. She lives in New York City with her husband, producer Robert Bradford.

Barbara Taylor Bradford

Unexpected Blessings

HarperCollins*Publishers*

This edition produced for The Book People Ltd,
Hall Wood Avenue, Haydock, St Helens WA11 9UL

HarperCollins*Publishers*
77–85 Fulham Palace Road,
Hammersmith, London W6 8JB

www.harpercollins.co.uk

This paperback edition 2005

A catalogue record for this book
is available from the British Library

ISBN 0 00 777595 4

Set in Sabon by Palimpsest Book Production Limited,
Polmont, Stirlingshire

Printed and bound in Great Britain by
Clays Ltd, St Ives plc

For my husband, Robert Bradford,
to whom I owe so much,
with all my love

THE THREE CLANS

The Hartes shown in line of descent

Emma Harte: Matriarch: Founder of the dynasty and business empire

HER CHILDREN

Edwina, Dowager Countess of Dunvale. Emma's daughter by Edwin Fairley. (Illegitimate). First born

Christopher 'Kit' Lowther. Emma's son by her first husband Joe Lowther. Second born

Robin Ainsley. Emma's son by her second husband Arthur Ainsley. Third born

Elizabeth Ainsley Deboyne. Emma's daughter by her second husband Arthur Ainsley. Robin's twin. Third born

Daisy Ainsley. Emma's daughter by Paul McGill (illegitimate). Fourth born

HER GRANDCHILDREN
Shown in line of descent

Anthony Standish, Earl of Dunvale. Son of Edwina and Jeremy Standish, Earl and Countess of Dunvale

Sarah Lowther Pascal. Daughter of Kit and June Lowther

Jonathan Ainsley. Son of Robin and Valerie Ainsley

Paula McGill Harte Amory Fairley O'Neill. Daughter of Daisy and David Amory

Philip McGill Harte Amory. Son of Daisy and David Amory. Brother of Paula

Emily Barkstone Harte. Daughter of Elizabeth Ainsley and Tony Barkstone. Half-sister of Amanda and Francesca

Amanda Linde. Daughter of Elizabeth and her second husband Derek Linde. Twin of Francesca, half-sister of Emily

Francesca Linde Weston. Daughter of Elizabeth and her second husband, Derek Linde. Twin of Amanda, half-sister of Emily

EMMA'S GREAT-GRANDCHILDREN

Tessa Fairley Longden. Daughter of Paula and Jim Fairley (Paula's first husband)

Lorne Fairley. Son of Paula and Jim Fairley. Twin of Tessa

Lord Jeremy Standish. Son of Anthony and Sally Standish, Earl and Countess of Dunvale. Brother of Giles and India

Toby Harte. Son of Emily and Winston Harte II. Brother of Gideon and Natalie

Gideon Harte. Son of Emily and Winston Harte II. Brother of Toby and Natalie

Natalie Harte. Daughter of Emily and Winston Harte II. Sister of Toby and Gideon

Hon. Giles Standish. Son of Anthony and Sally Standish, Earl and Countess of Dunvale. Brother of Jeremy and India

Lady India Standish. Daughter of Anthony Standish and Sally Harte, Earl and Countess of Dunvale. Sister of Jeremy and Giles

Patrick O'Neill. Son of Paula and Shane O'Neill. Brother of Linnet, Emsie and Desmond. (Deceased)

Linnet O'Neill. Daughter of Paula and Shane O'Neill (Paula's second husband). Half-sister of Tessa and Lorne. Sister of Emsie and Desmond

Chloe Pascal. Daughter of Sarah Lowther Pascal and Yves Pascal

Fiona McGill Amory. Daughter of Philip McGill Amory and Madelana O'Shea Amory. (Deceased)

Emsie O'Neill. Daughter of Paula and Shane O'Neill. Sister of Linnet and Desmond.

Desmond O'Neill. Son of Paula and Shane O'Neill. Brother of Linnet and Emsie.

THE HARTES CONTINUED:

Winston Harte. Emma's older brother and business partner

Randolph Harte. Son of Winston and Charlotte Harte

Winston Harte II. Son of Randolph and Georgina Harte

Sally Harte Standish, Countess of Dunvale. Daughter of Randolph and Georgina Harte. Sister of Winston Harte II and Vivienne

Vivienne Harte Leslie. Daughter of Randolph and Georgina. Sister of Winston Harte II and Sally Harte Standish

Toby Harte. Son of Winston Harte II and Emily Harte. Brother of Gideon and Natalie

Gideon Harte. Son of Winston Harte II and Emily Harte. Brother of Toby and Natalie

Natalie Harte. Daughter of Winston Harte II and Emily Harte. Sister of Toby and Gideon

Frank Harte. Emma's younger brother

Rosamunde Harte. Daughter of Frank and Natalie Harte

Simon Harte. Son of Frank and Natalie Harte. Brother of Rosamunde

THE O'NEILLS

Shane Patrick Desmond 'Blackie' O'Neill. Founding father of the dynasty and business empire

Bryan O'Neill. Son of Blackie and Laura Spencer O'Neill

Shane O'Neill. Son of Bryan and Geraldine O'Neill

Miranda O'Neill James. Daughter of Bryan and Geraldine O'Neill. Sister of Shane and Laura

Laura O'Neill Nettleton. Daughter of Bryan and Geraldine O'Neill. Sister of Shane and Miranda

Patrick O'Neill. Son of Shane and Paula O'Neill. (Deceased)

Linnet O'Neill. Daughter of Shane and Paula O'Neill. Sister of Emsie and Desmond

Emsie O'Neill. Daughter of Shane and Paula O'Neill. Sister of Desmond and Linnet

Desmond O'Neill. Son of Shane and Paula O'Neill. Brother of Linnet and Emsie

THE KALLINSKIS

David Kallinski. Founding father of the dynasty and business empire

Sir Ronald Kallinski. Son of David and Rebecca Kallinski

Michael Kallinski. Son of Ronald and Helen 'Posy' Kallinski

Mark Kallinski. Son of Ronald and Helen 'Posy' Kallinski. Brother of Michael

Julian Kallinski. Son of Michael Kallinski and his former wife, Valentine Kallinski

Arielle Kallinski. Daughter of Michael Kallinski and his former wife, Valentine Kallinski. Sister of Julian

Jessica Kallinski. Daughter of Michael Kallinski and his former wife, Valentine Kallinski. Sister of Julian and Arielle

CONTENTS

PART ONE

The Stormy Petrels
Summer 2001

The name 'petrel' is said to be a diminutive
of Peter: when feeding the bird flits and
hovers just above the water, often with feet
pattering on the surface, appearing to 'walk
on water' as St Peter did in the Bible story.
Field Guide to the BIRDS OF BRITAIN

CHAPTER ONE

Evan Hughes stood in the middle of the fashion floor of Harte's department store in London's Knightsbridge. It was seven o'clock in the morning and nothing stirred. All was silent at this hour. By eight the cleaners would be moving around this vast space, and by nine a few of the dedicated sales staff would be arriving to prepare for the store doors opening at ten. Now, though, she was totally alone.

She loved this store and this floor in particular. It was her domain. And hers alone. Last week she had been made head of fashion, a very big promotion which had thrilled her.

As Evan moved slowly across the floor, making for the new haute couture fashion displays, she couldn't help thinking about the first day she had walked into Harte's. January 2001. Eight months ago now. She had been very lucky that day. Quite by chance she had met the man of her dreams and had found the job of her dreams. She had never thought her dreams would come true that day. But they had.

Pausing for a moment, Evan glanced around, her light grey-blue eyes devouring everything: the fashion displays under bright lights, the elegance of the whole floor – such an important one in this prestigious department store, considered the greatest in the world.

Harte's of Knightsbridge had been founded by one of the most famous merchant princes ever known: Emma Harte. She had been dead now for thirty years and the store was run by Emma's granddaughter, Paula O'Neill. Paula, an elegant woman in her mid-fifties, had inherited her grandmother's great skills and brilliance as a retailer, and her two daughters Tessa and Linnet were following in her footsteps. Both of them worked at the store; Tessa was in charge of the first three floors which sold cosmetics, perfumes, leisurewear, lingerie and active sports clothes. Linnet, Tessa's half-sister, was in charge of the fashion floors and also worked with Paula on public relations.

It was Linnet O'Neill who had hired Evan to be one of her assistants, and for the first few months she had helped Linnet to put together a retrospective of fashion which had been a huge success and pulled many new customers into the store.

As a reward for all of her hard work and dedication, Linnet had given her this promotion . . . and Evan was in her element.

Evan stood in front of the couture fashion displays which had been finished late last night, looking at them for a few minutes. They were great, she decided. The display staff had done a good job with the clothes she had selected.

Turning away, she walked down the floor, making for her office. Tall, slender and dark-haired, she was good-looking, elegant. Back at her desk she glanced at the photograph of Gideon Harte . . . the man of her dreams. She had fallen in love with him, and he with her, that first day when he had bumped into her in the corridor. She had been looking for the management offices, and he had led her there, all the while firing questions at her. And it was Gideon who had told his cousin Linnet about her; Linnet had subsequently interviewed her and given her a job.

Sitting back in her chair, Evan thought about the past eight months, and all that had happened.

She had never expected to find a second family in England. Only a year ago the only family she knew were her mother and father, and her two adopted sisters who lived in Connecticut. But all that had changed because of her grandmother, Glynnis Hughes. On her deathbed her grandmother had told her to go to England to find Emma Harte, saying that Emma was the key to her future. And Evan had done exactly that, only to discover Emma was dead. But she had fallen in love with the store, and decided to get a job there.

And now here she was, working at Harte's, involved with Gideon, planning a future with him, and struggling to adapt herself to a whole new family. Because she herself was actually a Harte. It was Paula who had discovered that Evan was

5

another great-granddaughter of Emma Harte's, because Evan's grandmother Glynnis had given birth to a son fathered by one of Emma's sons. And that child was Evan's father.

They had welcomed her, treated her kindly, with enormous understanding, but at times things had been difficult for Evan. So many things to unravel, so much to accept, so many people to get to know. Sometimes it seemed endless to her, and problematical. She worried a lot, dwelled on all this for hours.

Most troubling of all was the knowledge she had about her father's biological father . . . facts she had been afraid to relay to him. Would her father Owen Hughes welcome the information? Would he really want to know that the man who had brought him up was not his father after all? She didn't know, and she continued to wrestle with these questions.

Evan knew she had to come to a decision. Her mother and father were coming to London in a week or so, to see her, spend time with her, and have a vacation.

Could she look her father in the eye and *not* tell him the truth? Could she keep it a secret? And should she? Nobody could advise her really. Gideon had told her to do what she thought best, and everyone else had been noncommittal.

The ball was back in her court.

And then there was Robin Ainsley, her new grandfather, the man who had been her grandmother's lover during the Second World War. He had been a pilot in the Royal Air Force, a Battle of Britain pilot, and her grandmother, Glynnis Jenkins then, had been a young woman from Wales who worked as Emma Harte's secretary, here in this very store.

She liked Robin; her feelings were even stronger than that. And she knew only too well that he longed to meet his son, Owen Hughes. But would her father want to meet this stranger – a stranger who was his real father? His mother's lover. *Oh God.*

Evan turned on her computer, and after a few moments started to work on it, but within an hour the troubling thoughts about Robin, Glynnis, and her father's imminent arrival began to intrude. Turning the computer off, she made a snap decision. She would take Linnet's advice and go to Yorkshire after all for a week's rest. And she would go to see Robin Ainsley, still needing to know about his relationship with her grandmother, and most of all to understand why Robin and Glynnis had never married.

'She was beautiful and glamorous: the most sexually potent woman I've ever known. But I realized we would be disastrous together in the long run. We would've ended up killing each other,' Robin Ainsley finished with a small sigh, and sat back in the wingchair, his eyes on Evan Hughes.

Evan was silent for a moment, digesting his words, and then she said slowly, 'Because you were so volatile together, is that what you mean?'

'Exactly. We never had a peaceful moment.'

'You weren't compatible?'

7

'Not in any way, except in bed. But one cannot build a lasting, lifetime relationship on sex alone.'

Evan nodded, and eyed him carefully, then confided, 'Gran was always pounding it into me that compatibility between a man and a woman was the most important thing of all. And I know for a fact that she was compatible with my grandfather, I mean Richard Hughes.'

'Please don't correct yourself, Evan,' Robin said in a quiet voice, shaking his head. 'Richard Hughes *was* your grandfather, just as he *was* your father's father. Glynnis was a wonderful young woman when I knew her, but put very simply, she wasn't suitable for me, nor I for her, not on a normal, everyday level. We were far too explosive. It was my fault as much as hers.'

'Is that why you finally broke up with her?'

'It is. At that time our dreadful quarrels were increasing, alarmingly so. Life with her was hell.'

'But she was pregnant, Robin, and you did nothing . . .' Evan's voice trailed off as she realized she might have sounded accusatory. She had not meant to place blame.

'We've already discussed this,' Robin responded patiently. 'But I shall explain one more time . . . we broke up, I started seeing Valerie Ludden. She and I were compatible, and became seriously involved. When Glynnis told me she was expecting my child, I had already made a commitment to Valerie. However, let me say this, so you truly understand. I would not have married your grandmother even if there had been no other woman in my life. We could not have led a worthwhile life and she knew that too.'

'I'm sorry, Robin, I am being a bit of a pest, aren't I?'

'That's all right,' he responded, a faint shadow touching his mouth. 'I understand your need to know everything.'

'I wonder why Glynnis wouldn't allow you to help her financially?'

'Pride, for the most part, so *I* believe.'

'She let Emma Harte come to her rescue, though.'

'She did. My mother loved Glynnis like a daughter and she knew this, and she knew how much my mother sympathized with her. When my mother was a young girl she had been in a similar predicament, pregnant by a man who wouldn't marry her, and obviously there was a great deal of empathy there.'

'Thanks for talking about this, Robin. I really needed to know exactly what went on between you and my grandmother all those years ago.'

'Sexual passion. I was also in love with her; it just wasn't enough for a steady, stable life.' He smiled at her then, his face softening with sudden tenderness, his faded blue eyes benign, loving.

Evan smiled back at him, reached out and took hold of his long, slender hand, squeezed it in hers. The two of them were seated on the large sofa in the library at Lackland Priory, Robin's house in Yorkshire, meeting for the first time in several weeks. They were glad to be together again, to have this chance to get to know each other better.

The old man and the young woman. Related by blood, but unknown to each other, total strangers, until recently. The grandfather. The granddaughter. Two people who had only just discovered the other's existence, who wanted to be friends, to understand each other, to find a certain kind of closeness, even the intimacy of family, if that was possible. The younger striving to comprehend the past and a disastrous long-ago relationship; the elder hoping that the past and his actions then would not damage him too badly in her eyes today, in the present.

The silence in this harmonious and peaceful room was broken by the sudden shrilling of the telephone, startling them both. Almost instantly the ringing stopped; the phone had been answered elsewhere in the house by a staff member.

A moment later the butler appeared in the doorway. 'Excuse me, sir, Dr Harvey's on the phone. He would like a word with you.'

'Thank you, Bolton,' Robin answered, and, excusing himself to Evan, he rose, striding over to the desk. Sitting down, he picked up the receiver. 'Good morning, James.'

Evan also rose and walked across to the French windows which opened onto the terrace of the ancient manor house. She stepped outside, closing the doors behind her, and took several deep breaths. The air was always clean and fresh up here in the Dales. It was a glorious morning in early August, the sky azure blue and without cloud: a sunny, golden day filled with pristine light, just as it had been yesterday and the day before. She had grown to love this crystalline light which she had discovered was so prevalent and unique to the north of England.

Now she sat down on the stone bench and stared out across the wide green lawns that splayed out from the house and were bordered by flower beds filled with colourful perennials. Her eyes finally came to rest on the copse of trees which stood slightly away from the house, to the right of the lawns. Beyond their opulent, leafy bowers she could see the rim of the moors, a dark smudge against the pale, blue-tinted horizon. It was such a beautiful spot, this long valley in the middle of the Dales where Lackland Priory had stood for centuries. Pennistone Royal was not far away and in the past few months she had spent a lot of time in this particular area of Yorkshire which was softer and much more lush than the surrounding higher land. Up there, on the high-flung moors, it was grim and bleak for most of the year, neither pretty nor welcoming. She knew Linnet would not agree; *she* thought the soaring fells were glorious in their stark and solitary splendour.

'I love those moors the same way Emma Harte loved them,' Linnet had once explained to her. 'My great-grandmother was a child of the moors, and she could never stay away from them for very long. I'm just like her. I *yearn* for them, as she did.'

Emma Harte.

Evan turned the name over in her mind. Dead though she had been for thirty years, Emma still lived on, her spirit and her presence almost as potent as it had been when she was alive. Emma Harte was *her* great-grandmother, too, although she had not known this when she had come to England in January. Just eight months ago now; how her life had changed since then. *She* was a Harte. And had been accepted by this unique family, made to feel one of them. She was still trying to come to grips with recent developments.

Almost immediately her thoughts swung to Robin Ainsley, favourite son of the legendary Emma: her father's biological father, her biological grandfather; a man she had met only a few weeks ago, but whom she had quickly grown to like and knew she could easily come to love. There was something endearing about Robin, even vulnerable, and she wanted to nurture and protect him. At eighty he seemed so alone and lonely in old age.

Robin Ainsley had abandoned her grandmother during the Second World War, but he had had his reasons, and it *was* over half a century ago now. And if she were honest with herself, she had to admit that her grandmother had probably had a much better and certainly a more tranquil life without Robin. After all, they had been forever at each other's throats, according to him. And Gran had a loving husband in Richard Hughes, who had married her some months before her baby, Owen, was born. Richard had brought up Owen as his son. He had been a good father; no man had ever had a better one, her father said that all the time.

Her father's face insinuated itself into her mind's eye, and she felt herself tensing. Yet again she wondered how to tell him what she had so recently found out? Owen had idolized Richard Hughes . . .

'I'm so sorry to have left you alone,' Robin murmured from the doorway, interrupting her thoughts. 'I'm afraid Dr Harvey can go on a bit at times.'

Evan jumped up and swung to face him. 'You're all right, aren't you? You're not ill?' she asked. Her voice echoed with sudden concern, and her eyes were anxious.

'I'm perfectly fine, my dear. In very good health, I do assure you. Dr Harvey was merely ringing up to confirm our dinner engagement tomorrow evening.' As he finished speaking Robin stepped onto the terrace. 'Let's stay out here for a while, enjoy Mother Nature. It's such a grand morning.'

'Yes, it is,' Evan agreed.

They sat down on the bench, and Robin went on, after a moment, 'You said earlier that you needed to talk to me about several things, but so far we've only discussed my relationship with your grandmother. What else do you have on your mind?'

'My father.'

'Ah yes, Owen. Have you told him about me? Does he know anything about . . . Emma's well-kept secret?'

'No.'

'Did you lose your nerve, Evan? Surely not. Not *you*.'

'No, not really. But I did decide it might be better to wait until he arrives in London later this month.'

'Don't you think you ought to give him an inkling about what's happened *before* he comes? About me, I mean? It would prepare him for what will no doubt be a bit of a shock.'

'It did cross my mind,' Evan responded, biting her lip, looking worried. 'But then I decided it would be smarter to tell him face to face.'

Robin frowned, stared ahead, his light-coloured eyes fixed on the distant horizon. After a moment, he began to speak slowly, thoughtfully. 'He's not going to like what he hears. It wouldn't surprise me if he were very angry. After all, some of his illusions are going to be shattered. He'll certainly be angry with me about the past.'

'And maybe he'll also be angry with his mother for not being truthful,' Evan suggested succinctly. 'Gran lied to him.'

'Oh, I don't know about that, my dear. Glynnis did the right thing. It was wiser not to tell him I was his father. Richard was married to Glynnis for some months before Owen's birth, and whilst he may not have made her pregnant, he loved that child as his own. Richard's behaviour was impeccable, and I think Glynnis did what she thought was best, you know.'

'That's true, but . . .' She let her sentence go unfinished.

'But what?'

'My father's not easy, Robin.'

A look of comprehension swept across his face and he exclaimed, 'I remember something, Evan. When Paula brought you here for the first time you told us you thought your father had come across some papers after Glynnis died.'

'I did. But he never actually said he found anything. It was just a feeling *I* had that sprang from his sudden, rather odd attitude towards the Harte family.'

'*Oh*. What kind of attitude?' Robin asked, his curiosity aroused.

'He became a bit . . . well, down on them. I guess that's the best way of describing it. He wasn't happy about my job at Harte's, and that was mystifying to me because he had agreed I should visit London to seek out Emma Harte . . . just as Gran had suggested on her deathbed.'

Robin ventured, 'I think he stumbled on a diary, or letters, or other items from long ago, which Glynnis had perhaps forgotten about.'

'That could be so,' she agreed. 'And what he found might have turned him off the Hartes. Is that what you're suggesting?'

'Yes, it is.' There was a pause. 'I wonder if it might not be wiser to let sleeping dogs lie, my dear? Why tell your father anything at all? He doesn't need to know the truth about his paternity. Perhaps it would be more prudent to let it remain the secret it's always been. Why not let him continue to think Richard Hughes was his biological father?'

'That makes sense,' Evan exclaimed, and instantly

felt as though a great weight had been lifted from her chest.

Almost as if he instinctively knew what she was feeling, Robin put his arm around her, held her close to him. '*We* know the truth, and that's all that really matters, isn't it?'

'Yes,' was all she said, and she leaned against his shoulder, closing her eyes, filled with relief.

They did not speak for a short while, lost as they were in their own thoughts. Evan was thinking about her boyfriend Gideon Harte, wondering how she would explain her sudden change of heart, yet knowing that whatever she decided to do he would back her to the hilt, would be on her side. Gideon had an understanding heart, and he was sensitive to her feelings about her father. In fact, he himself had suggested, only the other day, that maybe she would be better off not telling her father he was a Harte. She had been ambivalent; Gideon had then said he trusted her judgement and whatever she did ultimately would be all right by him.

As for Robin, his thoughts were centred on Evan Hughes. How glad he was that this young woman had come into his life. Very late in his life, that was true, but at least he had been fortunate to become aware of her existence. He had grown to know her over the past few weeks, and he liked what he had learned about her. Once before he had held her close like this, when she had comforted him, and he was glad to hold her again, to silently bond with her, and to comfort *her*.

The day she had arrived with Paula to meet him

16

for the first time he had feasted his rheumy old eyes on her lovely face. He had noticed that she looked like his twin, Elizabeth, when she had been twenty-seven, as Evan was now. *Evan*. His granddaughter. His only grandchild. His blood flowed through her veins, and one day, if she married and had children, it would flow in their veins . . . she ensured the continuation of his bloodline, his genes. It had always been important to him, the flowering of a family, but before the arrival of Evan this had not seemed probable.

Instantly, Jonathan sprang into his mind and a chill settled over him. He could only pray that his son would never harm Evan. Certainly Robin had made absolutely sure that Jonathan really did understand that his inheritance was intact, and not jeopardized by the advent of Evan. In fact, he had gone to extraordinary lengths to prove this to his son, taking steps that involved both their solicitors and the execution of various documents, which were binding.

On the other hand, Jonathan was unpredictable. For a long time now he had considered his only child a loose cannon and, even worse, a sociopath. There was no way of knowing what he might do. Or when.

'Are you all right?' Evan asked, feeling Robin's sudden tension.

'Yes, yes, I'm fine,' the old man answered, forcing a smile. 'But I must admit I do feel the cold even on a sunny day like this. Let's go inside, Evan. I have something I wish to show you.'

Together they walked into the library, and Robin murmured, 'Do sit down on the sofa, I won't be a moment.'

She did as he said while he hurried to the desk. Her eyes followed him. What a fine-looking man he was; tall, erect, and handsome in old age, and today he was much more robust and full of vigour. This pleased her. She had only just found him, and he was already eighty . . . the thought of losing him dismayed her.

A moment later Robin was sitting down next to her and handing her a photograph, a snapshot taken a long time ago. Staring down at it she exclaimed, 'It's of you and my grandmother. My goodness, what a gorgeous couple you were! So good-looking.'

He laughed in delight at her compliment. 'We did look wonderful together, you know, everyone remarked on that. As you can see, I'm wearing my RAF uniform and your grandmother is the height of fashion for the times, very much the glamour girl, as always. Well, anyway, it's for you, Evan.'

'Oh Robin, how lovely of you. But are you sure you want to part with it? You've had it for such a long time.'

'Who better to give it to than – *our* grand-daughter. I want you to have this picture of the two of us when we were young and in love and before things had gone so horribly wrong between us.'

She nodded, touched his arm affectionately. 'I shall treasure it always.'

His blue eyes lit up and he smiled at her. 'Now,

will you take pity on an old man and stay for lunch?'

'I'd love to,' she said.

But as she walked to the dining room with Robin, Evan knew there was nothing but trouble in store. Her intuition told her that her father would be difficult, and that the situation would more than likely explode.

CHAPTER TWO

Tessa Fairley Longden stood on the terrace, watching her small daughter bustling around like the proverbial mother hen, placing Daisy her porcelain baby doll, Teddy the bear, and Reggi the rag doll in the chairs she and Adele had just arranged around the small tea-table.

Once the child was satisfied she looked up at her mother, and said, 'Daisy is keeping Teddy company and I'll sit next to my Reggi.'

'That's a good idea, Adele. I'm sure they'll be happy wherever you've put them,' Tessa answered, smiling down at the three-year-old, who was looking up at her questioningly.

As she spoke Tessa made a mental note to wrest the rag doll out of her daughter's clutches as soon as possible. It was dirty and bedraggled, quite disgusting looking really, but the child loved it so much, clung to it, never let it out of her sight. Tessa had long realized it was like a security blanket to Adele, but it did need washing, by hand, of course, so that it would not fall apart. Tonight, she thought, I'll wash it tonight if I can get it away from her.

She was enjoying being here in Yorkshire with Adele, her first bit of peace since leaving her husband, Mark Longden.

Bending down, Tessa smoothed her hand over her child's silky, silvery-blonde hair, and murmured, 'I'll be in the library working, sweetheart, if you need me.'

Adele nodded, and said in a solemn voice, 'At your computer, Mumma.'

'That's right.' Tessa's heart overflowed with love for this extraordinarily beautiful child, so precious to her, the one person she loved the most in this world. Leaning over her, she kissed the top of her head, lingering for a moment longer on the terrace; but after a second or two she finally drew herself up, took a deep breath and walked briskly into the library, sitting down at the table she had pulled over to the French windows.

It was Elvira's day off, and the nanny had gone into Leeds, leaving Adele in her care. Tessa had toyed with the idea of taking Adele with her to the Harrogate store, but in the end she had changed her mind, had decided not to go after all. It was such a beautiful morning it seemed almost criminal to keep the child cooped up in an office; she could just as easily work here at Pennistone Royal on the plans for remodelling the Harrogate store, while Adele enjoyed the sunshine and the fresh air, playing outdoors on the long terrace at the back of the house.

Tessa had decided long ago that the library was the ideal place for her to work when she was here at Pennistone Royal. It was a long, spacious, airy room with a high-flung ceiling and walls panelled in light-coloured pine. Tranquil, a peaceful spot, it was well insulated with its many floor-to-ceiling shelves filled with leather-bound books.

Earlier this morning she had set herself up at the far end of the library, near the French windows. These opened onto the terrace where Adele could play happily until lunchtime. Tessa had pulled the library table over to the glass doors, creating a makeshift desk out of it. Adele was now in her direct line of vision; she could even hear the child chattering away to the teddy bear. Apart from being able to keep an eye on her daughter, she was readily available if the child needed her for any reason.

Tessa worked steadily at her computer for the next twenty minutes, glancing up from time to time, smiling to herself, thinking of how well Adele played alone, treating her dolls and the bear like real playmates, talking to them in the most natural way, as if they were alive.

Adele was a clever, inventive and imaginative little girl, and she could already read simple books even though she was not yet four. Tessa had come to understand that her daughter enjoyed learning new things, and she was extremely intelligent for her age, and in some ways rather precocious, at least when it came to learning. Not precocious in an irritating way, like some children were; Adele was sweet by nature, and a rather endearing child with her fey and somewhat whimsical traits and mannerisms.

Unexpectedly, Adele turned around and saw Tessa staring at her through the open glass doors, and she laughed, waved to her mother.

Tessa waved back before returning to her work. She concentrated hard, trying to pull together all of her ideas for the much-needed changes at the Harrogate store. This was her special project at the moment; her half-sister Linnet and her cousin India had been given the task of creating a new look for the Leeds store, along with Evan Hughes. Harte's were revamping everywhere.

The loud ringing of the phone brought Tessa's head up with a start. When it continued to shrill she wondered why no one was picking it up, and then remembered she was alone in the house at the moment. Elvira had already left for Leeds; Margaret had gone to do the marketing in Ripon, and she had seen Evan Hughes drive off well over an hour ago. As for Emsie and Desmond, her O'Neill sister and brother were off riding on the moors.

Jumping up, Tessa hurried across to the Georgian desk next to the sofa, and grabbed the phone. 'Pennistone Royal. Hello?' There was a great deal of static, and faintly, far away in the distance she heard a man's voice saying, 'Tessa –. Is Tess –' and then the voice faded out completely.

It's Toby, she thought; my cousin's calling me from LA. Holding the receiver tighter, she exclaimed,

'This is Tessa Longden! Who is it?' Much to her annoyance, the phone now went completely dead. She listened for a moment, said hello several times and then hung up in exasperation.

She had barely taken a few steps towards the makeshift desk when the phone began to ring once more. Snatching the receiver from the cradle, she said in a distinct tone, 'This is Tessa Longden. Who's calling?' There was no response, no voice at all, only static and sounds like lapping waves. 'Hello? Hello? I can't hear you! Who's calling?'

Her frustration echoed in her voice; she was positive it was her cousin, who had gone to Los Angeles to see his wife. He had promised to be in touch and no doubt this *was* Toby. On his mobile. The connection suddenly cut off, and with an impatient shrug she banged down the phone and headed back to her computer. No sooner had she turned away from the phone than its insistent shrilling brought her back to it, and she answered for a third time. *'This is Tessa. Who is it?'*

'Tess –' The voice broke up before the completion of her name, and then she was hearing only static and half a word here and there. She said 'Hello' several times, but whoever it was at the other end was not making himself understood.

She stood there with the phone glued to her ear for a few more minutes, and then with great irritation she hung up, mildly cursing Toby under her breath. Why use his mobile? Couldn't he have picked up a land line?

It suddenly occurred to her that perhaps Toby

had tried to reach her at the London store first, and so she dialled her new assistant's private line. It was answered immediately.

'It's me, Patsy,' she said at once. 'I think Toby Harte might be trying to get hold of me. From the States. Using his mobile. But it's not working, he keeps breaking up. Have you heard from him this morning? Has he been trying to get me?'

'No, he hasn't,' Patsy answered. 'In fact, you've had very few phone calls so far today. Only Jess Lister about a dress you ordered. It's ready. She's bringing it over. And Anita Moore. She called to say she wants to come in and see you, show you her new line of cosmetics and body products. I said you'd be in touch with her early next week.'

'Good. Well, look, if Toby does ring me from the States please ask him to phone me on a land line. I'll be here at Pennistone Royal all day, and this evening, too. I'm not going out. That'll be much easier.'

'I'll tell him. Talk to you later, Tessa.'

Tessa walked back to the library table and automatically glanced out at the terrace before resuming her work. And she caught her breath in surprise. Adele was no longer sitting at the tea-table.

Oh God, where is she? Tessa rushed through the French windows and out onto the terrace, looking up and down. Her daughter was nowhere in sight. And yet she was not in the habit of wandering off. Adele was an obedient child.

Instantly her hackles rose and alarm shot

through her. She swung around, glanced down at the tea-table as if seeking a clue, and immediately noticed that the rag doll was missing.

Where *had* Adele gone? Down to the old oak, perhaps? As this thought flew into her head Tessa ran over to the stone balustrade and looked out towards the dell at the bottom of the sloping lawns. Here an ancient oak spread its wide branches over a garden seat where Adele often went to play. But there was no sign of her there today.

How did she manage to get down the steps? Tessa now asked herself, and her alarm intensified as she raced along the terrace to the flight of steps. She dreaded what she might find; she fully expected to see her three-year-old child crumpled in a heap at the bottom of them. But Adele was not there either.

Panic spiralled into genuine fear as Tessa struck out towards the front façade of the house, looking around as she did, her face tense, her eyes filled with anxiety.

The driveway was deserted. There wasn't a soul in sight, not even the gardeners or the stable boys. It was ominously quiet, as if *everyone* had disappeared and she was the only person left there.

When she reached the heavy front door Tessa stood for a moment, frowning. The door was ajar and this surprised her. It was always locked for security reasons. Puzzled, she pushed the door open and went inside; her only concern was to find her child.

'Adele! Adele!' she called out in her loudest

voice, walking forward quickly. 'Are you here, sweetheart?'

No one answered.

No child came running to her on plump little legs, calling her name.

There was only the sound of Tessa's voice echoing back to her through the great Stone Hall. It struck her then that Adele might have gone to the kitchen looking for Margaret, wanting her favourite Cadbury's chocolate fingers for the dolls' tea party. Rushing down the corridor, she went into the kitchen. It, too, was deserted. Disappointment hit her in the face. Her heart sank and dismay lodged in the pit of her stomach. Unexpectedly, tears filled her eyes and she leaned against the door jamb for a split second, endeavouring to gather her swimming senses as she tried to imagine where the three-year-old could be. *Where?*

Taking a deep breath, Tessa swung out of the kitchen and made her way back to the front of the house, walked outside onto the gravel driveway, again looking around. And asking herself where she should begin to search for Adele. It now seemed obvious that her little girl had wandered off into the other garden, and Tessa suddenly understood that she would need Wiggs and his two assistants to start looking for her. And possibly the stable lads as well. The grounds at Pennistone Royal were vast and covered a wide area, and there were several dense woods beyond the fields and meadows.

'Miss Tessa! Miss Tessa!'

At the sound of the head gardener's voice, Tessa spun around. Wiggs was hurrying towards her and she saw that he had the rag doll in his hands.

She ran to meet him, exclaiming, 'Where did you find the doll?'

The gardener came to a standstill and handed it to her. 'Just around the bend in the drive.' He glanced over his shoulder. 'Yer knows that bend, Miss Tessa, it's just afore the house comes in ter sight.'

Clutching the rag doll to her, Tessa said shakily, 'I can't find Adele, Wiggs. She's suddenly gone missing, and I don't understand what she was doing out here. We must start looking for her in the grounds.'

Wiggs gaped at her. 'I thought she must've dropped the doll before she got in ter the car,' he said, frowning, his face puzzled.

'What car?' Tessa cried, her eyes opening wider, flaring with apprehension. 'There was a car *here*?' Her voice was unusually shrill and she gripped the gardener's arm.

'Yes. I heard the screech of tyres as it drove off. Almost run over one of the ponies, it did that, and two of the stable lads ran after it, shouting at the driver, telling him to stop. But he didn't.'

All of the colour had drained out of Tessa's face and she thought her legs would buckle under her as small ripples of shock ran through her body. *Mark*. It had to be Mark. Yes. *Oh, God, yes*. He had snatched their child. She snapped her eyes tightly shut, trembling inside, and brought one hand to her face, overcome by rising panic.

'You'd best go inside, Miss Tessa, and sit down for a bit,' Wiggs was saying to her. 'You look right poorly.'

And as Tessa opened her eyes and took a deep breath, she heard the clatter of horses' hooves in the distance and turned around swiftly.

Wiggs glanced behind him, and muttered, 'That must be Emsie and Desmond coming back from their ride.'

'Yes, it must,' she agreed, and she thought her voice sounded peculiar, oddly strangled in her throat. She was on the verge of tears again. Turning to Wiggs, blinking them back, she managed to ask, 'That car, Wiggs. What was it like? Did you see the driver? Was it Mr Longden, do you think?'

Wiggs shook his head. 'Didn't see the driver's face. But it was a man. Aye, it was. Car was black. A Mercedes . . . I think.' He nodded and his expression was suddenly confident. 'Aye, it *was* a Mercedes, Miss Tessa.'

At this moment Emsie and Desmond came around the bend, their horses walking at a slow pace. Emsie waved and called out cheerily, 'Tessa! Hello.'

Desmond also waved and his handsome young face was full of smiles.

Tessa raised her arm, beckoned to them to come over, then she changed her mind and ran towards them, Wiggs following in her wake.

Desmond, mounted on a superb black stallion, looked down at his eldest sister. Staring at her face, which was as white as her cotton shirt, noting her terrible strained expression, he asked, almost sharply, 'What's the matter, Tess?'

'It's Adele,' she began and shook her head in bewilderment. 'I can't find her. She's vanished. Into thin air.' Her voice was shaking and she stopped abruptly, turned to look at Wiggs. 'But she could have been taken from here.'

He had known her since she was a child, and he understood immediately what she wanted him to do. He had to explain. 'It's like this, Desmond,' Wiggs said. 'There was a car here. I don't know who was in it. But it drove off hell for leather, almost collided with a pony that'd strayed on ter the drive. Two of the stable lads ran after the car, shouting, but the driver paid them no mind, didn't stop. Just shot out of them there front gates like a bat out of hell. I was walking up the drive . . . when I spotted Adele's rag doll.' He nodded and finished, 'I thought Adele must've dropped it when she got in the car. Not that I'm sure she did that, yer knows. But it seems likely.'

'But you didn't actually *see* Adele in the car?' Desmond asked.

'No.' Wiggs shook his head. 'Still, what with the doll being there on the ground, well, I mean, I just thought she'd gone off in the car.'

Tessa took a deep breath, said in a worried voice, 'Wiggs, please arrange for the grounds to be searched, and talk to Joe. He might know who was in the car. Maybe they'd been to see him about something – to do with the estate.'

'I'll get a search going, Miss Tessa, but there's no way I can talk ter Joe. He's gone ter East Witton. And I don't think he's coming back. Not just yet. But nobody coming ter see Joe would drive like that, not with all the notices we've got posted, warning everyone ter go slow because of the horses. No, whoever was in that black car, well, them there folk were proper strangers, not from these parts. Locals don't go speeding around in cars when there's horses all over the place.'

'I agree,' Desmond said. He dismounted, went to Tessa, put his arm around her shoulders, wanting to comfort her. He was as concerned about her as he was about the situation. And what ought they to do, aside from searching the grounds?

Emsie followed suit, expertly jumping down from her horse. Turning to Wiggs, she said, 'Would you mind taking the horses to the stables, please? We'll be there in a few minutes, Wiggs, to rub them down.'

'Acourse I'll tek 'em back, Emsie,' he replied, accepting the reins from her, reaching for Desmond's horse. 'But the stable lads'll look after 'em. You should both be with Tessa.'

Emsie smiled at him, a faltering smile, and he noticed that her face was as white as her half-sister's. She looked frightened, as well. He patted the seventeen-year-old's shoulder. 'Try not to worry, lass. If she's around here, we'll find Adele.'

'I hope she *is* just lost,' Emsie murmured, biting her lip. 'I hope that's all it is.'

Wiggs hurried away with the horses, thinking

that Mark Longden had most likely grabbed the child. The whole staff knew all about the upcoming divorce; there was a good bit of gossip about Longden. None of them liked him. He was the child's father. Surely he wouldn't harm her. But Longden was a bit of a bugger, so he'd heard. A boozer. Also on drugs. And a wife-beater. A man who struck a woman was a coward, a bully and a thug in his opinion.

Desmond and his sisters went into the house, and as they hurried through into the Stone Hall, he took hold of Tessa's arm, and said, 'Shall I get you a brandy? You look as if you're about to pass out.'

'No, thanks, Des. A cup of tea and an aspirin is what I want. I have a splitting headache. Let's go to the kitchen.'

He nodded, and he and Emsie followed Tessa across the Stone Hall and down the corridor. Once inside the kitchen it was Emsie who filled the electric kettle with water, plugged it in, then found the brown teapot and three mugs in the cupboard.

Desmond and Tessa seated themselves at the round table in the bay window, and Desmond took hold of Tessa's hand, hoping to reassure her. He started to speak but stopped, noting the preoccupied look on her face. He had always been sensitive to her moods, and he understood that at this moment she was trying to think things through.

At fifteen Desmond O'Neill was mature for his

age, and looked older than his years. He was tall, over six feet, and powerfully built, a strapping young man with his father's height, broad chest and wide shoulders; he also had Shane's glamorous good looks. Hair and eyes the colour of jet stamped him Black Irish, and those in the know said that he was the spitting image of his great-grandfather Blackie O'Neill, long since dead, but well-remembered by many of the locals, friends and certain members of the three clans.

No one spoke. Emsie was busy making the tea, and Desmond was waiting for Tessa to relax, to say something. Only when Adele was found would his sister be at ease. She was a doting mother.

Tessa's mind was racing, and she felt sick, anxiety-ridden for her child. She did not know what to do at this moment. How could she just sit and wait until Wiggs and the others searched the estate? That could take ages. And wasn't time of the essence? If Adele *was* lost she would soon become frightened, and she might have an accident, could easily hurt herself. She wondered if she should go and join in the hunt for Adele? Could she have been grabbed by Mark? Did he have her? Or was Jonathan Ainsley behind this? She instantly pushed that thought to one side. The idea of Jonathan Ainsley being involved frightened her. If Mark did have their daughter, wouldn't he call Pennistone Royal to speak to her? Certainly he would never hurt Adele, he adored the child. But he wasn't himself these days, was he? Tessa shivered involuntarily.

Desmond noticed this, and said swiftly, in his most reassuring tone, 'I'm sure she was in that car, Tess. Wiggs might not have noticed. I don't think Adele is here, on the estate, lost somewhere, because Emsie and I would have spotted her on our way back. The only way to get to the fields is down the lane.'

Tessa did not respond.

Desmond remained silent himself, knowing Tessa in the way he did. Although his half-sister had a reputation in the family for being difficult, bossy and a snob, he knew another, very different side of her. He loved Tessa, and she loved him, and they had always been good friends; she wasn't really the ogre some of the family made her out to be. At least not in his eyes.

Rousing herself from her thoughts, Tessa suddenly said, 'I can't help thinking as you do she probably *was* in that car, Des. You're right. And she's so little, she couldn't have got very far.'

'Who would take her without telling you –' he cut himself off. His eyes met hers. 'Mark Longden. *Of course!* You think he's got her, don't you?'

'Yes.'

'So do I. That's the answer.'

Emsie carried the tray of mugs and the teapot over to the table and as she put it down she said, 'There's no one else to point a finger at. He might be trying to get his own back because of your nasty divorce, or to make trouble, hurt you.'

'Unless someone else has –' Desmond paused, took a deep breath, and finished, '*kidnapped her.*

For a ransom. This family's always been the perfect target for something like that.'

'I've considered the same thing. A kidnapping.' Tessa closed her eyes once more and sat very still, trying to control her trembling. 'That's why I've got to be here, near the phone.'

She was so white and her tension was so marked Desmond was convinced she was about to faint at any moment. He wished Linnet were here, she'd know what to do. But would Tessa listen to her? They were often at loggerheads.

Emsie looked across at her brother and her eyes caught his as she poured tea into his mug. These two had always been perfectly in tune with each other. At seventeen she was two years older than Desmond, yet it was he who was protective of her; they loved each other and were best friends. Like Desmond, Emsie was obviously Black Irish. She had inherited the striking O'Neill colouring – glossy dark hair and eyes as black and shiny as coal.

Silently, she mouthed, '*Linnet*. We need Linnet.'

Desmond nodded, looked across at Tessa, waiting.

Despite her fragile appearance and her delicate beauty, Tessa Fairley Longden had a great deal of inner strength and an enormous amount of resilience. As she often said, she was not Emma Harte's great-granddaughter for nothing; there was a certain toughness about her and she had a fair amount of determination.

Pulling herself together finally, she opened her

eyes and sat up a little straighter in the chair. 'Thanks for the tea, Emsie,' she murmured and took a long swallow of the brew. After a moment's thought, she glanced at the wall clock, continued, 'It's almost eleven here. Six o'clock in the morning in New York. No use phoning Mummy and Shane –'

Emsie cut in somewhat peremptorily: 'They'll still be asleep. What about talking to your solicitor?'

'No, no!' Tessa exclaimed, and gave Emsie a hard stare. 'You know very well what the family rules are. We deal with everything ourselves, for as long as possible, and with the help of the other clans if necessary. But no outsiders can be involved. Unless we have no other choice.'

'You ought to call Linnet immediately,' Desmond suggested, glancing quickly at Emsie, hoping Tessa wouldn't bite his head off. The strained relationship between his sisters often presented problems. Both wanted to run Harte's one day. But Linnet was the smartest in the family, other than his parents; he believed she was the best person to take charge in the absence of their mother and father.

Surprisingly, Tessa was not upset by his suggestion. Jumping up, she hurried over to the phone on the counter. 'I think I'd better do that, Desmond. Right away.'

Tessa was aware that Linnet had planned to come up to Pennistone Royal either today or tomorrow, and so instead of ringing Harte's in

London she dialled her sister on her mobile; Linnet was probably on the road already, driving to Yorkshire. It was answered almost at once with a crisp, 'Linnet O'Neill.'

'It's Tessa. I've got a problem here.'

'At the Harrogate store?' Linnet sounded surprised.

'No. At home. At Pennistone Royal.'

'A problem *there*! What's happened?'

'It's Adele. She's vanished. I can't find her, and I'm frantic. I think it could be Mark's doing.' Tessa's voice trembled and she swallowed hard.

'If you think it's Mark then it is,' Linnet exclaimed. 'Stay calm, I'm about an hour away. Don't call the police yet. We can deal with this ourselves.'

'I know the rules. Listen, Desmond thinks it could be a genuine kidnapping. For a ransom.'

'Oh my God! Let's hope not. Tell me exactly what happened.'

Tessa did as her sister asked.

When Tessa finished, Linnet said, 'The phone calls were to distract you. It's Mark who's behind this, I'm absolutely positive. You're right about that. Still, I'm glad Wiggs is searching the grounds. She *could* have strayed away from the house, but she couldn't have gone far. Who's there with you?'

'Just Desmond and Emsie. It's Elvira's day off, and Margaret went out shopping. And Joe's gone to East Witton.'

'Desmond's pretty reliable and responsible. So is Emsie. I'm glad they're there. Where's Evan?'

'I don't know. I saw her drive off several hours ago.'

'I'm sure she'll soon return. Now, stay there by the phone and if Mark calls tell him to bring Adele back immediately. Be firm with him but civil. Try not to have a row.'

'What if he wants to bargain with me? What if he wants something?'

'Promise him anything. Just get that child back in your arms. Mark can be dealt with later.'

'All right. But what if it's not Mark? What if it really is a kidnapping, and they call, making demands?'

'Listen to them. Agree to their demands, but explain it's going to take you a while to get money together. Because I'm sure they'll be asking for money . . . that's what most kidnappings are about.'

'I understand.'

'Tessa?'

'Yes?'

'Nothing's going to happen to Adele.'

'But –'

'I promise,' Linnet cut in. 'Don't go into the grounds. You must be there to answer the phone. See you soon.' With that she clicked off her mobile.

As soon as she saw a lay-by Linnet O'Neill pulled over and parked. She sat for a moment thinking about her sister's phone call and Adele's disappearance. She was filled with dismay, and extremely angry. I always knew that bastard wouldn't go quietly, she thought, her mind zeroing in on Mark

Longden. She had never liked him, had always believed him to be avaricious, ambitious, self-promoting. Years ago she had characterized him as a gold-digger who was after Tessa's money, not to mention her prestige as a Harte; she had never quite understood why such a beautiful and clever young woman as her sister had married him. And he wasn't a very good architect in her opinion, whatever others thought.

Their mother had told her recently that Mark Longden had physically and mentally abused Tessa, and much to her astonishment she had discovered she hadn't been in the least bit surprised. She had always been aware that underneath his smarmy, phoney charm he was a nasty piece of work.

Linnet sat thinking about Adele's sudden disappearance, and she realized she did not believe for one moment that the child had been kidnapped by strangers for ransom. She felt, deep within herself, that it was Mark Longden who had snatched his own child. Her gut instinct told her that it was a form of blackmail. He wanted something from the Hartes, and he was using his little daughter as a bargaining tool. The bastard, she muttered again, and cursed him under her breath.

'"Everybody has a price and it isn't always money," that's what Emma used to say to me,' her mother had once told her, and Linnet had never forgotten those words. They were absolutely true. When it came right down to it, everybody had some kind of vulnerability, something they wanted to protect at any price, and very often money never came into play at all. There were other currencies for dealing.

From remarks her mother had made recently, Linnet knew that Mark Longden was not only drinking very heavily these days, but was also on drugs. It had troubled her then; it was certainly more worrying now. A man under the influence could easily become irresponsible, even erratic, and quite possibly violent – and therefore dangerous. She was fairly certain that Mark wouldn't intentionally hurt his only child. But what if something went wrong with him, or others, and in the process Adele got hurt, albeit inadvertently?

It suddenly struck Linnet that thoughts of a similar nature must have occurred to Tessa. Never before had she heard her sister sound so vulnerable, nervous, and at such a loss about what to do than she had a few minutes ago. It seemed to her that the child's abduction, because that was what it was, had rendered Tessa helpless.

Normally Tessa was a take-charge person who wanted to be top dog, so that she could run everything and boss everyone around. And very often, because of Tessa's ambition to be their mother's heir-apparent, the Dauphine as she called herself, Tessa and she had locked horns. But there was a family rule that went all the way back to Emma Harte and her brothers, and it had never been broken. No matter what the circumstances, a Harte was always loyal to a Harte. They had been brought up to stand strong and steady together in a fight, to defend each other against the world. To kill for each other, to take the bullet for each other, if necessary. Linnet knew all the Harte rules by heart and lived by them.

The child was Tessa's vulnerable spot; Linnet was well aware of her sister's deep and unwavering love for her child. The entire family loved Adele. The three-year-old girl was like a Botticelli angel, with her silver gilt hair, silvery-grey eyes, and her exquisite little face. Beautiful and endearing, with genuine sweetness, she had touched them all in different ways. Linnet thought of Adele as one of those rare golden children, unique, almost spiritual. God forbid anything happened to her.

How to solve this dilemma? What to do? Linnet asked herself. And where to begin? Start driving for one thing, she decided, rousing herself from her myriad thoughts, releasing the brake and slowly pulling out onto the motorway.

Linnet knew she had to handle this. The very fact that Tessa had turned to her made her truly understand that her sister accepted that she herself was far too emotional to cope with the situation. I've got to deal with it fast, Linnet thought. Very fast. Today. It can't be allowed to drag on. I've got to find Mark. Find that child. Immediately. Before anything goes wrong.

There really was only her. Her parents were in New York with Aunt Emily and Uncle Winston, which meant the four senior and most powerful members of the Harte family were out of action for the moment.

Gideon Harte? She thought of her cousin, her best friend, for a moment. He could be extremely helpful. He ran the Harte newspapers, was brilliant and street-wise, and he had every kind of resource at his disposal. Owning and running an international newspaper chain spelled one thing. Power. *Immense power.* Yes, she might have to pull Gideon into this, but right now what she really needed was an expert. A genuine professional. A policeman who wasn't actually a policeman.

Jack Figg.

The name leapt into her mind at once. Harte's security adviser, he was considered a member of the family. She had known him since childhood, thought of him as a pal. And so the moment she saw another lay-by ahead, Linnet pulled in and parked. Reaching for her hold-all, she groped around in it for her address book, and quickly found his name.

A few seconds later she was dialling Jack's mobile number.

'Figg here,' he answered almost at once.

'It's Linnet, Jack.'

'Hello, Beauty. What do you need?'

'You, Jack. Please.'

'I'm yours,' he laughed, 'anytime you want me.'

'Remember what you said at Shane's birthday party in June – that I could count on you in an emergency?'

'I do. And you can.'

'Thanks, Jack. There's an emergency.'

'Tell me everything I need to know.'

She did so, and gave him her own thoughts about what had happened.

'The phone calls *were* meant to distract her, keep her busy. Where are you now, Linnet?'

'Parked in a lay-by, about an hour away from Pennistone Royal. Are you in Robin Hood's Bay?'

'No, I'm outside York Minster with a friend. If I leave York now I'll probably arrive at the house the same time as you. I'll meet you there. But please tell Tessa you've asked me to help. Just in case I arrive before you.'

'I will. And thanks, Jack.'

'Anything for you, Beauty.'

He was gone, and she was back on the motorway, picking up speed as she gunned the car forward, streaking along the empty road. There was hardly any traffic at the moment, and that was something in her favour at least.

Linnet concentrated on driving for the next twenty minutes or so, and then, slowing down, she phoned Tessa at Pennistone Royal. Her sister said there was nothing new, and no sign of Adele. Wiggs and his search party were still looking. Linnet told her about Jack Figg, and his imminent arrival, and fortunately met no resistance from Tessa.

A few seconds later she punched in Evan's mobile number, but it was turned off. No doubt Evan was with Uncle Robin, whom she had been wanting to talk to for several weeks. Linnet thought suddenly of her cousin India Standish. India had gone up to Leeds from London very early that morning, to start working on plans for revamping the store. Linnet was close to her cousin. In fact everyone in the family loved India. She had an understanding heart, was kind, with a loving nature. Many thought she was delicate, even frail, but her elegant aristocratic looks inherited from the Fairleys belied her character.

Linnet knew she was practical, down to earth, strong physically, and that, like their great-grand-mother Emma Harte, she was absolutely fearless. India worked with her in the fashion department of Harte's in London, and they had been close friends since childhood. India had grown up on her father's estate Clonloughlin in Ireland, but she had spent every summer at Pennistone Royal. And Linnet loved to boast of some of India's brave deeds as a child . . . like the time she rushed out into the backyard at Pennistone Royal wearing huge oven gloves in order to separate two dogs fighting over the dead body of a rabbit. Or the day Linnet's little sister Emsie had climbed into the big oak and got stuck in the upper branches. Undeterred by Linnet's warning that they would both fall out of the tree, India had climbed up it, had sat with Emsie, stopped her wailing and held her tightly until Linnet had come back with Joe, the estate-manager, carrying a tall orchard ladder.

Yes, Linnet decided, India would be helpful in this situation, and she got on well with the some-times difficult Tessa.

India would be staying at Pennistone Royal for

the next few days, as she usually did. I'd better warn her about the situation there, Linnet thought, tell her what's happened, before she goes over there later. She dialled her cousin, and waited patiently as the mobile rang and rang.

CHAPTER THREE

'That's *your* phone ringing, not mine,' Russell 'Dusty' Rhodes said, looking across at India, who stood next to the window.

She frowned, glancing around the bedroom, exclaiming, 'Heavens, where's my bag?'

'Over there, on the chair. Under your dress.'

'Oh gosh, yes, you're right.' As she spoke she ran to the chair, clutching the towel around her body; with her other hand she grabbed the bag, groped inside for the ringing mobile phone, turned it on, held it to her ear. 'Hello?'

'India?'

'Hi Linnet.'

'Where are you? At the Leeds store already?'

'No. I stopped in for a few minutes, then went to . . . lunch.'

Dusty grinned at her from the other side of the room and began to laugh.

She glared at him and silently mouthed, 'Be quiet.'

Linnet said, 'India, there's a problem. Adele's disappeared. Several hours ago, and Tessa's frantic.'

'Oh my God!' Alarm registered in India's eyes and she sat down heavily in the chair, concentrating on the phone call.

'She could be lost in the grounds, might have just wandered off,' Linnet went on, 'but somehow I doubt that. Personally, I think Mark Longden snatched her, and so does Tessa.'

'Yes, I agree. But surely he wouldn't hurt her –'

'True,' Linnet interrupted, 'but things sometimes do go wrong, so we've got to find her before anything untoward does happen. I've brought Jack Figg in to help, and there's a search party looking for her at Pennistone Royal. I should be there myself in half an hour.'

'Perhaps I'd better come too.'

'You might as well finish lunch, India. There's not a lot you can do except be there for Tessa. Obviously, she's very upset.'

'I can well imagine.' There was a slight hesitation on India's part, and then she asked worriedly, 'You don't think Jonathan Ainsley has anything to do with this, do you?'

'I sincerely hope not, but if he does it really changes the picture.'

'Yes, you're right. But what do you –'

'Let's not go *there*, India. At least not yet. I'll see you later.'

'I'll leave shortly.' India clicked off the phone and put it back in her bag. Her face was paler than ever, her eyes anxious.

'What's happened?' Dusty asked, sitting up straighter in the bed, looking at her alertly. 'You

47

sounded frightened. No, not frightened, you're not frightened of anything, are you? *Concerned* is possibly a better word. Or alarmed.'

India stared back at him, nodding. 'I am a bit alarmed, yes. Adele, Tessa's little girl, has vanished and Linnet says it could be Mark Longden's doing.'

'That's bad. What do *you* think?'

'I tend to agree. Mark's not very nice, and it's more than likely he took her.'

'She's not lost somewhere on that vast estate perhaps?'

'It's possible, I suppose. But I think she would've been found by now. She's still a toddler. How far could she get? Linnet says it's several hours since she went missing, and there's a search party out.'

'Why would he take her? Stupid question, Rhodes,' he answered himself, shaking his head. 'As a weapon in the divorce . . . he's using her against your cousin, using her in order to manipulate Tessa.' He ran a hand through his black wavy hair and a look of contempt crossed his face. '*People*. What shits they are, how they disgust me. He's a real bastard if he's using his child in that way.'

India sighed, stood up, reached for her clothes.

'You can be there in less than an hour, so come back to bed.' Dusty's voice was lower, suddenly tender, and he smiled at her seductively. She noticed yet again how white his teeth were against the tan of his face. 'Come back to bed with me, let's do it all again,' he insisted.

India shook her head. 'I do think I have to go,

Dusty,' she answered, but regret registered on her face.

He could not fail to miss that expression, knew at once that she wanted to stay. He saw the desire in her eyes, the look of yearning. He threw back the sheets and got out of bed, walked towards her purposefully, still smiling that beguiling smile of his.

India thought his blue eyes looked suddenly dangerous, almost predatory. Her stomach lurched and she felt weak; he always managed to make her feel this way at some point or other when they were together . . . shaking inside . . . swooning . . . trembling. She was always his willing partner in anything he wanted to do with her . . . sexually aroused by a mere glance from him, the touch of his hand.

As he drew close she thought how impossibly good-looking he was, almost absurdly handsome. It was as if a sculptor had spent endless hours shaping most of his face: straight, patrician nose, broad forehead, high cheekbones, perfectly rounded chin. And elegantly arched brows above those dazzlingly-blue eyes that became soulful with passion, could turn icy cold in anger. He did not have one of those pretty-boy, matinée-idol faces; it was ruggedly handsome, with sharp angles and planes, as if the sculptor had suddenly wanted to finish quickly and had become slapdash.

His face matched his body. He had a solid torso – broad chest, wide shoulders above slender hips. About five feet eleven, he gave the impression of greater height and strength because of his powerful build. From the moment she had met him she had been aware of his potency and masculinity. No other man had ever affected her the way he did.

Now he was standing in front of her, the smile still lingering on his mouth. He pulled her into his arms and held her close to his body; the towel and her clothes fell from her hands onto the floor in a heap, and her arms went around his shoulders. And as he bent his head towards her his mouth found hers. He kissed her deeply, passionately, and she felt his erection against her thigh, and for a moment she thought she would succumb, become an all-too-willing partner in his bed for a second time that day. And she clung to him, dissolving.

But then the brainwashing of years kicked in and she remembered the Harte rules and she knew she had to go to Pennistone Royal. Whatever her physical desires and needs were, no matter how much she wanted this man, her upbringing overrode everything else. A Harte was in trouble, and every other Harte must stand alongside, to defend their rights.

When they finally stopped their kisses, India gently pushed Dusty away, her hands resting on his chest. For a moment he resisted, and then quite suddenly he stepped back with an abrupt movement, looked into her face, his own questioning.

'You know the rules,' she murmured. 'I told you about them ages ago.'

'A Harte always goes to the aid of a Harte in

trouble!' he exclaimed. 'You don't have to embellish. I got it then, I get it now.'

'Please don't be angry.'

'I'm not,' he snapped, turning away, walking over to the window, where he stood looking out, his stance rigid, his face a mask of discontent.

Without another word she collected her clothes, went into the bathroom, tidied herself up, slipped into her bra and panties, pulled a black linen dress over her head, then slid her feet into high-heeled, black leather mules.

When she returned to the bedroom he was still standing at the window looking out, but he had quickly dressed, was wearing his jeans and a white t-shirt.

At the sound of her heels clicking on the parquet floor he swung to face her. 'Sorry,' he mumbled, and for once he looked shame-faced.

India walked over to him, touched his cheek gently. 'I *want* to stay, to be with you, you know that, and you also know how I feel about you. This sense of duty to the family is something I can't help.' She shrugged and finished, 'I suppose it's just . . . ingrained in me.'

He caught her hand in his, brought it to his mouth, kissed it. 'I know. And I'm a belligerent sod at times.' He laughed his deep-throated laugh. '*Most* of the time, wouldn't you say? Okay, I'll let you go.' He led her towards the door. 'On one condition.'

She caught the lightness in his tone, saw the sudden mischievous laughter in those amazing eyes.

'I agree to any condition,' she said, 'as long as it's a condition involving you.'

'You'll regret saying that when you know what it is.' He hurried her out of the bedroom and down the grand staircase.

'Will I really?' she asked, her expression suddenly flirtatious. 'So, tell me what it is, then.'

'You have to sit for me.' He stopped on the stairs, turned to look at her.

India gaped at him, her jaw dropping. 'You want me to sit for *you*? You want to paint me? *Me*?' She was flabbergasted.

He saw that he had startled her, and realized that her amazement was genuine, and for a moment or two he was baffled by this. They had paused in the middle of the staircase, were standing just underneath the domed glass ceiling. Light was streaming in, turning her hair into a silver halo and her silvery-grey eyes seemed to be lit from within. In contrast, her face was sensual, her mouth ripe and bruised. He caught his breath, wishing he could start painting right away. His fingers tingled.

She said quickly, 'You're staring at me, and you have the most peculiar look on your face.' Her hand came up to smooth her hair; suddenly, she felt ungroomed, self-conscious about her appearance. 'I know I look a mess.'

He took her face between his hands and gazed deeply into her beautiful, transparent eyes. 'I wish I could start painting you right now, capture you the way you look at this moment. So vulnerable and open, the sensuality still lingering. You look like a woman who has just been well and truly bedded.'

'I was.'

'You'll do it then? You'll sit for me?'

'If you really want me to, Dusty.'

He smiled and reached out, took hold of her fingers, and they went on down the stairs hand in hand. When they got to the bottom Dusty paused, gave her a long, thoughtful look. 'How will you explain it?'

India frowned in puzzlement, returned his steady gaze with one that was slightly surprised. 'I'm not with you.'

'How will you explain the painting to your father?'

'I don't know what you mean, Dusty.'

He peered at her more closely, wondering if she was being dense or perhaps even kidding him. And then he suddenly understood she was neither. Very simply, she just didn't get it. He shook his head and began to laugh softly. After a moment, he explained, 'Every one of my paintings is exhibited, even the portraits for private clients, and they are always photographed. Your father is bound to see photos of the picture I paint of you when they appear in the newspapers and magazines. He'll know I've been screwing you.'

She winced inside; sometimes his bluntness took her breath away, but she gave him a sweet smile and answered, 'Don't be so ridiculous, he won't know any such thing.'

'He will, because the painting I intend to paint

53

of you will be very sensual – the way you look now. It won't leave much to the imagination.'

'Oh Daddy won't care, he's . . . a man of the world.'

'He's also the Earl of Dunvale, and believe me he'll care. He won't want the world to know I'm . . . you know . . . having it off with his daughter. *Me*? The notorious, rabble-rousing working-class lad from the back streets of Leeds. Not 'alf he won't.'

'Now you *are* being silly. You're the greatest painter in the world today. Everyone knows that. Anyway, I actually don't care what my father or anyone else thinks. I'm twenty-seven and I can do anything I want. And I want to be painted by you, in fact I'm flattered that you asked.'

'It's a deal?'

'Of course.' She thrust out her hand. 'Let's shake.'

His boisterous laughter filled the air as he shook her hand, then he pulled her into his arms and embraced her. Against her hair he said, 'There's another condition. Before I paint you we'll have to be together, if you get my drift. You do understand that, Lady India?'

'Absolutely, Mr Rhodes. I'm in total agreement.'

He put his arm around her shoulder. 'Come on, I'll walk you to your car,' he murmured and turned the handle of the French windows. They opened up onto the terrace of the south façade of the house, which was very beautiful; there was a portico supported by four soaring columns, and the wide terrace stretched the length of the house and around the two end wings.

The heat of the August afternoon hit them as they stepped outside, and Dusty said, 'It's muggy, and it looks like rain.' He glanced up. 'Thunderclouds, India, but you'll get to Pennistone Royal before the rain starts.'

'I hope so,' she murmured, also glancing up, and instantly thinking of the search party out on the estate in rainy weather. But hopefully Adele had been found, or returned, by now. Involuntarily, she shivered when she thought of the missing child.

Dusty noticed and took hold of her arm as they walked along the terrace, heading for the courtyard. After a short silence, he said, 'Maybe I should go with you. You're just three women out there and –'

'Four with Evan,' India cut in.

'All right, four women. But you might need a bloke around. A bloke like me, who knows what's what. Mark Longden could show up making demands, you know. From what you've told me he's nasty.'

'Yes, he is, but we'll be all right, please don't worry. There's Wiggs, the head gardener, and Joe, who runs the estate.'

'And then there's that other rule, isn't there, India? No outsiders allowed.'

India eyed him through the corner of her eye, trying to ascertain his mood. He had sounded slightly annoyed; spotting the hint of mischief in his eyes, she laughed. 'Well, I will say this, you do learn fast, Mr Rhodes.'

'So do you, Lady India,' he shot back. 'How long do you intend to stay up here?'

'I'd planned to stay for a week before this happened. But who knows, I could be here longer now, if I'm out at the house and not at the store in Leeds. I've a lot of work there, and I'll have to stay until it's finished.'

'When can I start the painting?'

'Tomorrow. Hopefully. It all depends.'

He picked up on the concern in her voice, and said quietly, 'I'm sure Adele will show up, India, I really mean that. And certainly I hope so.'

'Thanks, Dusty . . .' Her voice trailed off and she searched in her bag for the car keys, found them and headed towards her car parked next to the barns.

'I do envy you this,' Dusty said when he drew to a standstill, patting the bonnet. 'An Aston Martin DB2-4, a piece of vintage mechanical art if ever there was one.'

She smiled up at him. 'Wasn't it nice of Daddy to part with his favourite wheels?' She kissed him on the cheek. 'But then I am his favourite, you know,' she added, getting into the car.

'Don't rub it in,' Dusty responded, his laughter rising. 'Give me a shout later.'

'I will.' After blowing him a kiss through the open window she turned on the ignition.

Once the Aston Martin had disappeared from sight, Dusty turned on his heels and crossed the cobbled yard, went down to the ornamental lake. He stood looking into its depths, taking pleasure at what he was seeing – a perfect reflection of the Georgian house on the hill, a mirror image clearly visible in that placid body of water as smooth as glass. How clever they were, those architects of the seventeenth and eighteenth centuries, he thought, nodding to himself. Whenever the topography allowed, they set the house on a hill and created a man-made lake at the bottom so that the house was reflected in all its glory. A double image. Very impressive indeed.

Dusty had studied architecture for a time, and he was particularly interested in the designs of Andrea Palladio. He considered it part of his training as an artist. And he had always thought that a Palladian villa set in a verdant English park was a very beautiful sight. He saw it as the perfect marriage of a building with nature. Dusty loved the classicism of the designs, because he loved all things classical, and of the Renaissance. William Kent, a follower of Inigo Jones, the great seventeenth-century architect, had designed and built his house, Willows Hall, over two hundred and seventy-five years ago, and it was pure Palladian. Dusty had fallen in love with it the first time he had seen it, although he had become concerned when he began to understand how neglected it truly was. The surveyors he had brought in had told him it was mostly surface damage, and that everything could be restored to its original state with some good repair work by master craftsmen.

He began to walk towards the house now, climbing up the grassy hill, and his thoughts automatically swung to India Standish. If anyone looked as if she belonged in this house it was she; after all, she had grown up in a very similar place – Clonloughlin in Ireland, a renowned Georgian house of impressive proportions and great beauty. And so of course she was at ease with the grand overtones of Willows Hall. He knew he looked right in it, too, even though he had been brought up in a back-to-back, a far cry from this place indeed.

Dusty had lavished a great deal of time, effort, care, love and money on Willows Hall over the past eight and a half years, and in doing so he had made it his own; he couldn't imagine living anywhere else.

When he reached the top of the hill he stood gazing at the south front façade for a moment, and he couldn't help admiring the way the pale stone gleamed in the afternoon sunlight; it looked as if it had been polished. It was perfectly beautiful.

As he lifted his eyes to the sky Dusty was happy to see that the thunderclouds had blown away; it wasn't going to rain after all. Turning, he walked down the length of the terrace, making for his studio. This stood a little away from the house on the left, and it was of his own design. From the outside it looked like a guest villa, echoing the main house since it was in the Palladian style.

When Dusty went inside he stood blinking for a moment. The studio was one vast, open space with a high-flung ceiling that seemed to soar endlessly upward, with many windows on both sides. There were a series of skylights set in the ceiling, and the whole area was filled with intense glittering northern light. Still blinking, he touched several buttons and electric window shades slid into place over the windows, dimming the daylight, cooling the room.

Moving lithely, he crossed to a drawing board, picked up a charcoal crayon and quickly made a series of dramatic and vivid sketches of India's face. Suddenly, he stopped, threw the crayon down and stepping away from the drawing board, went and lowered himself into an armchair.

Why was he painting her? The idea was ridiculous. It was really asking for trouble. In every way. Trouble for her. Trouble for him. Her father wouldn't like her association with him; whatever *she* believed, *he* knew he was right. They came from entirely different worlds. She was an aristocrat from very high altitudes; he was a working-class boy. Yes, he was famous. Very famous, in fact. And rich. All because of his talent, and doing something he couldn't live without doing. Painting. But as far as he was concerned, the Earl of Dunvale wouldn't care about those things. Other considerations mattered to a man like her father. Propriety and background, and stupid things like where he had gone to school, and what his father did, and whether he had a posh accent.

No, it wasn't fair to her, or to himself, actually, since he had no intention of becoming serious with India. *He* was wasting his valuable time with her, when he could be painting, and he was setting *her*

59

up to get hurt when he said goodbye. Yes, she was trouble. For a variety of reasons.

The red phone on the counter top began to ring. He looked across at it balefully, reluctant to answer it. But it didn't stop after six rings, so he got up in exasperation and strode over to the counter, snatched at the receiver.

'Hello?'

'Russell?'

'Hello Melinda.'

'How did you know it was me?'

'Recognized your voice.'

'I want out of this place, Russell,' she wailed. 'Get Dr Jeffers to release me.'

'You know I can't. You've got to stay there until he thinks you're properly de-toxed. Then he'll sign your release. I don't have anything to do with it, you know that.'

'Russell, please ask him.'

'You know very well he won't listen.'

'Please don't punish me this way.'

'I'm not doing that, Melinda. You signed yourself into the clinic.'

'I'll tell Atlanta what you're doing to me.'

'I'm not doing anything. Anyway, she's too young to understand.'

'Is she all right?'

'Yes, she's wonderful. I spoke to your mother yesterday and she said she's as happy as a lark. Look, Melinda, I've got to go. I'm working.'

'Will you talk to the doctor? *Please*.'

'Yes, I will. I'll give him a ring tomorrow. Now

rest quietly, and get well. 'Bye.' He hung up and stared at the phone. Now *that* was trouble if anything was. And then some.

He groaned. What was he going to do about Melinda and his child? He dreaded the thought of someone finding out about them. And yet he knew it would leak out some time soon . . . he was far too famous for it not to . . . He let this disturbing thought go, unable, suddenly, to cope with it.

Unexpectedly, his thoughts veered to Tessa Longden and her predicament about Adele. He fully understood how she felt, the agony of mind she was going through. After all, he had a three-year-old of his own, and he could well imagine how beside himself he would be in the same circumstances.

India drove along the motorway at a steady pace; she was soon leaving Harrogate behind and heading towards the village of Pennistone Royal. The sky had changed, the thunderclouds had drifted out to the North Sea and it was a lovely pale blue again. She was relieved. There would be nothing worse than tramping over sodden fields and meadows looking for a lost child.

Was she lost on the estate? No. Mark Longden had taken her out of spite. As a bargaining chip, as Dusty had suggested. *Dusty.* He was such a difficult man in so many ways, and so full of contradictions. He was loaded with baggage, most of it about *his* background and *their* class differences, all of which she found silly. He wouldn't listen to her. But no matter, she had fallen in love with him the night she had first met him, and nothing was going to change that. He was the only man she wanted, the only man for her, and she was determined to get him. Permanently. Long term. Marriage. That was her goal. It wasn't going to be easy, she was fully aware of all the problems.

Dusty was extremely independent, loathed being pinned down. Nor did he like to make commitments. That was obviously why he had never married or had a long-term relationship. 'Love 'em and leave 'em, that's always been my motto,' he had said to her when they first met several months ago, as if warning her. And then he had begun to laugh uproariously, seemingly highly amused by his own attitude.

He laughed a lot and she liked that. She couldn't bear glum people who sounded like the voices of doom with their dire predictions of impending disasters and gloomy outlook. He was usually in top form, cheerful, optimistic, raring to go, and ready to take a chance on life, except when it came to wedded bliss, of course. That was *verboten* even as a subject, not open for discussion at all.

Dusty liked being one of the boyos, as he called his male friends, who were numerous and varied . . . actors, writers, politicians, journalists, 'And,' as he often said, 'nobodies who I absolutely adore.' He fancied himself as Jack the Lad – Jack the *Bad* Lad. He enjoyed carousing and creating a stir, constantly referred to himself as a rabble-rouser. However, she had come to understand in the three months she had known him that much of this was a bit of an act. In point of fact, he drank very little, hardly anything at all, mostly nursed a Stolichnaya over ice all night, simply made a big noise about his consumption of booze. She was well aware that the men in the Harte family drank much more than Dusty. But then *he* needed a very steady hand the next morning in order to do his work. His style of painting was Classical Realism, and notable art critics around the world had hailed him right from the beginning of his career as the new Pietro Annigoni, proclaiming that he had inherited the mantle of the famous Italian painter who had died in 1988. They called Dusty a genius, and with the same awe and reverence they had called Annigoni a genius. Dusty's paintings were classical in style, very much in the manner of the great artists of the Renaissance, with precise attention to detail in the subject matter and background, whether these were interiors or exteriors. His portraits of the famous, and his paintings of landscapes and seascapes, were so detailed, his use of colour so breathtakingly beautiful, people simply stood and gazed at them mesmerized, unable to tear their eyes away.

Anybody who painted as precisely as he did could hardly afford to booze it up; she had said that to him once and he had grinned and winked at her. She felt the same way about his so-called rabble-rousing; even this was merely a form of jovial boisterousness, with much laughter, loud voices, arm-punching, back-slapping. Much ado about nothing, something which was totally innocuous but which the press played up. As he hoped they would. He loved his reputation as a wild hard-drinking hell-raiser, and did much to foster this characterization of himself. Especially in the papers.

When she had first understood his reputation was something of a myth she had burst out laughing. She had been walking through Harte's with Linnet when the truth dawned on her, and she had been unable to suppress her hilarity. Her cousin had stared at her and shaken her head, and said pithily, 'People who burst into gales of laughter for no apparent reason get taken away in strait-jackets. Especially when they're in the middle of a renowned and very posh emporium making a hulla-baloo. Drawing attention to themselves.'

'I'm sorry, Linnet,' she had spluttered, 'but I can't help it. I've suddenly realized my boyfriend is a bit of a phoney.'

This comment had instantly gained Linnet's undivided attention, and she had cried, 'Oh get rid of him. Immediately. We don't need anybody who's not true blue around here. Anyway, he'd get clob-bered by the lads.'

'What lads?'

'Julian, Gideon, Toby, and even young Desmond. They'd gang up on him.'

'That's true.'

'By the way, when you say boyfriend are you referring to the VFP?'

'VFP? What's that?'

'Very Famous Person. You told me you were

64

seeing someone very famous but you never confided who he is.'

'Russell Rhodes.'

'*Dusty* Rhodes? The painter?' Linnet's eyes had widened.

She had simply nodded in response but was pleased by Linnet's surprised reaction.

'He looks rather dishy, India.'

'He is, but complex.'

'Aren't they all,' Linnet had responded, grinning at her.

She had laughed and answered, 'But at least he's never been married, so there's no ex, or children to contend with. In fact he'd been unattached for quite a while before he met me.'

'You know, Dad loves his work, in fact we all do. He's always wanted Dusty Rhodes to paint Paula, but Mummy says she's too busy to sit all those hours for an artist. I wish she would, though, and so does Daddy.'

'I agree. Dusty's the perfect person to paint your mother. He could do a wonderful medieval portrait of her.'

Linnet had then asked her a lot of questions about Dusty as they had continued their walk through the store; she had answered some but had remained silent about others. She had discovered she didn't want to reveal too much about him or their relationship, at least not just yet. The real problem with Dusty was his attitude to her family. Without ever meeting any of them he had made a sudden snap decision and categorized them as aristos. 'Too posh. Snobs. Hoity-toity, idle rich folks,' was the way he described them. None of this was true, and she had tried to explain this, explain about her great-grandmother's impoverished beginnings, but he had swept her words away and changed the subject in his usual imperious manner.

At first she had thought he suffered from an inferiority complex about his own bleak and desolate background, growing up as a poor boy in the back streets of Leeds. Certainly he was always making reference to this. But she had quickly come to accept that he didn't have an inferiority complex at all – far from it, in fact. He was one of the most self-confident and self-possessed people she had ever met, in command of everything, exuding charm and displaying the most perfect manners when he wanted to.

Yet, nevertheless, Dusty believed her father would look down on him, wouldn't approve of him, would condemn their relationship out of hand. And so far she hadn't been able to convince him otherwise. But she would keep trying. And she knew her father and mother would like him, quite aside from the fact that they both admired his paintings, without even knowing she was involved with Dusty.

I have to give him time, she told herself, and slowed down as she came to the village. Within minutes she was leaving the small main street behind and heading for the road which would take her directly to the front gates of Pennistone Royal.

Her mind focused on Tessa and the situation she was likely to come across when she arrived. She had purposely not thought about it on the drive over from Dusty's house, but now she had to concentrate on the matter at hand. She had no idea what she would have to face. She prayed she would find Adele with her mother and not still lost. Or abducted. Prayed that tragedy did not lurk in the shadows.

Jonathan Ainsley crept into her mind, and she grimaced. From what she had learned lately, it appeared that Mark Longden was under his influence. How terrible that such a thing had happened. Could Jonathan be pulling the strings, was he the mastermind behind Adele's abduction? If that was what it was. She had no answers for herself.

CHAPTER FOUR

Linnet sat with Tessa in the upstairs parlour at Pennistone Royal, talking to her quietly, trying to reassure her that Adele was all right, that she would soon be home, silently praying that she was correct in this assertion, and that her assurances would not prove to be meaningless.

Evan was with them, seated near the lovely oriel window, but she was an observer rather than a participant at this moment, knowing it was best to let Linnet handle everything. Tessa could be touchy, even a little caustic, at the best of times, and today was the worst.

'Mark would never do anything to upset or hurt Adele,' Linnet said, touching her sister's hand, then taking it in hers. 'He does adore her, you know, that's always been most apparent.'

'Yes,' Tessa responded, 'but what if it's not Mark who has her? Perhaps Desmond was right when he suggested it might well be a kidnapping for ransom. She could easily be with strangers, and therefore in danger.'

'I really do doubt that,' Linnet answered in a stronger tone, wishing her younger brother had not voiced this opinion. It was a possibility but he would have been wiser to have kept it to himself. 'And you must *trust* Jack Figg. He's the best and the smartest private investigator there is, Mummy's said that for years and she's always relied on him in a crisis. And don't forget, he was head of Harte's security for years.'

'But he's been retired for some time now,' Tessa pointed out, a sudden shrillness in her voice.

'Semi-retired, to be exact. He still works full time for those who need him, such as former clients he's remained close to, like us. Anyway, you know very well our mother put him on a retainer and used him to do that in-depth check on Mark Longden several weeks ago. She filled us in before she went off to New York.'

'Yes –' Tessa's voice suddenly broke and tears welled in her eyes again. She wiped them quickly with a tissue and continued shakily, 'I'm so worried about Adele I can hardly bear it. She's such a little girl and she must be so scared, even if she is with her father. I mean, being snatched off the terrace in such an awful way will have frightened her. I feel so helpless, I don't know what to do.'

'Listen to me,' Linnet said in her firmest, most confident voice, 'we don't know *how* she was taken, whether it was awful or not. Actually, I'm sure it wasn't.' Hoping to calm Tessa, she went on talking. 'I'm sure Mark made it seem like a game to Adele, you know, waving to her, putting his finger to his lips so she would be quiet, smiling at her, beckoning. Yes, I'm quite certain that's what he did. It's obvious he wouldn't want to alarm her, frighten her. He knew he mustn't upset her since he was taking her without your permission. She would've made quite a racket, I think, if he'd just rushed in and grabbed her.'

'You seem so certain it *is* Mark. Like me.' Tessa gave Linnet a hard stare and her eyes narrowed slightly. 'I just hope to God we're right. What is Jack Figg actually *doing* right now?'

'He's working in the library, on the phone a lot, talking to people, mostly his operatives, I believe. I never question his methods and neither should you. Let it suffice for me to say that he has contacts everywhere in the world and in all walks of life. If anybody can find Adele, it's Jack, believe me it is.'

Glancing across at Evan, Tessa said slowly, '*You* had lunch with Uncle Robin at Lackland Priory today. Did he mention Jonathan Ainsley? Where he was living these days?'

Evan tensed. Tessa had sounded almost accusatory, but she kept her voice level as she answered calmly, 'No, he didn't mention Jonathan. I'm sorry, Tessa, I don't know anything about him. But he's more than likely out of the country. In Hong Kong. Robin would have told me if Jonathan were in England . . . you see he would have warned me. I know Robin worries a lot about Jonathan doing me harm out of spite.'

'And all of *us*, too, for that matter!' Linnet

exclaimed, her green eyes flashing. 'He's had it in for Mummy and her offspring for ages. In fact, I think he has it in for every one of the Hartes. He'd like to mow us all down with a machine gun and be rid of us once and for all. And all because he feels cheated by Emma Harte. He's a nasty piece of work, but Mums says he always was.'

'That's true,' Tessa agreed. 'And to think Mark let himself fall into his clutches.' Tessa sat back on the sofa, twisting the tissue in her hands, her face ringed with misery. At this precise moment she fervently wished she had never married Mark Longden. All he had ever done really was to create a ton of misery for her, not to mention the verbal and physical abuse he had meted out lately. Now he had stolen their child.

Suddenly the door flew open and India came into the upstairs parlour almost at a run. 'Hi, everybody,' she said and then made a bee-line for her cousin Tessa; she knelt down next to her and took hold of her hand. 'I'm so sorry this happened,' India murmured, looking at Tessa intently, wanting to convey her enormous sympathy and concern. Her face was full of compassion, her eyes warm and loving. 'I'm here for you, whatever you need. You only have to ask.'

Tessa nodded, attempted a smile. It faltered instantly, but she managed to say, 'Thanks, India, I'm glad you're here.'

Watching India commiserate with Tessa, Evan couldn't help thinking how very much alike they looked, like sisters actually, as if turned out from the same mould. It was apparent they were closely related; both had silver-gilt hair and silvery-grey luminous eyes, pale complexions and delicately-wrought faces. They were lovely looking in a soft, feminine way, and she knew their striking resemblance to each other came from their genes, their shared Fairley bloodline.

Evan had also heard the family legend that their great-great-grandmother Adele Fairley had been a famous beauty – stunning, elegant, aristocratic, and possibly slightly mad. And that it was from her that these two had inherited their unique silver-blonde hair and extraordinary eyes, as well as their angelic faces. Even little Adele had the same looks. She was part Fairley, and to Evan she did not appear to be anything at all like a Harte. The thought of the missing child made her shrivel inside, and she felt a sudden chill sweep over her. Involuntarily, she shivered. What if Adele were in some kind of danger? Everyone had mentioned Mark, or a kidnapper looking for money, but hadn't anyone thought of a paedophile?

Immediately Evan shoved that thought aside, it was too awful to contemplate. She glanced across at Linnet, who was a true Harte with her halo of red hair, green eyes and dynamic personality. Gideon had the same Harte colouring and upbeat attitude. Evan couldn't help but admire Linnet this afternoon. She had taken charge in a quiet but confident way and was handling everything with true diplomacy and efficiency. Not only did she convey great positiveness, she had managed somehow to keep Tessa calm. Evan knew how much the latter was suffering; furthermore, Tessa was at a loss, had no idea what to do, which was so unlike her.

Linnet's cell phone began to ring and she got up, walked over to one of the tall windows, stood talking for a moment, and Evan knew it was Julian on the other end. Linnet had asked her to be a bridesmaid at her marriage to Julian in the winter, and she had been thrilled to accept. Gideon was to be best man and India the other bridesmaid.

Her eyes wandered around the upstairs parlour . . . Linnet had once explained to her that this had been Emma Harte's favourite room, and she understood the reasons why. It was lovely, gracious, charming, and spacious, with a high ceiling and tall leaded windows. There was a carved mantel over the fireplace and the walls were a sunny daffodil colour. Two large comfortable sofas were covered in a floral chintz fabric vibrant with scarlet and blues, greens and pinks on a pale yellow background. The Aubusson rug underfoot was obviously rare, a valuable antique, as were the pieces of furniture made of mellow, ripe woods. Linnet had also explained that over the years the room had never changed in its decor; it was simply refurbished with the same fabrics and colours for a sense of continuity and as a reflection of Emma's great taste.

Evan loved art and she was particularly interested in English landscapes, and for a moment her gaze rested on the museum-quality Turner hanging on a side wall, then it swung to the oil painting above the mantelpiece. This was of Paul McGill, the love of Emma's life; he was wearing an army officer's uniform and it had apparently been painted in the First World War. What a handsome man he was, she thought. No wonder Emma had succumbed to his charms.

'Evan, let's go down to the kitchen and rustle up a pot of tea,' Linnet said. 'And Margaret will make us some smoked salmon sandwiches. I'm starved. I didn't have lunch.'

Evan sat up with a start, brought out of her reverie by Linnet's voice. 'Okay!' she answered at once, jumping up, moving across the floor swiftly, hating to be caught offguard in this way.

'What about you, Tessa?' Linnet asked.

'I couldn't eat a thing! Food would choke me!' she cried, shaking her head almost violently.

'India? Do you want something, darling?' Linnet's auburn brow lifted questioningly.

Her cousin nodded. 'Tea with lemon would be nice, and so would a smoked salmon sandwich. Thanks.'

'I thought you'd had lunch,' Linnet murmured, and then stopped short. 'Oh, but you never finished it, did you? Instead you drove here.' Linnet stared hard at India but her face was quite expressionless.

'That's correct,' India responded evenly, her own face as blank as her cousin's. But she couldn't help wondering if Linnet had guessed she had been with Dusty at lunchtime. No matter; Linnet was always on her side whatever she did.

* * *

74

Jack Figg was seated at the large Georgian desk in the panelled library, his eyes on the papers spread out in front of him.

After a moment he lifted his eyes and looked across at Linnet, who was seated on the sofa with Tessa. She was grim and intent, but holding her own as he knew she would. It was Tessa he was worried about.

She looked as though she would pass out at any moment; her face was stark, chalky, her eyes swollen and red-rimmed from weeping. He fully understood how anguished and worried she was, and his heart went out to her. Apart from being a kind and compassionate man, he had once lost a child to death and his grief had been searing, a sorrow he could not endure. Now he prayed that Adele was alive. Instinctively he felt that she was, and he wanted more than anything else to trust in those instincts. God damn it, she has to be alive, he thought, willing it to be so.

Seated on the other sofa near the fireplace were India Standish, whom he had known since she was a child, and Evan Hughes, the newcomer to the family, recently-discovered, and another great-granddaughter of Emma. He could see the concern on their faces as well, and he knew that all of these four young women had been waiting for hours to get an update on the situation from him.

So had young Emsie and Desmond, who had rushed after him when he had traversed the estate with Wiggs and Joe earlier. They were now sitting on the upholstered library fender, obviously being extremely careful about opening their mouths. He had warned them that if they wanted to stay in the library they had to remain totally quiet. 'Not one word,' he had cautioned and they had nodded their agreement.

Without preamble he began to speak, addressing himself to Linnet and Tessa who sat together. 'It's turning four-thirty, and it's just over five and a half hours since Adele disappeared.' He paused, his eyes sweeping over them, then he went on: 'I'm afraid I don't know where she is. But I do know where she *isn't*, and that's here at Pennistone Royal. She's not in the fields, the meadows, the woods or the gardens, which have all been thoroughly scoured. And I've even had Wiggs drag the pond. Fortunately, all he found were weeds. Nor has Adele been seen in Pennistone Royal village, although two or three people did notice a black Mercedes driving through at high speed around lunchtime. That's obviously the same car which was seen here in the drive by Wiggs and the stable lads.'

'What about Mark? What about Mark?' Tessa cried excitedly, repeating herself, and clutching the rag doll to her, as she had done on and off during the day. 'Have you tried to find *him*?'

'I have indeed,' Jack responded softly. 'I spoke to his secretary who told me he had taken a few days off –'

'He came up here to grab Adele!' Tessa interrupted, her voice rising. 'I bet anything he's in

Yorkshire. With Jonathan Ainsley. They're in this together.' She looked agitated, and her eyes flared.

'He could be up here, of course,' Jack said, 'but he's certainly *not* with Jonathan Ainsley. I've had one of my people check Jonathan's whereabouts and he's in Hong Kong at this very moment. And he's been there for several weeks.'

'Perhaps Mark took Adele back to London with him, *if* he grabbed her,' Linnet ventured, giving Jack a long, hard stare.

'He's not in his apartment nor is he at the house in Hampstead. Both places have been checked out.'

'But the house is locked up –' Tessa began, and then her voice faltered when she saw the irritated expression flashing across Jack's face.

'Yes, the house *is* locked up, Tessa, and so is Mark's apartment. But we do have our ways of checking things out.'

'I understand,' she said meekly, leaning back against the sofa, ignoring Linnet who had poked her in the ribs a moment ago, warning her to shut up, she had no doubt.

'I've phoned Mark's mother in Gloucestershire,' Jack continued. 'She was not at home, but was expected early this evening, according to someone called Dory.'

'Dory's the housekeeper,' Tessa volunteered. She cleared her throat and went on somewhat tentatively, 'Mrs Longden's a bit of a doting mother, but she's a decent woman. If Mark took Adele to her home she would insist he brought her back to me at once.'

'*If* his mother knew he had Adele without your permission,' Jack pointed out. 'Mark might not tell her. Anyway, I think that in all probability he's somewhere in Yorkshire. We must find him.'

'But how?' India asked, frowning. 'It's like looking for a needle in a haystack, isn't it?'

'Only too true,' Jack agreed. 'It's not going to be easy, even if we go to the police. We may have to do that, and soon. I've spoken at length to Gideon, I told him we might need to blast the news of Adele's abduction all over the media, starting with the Harte television network and the Harte newspapers. Gideon agrees with me. But we're not going to do that just yet. Before we go to those lengths, or go to the police, I want to give Mark a chance to bring Adele home to you, Tessa. Tonight, if that's at all possible.'

'But what if it's not Mark who grabbed her?' Tessa asked, sounding suddenly tremulous again. 'What if it's a kidnapping?'

'We'd have had a ransom note or some kind of communication from the kidnappers before now if that were the case,' Jack explained. 'By the way, Tessa, at my request Gideon spoke to Toby in Los Angeles this afternoon. Toby hasn't been trying to get hold of you today. So I'm positive it was Mark calling you this morning in an effort to distract you while he took Adele. Or it was someone else, someone who was helping him, working with him.'

'I didn't really recognize the voice,' Tessa replied. 'Although it did sound familiar, I suppose that's why I thought it must be Toby.'

Leaning forward in the chair, his arms resting on the desk, Jack was thoughtful for a moment before saying, 'In a short while I shall phone Mark's mother, explain what's happened. Hopefully she will cooperate, if she knows anything, that is. But if we don't have anything new or know where Mark is by about six-thirty, then I'll have no alternative but to inform the North Yorkshire police. I will also call Gideon to tell him to go ahead and issue a news bulletin about Adele's disappearance. I can't leave it much longer than that, I simply can't take that chance.'

Tessa pressed a hand to her mouth and stifled her sobs.

Linnet exclaimed, 'Once the Harte media companies go public here it will be on American television. Mummy will have to be told before she hears it from another source.'

Jack gave Linnet a fleeting smile. 'I'll be calling her after I've been in touch with the police, if that becomes necessary. You and Tessa can speak to her as well. But the main thing now is to find out whether or not Mrs Longden knows anything.' Jack leaned back in the chair trying to relax his tense muscles, and glanced across at the grandfather clock as he did.

There was a sudden silence in the room. No one spoke. Everyone was lost in their own thoughts.

Tessa's mind was in a turmoil, her senses swimming. It was almost six and she had no idea where her child was, and she was more frantic than ever. She felt nauseous, and making a snap decision she jumped up. 'I need some air!' she cried to the room at large.

Immediately India pushed herself to her feet and hurried over to Tessa, took hold of her arm. 'Come on, darling, let's go for some fresh air. After ten minutes outside you'll feel much better.'

'I think I will,' Tessa mumbled, pushing down the sickly feeling.

After Tessa and India had left the library, Evan cleared her throat and said to Jack, 'I didn't want to bring this up in front of Tessa, but what if it's neither Mark nor kidnappers but a paedophile?'

A long sigh escaped Jack and then he said, 'That had crossed my mind.' At this moment his mobile began to ring and he turned it on. 'Figg here,' he said, pressing it to his ear. Standing up, he walked over to the windows, and stood listening to his caller, eventually murmured his thanks and clicked off. Walking back to the desk, he told them, 'That was one of my operatives who's been checking every hotel in the area. Mark Longden was definitely in Yorkshire three nights ago. He stayed at the Queen's Hotel in Leeds. And last night he was at the Swan in Harrogate. However, he has checked out of both places. So far my chap hasn't found him registered anywhere else. Not yet.'

'Perhaps he's staying at a private home,' Linnet said, and gave Jack a knowing look, trying to indicate she needed to speak to him alone.

'I'm really frightened,' Tessa said quietly, staring at India, 'frightened that some harm might come

80

to Adele. She's such a delicate, sensitive little girl, so defenceless. But then all small children are defenceless against adults, aren't they?'

'That's right,' India agreed. 'But let's try and look on the bright side. I'm sure she's with Mark, not strangers, and therefore she's quite safe.'

Tessa shivered and goose flesh sprang up on her arms. 'You don't know what Mark's become, India! *A drunk, a drug-addict!* He's not been himself for a long time, and he's an abuser. I've feared for my life . . .' She peered at India. 'Did you know that?'

'Yes, your mother told me he'd been violent with you. It's shocking when you think about it – that he could become somebody else, totally different almost overnight.'

'When he's in control of himself he's fine. It's when he's under the influence of drink or drugs that he's dangerous, and quite inadvertently he could hurt Adele. That's what worries me.'

'I understand. But as I said, we've got to remain positive.' As she spoke, India got up from the wooden garden seat, and suggested, 'Why don't we go down to the old oak and sit there for a while? It's nicer there.'

'All right –' Tessa stopped, turned to India. 'Perhaps we ought to go back inside. I'm afraid of missing something.'

'Linnet will come and get us if there's any news. It'll do you good to be out of that room for a bit. It was becoming claustrophobic.'

Tessa nodded, and the two of them walked down

the path, past the long terrace; they crossed the sloping lawn and finally came to a stop under the ancient tree. They sat together at the wrought-iron table but remained silent for a few moments, each of them involved with their own thoughts.

It was Tessa who finally broke the silence when she said in a low voice, 'I don't know what I'll do if anything happens to Adele, I love her so much, she's my life. I'd just fall apart forever, everything would become so meaningless without her. Without my little girl my life would be over.'

'Come on, Tessa, don't talk like this,' India exclaimed briskly. 'Jack's going to get her back, you'll see. And you'll settle things amicably with Mark, the divorce will go through, and things will be normal.'

'Oh, India, I do hope you're right, but he's being very greedy, you know. He wants the house, a lot of money, and joint custody of Adele. I don't think I could agree to joint custody; the house yes. But not joint custody.'

'Once you've got Adele back I think you ought to try and move quickly, settle matters with him. You know very well you hate things hanging over your head.'

'You're right,' Tessa agreed, suddenly brightening. 'I'll talk to my solicitor, perhaps we can get everything moving faster. Much faster. But it's only a few months since I left Mark.'

'That's true, but so what. Anyway, Linnet and I both agree that Mark has always been avaricious, so he's got his price, in my opinion. Buy him off,

Tessa, it's the only way.' India peered across the table at her cousin. 'That's a Harte rule, remember.'

Jack and Linnet had walked out into the Stone Hall and stood talking quietly near the fireplace.

'Mark has friends in Yorkshire, where he could stay with Adele? Is that what you're suggesting?' Jack asked, squinting at Linnet in the dim, early evening light.

'Yes,' she answered and moving across the floor she turned on several lamps.

He stood watching her for a moment, thinking how much she resembled Emma Harte – well, a young Emma – with her red-gold hair and English-rose complexion. He'd gone to work for Emma when he was eighteen, forty years ago, and he had loved, respected and admired her, found her to be the most exacting, exasperating, charming, bossy and brilliant woman he had ever known. She had been his favourite boss. Now, here was Linnet, the spitting image of her, and just as smart, smart as a whip. She was his favourite amongst this younger generation because to him she exemplified so much of the past and her family's heritage as well as the present. It's as if she has a foot in both worlds, the old and the new, he thought, and that makes her unique, and very special to me.

'What are you thinking about, Jack?' Linnet asked, sitting in a chair. 'You look as if you've just had a most brilliant thought.'

'Not all that brilliant, but yes, I've had a rather interesting thought. Actually, it's a thought I'd had earlier and now it's come back. Look, Linnet, Jonathan Ainsley's in Hong Kong, that we know for certain, but the world's a village today, and he could very well be masterminding this situation with Mark and Adele. By phone, probably. He wouldn't want to put it in writing, in an e-mail or a fax. *And*, and this is very important, he's got a former girlfriend in Yorkshire, and she —'

'Of course, my mother's secretary, Eleanor! And what you're suggesting is that Jonathan is manipulating Mark long distance in order to hurt Paula and us, and that Mark goes along because he wants to spite Tessa. Good thinking.' She gave him a penetrating look. 'Are you wondering if Eleanor's in on it?'

'I am indeed,' Jack answered, flopping down in the chair opposite her, crossing his legs.

'If she is, she's being very foolish,' Linnet murmured. 'My mother's on to her. She has taken all power away from her. But she *is* an old flame of Jonathan's, and they've recently been in contact again. Look, I'm not suggesting she'd help Mark take Adele, but perhaps she's offering him —'

'A safe haven for a few days?' Jack ventured, cutting in, then smiling across at her.

'Yes, that's *my* thought.'

'But would she risk her job, I wonder? She might tittle-tattle about your mother, but do you think she would really help Mark? It would make her an accessory. And it *would* be construed as a kidnapping if we have to go to the police, resort to the law.'

'But not everybody's familiar with the law, or as astute as you are, Jack. Maybe she just doesn't understand. Also, there's another thing we have to think about. Ellie does rather fancy herself, and she's still a lovely-looking woman . . . so, perhaps she harbours the idea that Jonathan is going to get back with her after all. And if that's the case, does her job working for my mother at the Leeds store really matter to her?'

'You've got a point there, Linnet. And Mark could have taken Adele to Ellie's home without her knowing what's going on, if we're to give her the benefit of the doubt.' Jack now peered at his watch and stood up. 'Time to make that call to Mrs Longden, I think. Come on, Beauty, let's go on a fishing trip in Gloucestershire. Also, let's keep this conversation to ourselves, all right?'

'Absolutely,' she said.

CHAPTER FIVE

T he moment Jack walked back into the library with Linnet he immediately picked up on the tension in the air. Tessa sat as rigid as stone on the sofa, her face strained, her eyes filled with suffering. India was sitting next to her, also stiffly erect in her seat, her expression one of worry and anxiety. Evan, standing next to a window, was talking on her mobile whilst Emsie and Desmond huddled on the upholstered brass fender, whispering together.

Linnet gave Jack a quick look, and then hurried across to the other sofa, where she was instantly joined by Evan.

Jack strode over to the desk and stood behind it, suddenly conscious of six pairs of eyes fixed unwaveringly on him. I've got to get this moving along, he thought, I can't delay. Time is of the essence now. He knew he was going to have to bring in the police and the media if he didn't succeed with Mark's mother. And then there was the possibility that she didn't know anything, was an innocent bystander. If that was the case, he would have calculated wrongly. He prayed he had been right in his assumptions, that she *would* be able to help them solve this.

In his usual businesslike way, and without any idle chit-chat, he told them: 'I'm now going to call Mark's mother.' Fixing his gaze on Tessa, he added, 'I'm putting the phone on the speaker so you can hear her responses, but I want you to be perfectly quiet.' His eyes swept over the others. 'And that goes for everyone else, of course. One other thing, Tessa. Will you have a word with your mother-in-law? It might be necessary.'

There was only a moment's hesitation on Tessa's part, and then she nodded quickly. 'I'll talk to her, yes. We're not close, but as I said, she's a decent enough woman.' There was a little pause; Tessa frowned, then added, 'Mark's her only son and she'll always be on his side no matter what, even though he leads her a merry dance. But if you think it's necessary I'll certainly come to the phone.'

Jack nodded his understanding and sat down. Picking up the receiver he pressed the speaker button and then dialled.

A few moments later a woman answered. 'Camden Lodge. Hello?' Her cultured voice was heard by everyone in the library.

'Is this Mrs Hilary Longden?'

'Yes, this is she.'

'Good evening, Mrs Longden. My name's Jack Figg. I phoned earlier but you were out. You don't know me, Mrs Longden, but you do know my employer, Mrs Paula O'Neill.'

'Well, of course. Tessa's mother. Have we met, Mr Figg?' she asked, her curiosity apparent in her tone, her voice pleasant.

'Briefly. At Tessa's marriage to Mark. But to get to the point, we have a problem, Mrs Longden. I'm here at Pennistone Royal with Tessa, and the reason I'm here is because Adele, your grand-daughter, disappeared around eleven o'clock this morning and she still hasn't been found.'

'Oh my God! How terrible! Tessa and Mark must be out of their minds with worry. Oh dear, oh dear, why haven't they found her? Surely she's somewhere on the estate? Oh, my poor little Adele, she must be so *frightened*. This is very upsetting, just awful. Can I speak to my son? And Tessa?' Her voice had risen an octave or two, had become shrill, and it was obvious she was genuinely distressed. 'How can I be of help, Mr Figg?' she asked.

'By telling me where your son is, Mrs Longden,' Jack answered in a voice echoing with cold deter- mination.

'*Mark*? Do you mean he's not there with Tessa?' She was obviously startled by this fact.

'No, he's not. I have reason to believe that it's Mark who took Adele without informing Tessa,' Jack announced. 'I believe he has abducted her, and I must put certain things into oper –'

'Mark would never abduct Adele!' she cut in peremptorily and with great indignation. 'That's ridiculous! Preposterous! He's her father . . . what on earth are you suggesting? Going on about in this way, Mr Figg?'

'An abduction. Which will be construed as a *kidnapping* by the police and the law. Kidnappers get tough sentences, you know. And I *will* have to go to the police within the next few minutes. I can't put it off any longer. We've been unable to find Adele on the estate after several searches, nor can we locate Mark. He, too, has disappeared. So I have no alternative but to bring in law enforcement and also the Harte media companies. They can help by issuing news bulletins on television and the radio. We must find Adele as quickly as possible. *It's imperative.*'

'You're serious, aren't you, Mr Figg?' She sounded shaken, frightened.

'Very, very serious, Mrs Longden.'

'B-b-b-but I don't understand,' she began, stuttering, obviously more unhinged than before. 'Why would Mark take Adele without telling Tessa? I'm not following this.'

Intuitively, Jack knew the woman was telling him the truth, and he modulated his voice slightly, made it softer, as he explained. 'Because of the divorce. It's becoming extremely bitter, he's trying to use Adele as a weapon against Tessa.'

'*Divorce!* They're getting a divorce! But I don't know anything about that. Oh, this is so absurd, Mark would have told me. My son tells me everything. It just can't be,' she asserted.

'Oh it's true right enough,' Jack answered. 'Would you like to speak to your daughter-in-law now?'

'Y-y-y-yes please.' The stuttering had started again.

89

'Just a moment.' Jack beckoned to Tessa, who was by his side in a flash. Covering the mouthpiece, he said softly, 'Be careful what you say. We need her.'

Taking the receiver from him, Tessa murmured, 'Hello, Mrs Longden.' She was trying hard to keep a rein on her emotions, willing herself to be controlled, even though she was shaking inside. 'Jack is correct. Mark *has* taken Adele. There is no other explanation for her disappearance. She must be so upset and confused, not understanding what's going on, poor little thing.'

'Yes, yes, I know, you're right. But is it *true* about the divorce?'

'Yes, it is. I've tried hard with Mark, tried to keep the marriage together, but it's not been working between us. We've been separated since June.'

'Mark never told me!' Hilary Longden cried, tears in her voice. 'How could Mark do that to me?'

'I don't know, but he did. And we do need to find Mark,' Tessa repeated tensely. 'And Adele.'

'I don't know where he is, and I am telling you the truth!'

'Would Mr Longden know?' Tessa probed.

'No, no, of course not. Mark's not a little boy, he doesn't check in with us, you know that, Tessa.'

Tessa looked at Jack, made a facial grimace and handed the phone to him without a word.

'Jack Figg again, Mrs Longden. Since you have no knowledge of Mark's whereabouts I shall call in the North Yorkshire police. I do know Mark was in Yorkshire over the last few days, including last night, and I'm quite certain they'll find him fast enough. It's a pity, really, that I have to resort to this. And then there's going to be all the nasty publicity. That can't possibly do his reputation much good. Well, thanks for your courtesy, for hearing me out, Mrs Longden. Good night.'

'Mr Figg, please, don't hang up! I promise you I have no idea where Mark is, nor do I know anything about Adele's disappearance. However, I do have a mobile phone number which Mark gave me last week. I think it might be a new one.'

'Please give it to me.'

'Just a minute. I have to find it. Hold on, it's somewhere on this desk.' A split second later she was reciting the number to him and extracting a promise from him to keep her abreast of the situation.

Jack hung up and said to Tessa, 'Do you know this mobile number?' As he spoke he showed her the pad he had written it on.

She shook her head. 'His mother's right. I think it's a new one.'

Jack lifted the phone and dialled.

It was answered within a split second. 'Hello?'

'Mark?'

'Yes.' There was a hesitancy in the voice, wariness.

'If you cut me off I will immediately ask the North Yorkshire police to go into action. And I'll tell the media about your abduction of Adele.'

'What?' Mark exploded.

'Don't start with me, Mark. We know you have Adele. You've been spotted.'

'Who the hell *is* this?' he demanded, anger in the tone.

'Jack Figg here. I work for Paula O'Neill. I'm with Tessa at Pennistone Royal. We want Adele returned. *At once.*'

'I don't have her. It's the first I've heard about an abduction.'

'You don't sound too upset about your daughter's sudden disappearance today. Which means that you know exactly where she is. *She's with you.* How do charges of kidnapping sound, Mark? Should help your career and your reputation no end, eh?'

'I don't know what you're talking about,' he cried.

Tessa came to Jack, gave him a hard stare and motioned to the phone. He handed it over at once.

'Mark, this is Tessa. Please bring Adele back.'

'Why am I being accused in this way?' he demanded, anger echoing again.

'Because you took her this morning. We know you did. Wiggs saw you. Please, please bring her back to me. For the child's sake.'

'I told you, I don't have her!'

'Yes, you do. Don't play games with me, Mark.'

There was a silence and she wondered if she had lost him, been cut off, when he suddenly spoke again.

He said, 'You won't get her back until you meet my terms.'

'Anything you want,' she said swiftly, relief flooding through her. Obviously, he *did* have Adele.

'Joint custody, for starters,' Mark intoned.

'The solicitors will work all that out. But you can have the house in Hampstead, the cars, a financial settlement, as you wanted.'

'Joint custody,' he repeated, icy cold.

Jack's cell phone began to ring and he switched it on, walked closer to the window, speaking into it as he did.

Tessa's eyes followed Jack; she said into the phone, 'The solicitors will have to get together to work things out.' She took a deep breath and against her better judgement added, 'If not joint custody then certainly a lot of access.'

Suddenly Jack was hurrying towards her across the library, a grim smile on his face. He took the receiver from her unceremoniously, and said, 'Jack Figg here. I've just been speaking to the North Yorkshire police on the other line. They are on their way to pick you up. We know you are at the Spa Hotel in Ripon with Adele. Registered under the name of William Stone.'

Jack paused when he heard the surprised intake of breath at the other end of the phone. 'If you leave now you can be here at Pennistone Royal in half an hour, and deal with me. Or you can wait for the police to pick you up within the next fifteen minutes. Your choice, mate.'

'I'm leaving now,' Mark said abruptly, the bluster gone from his voice all of a sudden.

'With Adele?'

93

'Yes, I'm bringing her,' Mark mumbled and clicked off.

Jack replaced the receiver and looked at Tessa, a triumphant gleam in his light-grey eyes. 'That was one of my operatives on my mobile a moment ago. When he discovered that a man with a little girl was staying at the Spa in Ripon he double-checked with a contact he has there. The name William Stone didn't ring a bell with Pete, but he thought he'd better tell me, and of course I knew it was Mark at once.'

'Thank God!' Tessa reached out, touched Jack's arm. 'I feel as though I'm going to faint with relief that she's coming home. Thanks, Jack, thank you so much.'

In a sudden spontaneous gesture, Jack stepped closer, pulled her into his arms and hugged her to him. 'Before you can say Jack Robinson you'll have Adele back with you. Now, come on, we've quite a lot to do before he arrives.'

Tessa nodded and then promptly burst into tears, sobbing as if her heart would break. 'It's relief,' he said to her gently, and led her over to the sofa. Looking at India he went on, 'It's a normal reaction, she's been pent up with tension all day. Sit with her, look after her, she'll be fine soon.'

Beckoning to Desmond and Emsie, Jack continued, 'I need you two to do a couple of things for me.'

'Yes, Jack!' Desmond exclaimed, instantly jumping off the fender, rushing over to Jack, with Emsie following in his wake.

'What do you need us to do?' Emsie asked when they came to a stop near the Georgian desk. Her face was eager, her dark eyes bright with earnestness.

'Desmond, please go and find Wiggs and tell him that Adele should be back within half an hour. But don't say anything else, and don't mention Mark. Okay?'

Desmond nodded, and then volunteered, 'And Jack, when you talk to Mums, tell her we need to do something about security here. Anybody can come and go as they please.'

'I've made a note to do that, Desmond. I've a plan for a proper security system in the works,' Jack replied, and then looked at Emsie, smiled at her. 'Go and tell Margaret and Joe that Adele is coming back soon, and please ask Margaret to bring in some ice and a tray of drinks. I certainly need a vodka and I'm sure everyone else wants something, too.'

The two youngsters hurried out, and Linnet walked across to Jack and hugged him. 'Thanks Jack, thanks for everything you've done.' Her face was ringed in smiles.

'Thanks not necessary, Beauty.' He stared at her intently, said in a low voice, 'I pushed it a bit, but I felt I was doing the right thing. Thank God it worked out all right. Mark became scared when I said the police were on the way. It sobered him up.'

'Why? Was he drunk?' Linnet asked swiftly, raising a brow.

'Just a manner of speaking.'

'*Had* you called the North Yorkshire police, Jack, or were you bluffing?'

'Bluffing, Beauty. But when Pete, my operative checking the local hotels, mentioned the name William Stone I remembered what you'd told me about Mark using that name as a pseudonym for his client Jonathan Ainsley.'

'I'm glad I told you.'

He smiled, went to the desk, sat down, looked at the pad where he had made voluminous notes.

A moment later Evan was standing in front of the desk, and he glanced up, his eyes questioning.

'Thanks for being such a calming influence, Jack. Would it be all right if I told Robin that Jonathan *is* in Hong Kong? He was wondering where his son was when I had lunch with him today. It will ease his mind knowing Jonathan's not in the country.'

'By all means. Be my guest, Evan.'

A moment later Linnet and Evan went to sit with Tessa and India, gently talking to Tessa, re-assuring her that everything was going to be all right. She accepted their words, their kindness, their reassurances, and tried to smile, tried to bring herself back to a normal state. But the tension was deeply imbedded in her, and she was also aware that her life had been changed forever by the events of the day. She also knew that no easing of her pain would come until her child was safely by her side.

Gideon Harte sat at his desk in the offices of the Yorkshire Consolidated Newspaper Company, in

South East London, not far from the famed Fleet Street of yesteryear. Although the renowned street of ink was still there, many of the great national daily newspapers had moved to quarters elsewhere as the Hartes' newspaper company had.

Overlooking a portion of the Thames, Gideon's office was spacious, light-filled and airy, with lots of plate-glass windows, shaded by silver metal-mesh panels. It was discreetly decorated in shades of white and grey, and there were lots of books banked in low-slung black-lacquered shelves that rode across a long back wall. His black-lacquered desk was empty, the way he liked it, with a few memos in simple black trays, a dictionary, a thesaurus, and antique crystal inkpots on a silver tray.

Pushing his chair back, Gideon lifted his feet to the desk and leaned back in the chair, watching the large modern clock on the wall straight ahead. Once the hands hit six forty-five he lowered his legs, sat up straight and picked up the phone. He dialled the Peninsula Hotel in Beverly Hills and waited.

When the operator answered he said, 'Toby Harte, please.'

A moment later his brother was saying, 'Hello? Toby Harte here.'

'It's me, Toby. Gid. And it's good news. Jack's found Mark. He's admitted he has Adele, and he's on his way to Pennistone Royal now bringing her back to Tessa.'

'Thank God! What a bastard he is, Gid, taking

his own child in that way, and all to get back at poor Tessa. He should be – well, I can't think of anything quite bad enough to do to that shit!'

Gid laughed. 'How about horsewhipped, to use an old-fashioned phrase? Or even better, what about hung, drawn and quartered?'

Toby also laughed and said, 'I'll punch him in the face a few times myself and I'll be relieved when I know Adele is actually with Tessa at the house. Only then will I relax, I don't trust that bugger.'

'I agree with you. But I promised to let you know as soon as I had *some* news, and I just hung up on Jack. Evan had called me a few minutes before, to pass the word for him. But then Jack called himself, wanted to talk to me about security. Not only at Pennistone Royal, which is very vulnerable, as we now know, but all of our homes, and I think he's right. They should have more protection.'

'Agreed. And Jack's the right chap to set everything up. By the way, do Paula and Shane know anything yet, Gid?'

'God, no! And don't get involved. Don't tell our parents, because you know our mother will pass it on to Paula. They're as thick as thieves.'

'Well, *all* of them are. Mother and Dad. Shane and Paula, Sally and Anthony Standish, Amanda. And Sarah, now she's back in the fold. They grew up together, for God's sake,' Toby reminded his brother. 'We all know about Heron's Nest, the summers they spent there, now don't we!'

'Listen to this. Jack told me that one of his operatives found out that a man with a small child was registered at the Spa Hotel in Ripon – your old hunting ground, if you recall. Anyway, the man had registered under the name of William Stone. It meant nothing to Jack's chap, but the minute Jack heard it he knew it had to be Mark. William Stone equals Jonathan Ainsley. That's his pseudonym.'

'Oh Christ, you're right! Was Jonathan involved, do you think?' Toby wondered out loud.

'I've no idea,' Gideon answered, 'but it's crossed Tessa's mind and Linnet's, not to mention Jack's as well, so Evan told me.'

'I see. Paula will have to be told eventually, you know, something like this can't be shoved under the rug.'

'It couldn't be anyway, because Tessa's promised Mark Longden the earth to bring Adele back to her, and she's going to have to discuss all that with her mother and Shane. It could involve millions, according to Linnet. I guess right now Longden is harping on about joint custody, so Tessa is trying to buy him off. Everybody has a price, according to our great-grandmother. Emma's rule.'

'Emma was right. And that joint custody bit won't sit well with Tessa. Thank God Adrianna and I don't have any kids, it certainly makes things easier.'

'Are you and Adrianna definitely getting the divorce, then, Toby?' Gideon asked.

'We are, but at least it's amicable. We both want it, Gid. She's decided she prefers to live and work in Hollywood, and I want to be in London. Have to be, as a matter of fact, when you consider my responsibilities. The marriage was a big mistake, in all truthfulness. But she's being decent, believe it or not . . . she's not a gold-digger, far from it. Adrianna doesn't want alimony. She'd like me to buy her a small flat in London, so she can have a base: you know, one foot each side of the Atlantic, and I agreed. Actually, though, I'm thinking of letting her have our flat. I've never really liked it, and she has always loved it.'

'I felt you wanted a divorce, so am glad for you, Toby. And Dad will be, too. He's looking for grand-children from you, Toby, and he never thought Adrianna was the motherly type.'

Toby began to chuckle. 'Never a truer word spoken by our dear dad. The old man's right on the ball.' There was a moment's hesitation before Toby went on. 'Do you think I can call Tessa? I've been so terribly worried about her, and I do want her to know I'm here for her, whatever she needs.'

'Why shouldn't you phone her, Toby? You and she have been joined at the hip all of your lives. And she knows you're there for her. Of course, give her a ring, for God's sake.'

'I wouldn't want to call her just when she was getting Adele back, I wouldn't want to interrupt that. Knowing Tessa the way I do, she's suffered horribly today, not knowing where Adele was.'

'You've got a few minutes before Mark arrives

at the house. So call her now and give her my love.'

'I will. Everything's all right between you and Evan, isn't it, Gid?'

'Absolutely. Never been better. Talk to you later.'

'Sure thing, Gideon.'

Gideon leaned back in his chair, after hanging up on his brother, propped his feet on the desk again and closed his eyes. He began to think about Evan Hughes.

Things *were* better between them, even though she was constantly worrying about her father and his impending trip to England. But she's really worrying about what he'll think of *me*, and of Robin Ainsley, Gideon suddenly decided, and wished then that she wouldn't wrestle with those sort of things, inventing problems when they didn't exist. The problem was Evan herself, Gideon decided. She needed everybody to like the people she liked, and that wasn't the way the world was.

He knew he wanted to make a life with Evan, wanted her on a permanent basis. And ever since the beginning of their relationship he had felt she wanted to make a life with him. But he had come to the conclusion she couldn't make that commitment to him because of her father and his peculiar attitude towards the Hartes.

Gideon sighed. He would be delighted when her father finally did arrive from New York. Then everything would be out in the open.

In the meantime, he had a national daily to get out. With his father away, *The Daily Gazette* was under his aegis. Opening his eyes and swinging his feet to the carpet, he stood up, retrieved his mobile from the desk and left his office, heading for the newsroom, one of the places he always loved to be.

Tessa could hardly sit still and finally, in her agitation, she stood up and exclaimed to Jack, 'I just can't stand it! I've got to go to the front door, wait for Adele there.'

'I know, I know. Go ahead, Tessa. Mark should be arriving at any moment now. Come to think of it, I'd better accompany you.' Jack joined her, took hold of her arm and led her to the Stone Hall.

After taking only one step into the Stone Hall, Tessa stopped dead in her tracks and stared at Jack. 'The rag doll! The first thing she'll ask for is her Reggi. Hang on a minute, Jack, whilst I go and get it. I left it in the library.'

He nodded, his eyes following her as she retraced their steps. She had hugged that doll to her for half the day, saying time and again to them all that Adele was undoubtedly heartbroken because she'd lost it. He sighed to himself. This was one hell of a mess, a bitter separation that would only become more and more acrimonious as time passed.

When Paula had brought him in a few weeks ago to investigate Mark Longden, he had realized at once how troubled she was about her daughter's husband. Paula was not the type of person to pry into people's lives, have them checked out, rather she had great respect for everyone's privacy. Once he had begun to dig, Jack was glad she had taken the steps she had; he hadn't liked what he had discovered about Mark Longden and he had lost no time in bringing the information to Paula.

Longden was very entangled with Paula's cousin, Jonathan Ainsley, her great enemy and the enemy of the entire Harte family. Ainsley had hired Longden as the architect of his new mansion in Thirsk, and Longden had soon fallen under Jonathan's bad influence. Booze and drugs and other women were the perks Mark was being offered. He had indulged and become addicted. Paula had been as appalled as he was, and worried for Tessa because of Mark's violence towards her in the past. Even though they had already separated there was no telling what Mark Longden might do to her. Witness today. Snatching Adele was both cruel and dangerous, and yet Mark hadn't hesitated. It's blackmail, Jack thought, he set out to blackmail her and he succeeded. He's after money, big money, as well as joint custody. He won't get that, not with the evidence I have about his private life. But Paula will give him the money just to get rid of him. And good riddance to bad rubbish.

'Here I am!' Tessa exclaimed, hurrying into the Stone Hall, the rag doll in her hand. 'You don't know how she loves this bit of nothing. To her it's the most precious thing in the world . . .' Tessa paused, looked at Jack and said softly, 'As she is the most precious thing to me. Thank you again, Jack, for getting her back. She's the most important part of my life.'

'I know that, Tess. And you ought to know by now that I'll always help you any way I can. Why, I've known you since you were Adele's age, and you looked just like she looks now.'

'Mummy always says she's the spitting image of me.'

They crossed the small entrance hall and Jack unlocked the front door and opened it; they both stepped out onto the top step. The sky was pale blue and bright, the light crystalline on this August evening, and it was warm. Yet despite the mugginess he noticed that Tessa shivered slightly as she stared towards the drive, and he saw the strain settling on her face once more, picked up on her sudden tension. She had relaxed for only a brief moment and he knew she could barely contain herself as she waited for Adele.

They glanced at each other as they suddenly heard wheels on the gravel drive, and within seconds a black Mercedes was turning the bend. Tessa started to move but Jack restrained her.

'I know you long to hold her in your arms, but let us wait for a moment, Tessa. I need to see how Adele behaves when he takes her out of the car. I need to know if she's frightened or upset, and, most importantly, if she's afraid of her father. Those things are important for the divorce, you see.'

'I understand,' Tessa mumbled, but her agitation was growing and she was trembling excessively, could not keep a limb still.

The car finally came to a standstill in the area near the privet hedge which was always used for parking. She wished he'd driven up to the front door, so anxious was she for her daughter's return.

Mark alighted, glanced across at Tessa and Jack in the doorway, then went around and lifted Adele out of the car.

For a moment it seemed as though he was going to carry her over, but Adele began to struggle in his arms, and he had no option but to put her down on the ground.

The child shot away from him, running to her mother, shouting, 'Mumma! Mumma!', moving as fast as her little legs would carry her. 'I lost Reggi,' she shouted and began to sob loudly.

Tessa ran to meet her, afraid that the three-year-old was going to stumble and hurt herself, and as she drew close Tessa noticed how dishevelled Adele looked; her silver-gilt hair was a tangled mess, her face had black smudges on it and what looked like raspberry jam around her mouth, and her pale blue shirt and shorts were grubby.

A split-second later Tessa was showing Adele the rag doll, exclaiming, 'Look, here's Reggi, I found her for you, darling.'

'Oh Mumma. It's my Reggi!' Adele's sobbing instantly stopped, and she lifted her tear-stained face to her mother, gave her a huge smile as she clutched the rag doll to her.

Tessa, who was kneeling, pushed away her tears, smiled back and took Adele in her arms, hugged her close, filled with love for her small, defence-less little girl. And mingling with that love was enormous relief that she was now safely home. Out of the corner of her eye Tessa saw Mark approaching, coming to join them. Instantly, she let go of Adele and stood up. Then she scooped the child into her arms and took a step backwards, wanting to put distance between herself and Mark.

When he drew to a standstill he glanced at Jack, and then addressed Tessa. 'Shall we have our little talk?'

'Let's do it later. *Please*. Adele must be awfully tired, and perhaps even hungry. Have you fed her today?'

'Of course I've fed her, you stupid fool! I love my child, why wouldn't I feed her!' he cried, glaring at Tessa, his face flushing.

She glared back at him, hating every fibre of his being. Not only for all that he had done to her, but also for his cruel abduction of Adele, which could have so easily gone wrong, causing additional heartache for them all.

'Now, now, Mark,' Jack said quietly, stepping forward protectively, motioning for Tessa to go into the vestibule. 'Angry words aren't going to get you anywhere. And certainly we shouldn't be doing business in front of your daughter. Or on the doorstep, for that matter.' Looking over his shoulder at Tessa, who stood just behind him, he asked her, 'Perhaps we could talk to Mark for a few minutes? Inside?'

Filled with anger, and anxious to bathe and feed her daughter, Tessa simply nodded, swung around, walked through the vestibule and into the Stone Hall.

Jack was very close on her heels and he caught up with her and said, 'Why don't you take Adele into the library? She'll be all right with the others for a few minutes, and that's all this is going to take, I can assure you of that. Just leave it to me.'

'All right, Jack, but I hope it is only a few minutes.' She hurried across the vast hall made of local Yorkshire stone, heading for the library. When she pushed open the door and went in everyone clapped and laughed and surged around her and the child, making a big fuss of Adele, who laughed happily, her eyes sparkling, and accepted all of their kisses.

And then a moment later, just as Tessa was turning to leave the room, Elvira rushed in, her face drained of all colour, her eyes filled with apprehension.

'Elvira!' Tessa cried when she saw the nanny. 'Did you just get back from Leeds?'

'I did, Mrs Longden, and Margaret and Joe told me what happened to Adele today. Oh Mrs Longden, I'm so sorry, I wish I hadn't taken the day off, I wish I'd been here . . .' Her voice trailed off, and she looked suddenly uncertain what to do next.

'Elvi,' Adele said, smiling at her, 'I lost Reggi. Mumma found her. Look.' She showed Elvira the rag doll.

'I'm glad she's safe,' Elvira murmured to the child, but looking up at Tessa as she spoke.

'Take her for a few minutes, Elvira, please, I have to speak to Mr Longden,' Tessa said, and handed Adele to the nanny.

Glancing at the others, Tessa's eyes finally settled on Linnet. 'I'll be right back. Jack's in charge out there, and he knows what he's doing.'

'He certainly does,' Linnet concurred. 'He's the best.'

Returning to the Stone Hall, Tessa found Jack and Mark sitting opposite each other near the fireplace. Mark was angry, while Jack seemed remarkably calm, cool, and unperturbed. He's holding all the cards, she suddenly thought, remembering some of the things he had told her mother.

Not wanting to sit down, to make it appear that she was ready to have a long discussion, Tessa remained standing, positioning herself near the soaring stone fireplace.

Jack looked across at her and said in a soft but distinct voice, 'I told Mark you would be quite happy to reiterate the terms you had given him earlier on the phone. Seemingly he'd like to hear them again.'

'You can have the house in Hampstead,' Tessa began, 'which is actually *mine*, since my mother gave it to me, not to us. You can also have the two cars which are garaged there. I'll throw in all of the contents of the house, as well, except for a few paintings and personal items which are mine, and my other personal possessions such as clothes, that sort of thing. And I will make a financial settlement on you.'

'I want the jewellery back. The pieces I gave you.'

'*Fine*. That's certainly very fine by me,' she

said, thinking that every piece was a worthless nothing.

'And I want joint custody of Adele.'

'That I can't promise,' Tessa said, her voice suddenly trembling unexpectedly, 'but I will give you fair access.'

'Joint custody,' he snapped in a nasty voice.

'No, Mark, I can't agree to that. Not after today.'

'We'll see what the divorce courts have to say,' he threatened.

Jack cleared his throat. 'If you don't mind me saying so, I think the divorce courts will be in Tessa's favour.'

'No way! A father has as many rights as the mother these days, and let's not forget that.'

'But you *are* rather a problematic father, I would say.'

'What the hell does that mean?' he demanded furiously, staring at Jack through blazing eyes.

'I don't want to go into it now, since your solicitor and Tessa's will be discussing everything shortly. But perhaps I should just add that we have quite a lot of information about your private life, your indulgences, your preferences, your rather . . . *decadent* lifestyle, shall we call it? Do I need to say more?' Jack gave the younger man a hard look, rose and went to stand next to Tessa.

Leaping to his feet, Mark cried, 'This sounds like bloody blackmail to me!'

'Call it what you will,' Jack murmured. 'But I do have the evidence to prove that I am speaking the truth. And by the by, it's certainly the kind of evidence that a judge would be interested in hearing, especially since a child's welfare is at the heart of the matter.'

Glaring first at Jack and then at Tessa, Mark shouted, 'You haven't heard the last of me!'

'Nor have you heard the last of me, mate,' Jack retorted. 'And now, under the circumstances, I think it's about time you left. I'll escort you to the door.'

CHAPTER SIX

Paula O'Neill stood at one of the windows in the bedroom of the Fifth Avenue apartment, looking out at the view of Central Park. It was sunny and hot but not humid outside, and there was a sparkle to the day. The leafy domes of the trees in the park were brilliantly green against the azure sky, and rising upward beyond the trees the skyline of Manhattan looked superb. Brilliant sunshine glanced off thousands of windows, making the skyscrapers appear to gleam, almost shimmer in the clear light.

There's no city like it anywhere else in the world, she thought. She had always loved New York ever since she had first come here as a child with her grandmother; Emma had also been addicted to this busy, electric, exciting, whirlwind city – where anything was possible, Emma frequently said to her, adding, 'The sky's the limit here, Paula. And don't you ever forget it.'

Turning away from the window, Paula walked across the bedroom and out into the entrance foyer, her high heels clicking against the black-and-white marble floor as she headed towards the library, one of her favourite rooms in the apartment. It had been her grandfather's favourite, too, according to Emma, who had once confided that he had loved the dark-wood panelling on the walls, the books bound in red leather, the Georgian antiques she had chosen, the warmth of dark-rose brocade hanging at the windows and used on the sofas. 'He used to say it was masculine without being stuffy and heavy,' her grandmother had explained, 'but then he usually did like the way I decorated our homes.'

Paul McGill had bought the Fifth Avenue apartment for Emma and himself in the 1930s, and it was a spacious and lovely duplex designed by the renowned architect Rosario Candela in 1931. After Paul's untimely death in 1939 Emma had contemplated selling it but only briefly. There was a war on, and she was far too preoccupied with other matters and the Blitz in London to worry about the apartment in Manhattan. 'And I'm glad I didn't sell it,' Emma had once told her, 'because it means we can live here in comfort and privacy when we come to the States instead of having to stay in hotels.'

Paula and her brother Philip had inherited the apartment jointly upon Emma's death, but it was also used by other members of the family whenever they came to America, particularly her cousins Emily and Winston Harte, and Emily's sister Amanda Linde who flew in all the time. Everyone loved it, took great pride in its uncommon beauty; luxurious and comfortable without being ostentatious, it truly bore Emma Harte's imprint in every way and was a reflection of her great taste, her critical eye for colour and the finest in antiques and paintings.

Now, as she seated herself at the desk, Paula felt a sudden, unexpected sense of awe when she thought about her grandmother and her most remarkable achievements. It was mind-boggling really when she considered everything that Grandy had accomplished in her life — and she a poor girl from Fairley, a mill village on the Yorkshire moors, who had started working at the age of twelve as a servant for the Fairleys of Fairley Hall.

However did she do it? Paula wondered. Where did it come from, this talent, this infallible taste, this sense of style and scale, this understanding of art, and colour and fabrics? And where did her drive and energy, her strength and stamina come from? How did she summon up that unique will, that indomitability, that desire to scale the mountain tops? How on earth did that little servant girl become such a great lady, such a successful tycoon, so powerful, unbeatable, and absolutely inimitable? Emma Harte almost single-handedly had created a business empire worth many billions of pounds today, and had left her descendants an extraordinary legacy of power, wealth and privilege, not to mention that successful, thriving business empire that circled the globe.

There has never been anyone like her, Paula thought, shaking her head in wonderment, still gazing into space. Emma was a one-off; they threw away the mould after they made her. And again she wondered to herself how Grandy had done it . . . what extraordinary gifts she had had . . .

As the phone rang Paula automatically reached for it. 'Hello?'

'Hello, Mummy, it's me, Linnet.'

'Darling, what a nice surprise! How's everyone? How's the remodelling and revamping of the stores coming along?' Paula asked, her joy at hearing her daughter's voice echoing in her own.

'Oh very well, I'm pleased . . .' Linnet paused, took a deep breath, said quickly, 'Mummy, listen, something happened today. But it's all right now, everything's fine. Honestly. But I thought I'd better fill you in. And —'

'What happened, Linnet?' Paula cut in swiftly, sensing trouble at once. 'I hope everyone's all right?' As she spoke Paula had a sudden remembrance of the day her cousin Winston Harte had called Shane in Connecticut, to break the news that her father and her husband were dead, killed in an avalanche in Chamonix. Goose flesh speckled her arms and she felt cold all over; she tensed, wondering what bad news was coming now.

'Yes, yes, all's okay,' Linnet exclaimed, and told her what had happened earlier.

'Oh God, no! Not Adele! But she *has* been found? You did say everyone was all right?'

'Yes, she's safely home at Pennistone Royal again, with Tessa.' There was a pause and Linnet added, 'I brought Jack in, and here he is, Mummy.

I'll come back to you in a few minutes. Jack needs to talk to you.'

'Hello, Paula,' he said.

'Hello, Jack, I'm so glad you're there,' Paula answered, and she thought her voice sounded unnatural, strangled in her throat.

'Everybody's quite safe,' Jack went on calmly in his most reassuring voice. He had always adored Paula, and there were those in the family who actually believed he'd been secretly in love with her for years. 'As Linnet just told you, the child is unharmed. Now, Paula, I must insist you do something about security here. You don't have much at all. Just burglar alarms . . . it's downright dangerous.'

'Shane's mentioned it several times lately. I don't think any of us envisioned something like this . . . *kidnapping* happening though. But you're right, security has become extremely important. Can you do it for us, Jack? Can you set it up?'

'Yes, I'll get the best security experts on it at once. Tomorrow, in fact.'

'That's a good idea, and thank you for everything you've done for us. I'll be forever grateful.'

'Just know I'm always here for you,' he said.

'Can I speak to Tessa, Jack?'

'Yes indeed, she's standing right next to me. I'll talk to you later, Paula.'

'Hello, Mummy,' Tessa began and stopped abruptly, choking up.

'Tessa darling, I'm so sorry this happened, so very sorry. You must have gone through hell today.'

'I did,' Tessa answered, her voice tearful. 'But I'm happy to say Adele is perfectly fine, and she doesn't seem at all upset, other than she thought she'd lost her rag doll. She's fast asleep now, and Elvira is sleeping in her room tonight. Mummy, Mark was beastly, so cruel and hateful. He did this because he wanted to get at me, wanted a weapon to use, to gain advantage over me. It was wrong that he used Adele in this way. Oh, and he wants joint custody.'

'He'll never get it, Tessa, please be assured of that. When Jack investigated Mark he came up with quite a lot of unsavoury information, and I feel certain he will be viewed as an unfit father by the courts. What did you promise him, darling, in order to get Adele back?'

'Only those things we'd discussed earlier. The Hampstead house, the cars garaged there, and a financial settlement. Nothing more, and I was wary about the custody. I said the lawyers will have to talk it through.'

'Good girl. And do let the legal team handle things from now on.'

'Oh I will, Mummy, but I had to offer something to get him to bring Adele home.'

'I know you did. I think you did very well indeed. And one thing we must do is make sure the price is right. You don't want Mark around your neck for the rest of your life like an albatross.'

'Can I stay up here? Jack says it'll be perfectly safe, that Mark won't come around troubling me again. And he has the front and back gates locked tonight. He can make it really secure here.'

'Yes, I think you should stay, as you'd planned, and of course Jack is right about it being made secure, and also about Mark Longden, who's probably already regretting that he did this terrible thing. How're Emsie and Desmond? I suppose they were there when this happened?'

'They were out riding. But they want to say hello. I'll pass the phone, Mummy.'

After she had hung up Paula sat for a while at the desk, mulling over everything Jack and her children had told her; she had also spoken to India and Evan, heard their opinions as well. It seemed to be the general consensus that Jonathan Ainsley was involved, somehow, in the events that had transpired at Pennistone Royal earlier in the day.

Jonathan Ainsley. Her first cousin and bitter enemy. Enemy of her immediate family. Enemy of the entire Harte clan. And the O'Neills and the Kallinskis as well, since they were all so closely connected.

Lately he had been clever. He had pulled Mark Longden into his orbit by hiring him to design his new home in North Yorkshire. Mark had taken the bait, flattered; he had quickly been lured into Jonathan's decadent social life, and, inevitably, he had become Jonathan's pawn.

Her cousin hadn't had to do anything himself to hurt her – simply whisper a few choice words in Mark Longden's ear about Tessa. And the die was cast.

She did not know how to deal with Jonathan

at this moment, though she would eventually find a way to outwit him. But she did know how to handle Mark, render him powerless against her daughter and grandchild. And she would put her plans in motion tomorrow.

She glanced at the carriage clock on the desk, saw that it was after five and wondered what had happened to Emily. She couldn't still be at the board meeting at Harte Enterprises, could she? But of course she could. Emily was diligent and –

'Sorry I'm so late getting back!' Emily exclaimed, hurrying into the library looking warm, her face slightly flushed. 'Oh good, it's lovely and cool in here. It's a furnace outside –' Emily suddenly broke off, staring at her cousin and frowning. 'What's wrong, Paula? You look quite awful.'

'Hello, Emily,' Paula answered, rising, walking around the desk, kissing Emily on the cheek. 'I just had a little bit of a shock actually, but everything's all right. I'll tell you about it in a moment. Shall we have a cup of tea? Or do you want iced tea?'

Sitting down on the sofa, without taking her eyes off Paula, Emily said, 'I think I'd like iced tea for a change. Shall I go and tell Alice?'

'No, no, I'll do it. And will Winston be back from Toronto or not? I need to tell her how many we'll be for dinner.'

'It's still just you and me, darling. Winston won't make it out today. Maybe tomorrow, and I'm assuming Shane is coming on Friday as planned.'

'That's correct. He's taking the morning plane from Nassau. So yes, we're a couple of grass widows tonight.' As she spoke Paula glided out of the room, went to the kitchen, spoke to Alice, the housekeeper, and returned within seconds.

She went over and sat down in a chair facing Emily, and explained, 'There's been a bit of a fuss at Pennistone Royal today.' Speaking swiftly, and with her usual conciseness, Paula told Emily everything that had happened in Yorkshire.

'What a ghastly day poor Tessa must've had, and thank God it all ended well. Almost anything could have gone wrong, you know. And listen, Paula –' Emily leaned forward and continued in a much quieter, confiding voice, 'I tend to agree with Linnet and Tessa, bloody Jonathan probably *was* involved. He *has* to be dealt with – somehow.'

'I agree, but I'm not sure what to do about him at this moment, Em. However, I think I have a way to make Mark Longden toe the line and behave himself. I've come up with a plan in the last half hour and I think it will work. I certainly intend to set it in motion tomorrow.'

'Oh please tell me about it,' Emily said eagerly, her face lighting up.

And Paula did.

After Emily had gone to her room to relax before dinner, Paula sat for a while at the desk, going over her engagements for the next few days. But at one moment the striking of the clock in the hall made her sit up with a start, and her concentration fled.

Leaning back in her desk chair she sat thinking

about Tessa and her granddaughter Adele, and the things that had happened at Pennistone Royal that day. Thank God they were safe. She wished Shane were here. Turning her head, she looked at the photograph on a nearby circular table, rose, and walked over to it.

Seating herself in the adjacent chair, she picked up a silver-framed picture of Shane, and a smile broke across her face. It had been taken many years ago, when he was about twenty-six, and she couldn't help thinking how wonderful he looked, so handsome, debonair even then. What was it Emma had always said about him? That he had glamour. And that was the truth. She had never known anyone with that kind of glamour, man or woman. Dark-haired, dark-eyed, he was Black Irish through and through, and she had always teased him, said he had kissed the Blarney Stone. 'Inherited the gift of the gab from my grandfather,' he answered back, and she responded, 'Emma says Blackie's kissed *three* Blarney Stones!'

It's funny how life works out, she suddenly thought, her eyes settling on a photograph of Tessa and Lorne with Shane. He had brought them up as his own since they'd been toddlers, and she knew how much Lorne loved Shane, but she sometimes wondered about Tessa's feelings for him.

Of course she loves him, Paula told herself. Everyone has always loved Shane. Grandy. My mother. Winston Harte, his best friend and sparring partner since they were boys. And Emily. And Sally and Anthony Standish. Shane, if the truth be known, was the most popular person in the three clans, and anywhere else!

Her eyes moved on, and she literally laughed out loud when they fell upon a photograph taken when they were all teenagers: a picture of them at Heron's Nest one summer, Emma's house in Scarborough by the sea. It had been taken the year the boys had formed their own band. The Herons they called themselves, and of course it was Shane who was the band-leader. He also played the piano and was the vocalist. Alexander, her beloved Sandy, now sadly dead these long years, had played the drums and cymbals; Michael Kallinski had warbled the harmonica; Jonathan scraped the violin; Philip blew the flute. But it had been Winston who considered himself the most important, the most talented member of the ensemble. He had modelled himself on Bix Beiderbecke, after seeing the film *Young Man With A Horn*, and thought he was the bees' knees. They had wondered out loud where he had learned to play the trumpet, and Emma had smiled thinly and said he hadn't, and that was the trouble. What fun they had had together in those days.

Shane had been part of her life for as long as she could remember, since her childhood. She had become conscious of him when she was four and he was eight, and had tagged along after him.

One summer afternoon, Shane had told her he had a wonderful idea. He said she was to become Queen Boadicea, and he would be her consort, her lord. 'But we have to look right,' Shane had confided. 'How should we look?' she had asked him, her violet eyes full of love and pride at being his friend even then. 'We have to be blue,' the eight-year-old boy had explained. And had then proceeded to paint her blue all over, after he had undressed her. She had insisted on keeping her knickers on, being a modest child. And later Emma had been thankful she had. At least some pores had been allowed to breathe, and so she had stayed alive. Somehow, Shane had coaxed her into painting him blue to match, and there was hell to pay when Blackie came over at Emma's request to chastise his grandson. 'Young scallywag,' Blackie had pronounced.

Remembering all this, Paula smiled, thinking of the turpentine baths Emma and Blackie had given them . . . worse than any thrashing.

Blue, she thought, seeing in her mind's eye her lovely blue marbles which Shane had managed to lose. He had presented her with some new ones but they weren't as nice, and she had been put out with him for a long time.

And then one day, when they were grown up, he had given her a small leather box, and when she had opened it she had been entranced by the sapphire earrings inside.

Leaning down, kissing her, Shane had said, 'I hope these will now satisfy you . . . they are in place of those blue marbles I lost when you were all of six.'

And one day much later she had married Shane.

Yes, life *is* strange, she thought again. They had grown up together, had been inseparable even as teenagers, and then he had gone off to boarding school, later university, and she had seen less of him.

And she had met Jim Fairley, who worked for Emma, and they had fallen in love. Or so she thought. She had married Jim, had had the twins, Tessa and Lorne.

Shane had moved to New York to run the O'Neill Hotel chain on that side of the Atlantic. But he had never married, and one day, when her marriage was falling apart, they had suddenly understood that they were in love with each other, and always had been.

They had discovered this in Shane's wonderful old barn in New Milford, an oasis of peace in the Connecticut countryside. And they had vowed to be together always. *Somehow*. Because it was meant to be.

Life plays funny tricks, she murmured to herself. Jim Fairley and her father David Amory, on a skiing holiday in Chamonix, had been killed in an avalanche. Winston and Emily had decided not to go skiing that day, and had narrowly escaped death. Their time wasn't up, Paula whispered to herself. That's what Emma always used to say: 'You go on living until your time's up.'

For a long time she had grieved for Jim and her father, and suffered the most devastating guilt. She had sent Shane away because of her guilt. But eventually she had realized how much she loved him and needed him, had understood he was her entire life. He still was.

* * *

Evan's mother, Marietta Hughes, was furious.

Once again Owen had behaved in the most high-handed way and she felt like strangling him. But because her mother had always told her no man was worth murdering because of the dire consequences to oneself, she had decided against this rather harsh and drastic solution.

Flight for several hours was the only way she could settle the score and calm herself. And so she grabbed her handbag, picked up the shopping bag she had just taken out of the wardrobe, where it had been hidden behind her clothes for days, and left the suite. She didn't even go into the bedroom to say goodbye to him. And so he would worry when he discovered she had gone.

As she took the lift down to the hotel lobby she prayed she wouldn't run into the hotel proprietors, George or Arlette, especially Arlette, who constantly wanted to take her for tea or coffee in order to gossip about Evan. She knew the Frenchwoman adored Evan, had been kind to her, and meant no harm, but Marietta usually felt a degree of discomfort if forced to discuss members of her family, particularly Evan who was very special to her.

Fortunately she was not waylaid, made it safely out into the street, where she stood looking for a cab. It was a nice day, if a little too humid, but she was relieved it wasn't raining. It had poured yesterday.

A cab slid to a stop in front of her and she got in, gave the cabbie the address of her bank, then sat back. She was relieved that she had escaped from the hotel without having to deal with George or Arlette, and, most importantly, that the shopping bag had gone undetected in its hiding place in the wardrobe.

Marietta placed her handbag on the cab seat next to her, but kept the shopping bag on her lap. The package inside it was precious – ever since finding it she had believed it to be dynamite – and she must keep it safe. She wasn't sure if she could use it to her advantage, but she certainly was aware of its true value.

It suddenly struck her how wise she had been to keep her account open at Barclay's Bank. There wasn't much money in it, because she hadn't transferred any, but they knew her at this particular branch, and renting a safe-deposit box had presented no problem. How relieved she would be when the package was safely in the bank. Then she would go to Fortnum and Mason's and have coffee in the restaurant, and perhaps browse around in the store. She might even buy herself a hat, although she knew she wasn't going anywhere special to wear it. But she'd always loved hats.

Normally she would have gone to Harte's in Knightsbridge for coffee, but she was afraid of running into Evan. They were supposed to be in Connecticut, not here, were not due in London until next week. Owen had decided to come earlier than planned. 'To give us time to get over our jet lag,' he had said, but she knew this was just a ploy. He had wanted to arrive sooner than expected in order to take Evan by surprise, to catch her off-guard.

Marietta hadn't liked that at all, but she had kept quiet. Long ago she had learned not to argue with Owen. So most of the time she kept her own counsel; however this did not prevent her from drawing her own conclusions and she knew she was right when it came to his attitude towards their daughter.

Owen had always believed he owned Evan. Certainly he behaved as if he did. He had taken their daughter over years ago, when she was very young, and he had pushed *her* out. She had lost Evan because of his possessiveness, and also because of her own mistakes, perhaps. She gripped the shopping bag tighter, her knuckles whitening over the handles as she thought of the past. Sometimes you did something, just a small thing, and yet it could have the most terrible and far-reaching consequences.

The cab came to a stop, and she alighted quickly, paid the driver and went into the bank. It was all so easy . . . within minutes she was placing the precious package in the safe-deposit box and putting the key in her handbag. Now no harm would come to it; nor could it be lost or stolen.

It was only much later, when she sat sipping her coffee in Fortnum's that a terrible thought occurred to Marietta. What if she got sick and died, or was killed in an accident, or became senile? What would happen to the package in the safe-deposit box at the bank? No one but she knew it was there. She would have to tell someone. But who could she confide in?

Marietta's mouth twitched slightly in a wry smile. There was nobody she could make her confidant because she did not trust anyone she knew.

A lawyer, she thought, I need a lawyer. To make a will. Yes, that's what I have to do. She had a few things of real value to leave. As well as the package in the safe-deposit box. For her daughter Evan. The person she loved the most in the entire world.

Tomorrow that would be her project. She would set out to find a lawyer. It was imperative.

CHAPTER SEVEN

The four of them walked slowly around the perimeter of the estate – Jack Figg, Gideon Harte, Evan Hughes and Desmond O'Neill. Jack had a captive audience and he was in his element. He was talking about his favourite subject, Security with a capital S, and he did so enthusiastically.

'For years all that's ever been needed here are burglar alarms, because there are so many people around most of the time . . . Wiggs and his gardeners, the stable lads, Joe and his estate workers. But it's very different now. We're living in dangerous times, things are not the same anymore. England's changed and *not* for the better,' Jack pointed out.

'You're absolutely right in everything you say,' Gideon answered. 'It's the same at Allington Hall, by the way. My father hasn't got proper security either, except for alarms, and it's downright neglectful when you think about it . . . all those horses, valuable horses, for example.'

Desmond said, 'Uncle Winston *has* been talking about security with Dad. I heard them wittering on about it a few weeks ago. But I think Dad and Uncle Winston are very trusting.'

'Perhaps that's true when it comes to their homes,' said Gideon. 'But I know for a fact that your father is extremely high on security for all the O'Neill hotels, and certainly Dad knows it's a priority at the newspaper offices, the television network and our radio stations.' He glanced at Jack. 'I'm hiring you right now to overhaul the security system at Allington Hall. And I'd like you to tackle the newspaper offices, television studios, radio stations as well. Make sure we've got the latest.'

'Thanks for your vote of confidence, Gideon,' Jack said, 'but I *will* be hiring outside companies, if that's all right. Of course I'll be working with them, supervising.'

Gideon nodded.

'One thing's for sure, the store has huge security in place,' Evan volunteered, smiling at Jack. 'And I know you're responsible for that.'

'Yes, it was always at the top of my list when I was head of security at Harte's.'

At this moment Evan's mobile phone began to ring; she reached into her pocket and pulled it out. Bringing it to her ear, she said, 'Hello?'

'Hi, Evan honey, it's me,' Owen said.

'Dad! Hi! It's nice to hear your voice.' As she spoke she walked away, giving Gideon a wide smile, went to sit on a drystone wall. She watched the three men as they moved on, talking between themselves in an animated way.

'I can't wait for you to get here. I'm dying to see you and Mom,' she continued.

'We're here already, honey,' Owen announced, a chuckle in his voice.

'You are! But why didn't you let me know you were coming earlier?' she exclaimed, startled by this news but not unduly put out. 'When did you get to London, Dad?'

'Wednesday night. Three days ago. I decided to change the date so we could recover from our jet lag before we started running around. Anyway, we'd love to see you today if you can make it. Your mother's excited about your new apartment, and so am I. We thought we'd come over later.'

'Oh Dad, it would have been great, but I'm not in London. I'm in Yorkshire.'

'Oh, are you working up there?' he asked.

'No, not today, not on Saturday. I came up for a few days of rest, and I'll be here until next Wednesday, since I do have to help India with certain things at the Leeds store. I have to spend three days there, so I guess I won't see you until next Thursday, which is when I get back.'

'I see.' He sounded disappointed, his voice suddenly flat. 'Too bad, honey,' he added. 'Thursday it is then.'

'I'm so sorry, Dad. I didn't know you were coming early and I made my plans around your original date. Gee, I don't know if I can change things –' Her voice trailed off as she wondered how to reschedule everything; she knew she couldn't do so, at least not very easily.

'Your mother wants to talk to you, to say hello, Evan.'

'Put her on, Dad.' A moment later she was exclaiming, 'Hi, Mom, it's so good to hear you. How are you?'

'I'm very well these days, Evan,' her mother said, her voice loving and warm. 'I gather you're not around.'

'No, I'm in Yorkshire. I didn't expect you until next week.'

'I know, I know. I told your father you'd probably be busy, but you mustn't worry about us. We'll see you as soon as you return. At least, I hope we will.'

'Absolutely. The hotel's nice and cosy, isn't it, Mom? I know George and Arlette must've made you very comfortable there, haven't they?'

'Yes to both your questions. They miss *you*, of course, now that you've moved out. But I don't blame you, it's nice to have a place of your own, isn't it, Evan?'

'Yes, it is,' she laughed. 'Oh Mom, I can't wait to get back to town now I know you and Dad are there.' She meant this, and she was particularly pleased that her mother sounded so *normal*. That was the only word for it. Normal. And yes, *happy*. Actually happy. She who was always depressed.

They went on talking for a few more minutes, and after promising to phone them at the hotel tomorrow, Evan clicked off the cell. She hurried after Gideon and the others, whom she could just see in the distance, heading for the front gates of Pennistone Royal.

It was true, she *was* glad her parents had arrived in London. She hadn't seen them since January, and it was now August. Eight months in which so much had happened. Her life had changed in many different ways. And, in a sense, she had changed. She was a different person. She couldn't wait to see them, but at the same time she *was* slightly apprehensive. Although she and Robin had agreed, only a few days ago, that she would not tell her father about him, there were, nonetheless, many other things she had to discuss. Difficult things.

Tessa stood at the window of her bedroom, looking down at the driveway, her eyes on Jack Figg. He stood talking to Gideon, gesticulating, obviously explaining something to him and to Desmond who was with them.

She guessed it had to do with security. Jack had brought in a number of experts since Adele's disappearance on Wednesday, and for the past few days scores of men had been digging, laying cables, hauling in cameras and monitors and all manner of other devices. Linnet said they had been invaded by an army, and that's how it seemed to her, too. Parts of the estate had been mangled, but she didn't care about the mess they had made. Things could be put right once they had completed their task and left; Wiggs had told Linnet and her not to worry about it. And so she wasn't going to, kept reminding herself the most important thing was that Pennistone Royal was being made impenetrable.

Turning away from the window, Tessa moved through the bedroom and went into her small sitting room which adjoined. She glanced around, as always filling with pleasure when she was in this intimate room, loving the way it looked. The walls were primrose, there were yellow-and-red draperies at the windows made of a toile de Jouy cotton, and the small loveseat next to the fireplace was upholstered in a yellow-and-white flower print. It was a cheerful, sunny room, and it had been hers since she was a little girl; it was her safe haven now as it had been then.

She paused in front of the Victorian mirror hanging on the side wall, staring at herself, not liking what she saw. She felt totally drained and she realized she looked it; her face was a ghostly white and there were dark smudges under her eyes. Because she had not eaten much over the last few days her face seemed narrower, and it was taut with lingering tension. Only her silver-blonde hair was as beautiful as it always was.

Sighing under her breath, moving away from the mirror, Tessa went and sat down at her desk, the French *bureau plat* which had stood in the same spot for as long as she could remember. Next to the big yellow porcelain lamp was a photograph of Adele taken earlier in the summer, and she reached out, touched the child's image with one finger. An overwhelming feeling of the most intense love for her daughter surged through her and Tessa was more deeply aware than ever that her child took precedence before anyone on this planet, and certainly before anything else in her life.

Mark's abduction of Adele had changed her forever. Tessa had understood that within a few hours of her little girl's disappearance. Now she realized that in the next few days she would have to start assessing her entire life, in order to decide what to do, what changes to make. And there would be changes. She wasn't prepared to sacrifice her daughter's well-being for her career. Suddenly, being the boss of Harte's one day lost its lustre, at least for the moment. Perhaps her attitude would change when everything settled down, when Mark had been neutralized, although she was sure . . .

A few gentle taps on the door interrupted Tessa's chain of thoughts, and she exclaimed, 'Come in!'

The door opened and Elvira's face appeared around it. 'Could I have a word with you please, Mrs Longden?'

'Yes, of course, Elvira.' Noticing at once that the nanny was alone, she asked swiftly, 'Where's Adele?'

'She's fine, Mrs Longden, perfectly safe. She's with Margaret in the kitchen, giving a tea party for her dolls.'

'I'm sorry, Elvira, you did tell me that was what you'd planned.' Tessa forced a smile. 'I think I'm getting paranoid.'

'No, you're not, and anyway it would be natural, wouldn't it?' Elvira hovered in front of the desk, twisting her hands together and looking worried.

'What's wrong, Elvi?' Tessa asked, using the diminutive, hoping to put the nervous young woman at ease.

'Mrs Longden, there's something I need to tell you . . . I saw Mr Longden on Wednesday morning, just after leaving the estate. He was sitting in a car with another man, about halfway down the road, and he . . . well, he flagged me down. I think he recognized my car.'

Tessa's eyes narrowed instantly and she asked in an urgent voice, 'Who was the other man? Did you know him, Elvi?'

The nanny shook her head. 'No, I didn't, Mrs Longden. I'd never seen him before. Anyway, Mr Longden just said hello, told me he was on his way to see Adele, and asked if you were about or had you gone to the Harrogate store? And I said no, you were at Pennistone Royal, working in the library and that Adele was on the terrace playing –' She broke off. Tears sprang into her eyes, and she tried to flick them away with her fingertips. 'I wish I hadn't stopped, just driven on, I feel so responsible for what happened.'

'Oh, Elvira, you *mustn't*. It wasn't your fault,' Tessa replied, her tone kindly. 'But why didn't you tell me before? After all, you were back on Wednesday evening, just when Mr Longden returned Adele. Surely that was the time to say something?'

'It was, yes, you're right, but you were agitated, and exhausted, and I was very distressed myself, *thrown* if you know what I mean.'

'Today's *Saturday*, Elvi.'

'I know, but on Thursday and Friday you were ever so preoccupied and busy with Mr Figg. I didn't really like to disturb you. I did keep trying to find the right moment, but there just wasn't one. Besides, I was a bit afraid, to be honest, I felt very guilty about talking to Mr L. And I thought you'd be angry with me.'

'Never mind all of that. Now, tell me, Elvi, do you think Mr Longden was parked down the road here actually waiting for you? Do you think he was expecting you to leave Pennistone Royal around the time you did?'

'I don't know, Mrs Longden, but I always have the same routine on my day off. I usually leave about ten or ten-thirty. And he knows Wednesday is my day off, I've always taken Wednesday ever since I began to work for you when Adele was a baby.'

Tessa inclined her head. 'I understand, and let's forget it. However, Elvira, if anything ever happens, anything at all, that you think is strange, you must tell me.'

'I will, Mrs Longden, I will, I promise.' The nanny attempted a smile but it didn't quite materialize, and she added, 'Well then, I'd better get back to Adele.' Without another word she scurried out.

Left alone in her lovely sunny room which she had always loved, Tessa felt oddly alien and chilled, and just a little frightened once again. Mark had obviously planned the abduction very carefully, right down to the last detail . . . waiting for Elvira on the roadside, quizzing her, and then swooping in and scooping up Adele. While his accomplice, whoever that was, did all that dialling on a mobile phone. She shivered involuntarily, and bit her lip, and suddenly her eyes filled with worry.

After a few moments Tessa managed to calm herself and she made a vow to outwit Mark Longden. Whatever it took that was what she was going to do. *Outwit him.*

'My parents are here,' Evan said, staring at Gideon.

A look of genuine surprise crossed his face, and then his brows met in a puzzled frown. 'I thought they were coming next week?'

'They were. Dad changed the date, he said he wanted a chance for them to get over their jet lag. Anyway, they're in London. At the hotel. That was Dad on my mobile when we were walking with Jack.'

Evan and Gideon were seated at the table under the old oak tree at the bottom of the lawns which sloped away from the back terrace of Pennistone Royal. Gideon Harte put down his glass of white wine and leaned across the wrought-iron garden table. 'So when am I going to meet them?' he asked. When she didn't immediately answer, he said, 'I *am* going to meet them, aren't I?'

'Of course. But I thought I'd better see them by myself first. On Thursday when I get back to London. It *has* been eight months and there's a lot to catch up on, and I just think it's better that I see them alone.' Evan didn't add that they might resent his presence, although she was thinking that.

'I understand,' he said, and went on swiftly: 'Tell you what, I'll take the three of you to dinner on Friday evening. Somewhere really nice.' He spoke in a firm voice that forbade argument and looked at her very intently. There was a steely glint in his eyes.

'That'll be great,' Evan responded softly, realizing it was better to acquiesce rather than refuse for the time being.

Gideon experienced a small stab of dismay at her lack of enthusiasm which was obvious and made him feel suddenly awkward, and he reached out, took hold of her hand. His green eyes bored into hers. 'I know I've said this before, but I'm in love with you, Evan.'

'I know that.'

'And what about *you*? How do you really feel about me?'

'I'm in love with you, Gideon,' she replied, her voice suddenly intimate, very loving. 'You know I am.'

He realized she was being sincere, and now he relaxed, smiled, squeezed her hand. 'I want to spend the rest of my life with you, as if you didn't know that, and I want to marry you. I know I've said that to you before, but I'm asking you again . . . Evan, please marry me.'

There was only a fractional hesitation on her part before she agreed. 'Yes,' she said. 'I will, Gideon.'

'Let's tell your parents on Friday over dinner! Then it will be official and we'll phone my parents in New York to give them the good news. Do let's get engaged.' Without waiting for her reply, he grinned and rushed on, 'I've got a confession to make. I've had your engagement ring for ages.'

'You have?' Evan's grey-blue eyes sparkled and she began to laugh. 'Gee, you sure are sure of yourself, aren't you?' Her voice was teasing, full of laughter.

'I could only hope, my love, I could only hope. Actually, I can't give it to you at this moment, because it's not in my pocket. But I wish it were, so I could slip it onto your finger immediately. Unfortunately, it's locked up at Allington Hall.'

'Well, at least it's good to know it's in Yorkshire,' she quipped.

'I'll give it to you tonight, and *can* we tell your parents next week?' he pressed.

Evan took a deep breath and blew out a few puffs of air. 'I'd like to tell them when we have dinner, but I'm still a bit worried about the Robin–Dad situation. I haven't made my mind up . . . I don't know what to do about that yet.' She frowned and shook her head, groping for words that would accurately describe what she felt. 'I'm so *ambivalent*, and having to tell Dad that his father wasn't his biological father is going to be –'

'Let's not go there, let's not get things confused,' Gideon exclaimed, sounding impatient. 'Our engagement doesn't have anything to do with Robin, your father and Richard Hughes.'

'But it does, because my father –'

'Evan, please don't start with that whole business of us being related. My grandmother Elizabeth and your grandfather Robin are brother and sister, but that isn't troublesome. A genealogical chart would show that we are cousins a few times removed. So what! In this country it's not illegal to marry even a first cousin, so *we're* certainly within the law. And I don't believe those old wives' tales about children of cousins being born afflicted with something. My parents are cousins, yet Toby, Natalie and I are perfectly all right. Not that you've met Nat yet, what with her being in Australia at the moment. But you can take my word for it, my sister's as perfectly healthy and sane as me and Toby.'

'Oh Gid, don't get angry, please don't. I do love you very much, and being related has nothing to do with it. I *do* want to marry you. It's just that my father seems to bear a grudge against the Hartes, and I want to find out *why* that is, Gideon. Can't you understand that?'

'Yes, I can. I know it's important to you that my parents like you, and they do. In fact, they really approve of you. However, please understand that even if they didn't like you, I would still marry you. They can't live my life for me, and I would never permit them to influence me about my choice of a wife.' He frowned, his eyes scanning her face as he finished. 'Don't you feel that way, too? Surely you believe in your own convictions, your own choices, don't you?'

'I certainly do. I'm my own person. But I want to get to the root of his *dislike* of the Hartes, so please try and accept that. Ultimately, whatever he says, and what my mother says, won't alter my decision. I am going to marry you.' A few moments ago he had released her hand; now it was Evan who reached out and grabbed his. 'I think I know what it's about, Gideon.'

'You do? Then for God's sake tell me, don't keep me in the dark.'

'It's all to do with class differences, I think. Money, privilege, upbringing, background, those kind of things. *Your* life as opposed to *mine*. Look, my family wasn't, isn't, dirt poor. Not rich either, but there was always enough money for the things we needed. Not a lot of disposable income, I'm sure of that, but my sisters and I never wanted for anything. We had decent if somewhat plain clothes, yearly vacations, and we went to good schools. But in my father's mind I come from a different world from yours, Gideon, and he believes there will inevitably be a clash, that a relationship with you will only end in unhappiness for me. In a way, I think he believes I'm not good enough for you, that I don't have the right pedigree.'

Gideon was startled, and finally he said in a very quiet voice, 'He sounds as if he's extremely prejudiced, Evan, and a little bit out of date.'

'Dad *is* old-fashioned. Stubborn and opinionated as well. And, yes, you're right, he's very prejudiced.'

'And what about your mother? How will she react to our engagement?'

'I'm not sure . . . I think she'll be pleased if she knows I'm happy. But to be truthful, I don't know my mother very well. All those years of . . . of her being ill, being a manic depressive, those years took their toll on our relationship, Gid. We missed out on such a lot when I was growing up, and I regret that. I wish we'd been closer then, I really do.'

'I can understand that. Did you speak to her this morning?' he asked.

'Dad put her on, and you know what? I thought she sounded *different*. Much more like a normal person, no hint of depression, at least not in her voice, and it struck me that she sounded real happy. I can barely remember her sounding, or being, *happy* ever in my life. It was such a peculiar feeling, I was taken aback. But I was happy that she was happy.'

Gideon found this last statement so sad he didn't speak for a moment, contemplating Evan's mother and her illness. How terrible for someone to have lived that way for most of their life, virtually a prisoner trapped inside their own pain. A sudden rush of sympathy for Evan made him exclaim, 'It can't have been easy for you as a child. I'm so sorry, Evan.'

There was a moment's silence; Evan looked off into the distance, staring up at Pennistone Royal, that great stately home sitting atop the hill, thinking about her childhood in Connecticut . . . It had been so bleak in many ways, and yet there had been her father, and of course her grandmother, who were her great boosters.

Evan's face brightened and she exclaimed, 'There was always Glynnis. She was there for me, my lovely gran. It was she who really brought me up, and she was – just *wonderful*.'

'I bet she was. And she was truly beautiful, if that snap you showed me this morning is anything to go by,' Gideon murmured.

Evan nodded. 'It's amazing to think that Robin kept it all these years.'

'It's obvious he had a real big *thing* about her, my sweet, just as I do about you. I wish we could go back to Allington Hall and make love.'

She laughed, shaking her head. 'I do, too, but we can't.'

'I realize that. I have a sinking feeling that we're stuck here for lunch. With Tessa.'

'Yes, and Jack Figg. Just the four of us.'

'Oh. Where're Linnet and India?'

'Linnet told me she was going to the Harrogate store, and later to see Sir Ronald. Julian's brought him up from London, but he's not well apparently. Julian's worried about his grandfather. She was going over for lunch with them, and India's meeting a friend.'

'Thank God Jack's here, he's good company,' Gideon said. 'Tessa can be hard to take. How is she, by the way? I guess it was some ordeal on Wednesday.'

'It was. She really suffered, as I told you. There were moments when I thought she was going to pass out from anxiety. She was frantic. Yesterday she seemed a bit better, less agitated, but so quiet. She seems to alternate between looking worried and being preoccupied. Linnet thinks she's changed a lot in two days, but I'm not sure.'

'I hope it's for the better,' he shot back succinctly.

They sat and finished their drinks in silence and then Gideon said suddenly, 'I guess we'd better wend our way.' They rose, picked up their empty glasses and began to walk slowly up the hill. It was still scorching hot and the blue sky and brilliant sunlight combined to make it the most gorgeous August day.

Gideon stole a look at Evan, thinking how young and fresh she looked in her strapless cotton sundress and sandals. She was not wearing any make-up except for a touch of lipstick, and she suddenly seemed vulnerable and tender and he wanted to protect her, cherish her. He couldn't help thinking what a strange childhood she must have had with a depressive mother. Several times she had expressed worry about her own chances of inheriting her mother's illness, wondering aloud to him if it was genetic. He wasn't sure about that, but after eight months he knew her well now; he was quite certain she had not inherited that troubling disease, would not fall prey to it.

As for Evan, she was also thinking about her mother, wondering what had brought about this change in her . . . at least what had made her sound so . . . *upbeat.* There was just no other word for it. Her thoughts flew to her father: she dreaded the idea of telling him he was part Harte, that she was part Harte, and that she was contemplating marrying a Harte. Trouble lies ahead, she thought. I'm going to have trouble with Dad, especially about Gideon.

She stole a surreptitious look at him through the corner of her eye, and her heart seemed to melt within her. He was the nicest, kindest man she had ever met, not to mention charming and good-looking with his reddish-blond hair and green eyes. Emma Harte's colouring, she thought, the same as Linnet and his father. He was a full-blooded Harte and she was half Harte, but so what? She loved him very much and she had every intention of marrying him, no matter what her father said. Well, I've finally made up my mind, she thought, at least about Gideon. And she smiled to herself, pleased.

'Where have you been, Emma? Dad's been looking for you all over the place. It's about Lady Hamilton Clothes.' As he spoke Sir Ronald Kallinski adjusted his glasses and peered at the couple standing in front of him. The sun was behind them and he could not see them properly; he blinked several times, focusing first on the woman and then on the man.

'Is that you, Michael? What are you doing with Emma? You're delaying her.'

'Grandfather, it's me, Julian, not my father. And this is Linnet, my fiancée, not Emma. You know Linnet, Grandfather, she's *Paula's daughter*, Emma's great-granddaughter. We're engaged, remember?'

'Yes,' the old man said vaguely, sitting up straighter on the sofa.

'I think you must've been dozing, Grandfather, and having a dream perhaps – about the old days, eh?' Julian smiled at him.

Sir Ronald blinked again and peered at the couple. 'Of course it's you, Julian, and Linnet! I suppose it's possible I *was* daydreaming about the past, that's what you do when you're over ninety: dream about the days long ago, live with the memories. I'm one of the last, you know, except for Bryan O'Neill, Linnet's grandfather, and Edwina, Robin and Elizabeth. All of the others are gone now. Yes, I'm one of the last.'

'That's true, but you're pretty *healthy*,' Julian said in a strong, reassuring voice, motioning for Linnet to sit down next to his grandfather on the sofa. He took the chair opposite them; he was worried about his grandfather, to whom he was close, and cared about his well-being.

Sir Ronald turned to gaze at Linnet, and said in a voice tinged with awe, 'But my goodness, Linnet, you could be *her*. Now, when I look at you, I feel as if I'm seeing a ghost, a reincarnation. You're the spitting image of Emma, lass.'

'I know, Uncle Ronnie, everyone tells me that.' She smiled at him and went on, 'Julian and I have come to have lunch with you, and tell you about our marriage plans.'

'Although I'm a bit doddery on my feet, I'll be there!' Sir Ronald announced in a voice much stronger. 'You can be damned sure of that. I've not made any plans for dying, oh no, not just yet. I still have too much damage to do.' He began to smile. 'It's going to be the joy of my life, seeing you two get married. It was always a dream of Emma's . . . that a Kallinski and a Harte would wed one day.'

'And don't forget I'm also part O'Neill,' Linnet reminded him. 'So Julian and I will be linking the three clans when we tie the knot.'

He nodded. 'That's fantastic, my dear. And what's the date then? Last time I asked, you said you didn't know. Julian, do *you* know yet?'

'We haven't settled on the actual date, Grandfather. But it will be during the first week of December, probably the first Saturday. We'll make a final decision in a few days.'

'And where will you be wed?' he asked, beaming at them. Their arrival had cheered him immensely. Nothing like the young to keep you young.

'Mummy wanted it to be at the church in Pennistone Royal village, but now we're not too sure about that . . . there seem to be a lot of people to invite. So Dad's been talking about Ripon Cathedral.'

'Aye, that's a grand place, a very beautiful cathedral indeed. Your father sang "The Minstrel Boy" there, long, long before you were born, Linnet.'

'Yes,' she said softly, 'at Emma's funeral, wasn't it? He told me about it once.'

'Aye, it was. Where's your father, Julian? I thought he was coming up here this weekend.'

'He is. He said to tell you he'll be arriving in

time for dinner, Grandfather. Now, would you like to go in for lunch? Mary told me when we arrived that we can sit down any time you wish.'

'Well, all right, why not. Got to eat a bit, keep myself alive and kicking for your impending nuptials.' He smiled benignly at them both. 'I think you'll have to help me up,' he muttered, staring at his grandson. 'My bones ache, you know. I'm living on borrowed time, I suspect.' He chuckled and turning to Linnet, he said, 'That's what your grandfather's always telling me, so it must be true.'

CHAPTER EIGHT

'Don't move!' Dusty exclaimed without looking up, his eyes focused on the canvas propped on the easel. 'It'll just be another few minutes, and then you can have a stretch. Perhaps a few seconds even.'

'It's all right, I'm not going to move a muscle,' India answered. 'In fact, I'm fine, really I am.'

'Good girl, good girl!' He still didn't look at her, concentrated on the painting, and then quite suddenly he exclaimed, 'There, that's it! I've got it! Just those last few strokes were what I needed. Okay, sweetheart, you can stand up and stretch those lovely limbs of yours. I know you must be bloody cramped by now.'

Dusty put down his brush and wiped his hands on a paint rag, then dropped it on the work table and stepped around the easel. He walked over to the chaise where India reclined and taking hold of her hands he brought her to her feet. 'You're a marvellous model,' he murmured, pulling her into his arms. 'Absolutely bloody marvellous.

You didn't even flick an eyelash.'

'I tried very hard to keep perfectly still,' she said, laughing, looking up into his face.

'Oh God, are you luscious today,' he murmured, bending towards her, finding her mouth with his own. His lips lingered on hers; she wrapped her arms around him, found herself leaning into his body, longing for him again even though they had only just made love two hours ago. He devoured her mouth, slid his hands down her back and onto her buttocks and pressed her even closer.

He brought one hand to her breast, played with her nipple, visible under the filmy black chiffon top she was wearing. Carefully, he lifted the top, bent over her breast, kissed her nipple, and then stopped abruptly, stared up at her and said, 'Let's go back to bed. I can't stand fooling around like this when I want you so badly.'

'Yes,' was all she said, and then she smiled at him and whispered, 'but the painting will never be finished at this rate, Mr Rhodes.'

Holding her away from him, he looked down into her large, shining eyes and murmured, 'Only too true, Lady India, only too true. But this lad wants to –'

She stopped his words with her mouth, kissing him deeply, and then pulling away she said softly, 'I'll be here for the rest of the day. And tonight. I can stay as long as you want me to stay, Mr Rhodes.' Her smile was inviting, her eyes provocative.

He smiled back at her, enjoying the way she was flirting with him.

'It's the weekend, and I'm free as a bird. I can be here with you. And whatever you want to do with me you can – paint me, feed me, talk to me, and love me, love me, love me,' she finished, her voice teasing. 'Yes, please, to the latter.'

'You've got *that* exactly right, my lady.' Dusty hugged her to him and added, 'You're the best, India, just the best. I can't begin to tell you what it's like making love to you . . . it's the nearest thing to ecstasy I've ever experienced.' When she remained silent he said in a low voice, 'I mean that, you know.'

'Yes,' was all she could manage, feeling weak at the knees. His words filled her with happiness, thrilled her. She wanted him to love her in the way she loved him, with all his heart and soul and mind.

Dusty released her, and looked down into those silvery eyes. 'All right, a bit more work and then we'll have a lovely break. Later I'll paint you for another hour or two and then I'll make you dinner. I'm glad you're not planning to abandon me, it's great we've got the whole weekend together.'

'I'm glad too,' she agreed and raising her arms, reaching for the ceiling, she stretched her long lithe body. She *was* a little cramped after reclining in one position without moving for almost two hours, yet the time had passed quickly. She enjoyed being with him in the studio, watching him as he painted.

She was so much in love with him she couldn't see straight; he was the only man she had ever cared about in this way and the only man she wanted forever, and that was the truth.

Dusty began to move around himself, stretching, breathing deeply, bending, touching his toes, and saying, between movements, 'Thank God for the air conditioning. If I hadn't put it in just think how stifling it would have been on a day like this with all these windows. Are you all right, India? How about a glass of water?'

'Thanks, but I'm fine. This black chiffon blouse is as light as air, and so are the harem trousers.' She laughed and looked down at them, making a little grimace. 'All I need are bells on my ankles, bells on my toes and a tambourine and I'd be quite exotic.'

'Don't knock it. You look very sexy in that outfit, and those trousers! Wow! *They* don't leave much to the imagination.' He rolled his eyes theatrically.

'Oh Dusty, you're priceless,' she said and ran over to him, threw her arms around him. 'I do adore you so –'

The door of the studio flew open with such force and a rattling noise so loud it startled them, and they swung their heads, gaped at the young woman who had suddenly appeared on the threshold. They were horror-struck. The woman looked demented, her face twisted in rage, her eyes blazing, her hair horribly tousled; even her clothes seemed all awry on her body, in disarray.

'Get away from him, you bloody whore!' she shrieked at India, her voice high and shrill. 'Get away from him. He belongs to me.'

The woman came into the studio at a run, her eyes swivelling around, taking in everything – Dusty's paint-stained t-shirt, India's flimsy costume, the rumpled bed at the far end of the room. Finally she spotted the canvas on the easel, the beginning of a life-size portrait of India.

Rushing across to Dusty's work table she grabbed the first knife she saw, a jackknife he used for cutting canvas, and made a run at the painting, the knife raised and pointed at the portrait. 'Whore! Whore!' she screamed.

Dusty had been frozen to the spot in shock, unable to move for the last couple of seconds, but now he went into action, suddenly realizing that she was about to rip his work to shreds. Pushing India to one side, he dashed over to the easel, stood in front of the painting to protect it, and took the thrust of the knife, which had been intended for the canvas, in his left upper chest. Instantly blood spurted, and then gushed, staining the white t-shirt, staining it vivid red.

India cried out in dismay and fear.

The woman, who had the knife raised to strike again, began to scream when she saw the blood on the front of his t-shirt. Instantly dropping the knife, she swung around and flew out of the studio, banging the door behind her.

Dusty stepped over to the work table, grabbed the paint rags and pressed them to his upper chest, steadied himself against the table, cursing under his breath.

At once, India raced over to him, her face pale, her eyes wide with horror. 'Oh God, Dusty, this looks really serious!' she cried and ran to the bathroom, came rushing back with a pile of small hand towels. 'It's bad,' she said, taking the paint rags out of his bloody hand, pressing two of the clean towels against his chest, then placing his hand over them. 'Keep the pressure on,' she instructed. 'We must staunch the bleeding the best way we can.'

'I think she's severed the artery,' he said in a strangled voice, and suddenly his face crumpled; he stiffened, biting his lip. 'Jesus! That's a bloody blinding pain!' he gasped, and sat down heavily in the nearest chair. Quite aside from the excruciating pain he felt suddenly and unexpectedly weak in the legs.

'Get dressed, India. *Be quick*. I need to get to Harrogate hospital. I need surgery, I'm sure. Please hurry, I'm losing a lot of blood. I could bleed to death with a severed artery, and I'll certainly go into shock very soon.'

'Give me a minute,' India exclaimed, aware of the pain in his bright blue eyes, the agony twisting his mouth into a grimace. She threw off the black chiffon outfit, scrambled into her cotton trousers and t-shirt, grabbed her handbag and rushed back to him.

Taking hold of his right arm, she helped him to stand. 'Come on, let's go. I'll grab some more towels as we leave. Where did you put the door keys? I must lock up.'

'Table. Near the door,' he gasped.

He sounded so terrible India tightened her grip on his arm, and glanced up at him. He was chalk-white now and beads of sweat stood out on his face.

'Don't pass out on me, darling,' she said in a strong voice. 'I've got to get you to the car and then to Emergency.'

'I'll just about make it . . . I hope,' he groaned.

Brilliant sunlight blinded India as she and Dusty came out of the studio, and she was glad she had parked close by, just behind this building, instead of near the barns. Helping him along as best she could, she soon had Dusty seated in the Aston Martin, the seat belt across his chest and buckled. Groping in her bag, she pulled out two more hand towels she had grabbed from the bathroom as they had left, put them under the seat belt and on top of the other towels already there.

Once she had finished she looked at him, noted the pain glazing his eyes, the intense pallor of his face. Now he was ashen, still perspiring profusely, and she knew she had very little time to get him to Emergency before he went into shock. And the loss of blood was frightening. After closing the door she ran around to the other side of the car and got in, put the key in the ignition.

'The studio door,' he mumbled, partially turning his head to look at her. 'Lock it.'

'It's double-locked, Dusty, don't worry,' she reassured him, turned the key and started the car, then backed up the dirt road and headed around the house to the main driveway. At one moment she said, 'The seat belt's holding the towels in place, darling,' but he didn't seem to hear her. His eyes were closed, and his right hand was still pressed down on the towels covering the wound.

Slowing the car as she came to the main gates of Willows Hall, she took out her cell phone and punched in Linnet's number. It was answered after only a few rings. 'Hello?'

'Linnet, it's India. Don't talk, just listen please. I've got a very serious problem. Dusty's been stabbed. Badly. An artery's been severed, I think. He's losing lots of blood. I'm just leaving Willows Hall. I should make it to Harrogate District Hospital in about twelve minutes, unless there's more traffic than usual. Call Emergency would you please, Linny? Tell them I'm coming. That way they'll be ready for us.'

'God, how terrible! I'll call immediately. Then I'm heading there myself. I should make it in five minutes if I leave now. I'm at Uncle Ronnie's house.'

'Thanks, Linnet.' India clicked off, and glanced at Dusty. His eyes were closed and he seemed to have slumped down in the seat, looked out of it. And blood was seeping through the towels onto his hand and trickling down his arm.

As she started up the car again, India noticed that her hand trembled and she had to take several deep breaths to steady herself. Now was not the time to panic. Or lose her nerve. She knew he was about to go into shock, if he hadn't already, and speed was of the utmost importance. Gripping the wheel, she edged out onto the road which led into Harrogate, was filled with relief when she saw that it was empty, except for a lorry and a cyclist. She put her foot down on the accelerator and concentrated on driving, exceeding the speed limit.

She made it to the hospital in exactly nine minutes, and as she slowed down at the hospital gates she could see several people clustered at the Emergency Entrance door; three nurses and a couple of doctors, she thought, all standing next to a stretcher. Linnet was with them, looking pale and extremely anxious.

Slowing to a standstill, India braked and alighted, motioned to the doctors, then ran around to the passenger door. Before she had even opened it they were rushing towards her with the stretcher, and Linnet was not far behind.

India stood to one side, allowed the professionals to take over, to lift Dusty out of the car, but she said to one of the doctors, 'My friend thought the knife struck his artery, maybe even severed it.'

He stared at her, frowned. 'Is he a doctor?'

She shook her head. 'No, he's an artist. But he studied anatomy in art classes.'

'I see.' He nodded and added, 'He's probably correct. Right now he's in shock and there's obviously enormous blood loss. Try not to worry,' and with that he ran after the stretcher which was already being trundled at top speed into Emergency by the hospital staff.

Linnet came over to her, took hold of her arm, and said, 'Let's go inside and sit down. I gave them as much information as I could, but they'll want to talk to you, India, I've no doubt.'

She nodded. 'I know. I suppose they've already called the police.'

'It's routine, isn't it, with something like this?' Linnet murmured, eyeing her closely.

'I expect so.' India suddenly began to shake uncontrollably and brought her hands up to her face. 'It was so awful. Terrifying, Linny.'

After opening the Emergency Entrance door, and leading her over to a chair, Linnet sat down next to her cousin, and asked in a low voice, 'What the hell happened? Who stabbed Dusty?'

'A woman. I don't know who she was, so don't ask, and I certainly wasn't able to question Dusty, under the circumstances. Perhaps he knew her, I'm not certain. She burst into the studio and just went berserk when she saw me.'

India now told Linnet everything that had happened less than an hour ago, not pausing for breath until she had finished, and then she let out a long shuddering sigh. 'Oh God, Linnet, I hope he's going to be all right. What if he dies? God, I couldn't bear it if anything happens to him.' India took hold of Linnet's arm, stared at her intently and burst into tears.

At once Linnet put her arm around India and

brought her close, soothing her softly. 'Dusty will make it, darling. He's young, strong, and they can work miracles today. Modern medicine's quite incredible.'

'But he's lost so much blood. It just . . . spurted out of him. It was frightening to see –' She broke off, and her face underwent a sudden change. Then she exclaimed, 'I could give him blood, if he needs a transfusion. Would you do it, too, Linnet, if it were necessary?'

Momentarily startled by this request though she was, Linnet said, after the merest pause, 'Yes, of course, if he needs it.'

India now sat up a little straighter, and her face seemed to lose some of its tension. Giving Linnet a half smile she murmured in a very low voice, 'I love him very much, you know. I've never felt like this about any other man. He's the only one I've ever wanted to marry.'

This announcement did not startle Linnet; she had known, right from the outset of India's involvement with Dusty Rhodes, that she had fallen heavy and hard for the artist, and Linnet was pleased for her. Her only worry had been his well-known reputation as a bit of a carousing and volatile rabble-rouser, but India had assured her this was all a big put-on by Dusty. On the other hand, hysterical women wielding knives was another thing altogether, and smacked of an unsuitable, and perhaps even an unsavoury background. And this thought troubled her. Other women who had been rejected could cause untold problems.

Linnet looked up as a voice said in careful tones, 'Lady India, could you come and give us some details about Mr Rhodes, please.'

India rose at once, and said, 'Certainly,' and followed a woman in a white coat holding a clipboard and a pen. A moment later two police officers walked into Emergency, and Linnet groaned inside. There was no question in her mind that they had come to talk to her cousin about Dusty's stabbing. Of course they had. And if Dusty died then it would be murder they were talking about.

The woman in the short white jacket holding the clipboard turned out to be Mrs Anita Giles from Administration, and after introducing herself to India she led the way to her office off the Emergency Entrance lobby.

Once they were seated, Mrs Giles explained, 'Now, Lady India, if you could fill in the gaps for me I'd be very appreciative. Your cousin Miss O'Neill just gave me the name Russell Rhodes and said he'd been stabbed. I'm making the assumption that Mr Rhodes is the well-known artist. Am I correct?'

'Yes, you are, Mrs Giles. His full name is Russell Cecil Rhodes, and he lives at Willows Hall in Follifoot. He's forty-two years old. Is that the kind of thing you want to know?'

Mrs Giles nodded, continued to write on the form attached to her clipboard; once she had jotted down these salient facts, she asked, 'Does Mr Rhodes have any medical problems that you know of?'

'No. At least, I don't think so. He's very fit as far as I know. He exercises, watches his diet, drinks very little.' India smiled when she saw Mrs Giles raise her brow, and added, 'His reputation for being something of a roué is quite false, I can assure you of that. Somewhat self-engendered, if you know what I mean, and wildly exaggerated.' Leaning forward, India asked, 'He *is* going to be all right, isn't he? I mean, he said he thought an artery had been severed.'

The woman's face was quite unreadable when she said, 'Everyone at the hospital will do their very best for him, Lady India, and I'm sure you'll understand that I can't even hazard a guess under the circumstances. Now, could you tell me exactly what –'

At this moment there was a knock on the door, and Anita Giles stopped in the middle of her sentence and said, 'Come in.'

The door opened to admit two policemen. 'Hello, Mrs Giles,' one of them said; the other simply nodded, smiled across at her.

'Good afternoon, officers. This is Lady India Standish, a friend of Mr Russell Rhodes, who is the victim of the stabbing reported earlier. Lady India brought him to the hospital.'

India immediately stood up, went and shook hands with the two policemen, who introduced themselves as Constables Hobbs and Charlton.

'If you'd be so good as to leave us alone with Lady India,' the one called Hobbs said, staring hard at Anita Giles, nodding at the door.

'Oh yes, of course. I do realize you wish to speak to her ladyship alone.' Smiling at India, she hurried out of the small office, softly closing the door behind her.

India said, 'There's not much I can tell you, Constable Hobbs.'

'Just give us the details, Lady India,' Constable Charlton suggested, and gestured for India to sit down.

'Thanks, but I'll stand,' she answered, and told them, 'Mr Rhodes is a well-known artist, as I'm sure you know, who lives at Willows Hall in Follifoot. He has his studio there, and he's painting my portrait . . . for my father, the Earl of Dunvale. A short while –'

'You're related to the late Mrs Emma Harte!' Hobbs exclaimed, eyeing her with sudden unconcealed interest.

'Yes, I'm her great-granddaughter. And her other great-granddaughter is Linnet O'Neill, my cousin, who's waiting outside.'

'Both my mother and grandmother worked at the Harte store in Harrogate,' Hobbs explained with a small smile, and then continued, 'So Mr Rhodes was painting you and suddenly someone came in and stabbed him, is that what you're saying?'

'No, it isn't what I'm saying at all,' India answered briskly. 'We had stopped because I'd been sitting for over two hours without moving, and I needed to stretch myself, and Dusty, er, Mr Rhodes, was also a little stiff. He said he wanted to do some stretching before continuing. Anyway, we were doing our exercises and chatting when the door of the studio flew open and this young woman came in. I don't know who she was, and I'm not certain that Mr Rhodes did either.'

'And she rushed up and stabbed him, is that it?' Charlton asked, sounding sceptical.

'Oh no, she saw me and started shouting at me, calling me names. She was a bit out of control. And then her eyes lighted on the portrait, and she seemed to go berserk, ran forward, grabbed a knife from the work table and made a beeline for the portrait, the knife raised.'

'And she slashed the painting, before stabbing Mr Rhodes?' Hobbs asked, his brows drawing together in a frown.

'No, no, it didn't happen that way at all! Dusty and I, well, we were both sort of stupefied, yes, that's the best word. We were *utterly stupefied*, in fact, and suddenly he obviously realized she was heading for the portrait, and he ran forward, stood in front of it, to protect it, and that's how he got himself stabbed. The woman meant to damage the painting, not Mr Rhodes. It was an accident.'

'I see,' Hobbs murmured thoughtfully and glanced across at his colleague. Hobbs said to India, 'We hope to speak to Mr Rhodes soon, once he comes out of the operating room.'

India clenched her hands, digging her nails into the palms, her anxiety rising. 'Have the doctors told you anything, Constable Hobbs? He's not going to die, is he?'

'I dunno,' Hobbs said, shaking his head. 'I hope not. Dr Palmerton is a wonderful surgeon. If anybody can make Mr Rhodes right, he can. But we'll just have to wait, won't we?'

CHAPTER NINE

'Where is my beautiful other half?'

Tessa, buried in one of the big wingchairs in the library, threw the folder of balance sheets on the floor, jumped up at the sound of her brother's voice, and ran to him.

Lorne Fairley stood leaning against the doorframe, looking every inch the actor he was, handsome and debonair. 'Hello, darling girl,' he said in his beautifully modulated actor's voice.

'Oh Lorne, you made it! Thank God you're here!' She flew into his outstretched arms and he held her tightly, filled with relief that she appeared to be perfectly calm and in control after her ordeal.

They stood together in a long and loving embrace, as close to each other emotionally as they had always been. They were of similar height, had the same blond colouring and sculpted, pristine features. There was no mistaking that they were twins, carried the Fairley genes of their late father, Jim Fairley, their mother's first husband.

Tessa, who had been born a few minutes before

Lorne, considered herself to be the elder and never let him forget it; Lorne, sincere, good-natured, loving, and easy-going, simply laughed when she pulled rank. From childhood he had called her 'the Ancient One', much to her irritation even to this day.

'I'm so sorry you had to come back all the way from Turkey, but –'

'My few days of holiday were almost over,' he interrupted, standing away from her, his eyes roving over her face before he kissed her on the cheek. 'And to be honest I was getting bloody bored. Anyway, I wouldn't leave you in the lurch, we're always there for each other, aren't we?' Putting his arm around her shoulders, he walked her over to the sofas and went on, 'I gather Ma's not coming back just yet.'

'No, she's not. I insisted she kept to her schedule, stayed on in New York with Shane.'

'I know. I spoke to Dad and he said everything was under control here, so they weren't making any changes in their plans. And how's my sweet Adele?'

'She's fine, Lorne, none the worse for what happened, thank heavens.' At the thought of her daughter Tessa broke into smiles, and added, 'She's such a happy child.'

'And where is the little tyke? I want to see her at once.'

'She's taking her afternoon nap, so you'll have to wait a bit.'

They sat down together on one of the sofas and

Lorne peered at her again. 'What's the latest on that bloody awful husband of yours?'

'He's about to become my ex!'

'So fast?' Lorne stared at her, a sceptical look crossing his face. 'Don't tell me he's being acqui escent for once?'

'No, he's very demanding and arrogant, and naturally the divorce will have to take its course. But our solicitors, his and mine, are doing a lot of talking, and incidentally *his* are pretty annoyed with him for snatching Adele the way he did. Obviously it puts *him* in the *wrong*, and they don't like that one bit.'

'It was a ridiculous stunt he pulled. As *you* well know, I've never really liked him, Tessa, and I've always thought he was two bricks short of a full load.'

She began to laugh. 'You remind me of Jack Figg with all your old-fashioned sayings. They're forever on *his* lips.'

'They always were. Where do you think I learned them? At the knee of the master himself. Whom I just saw when I drove in. He was his usual warm and loving self, but he's a tough bugger, Tess, and thank God for that. He told me he's making this place impregnable and if the number of chaps around here installing things are anything to go by, I believe him.'

Tessa nodded. 'He told me he's staying on until Monday, then he's going back to Robin Hood's Bay for a couple of days. He'll be back in the middle of next week. Anyway, I thought I'd cook for us all tonight, I want Margaret to have the evening off. She and Joe have been so worried. All this trouble . . . it's sort of . . . done them in a bit.'

'I'm not surprised, and talking of Margaret, I went to the kitchen when I got here and asked her to make me a sandwich. I stepped off the plane at Heathrow and drove straight up here. And I'm famished. So come on, let's go see what she's managed to rustle up. And as far as tonight's concerned, I can't wait for one of your gourmet specialities.'

As they crossed the Stone Hall together they ran into Margaret who was coming to find them. 'There you are!' she exclaimed, and, addressing Lorne, she explained, 'I've put your sandwiches in the morning room, along with a pot of tea for you both.' She nodded and hurried off towards the kitchen, thinking about Lorne. He had always been her favourite, and she was pleased he was back at home to look after his sister, if only for a short while. She always wished he would stay longer, he was so special to her, like her own, in a sense. He was the kindest, sweetest of men and his fame as an actor had not changed him one bit. He was the same as he'd been as a boy when she'd bounced him on her lap.

Until last winter the morning room had been an office which Emma Harte had used for many years whenever she was at Pennistone Royal. But this past December Paula had finally decided it was wasted space, and had transformed it into a charming spot for breakfast and casual meals.

As they went in, Lorne glanced around, thinking how cool and restful it looked on this hot August Saturday. The walls were a soft apple-green and there were rafts of white everywhere; the lovely, curving bay window was treated to airy, puffed-up balloon shades made of a green-and-white striped silk, while the chairs around the walnut table were covered in a green-and-white checked fabric.

'Mother did a great job with this room,' he remarked as they sat down at the circular table which Margaret had just set. 'I'm going to take her up on her very generous offer to redo my flat.' Staring at the plates of sandwiches, Lorne now shook his head and smiled. 'She's a wonder, that woman! Look, Margaret's made all of my favourite nursery sandwiches.'

'Yes, she always did spoil *you*,' Tessa said succinctly, giving him an old-fashioned look.

Lorne did not rise to the bait, merely grinned, took an egg salad sandwich and munched on it, watching his twin as she poured tea into his cup and added a slice of lemon. She had sounded so upset and terrified when she had called him on Thursday; she had reached him in Turkey, where he was spending a few days with friends before starting a new film at Shepperton Studios outside London.

Even if he had been having the best time in the world, he would have left immediately, once he knew his twin sister needed him. As it was, he was fed up, itching to head back to London, which he had done with alacrity after her phone call. Because of the heavy holiday air traffic he had not been able to get a direct flight. So he had jetted to Paris, spent the night at the Paris O'Neill Hotel on the Avenue Montaigne, and flown to London today.

There was nothing he wouldn't do for her; they were extremely close. Yet he was fully aware of Tessa's faults . . . her extreme rivalry with Linnet for supremacy at the Harte stores, her terrible jealousy of their half-sister, which he considered to be totally unreasonable. And then there was her snobbery about being a Fairley, her desire to be known only as Fairley. This he found a bit silly. After all, they were Hartes and McGills and Amorys as well, and in fact they owed everything they had to their great-grandmother Emma Harte, and to their great-grandfather Paul McGill.

Lorne wished Tessa could see things his way but apparently she couldn't, or perhaps wouldn't, he wasn't sure of which. She was obstinate in her views, vociferous in her opinions, but he had ceased long ago to chastise her. There was no point really, since he was convinced she would never change. He had long ago made up his mind not to waste his breath needlessly. And he continued to adore her as he had since their childhood, accepted Tessa as she was, tried not to make judgements about her. Or anyone else, for that matter. His motto had always been live and let live.

However, he now stared at his twin in surprise when she announced: 'Linnet was on top of everything, Lorne. She really was. I don't know what I would have done without her.'

'*You're* suddenly singing a different tune!'

'Don't be mean.'

'I'm not being mean, just truthful, my pet. You're the one who's constantly complaining about Linnet. I realize that you're determined to be the supremo at Harte's, but there's a place there for Linnet, too.'

'I know, I know. Don't go on about it, Lorne. I'm really grateful that Linnet had the presence of mind to do the things she did, like get Jack Figg on the job, for instance. You see there was no one here when Mark snatched Adele . . . well, only Wiggs and his gardeners.'

'Where the hell was everybody?' Lorne's voice had risen and he looked even more taken aback. 'This place is teeming with people usually, it always has been since our childhood. Odd that everyone was gone that morning, don't you think?'

'Nothing sinister, Lorne. Just a coincidence. Margaret had decided to go shopping, Joe had driven over to East Witton on estate business, and Elvira was on her day off . . .' Tessa paused, sat back, and thought for a moment about her encounter with Elvira earlier. In a way it still bothered her that the nanny had waited so long to mention Mark's conversation with her on the roadside.

'What is it? Something's troubling you, Tess.'

'No, I'm fine. It's just that Elvira told me this morning that Mark had been waiting for her on the main road outside Pennistone Royal –'

'How the hell did *he* know she'd be leaving when she did?'

'Because it was *Wednesday*, and she always has that day off. Anyway, apparently he flagged her down, she stopped, and he asked her where I was, where Adele was, said he was on the way to visit us.'

'And she told him, gave him all the details.' Lorne nodded and a reflective expression settled on his face. 'They weren't in cahoots, were they? Do you trust her?'

'I'm quite certain they weren't in cahoots, and yes, I do trust her. She's a creature of habit, Miss Elvira is, and she has never changed her day off. Always Wednesdays. Everything else is done in the same way, almost by rote in a sense, although it's not really that – banal.'

'And Evan? Where was she? You did say she's staying here.'

'She'd gone over to Lackland Priory to have lunch with Uncle Robin.'

'And where is the dastardly Jonathan, the elusive Jonathan?' Smiling acidly, not waiting for her answer, Lorne declaimed, in a highly exaggerated upper-class English accent, 'They seek him here, they seek him there, those Frenchies seek him everywhere. Is he in heaven, or is he in hell, that damned elusive Pimpernel?'

Tessa began to laugh; her brother had always had the ability to bring a smile to her face, and she loved listening to him when he put on his actor's face and voice and adopted appropriate mannerisms. 'Jonathan's in Hong Kong, according to Jack, who just had him tracked by one of his top operatives.

But as Jack pointed out, where he happens to be is meaningless, of no consequence in this Age of Communications in which we live. Mr Ainsley can direct the traffic from anywhere.'

Lorne nodded his understanding. 'Mark and Jonathan, what a pairing up *that* is, very hard to believe. My God, Mark's a bloody fool, Tessa, when one thinks about it. How could he let himself get . . . conned by Jonathan?'

'You just said it yourself, Lorne. He's two bricks short of a full load.'

Lorne picked up his cup, took a swallow of tea and remarked, 'I wouldn't want to be in Evan's shoes . . . Jonathan must detest her.'

'Absolutely true, I'm sure. She's very, very close to Gideon, you know. I think they might –' Tessa sat back, gave her twin a long knowing look, and finished, 'be very serious about each other.'

'I thought they were, at Dad's sixtieth birthday party, didn't you?'

She simply inclined her head, suddenly filled with a strange aching feeling, a sadness really, when she thought of Shane's birthday celebration. She had been alone that night, without an escort, having so recently left Mark, and she felt empty inside, awkward and somewhat lost. It had been her cousin Toby Harte who had come to her rescue, who had looked after her, just as he had done when they were little. They had been close all of their lives; Toby truly understood her. Wasn't it funny how life worked out? He was in a mess himself, just as she was, getting a divorce from Adrianna.

Divorce. She rolled the word around in her head like a small glass bead. She hated the idea of failure; she had failed at marriage. But she wasn't going to fail at motherhood. Oh, no. Whatever it took, whatever it cost her, she was going to make sure Adele had a happy childhood and a wonderful life, and certainly without any interference from Mark Longden.

Tessa picked up her cup, took a sip of tea, and with a small shock she noticed her hand was shaking. Swiftly replacing the cup in its saucer, she turned her head and gazed out of the window, her mind awash with memories of Mark and the early years of their marriage.

She had had such great hopes for it. How had it gone so very wrong? Was it somehow her fault? Had she not pulled her weight? Why had Mark fallen under the influence of Jonathan Ainsley, a man whom he knew the entire family despised? Was he motivated by greed? Dissatisfaction with her? Or was he, very simply, a weak man?

Unexpectedly, her silver-grey eyes filled. She tried to choke back the tears, felt a burning sensation at the back of her throat and tried to swallow . . . now the tears were falling unchecked, spilling out of her eyes. Bringing a hand up to her face, she attempted to hide behind it, but didn't succeed.

Instantly Lorne noticed how upset she had become, and he was filled with a mixture of dismay and concern for her. Leaping to his feet, he went and stood next to her, bent down, placed an arm around her shoulders. 'Oh, little pet,' he said, using his childhood name for her, 'don't, don't, Tess, he's just not worth it. Nobody is, you know.' When she remained totally silent, he added, very softly, 'Did you give him your heart, Tess?'

Clearing her throat, she wiped her face with both hands, and shook her head, then looked directly at her brother. 'I'm fine, do go and sit down, Lorne dear, and finish your sandwiches.' Sighing to herself, she remarked, 'And no, I didn't . . . give him my heart.'

'But you did fall in love with him,' Lorne asserted, returning to his chair.

'I suppose I did. Well, I *thought* I was in love with him. Maybe it was just an infatuation.'

'Perhaps it was, I've been there.'

'Oh. You're thinking of your last girlfriend, are you? Did you give Miriam Delaney your heart?'

He smiled at Tessa, and it was a rueful smile, very fleeting, barely settling on his mouth before it was gone. 'Oh yes,' he said.

'So what happened?'

'She trampled on it.'

'I'm so sorry. I knew you cared deeply for her, were very much in love with her. I hadn't realized it was so one-sided.'

'Neither did I, at first.' He shrugged, then lifted his hands in a Gallic gesture. '*C'est la vie, chérie.*'

A small silence fell between them, but it was an easy silence, and they were as comfortable with one another now as they had been since childhood. On the same wavelength, thinking the same thing.

Suddenly Tessa said, 'I'll never get married again. It's not worth it.'

'I do sincerely hope you don't mean you're going to remain celibate for the rest of your life. Surely you don't mean that?'

'Why not? There are worse things.'

Leaning across the table, Lorne exclaimed, 'Listen to me, Tessa Fairley, I'm not going to permit you to lead a bleak, empty, unfulfilled life without love. You must be fair to yourself. I agree that marriage might be too much for you, after your recent hassles with Mark, but there has to be a lover. I won't let you spend the rest of your life alone without a man in it, a loving, caring man who will treat you the way you deserve to be treated. Actually, if it's anything to do with me, I'll see you have a string of devoted lovers,' he finished on a teasing note.

Tessa had the good grace to laugh, and she also managed to push her troubles to one side. 'And that goes for you, too. Put Miss Delaney behind you and find yourself a gorgeous girl. Perhaps you'll meet somebody wonderful in Paris when you're over there filming. A beautiful mademoiselle perhaps.'

Lorne was relieved that her mood had lightened, and he caught hold of her hand, kissed it. 'Now you're sounding better, much better indeed. Like your normal self.'

'This is an extraordinary studio, India,' Linnet exclaimed, glancing around. 'Dusty did a wonderful architectural job . . . you did say he designed it himself, didn't you?'

'That's right,' India replied, sounding preoccupied as she let her eyes roam around the room, taking in everything. There were a lot of blood splatters on the floor near the painting, and she hurried over to check the portrait and saw, with great relief, that none of the blood had hit it.

It was at this moment that she noticed the knife on the floor where the young woman had dropped it, and she said, 'Look, Linnet! Over there! It's the knife.' She pointed to it and immediately added, 'I mustn't pick it up or touch it. *Her* fingerprints have to be on it, not mine.'

'You're right about that,' Linnet emphatically agreed. 'And I just want to say this, India. I thought the two policemen were nice to us, but just a little bit suspicious of you, wouldn't you say?'

'Yes. Constable Charlton was suspicious of my story, I agree. But not Hobbs. I know those who are closest to a victim, especially of the opposite sex, are usually suspected of being the perpetrator. So they most probably do have me in their sights.'

Linnet glanced at the big clock on the wall. 'Those two will be arriving soon. Are you sure you don't want me to ask Jack Figg to drive over, be here for you in case you need him?'

'No, no, honestly, it's fine. My prints aren't on the knife, and I know that when Dusty comes round he'll tell exactly the same story I've told. Because it's the truth. Also, Paddy Whitaker will be back by four, or thereabouts. And maybe he can throw some light on what happened. He's the house-manager I mentioned earlier –'

'Isn't that simply Dusty's more plebeian name for a *butler*?' Linnet asked, an auburn brow lifting.

India half smiled. 'You're correct in that assumption. Anyway, Paddy had to go to Manchester this morning, but I heard him tell Dusty he'd be returning around teatime.'

'And where did you say the housekeeper was?' Linnet probed, and continued to prowl round the studio, filled with curiosity.

'I explained before, it's her weekend off,' India answered, sounding slightly impatient, 'that's why we'd been looking forward to being here together. *Alone*.'

'So you think the house-manager might know who the young woman was, or rather, is? Isn't that what you're saying?'

'Yes,' India answered, quietly, her sharpness receding. 'If it was somebody from Dusty's past . . . or present. But she could have been a total stranger, you know.'

Linnet glanced across at her cousin and shook her head. 'That's stretching it, love. Why would a stranger attack him? Or rather, attack the painting?'

'Perhaps she was a deranged fan.'

'India, really! He's not a film star or a rock star. Fans of artists aren't – *stalkers*, for God's sake. They don't go bursting into studios and stabbing people, or rather stabbing paintings.' Linnet threw her an odd look, shaking her head, nonplussed.

'She *could* be a deranged fan. Or a former girl-friend, a lover, even. But I trust Dusty and he would have told me if there was anyone important still hanging around in his life. I just know he would, Linnet.' India's voice had risen several octaves.

'Okay, okay, don't get upset. I trust you and your judgement, India, so if you say he's above board and all that, then of course I'll take your word for it.' Moving towards one of the tall side windows, Linnet continued, 'I think I'd better call Julian, he'll be wondering what's happening.' As she spoke she pulled out her mobile and punched in her fiancé's number.

India half smiled, nodded, and walked over to the portrait, stood looking at it, her head on one side. Her thoughts went to Dusty in the hospital, strung up with wires and drips and God knows what else. He had rushed to protect this painting, and that's why he was where he was at this moment. He could have died for it, actually, and the terrible thing was it was still in the early stages, *incomplete*. He had only been working on it for three days, and he could have surely started it all over again, couldn't he? Perhaps he had acted on impulse, his reflexes automatic and in high gear.

Thankfully he was going to be all right; the doctors had told her that before she had left the hospital to come to the studio. The 'crime scene', the police called it, but there was nothing here of great interest to them, nothing of real importance, except the jackknife on the floor where the woman had dropped it, and Dusty's blood. Just before she had left Harrogate District Hospital, they had allowed her to see Dusty in the ICU. She had stood alone by the side of the bed, looking down at his drawn face, swept free of all colour, chalk white, as if his essence had been drained away. Well, it had, she supposed. The blood loss had been acute; he had had to have transfusions. Fortunately the artery had been successfully repaired. Since he was still unconscious from the anaesthetic, she had simply leaned over him, touched his face gently with two fingers, whispered that she loved him. And then the nurse had put her head around the door and beckoned for her to leave the room.

India's sense of relief was enormous, and her anxiety had begun to ease. *He was going to live.* And so, after seeing him, she had been quite willing to drive over to Willows Hall and open up the studio for the police.

Who was the woman? This question hung there in mid-air, as it had for hours. Was she a stalker intent on doing harm? Or a former lover? And would she come back to do more damage?

CHAPTER TEN

Gideon expected the kitchen door to be locked. But when he turned the knob it opened at once and he walked straight in, fully anticipating a cheery greeting from Margaret and Joe, who were usually sitting here having a cup of tea at this hour. Much to his surprise the room was empty.

He paused in his tracks, glancing around, then stood inhaling the marvellous smells. The air was redolent with the scent of mixed spices that brought memories of North Africa rushing back, of meat simmering and vegetables steaming and glorious mouthwatering aromas of a special gourmet meal in the process of being made. He knew it would be a delicious feast tonight because Tessa was the best chef he knew, bar none. *She* missed her calling, he thought, as he hurried across the spacious kitchen and went into the back service corridor.

A steep staircase led to the first floor, which was mostly Paula's domain, and then continued up to the second floor where so many of the bedrooms were located. No security here, he decided, anybody could've walked right in, just as I did, and made it to the main part of the house. Everyone was going to have to get used to locking outside doors, or they would have Jack Figg to contend with. He sighed as he climbed the back staircase which long ago had been used by servants when the house had been staffed to the hilt.

It was a steep climb and he thought of those little housemaids of long ago carting breakfast trays up to the rooms. They must have been worn out by mid-morning. But the world was full of genuine inequities in those days; in certain ways, things *had* changed for the better.

On the second floor every door had a small brass plate with the name of the suite engraved, announcing Yellow, Blue, Crimson, or Gold, and so on; this way of identifying each room by a colour had been Emma Harte's invention and he had always thought it a charming idea. Finally he arrived at the Yellow Suite, tapped on the door and walked in before he was bidden to enter.

'Oh my God!' she exclaimed, 'you startled me!' She clutched the towel to her naked body as she stood and gaped at him.

'Sorry,' he apologized and walked towards her, his step determined. When he came to a standstill he took hold of her hand purposefully and pulled her into his arms in the most proprietary manner. Holding her close, he kissed her deeply, and then swiftly led her across the room.

She endeavoured to keep the towel around her;

the expression on her face was one of uncertainty. 'What's going on?' she demanded quietly, staring at him, trying to break free of his tenacious grip.

Not answering her immediately, he went on manoeuvring her towards the bed. 'Now sit there, and stop struggling, I'm not going to rape you.'

'Are you sure you're not?' she asked, but dutifully sat on the bed as he had suggested, and watched him as he struggled out of his clothes. When he walked towards her she realized at once that they were going to be on this bed for some time, and that would mean they would be late for dinner. But she didn't have a chance to mention this, or protest, because he was on the bed next to her before she could even blink, and kissing her passionately. And, of course, she immediately responded, ardently, matching his passion, since she did love him with all her heart.

After a moment or two they stopped kissing, and he pushed himself up on one elbow, looked down into her face. 'I know what you're going to say, that we'll be late down to dinner, and all that stuff. But I haven't been alone with you for over a week, and I do have the need to be close to you like this, and *very* intimate.'

'I know, I know,' she murmured, her hand going up onto the nape of his neck and then reaching into his thick hair. 'I've missed you, too, missed being with you, making love like this.'

Gideon looked down into her large, luminous blue-grey eyes, and smiled at her, and then quite unexpectedly, almost involuntarily, he sat up with a jolt, jumped off the bed and went over to his clothes piled on a chair. A moment later he was back on the bed with her and taking her hand in his. 'I wanted you so much I couldn't wait to get you into bed, but we've got the rest of our lives to make love. It's only once that a girl and a boy get engaged.' He began to laugh. 'Well, let's hope it's only *once*,' he said and slipped the sapphire ring he was holding onto her finger, and then announced, 'Now we are really engaged, Evan, and that's all that matters.'

Evan sat bolt upright on the bed and stared at him and then at the third finger of her left hand, her eyes brimming with surprise and delight. 'Thank you for such a gorgeous ring,' and leaning forward she kissed him on the lips. 'And yes, we really *are* engaged.' There was laughter in her voice as she added, 'Whether my father approves or not, we're engaged! *I* certainly approve! Oh, yippee!'

Gideon laughed with her, enjoying her happiness, excitement and enthusiasm. 'I'm glad you like your ring.'

'I love it. Oh, Gid, you really have taken me by surprise, and it's all so great, and I'm so happy.'

'And so am I.' He beamed at her. 'Now, let's seal our bargain with a kiss, shall we?'

She smiled back at him and slid her arms around his neck, pulled him down so that he was laying on top of her body. They kissed deeply, hungrily, and they touched each other in intimate places, and swiftly his passion soared. And so did hers; she felt sudden heat rushing through her, and she clung to him, loving him so much, and then her legs went around his back as he entered her, and she cried out as she always did, as if she were taken by surprise. This thrilled him, added to his pleasure, and when she began to thrust her body vigorously against his he thought he would explode with excitement. Within seconds they were moving together in unison, had quickly found their perfect rhythm. It was a rhythm that swiftly increased, and the faster they moved the more excited they both were. And as she came in ecstasy she cried out his name, and he called hers a mere split second later, telling her how much he loved her over and over again.

After they had calmed down they took a shower together, stood under the running water wrapped in each other's arms. It was as if they were unable to pull apart.

But they finally did so, and Evan went into the bedroom to dry her hair and brush it into shape. She was still wrapped in a towel, putting on a few touches of make-up when Gideon came back into the bedroom and quickly got dressed. Then he sat down in a chair and watched her, loving her, counting his blessings that he had found her. Yes, he had found his true love in this uncertain world and he felt very lucky he had. He was truly fortunate that this woman was a perfect fit in every possible way, that they were in tune with each other, so compatible.

After she had put on a pretty muslin summer frock and a pair of sandals, Evan swung to face him, and said, 'What is it? You sure are staring at me. *Hard*.'

'Just admiring, darling, that's all,' he murmured languidly.

She walked towards him, holding out her left hand. 'It's gorgeous, Gideon, isn't it? The most perfect engagement ring.'

'I think so, and you *are* wearing it tonight, aren't you? Downstairs, I mean?'

'Yes, if you want me to . . . everyone will know we've become engaged . . .' She paused, looked at him carefully, waiting for his reaction.

'Naturally. But since we *are* actually engaged why shouldn't they know? They're family, yours as well as mine. And listen, I don't want you taking it off, not even when you see your parents next week. Okay?' His green eyes narrowed slightly, were piercing as they gazed at her.

'Okay, okay,' she answered quickly, meaning it, but also detecting something in his voice and in his eyes that would brook no argument. And he was right. Since they were indeed engaged to be married why should they hide it from her parents? Her father wouldn't be pleased, she was fairly certain of that, but it was her life not his; conversely, she knew Gideon's parents would be delighted, because Emily and Winston had already told her they hoped she would marry their son. Something suddenly occurred to her, and she exclaimed, 'Can we go over to see Robin tomorrow and tell him, Gid? Oh let's do it. I'd really like him to know we've made it official.'

'Why not? Anyway, he's a bit of a romantic, isn't he, so he'll be happy that we've told him first. Imagine, Evan, that he kept that snap of your granny all these years.'

Evan started to chuckle. 'She was no *granny*, not my Glynnis! Not even when she was old. And anyway over fifty years ago she was one helluva glamour girl.'

'I saw the picture, didn't I? She was a true beauty and so are you. *My* beauty. *My* beautiful wife-to-be.'

Tessa stood at the stove, hovering over several pots, so concentrated that there was no way she was going to turn around at the sound of footsteps in the kitchen. She simply called out, 'Where have you been? I thought you were coming to chat to me ages ago, Lorne.'

'It's not Lorne,' Jack Figg said, as he drew closer. 'Lorne sent me to ask if you'd like a drink.'

Now Tessa swung around, and nodded. 'That would be nice, Jack.'

'Lorne's busy opening a bottle of champagne in the Stone Hall. Is that all right? Or would you prefer something else?'

'Champagne, thanks.'

'Back in a moment,' he replied and disappeared through the door.

Alone again, Tessa busied herself with her pans once more, stirring the meat gently, which was on a very low light, lifting lids, peering into pots, nodding to herself, and then turning some of them off. A moment later Jack returned, was instantly by her side, offering her a flute of champagne. 'Thanks,' she said, taking it from him.

Bringing his glass to touch hers, he said, 'Cheers.'

'Cheers,' she answered, and took a sip. 'That's crisp. Tastes great.'

'All of this smells mighty good. What're you making for dinner?'

Turning off several more burners on the stove top, Tessa walked over to the kitchen table, sat down, and sipped her champagne; Jack followed, stood looking at her. 'Or is it a secret?'

'No, it's not. I've steamed a batch of white asparagus to start with, and I'm going to serve it warm with Hollandaise sauce. The main course is couscous. I know that perhaps this sounds like a strange dish on a hot night, but it's not really. After all, couscous is Moroccan in origin and Morocco's a warm country. The couscous grain is very light, a type of semolina, you know, and I've used veal instead of lamb, which is a much lighter meat. I've made a sort of Moroccan-style *blanquette de veau*, but with a brown sauce, not a white one. You'll enjoy it, Jack.'

'I know I will,' he answered, sitting down finally at the table. 'The aromas are wonderful. What exactly am I smelling in here?'

'Lots of spices melding together, for one thing. Turmeric, ginger, saffron, cumin, and I've used onions, so you can smell those, as well as vegetables steaming, and meat juices. I hope you're hungry because I've made loads of it.'

Jack laughed. 'Sitting here has certainly got *my* taste buds going. My mouth's really watering. To be honest, if I was starving before I'm now *ravenous*.'

'It's almost finished. Is everybody downstairs?'

'Gideon and Evan haven't appeared, nor has India, but the others are out there in the Stone Hall quaffing cocktails.'

'Gosh, I'd better get back to my pots and pans.' She half rose.

Jack reached out, put his hand on her arm. 'Give me a couple of minutes, Tessa, sit here with me. Or is something going to spoil? I'd hate to be the one to ruin a dinner you've spent hours preparing.'

'No, no, nothing will spoil, as long as it *is* only a few minutes.' She threw him a curious look, and sat down again. 'You want to talk to me about Adele, is that it?'

Now it was his turn to give her an odd look. 'How did you know?' he asked, momentarily startled.

'Because you've not mentioned her since Thursday, not asked me anything about her, and I just thought that was very strange. You see, Jack, no one's asked me what happened when she was with Mark, and I suppose this struck me as rather peculiar. Maybe not the family being quiet, but I wondered why you hadn't brought it up.'

'I wanted you to calm down. Also, I knew you would tell me if there was something I ought to know. And to be honest, you've seemed very much on . . . an even keel, and I realized if Mark had treated her badly, or hurt her in any way, you would have come running to me.'

'That's true, and you're right, nothing much happened according to Adele. He drove her around the countryside for a while, and then he took her to Harrogate, to Betty's Café for lunch and after that they went to Ripon. I think mostly she was terribly bored, and upset as well, crying about the loss of her doll. And of course she became tired in the afternoon, so he had to take a room at the Spa Hotel so that she could have her afternoon nap. God knows what he was thinking, pulling such a stunt. Well, to upset me, scare me, I must presume.'

'That's absolutely correct. Did Adele mention the other man in the car? A name perhaps? Did she know him?'

'No, she didn't know him, and she seems to have a good memory for a little girl. She said there was a friend of Daddy's with them. His name was Buddy. But I'm not sure this really *was* his actual name.'

'Oh, what do you mean?' Jack asked, looking at her alertly.

'Because when I questioned Adele about the man she said her father had told her, "This is my buddy," and I suppose she thought that was his name, because he called the man *buddy* several times later. I've no idea who it was with him, Jack, unless it was one of his sidekicks from the office.'

Jack nodded. 'That's a thought. I'll have it checked out on Monday morning first thing, ascertain if any of his assistants were off on Wednesday.'

Tessa jumped up, and exclaimed, 'I've got to start getting the food onto the plates, Jack, otherwise everything will fall apart. Is that it, more or less? I mean what you wanted to ask me?'

'Yes, it is, Tessa. Now, can I help you?'

'Not really, but you could carry the food into the dining room in a few minutes.'

'I'd be delighted to do so.' He took a sip of his Dom Pérignon, sat watching her move around, emptying pans, scooping food onto the big platters she had taken out of the two ovens. Lithe, energetic, efficient, totally in control. Observing her acutely, he thought she had never looked better. Normally as pale as a ghost, tonight she seemed to glow. Her milky complexion had a flush to it, a shell-pink tint which obviously came from exertion and the heat of the kitchen, yet it was becoming to her. Also, she had been very busy all afternoon into early evening, and he was aware she was usually in much better spirits when she was working hard. In this she was like her mother, Paula O'Neill. Paula functioned best when she was under great pressure. She fell apart when she had nothing to do, became morose, lethargic, lost all of that superwoman energy. Tessa and Linnet both took after their mother, but he also knew it was a characteristic all three of them had inherited from the founding mother of the dynasty, Emma Harte. As long as he had known and worked for Emma she had been pulled down by inactivity and boredom; she was at the top of her form and full of energy when she was working like a galley slave.

And there was another thing – Tessa did love cooking, drew enormous satisfaction from preparing gourmet meals for the family and friends. In his experience, someone who loved their work was bound to thrive. And she looked as though she were thriving tonight, despite her worries about Mark and the impending divorce.

Tessa interrupted his thoughts when she said, 'Jack, would you mind going into the dining room and lighting the candles on the table? And perhaps you could check the hotplates on the sideboard, please. I put them on low about half an hour ago, so they should be pretty warm by now.'

'Yes, General, sir!' he exclaimed, jumping up swiftly, saluting her and hurrying out, chuckling to himself.

Her gaze followed Jack as he left the kitchen. If he loved her mother and adored Linnet, whom he had always called Beauty, he nonetheless did *like* her, that she knew for a certainty, and he was kind to her, had been since her childhood. But he was an enigma, a man who spoke little about his personal life, gave nothing away. Her mother had told her once that he had been married years ago, and there had been some kind of tragedy. But that was all she knew about his private life, which was actually nothing. He had let things drop from time to time – how much he loved sailing in Robin Hood's Bay, the picturesque Yorkshire seaside town where he lived, that he was keen on the theatre, and was an amateur painter in his spare time. But not much else. She knew he was devoted to the Hartes, on a retainer with Harte Stores, and he had been around a lot lately, ever since the trouble with Mark had first started. She was glad about that. He was a reassuring presence, familiar, comforting, very reliable, and like a member of the family. And yet there was so much she didn't know about him. Some mystery man, she thought, and began straining the vegetables.

Jack returned to the kitchen when she was heaping couscous onto an extra large platter; he stood watching her with interest as she formed it into a grand mound in the centre.

'What are those other things in the couscous?' Jack asked, leaning forward, peering at it in order to see better.

'Chickpeas and large raisins, which is the traditional way of preparing it. Now I'm going to add the steamed vegetables around the mound.' As she was speaking she had begun to spoon carrots, turnips, parsnips, zucchini and pearl onions around the couscous, and then turning to him she explained, 'I'd like you to pop this in the big oven over there to keep warm, please. I've got to dish up the veal stew and warm the Hollandaise sauce for the asparagus, and then I'm all set.'

'Glad to be of help, Tessa, and congratulations, the dinner looks splendid.' He walked over to the oven with the huge plate of couscous, and then thought to ask, 'How do you plan to serve?'

'After we've had the asparagus I thought you and Desmond and Linnet and I could carry the big platters into the dining room and put them on the hotplates. The dinner will be served buffet style; everyone can help themselves.'

'It's the only way,' he answered, 'and certainly the easiest.'

The room was unfamiliar.

So much so he felt completely disoriented.

He blinked in the dim light and looked around, slowly began to make out shapes and objects juxtaposed against each other: a chest, a chair, a clock on the wall, and to the right, a window. Where the hell was he?

Dusty Rhodes blinked again, and adjusted his eyes. And very slowly he began to get a better picture of the room, a whole picture, not fragmented parts. It was a hospital room. And he was in a hospital bed . . . hooked up to a drip. Or something. What the hell was he doing here?

For a moment he could not remember anything. And then with a sudden flash of vision he saw himself in the studio that morning, rushing to stand in front of the painting, protecting it from the raised knife.

Once again he felt the sudden sharp pain of the blade entering his body. A blinding pain. Excruciating. Blood. A lot of blood. Spurting out. All over him. Covering his shirt. On his hand. Running down his arm. On the floor.

She had driven him here. Harrogate District Hospital. That's where he was. Now he remembered it all. *India.* Lady India Standish, daughter of an earl, a lady in her own right. A wonderful girl. An angel. The best girl in the world. She had saved his life. No question about that. She had remained calm. He could see her in his mind's eye. Calm. Controlled. Practical. She had wadded him up with towels. Driven him here. At breakneck speed. He remembered cringing at the speed. She had delivered him in one piece to Emergency. Yes, that's why he was still alive, hadn't bled to death. Because of her.

She had come back to see him a short while ago. He had still been out of it. He had opened his eyes once and seen her sitting there. Next to the bed. Holding his hand. Mouthing soothing words. White and ghostly, the pale hair in disarray. He had tried to speak to her. But he had been too weak. Then he had passed out again.

He had just awakened. But she was gone. Was she gone forever? He hoped not. He wanted her in his life. Would she stay? He didn't know the answer to that.

It would all come out now. About his affair with Melinda. His long relationship with her. The press would know about his child. Atlanta. Just a very little girl. Beautiful Atlanta. He didn't want that to happen. But he knew it would. And the police would be on top of him. They hadn't talked to him yet. Because he had been incapacitated by the anaesthetic. But they would be back tomorrow. To ask their questions. Sure as God made little green apples they'd be back. With their notebooks. Writing everything down. It would all read so badly. But Melinda hadn't meant to hurt him. It was an accident. She'd been after damaging the painting. Wanted to spoil it. Incensed by the sight of another woman in his studio. How had she managed to get out of the hospital? Get into his studio? His fault, that. He hadn't locked the door this morning.

What to tell India? All of it, that was the only way. Real honesty. *How* to tell her. That was the question. Find the right time. Tell her about Melinda. Tell her about Melinda's sickness. Her drug-addiction. Tell her about their child. His beautiful little girl. He loved her. Atlanta. India. He loved them both.

What to do about Melinda? How did he get her well? Get her on her feet? And get her out of his life? Thank God he had never married her. Still, he had to be responsible. Help Melinda. Get Atlanta. Keep India . . .

When the nurse looked in a short time later she saw that Russell Rhodes, the famous artist, was sleeping soundly again. Best thing for him, she thought, knowing that it had been touch and go for a while, earlier that day. There was a moment when he might easily have died. Thank God he hadn't. Luck was on his side. Everyone needed luck sometime in their lives, Nurse Paston thought, and she quietly closed the door of the room and went about her other duties.

CHAPTER ELEVEN

The buzzing of the intercom brought Evan's head up with a start and her eyes flew to the clock on the mantelpiece. It was exactly twenty minutes to seven and her parents weren't due to arrive until seven, but she knew it was them. A moment before, she had pulled on a pair of black linen trousers; now she slipped her feet into black patent high-heeled mules and quickly buttoned her white cotton sleeveless blouse as she ran to the door.

The buzzer was shrilling again, and she snatched up the small wall phone and said, 'Hello?'

'It's us,' her father's slightly disembodied voice informed her from the street.

'Hi, Dad! I'll buzz you in. Just push the door open. I'm on the third floor.'

'See you in a minute.'

She replaced the receiver, ran back to the bedroom, put pearl studs on her ears, turned to run out again, then dashed back to the dressing table to get her sapphire engagement ring, which she slipped onto her finger. Finally she hurried back to the front door, opened it, stood poised on the threshold waiting – waiting for her mother and father to get out of the lift. It was almost but not quite opposite her front door, and as they suddenly appeared, stepped into the hall, she broke into smiles; excited, thrilled that they were here, she ran across to greet them, hugging her mother first and then her father.

After a big all-encompassing bear hug, Owen Hughes held her away from him and searched her face, his own wreathed in smiles. 'It's great to see you, Evan!' he exclaimed. 'Just wonderful.'

Her mother, also smiling, said, 'We missed you, honey.'

'And I've missed you, and it's lovely to see *you* both after all these months,' Evan responded, glancing first at her mother and then back at her father.

She stared at him intently for a split second, her stomach lurching, instantly thought: My God, he's a younger version of Robin Ainsley. I always believed he resembled Richard Hughes. How peculiar he should resemble both men: one his biological father, the other the man who adopted him as a newborn. Except that Robin and Richard *were* exactly the same type – tall, lean, almost rangey, with bright blue eyes and dark hair. Well, Robin's wasn't exactly dark anymore, and Richard's had turned pepper and salt long before his death.

Seemingly her grandmother Glynnis had fallen for the same type of man: men of similar physical appearance at least, like most women usually do, she had realized long ago. Suddenly becoming aware of the growing silence, a slight awkwardness between them, Evan said swiftly, 'Well let's not stand here in the hall . . . come in, come in.' So saying she turned and led them into her apartment.

They followed rapidly on her heels, and she was instantly aware that their eyes were taking everything in as she closed the door and joined them. 'This is the living room,' she explained, 'and there's a small kitchen down at the far end. That's where the room turns into an L shape, and becomes a small dining area. I have a bedroom and bathroom, and that's it. It's not very grand I know, but I love it.'

'Somehow I thought it would be much larger,' her father murmured as he continued to glance around. 'The way you spoke about it . . .'

Evan thought he had sounded slightly critical and somewhat defensively she exclaimed, 'It's a lovely flat, Dad!'

'Oh yes,' he said, nodding, and walked the length of the room, still looking around. He remained silent, as if he were at a sudden loss for words, then made for the sofa near the fireplace.

Her mother said in a warm and confident tone, 'I think it's very nice, very nice indeed, Evan. Comfortable, cosy even, and perfect for you.'

'Yes, it is, Mom.' Evan was really surprised that her mother had sounded so firm, positive, and perhaps not quite as intimidated by her husband as she had been in the past. Taking hold of her mother's arm affectionately, she led her over to the chairs placed opposite the sofa, where they both sat down. 'I didn't want a large apartment, Dad. Anyway, I was extremely lucky to get this. It's a sub-let, furnished, and it's ideal. It doesn't need a lot of upkeep and it's easy to keep clean. Besides, it's near the store, and I can walk to Harte's every day.'

Once again, it was her mother who spoke up. 'I like it very much, honey, and I can see so many of your own little touches in evidence. Lots of plants and flowers, which you always love to have around you, the photographs of us all, your favourite books, the fashion and news magazines you enjoy, and bits and pieces I recognize. And I bet all of these cushions are yours, that you just bought them recently. Yes, you've really made it your own.' When Evan was silent, Marietta asked softly, 'I am right, aren't I, Evan?'

'Yes, you are, Mommy, and thanks.' She grinned at her mother. 'And I did just buy those cushions, you're right. I tried to superimpose a little of my own taste, put my stamp on the flat. You see, the owner had taken out all of the small objects and accessories, so it was quite impersonal, almost cold. I had what I thought of as a blank canvas to work with. Anyway, it's not forever, just a temporary place.'

'The furniture's very nice,' her father remarked, obviously wanting to make amends for his first rather churlish words of a few moments ago. 'That's an extremely good-looking Georgian desk over there, and I'm sure the bookcases are Georgian, too.' He got up, walked over to the bookcases, looked them over with an expert eye. 'Yes, just as I thought.' He glanced at the mirror hanging on the long back wall, and added, 'That's definitely a Georgian mirror. All very valuable pieces. Who owns this place?'

'I don't actually know,' she answered swiftly, resorting to a fib, deciding that a small white lie of this nature didn't matter if it kept the peace for the moment. 'I made the deal through a real-estate agent. The young woman who owns it is living abroad.'

'I see. Well, yes, it's very nice,' he murmured, obviously extremely impressed by the antiques, and returned to his seat on the sofa.

'Now can I get you both a drink?' Evan asked, rising. 'A soft drink? Scotch or vodka? Wine? I've even got champagne.'

'I'll have a glass of white wine, Evan,' her father said. 'Thanks.'

'And I'll have one, too, please,' Marietta announced in a light, clear voice.

Startled though she was by her mother's request, because she never drank alcohol, Evan nonetheless managed to keep a neutral expression on her face. 'Coming right up,' she said, and hurried across the living room, making for the kitchen.

Once she was alone, Evan immediately took off her sapphire engagement ring and slipped it into the pocket of her trousers, hoping they hadn't spotted it on the third finger on her right hand. But her father would have remarked on it if he had. He would have been unable to resist asking a few potent and probing questions.

As she opened the bottle of Sancerre she admitted to herself that she was afraid to discuss her engagement to Gideon, explain about him to her parents. And how furious *he* would be if he knew she had taken off his ring. But she felt easier within herself holding back this news. At least for the moment.

Pouring white wine into the elegant crystal goblets she had taken out of the cupboard, she thought about the changes in her mother. They were startling.

Firstly, Marietta looked very different. Her general appearance was much smarter than usual, her hair better groomed, her make-up nicely applied, and surprisingly she was well dressed. The navy-blue linen dress she wore was obviously expensive, superbly cut and styled, and more than likely it had cost much more than her mother was used to spending on herself. No, this was not her mother's normal way of dressing, she who favoured t-shirts and slacks most of the time, and often looked sloppy and dishevelled.

Secondly, her mother was somehow managing to assert herself with Owen. Evan had been taken aback, and still was, because she had never seen her mother stand up to her father in her entire life. Certainly not in the way she just had, overriding his comments with opinions of her own. Why, she had practically pooh-poohed his opinion of the flat.

It struck Evan now that her mother seemed not only much better in health, but much more independent, even *spirited*. Evan couldn't help wondering what had brought about this extraordinary change in a woman who had always seemed cowed, unhappy and depressed. She was just the opposite this evening. And this pleased Evan, made her happy for her mother, who had been a manic depressive for years and years. It's amazing, she thought. And also puzzling. Was it a new medication finally kicking in? Or something else?

Opening the refrigerator, Evan took out the platter of hors d'oeuvres she had made earlier, and began to peel off the plastic wrap, thinking about her father. She had known Owen would spot the genuine antiques in the flat; after all, he was a leading antiques dealer in Manhattan and Connecticut, and a well-known expert in Georgian furniture, even gave lectures.

And everything in the flat *was* Georgian and valuable, he was correct in that assessment. It all belonged to Emily Barkstone Harte, Gideon's mother; she also owned the flat which was normally occupied by her daughter Natalie, Gideon's sister. Since Natalie was currently doing a stint at the Harte newspaper company in Sydney, Gideon had arranged for her to move in for a few months until Natalie returned to London.

Evan had been anxious to leave the charming little hotel where she had lived since her arrival in London in January until a few weeks ago. And Gideon had wanted her to leave, to have a place of her own, and blessed privacy. The hotel belonged to her father's great friend George Thomas, and they both agreed that whilst Arlette, George's wife, was a lovely, loving and motherly woman who doted on Evan, she was far too keenly interested in their relationship for comfort.

Evan constantly had the feeling that her comings and goings were noted by Arlette and reported to her father, albeit in the most innocent way, with no malice aforethought. But nonetheless she believed it wiser to move on, so that she was totally removed from Arlette's scrutiny and her never-ending questions about Harte's store and her private life.

There was no reason for her parents to know anything about her reasons for leaving the hotel, other than that she wanted a place of her own to call home. Or to know about the ownership of this flat filled with these beautiful Georgian pieces. It was nobody's business but hers. She was, after all, free, white and twenty-one. Twenty-seven actually, self-supporting and therefore her own boss. She did not have to explain or answer to anyone.

Feeling more comfortable now that she had removed the engagement ring, Evan carried the tray of drinks into the living room and put it down on the coffee table near the sofa.

After handing her mother and father a glass of wine she turned and went back to the kitchen, saying over her shoulder, 'I made a few little snacks, I'll only be a moment.' And she was, hurrying back within a second or two, her face full of smiles.

Placing the platter she was carrying on the coffee

table, she sat down next to her mother and reached for her glass. 'Cheers, Mom, Dad, and welcome to London.'

'Cheers,' her parents said in unison, and both of them took a sip of their wine.

'Help yourself to the smoked salmon and little sausage rolls,' Evan instructed, love and warmth echoing in her voice. 'I made them myself.'

Her mother beamed at her. 'You've gone to a lot of trouble, thank you, honey.'

Her father said, 'So fill us in, Evan, tell us your plans. We're dying to hear what you intend to do for the rest of the year.'

Evan stared at her father in surprise, and exclaimed, 'But I talk to you once a week, every week, and you know my plans, Dad. I love working at Harte's, and that's what I'm going to do for the rest of the year.' She felt like adding, and the rest of my life, but refrained. She sat back, her eyes on her father.

'I see. But a moment or two ago you said this flat was only temporary . . .' His voice trailed off and he looked suddenly baffled, uncertain.

'I did say that, yes, but what I meant was that this flat was only temporary until I find a place I really like, which I will then buy.'

'That's a good idea,' Marietta said. 'It will be a good investment.'

Her father threw her mother a reproachful look, then said in a quiet, rather subdued voice, 'Do you mean you're planning to live in London indefinitely, Evan?'

'Yes, I do.'

'But when you came here in January it was my understanding it was only for a year, a sort of sabbatical, like the one I took myself years ago.'

'Perhaps that's what I meant *then*, Dad, but I do love working at the store. In fact, I love the store. It's great, probably the greatest department store in the world, thanks to Emma Harte and her heirs, and I'm thrilled to be a part of it.'

'I hope they're not working you too hard there. You look to me as if you've lost weight. You're very thin, Evan.'

Something inside Evan rose up like bile, a bad-tasting bile, and several sharp retorts sprang to her lips. But she knew it was wiser not to respond, even though she resented her father's comments enormously. But the anxiety suddenly clouding her mother's face was another reason she held her tongue, at least as far as sarcastic remarks were concerned. Instead, she said, 'No, they're not working me too hard, Dad. In fact, they all work much harder than me and every other employee. And they're wonderful people, the Hartes. I can't understand why you have this hatred for them.' There, it was out. She hadn't meant to say it, at least not yet, but she had and she wasn't going to retract it.

'I don't hate the Hartes!' he cried, his voice rising slightly. He looked at her askance. 'I don't even know them. Why would you say a thing like that? You're being silly, over-imaginative.'

'No I'm not, Dad. You have continually made

remarks about them for the past eight months, ever since I started working at the store, and you continue to make strange comments about Gideon, a man you don't even know.'

'Is that what this is all about? Your boyfriend?' he asked, his voice suddenly chilly.

'No, it isn't. You started it by implying my bosses made me work too hard, that I looked too thin, that I've lost weight. Maybe I have, because I want to be thin and elegant, wear the nice clothes I have with a degree of self-confidence. Anyway, I've always been pretty slender. As far as Gideon's concerned, he's a very nice young man. And he's been kind to me every day since I arrived, which is when I first met him.'

Marietta, sensing a row brewing, injected herself into the conversation, saying, 'I think it's nice that you have a boyfriend, Evan, a man who is kind and understanding, and obviously devoted to you. I hope we're going to meet him while we're here in London.'

Evan gave her mother a grateful smile, thankful that she was present, had so diplomatically poured oil on troubled waters. 'Of course you are. I *want* you and Dad to meet Gideon. In fact, he would like to take you out to lunch on Sunday –'

'Oh, I don't think we can do that,' her father cut in a little peremptorily. 'I promised George and Arlette we would join them for lunch on Sunday. At the hotel. You know how much they care about you, Evan.'

'I suppose it'll be all right,' Evan murmured,

disappointed but glad the tricky situation had been defused by her mother. 'I'll tell Gideon about the change in plans. I think he'd enjoy seeing George and Arlette again. He likes them.'

'Oh, but I don't believe George was including your friend,' her father said. 'He meant just the three of us.'

Evan was furious and sat back, gaping at her father. She was about to remind him that they had come to London to see *her*, not the friend of his youth, when her mother put a hand on her arm soothingly, cleared her throat, said quietly, 'Don't be upset, Evan dear.'

Leaning forward in her chair, Marietta focused all of her attention on her husband. 'No, Owen, I'm afraid we won't be accepting George's invitation for lunch on Sunday. At a later date perhaps, while we're here, but not this Sunday. Oh no, we are going to go out to lunch with our daughter and her boyfriend. We don't need other people along, not if we're going to properly get to know Gideon Harte.'

'I don't wish to offend George,' Owen began, glaring at his wife, but before he could finish his sentence, Marietta was speaking once again.

In an extremely firm voice, she said, 'Oh, it won't offend him. He'll understand, I'm sure. Anyway, I can always go alone with Evan to meet Gideon, you know. And you, Owen, can have lunch with your old pal George, and Arlette, if you prefer.'

Evan was once more surprised, and delighted

as well. Her father had opened his mouth to say something and then promptly closed it. He looked mortified, but she didn't care. She was silently applauding her mother. God knows what's happened to her, but she's a different woman. And quite wonderful, Evan thought, smiling to herself.

Suddenly her mother was continuing in that lovely newly-confident voice. 'Now, Evan, you said yesterday that you'd booked a table at a special place for dinner tonight. So . . . where *are* we going, honey?'

'To Rules, Mom. It was Glynnis's favourite restaurant, and she and Grandfather used to take me there when I came to London with them. And you and Dad came with us once to Rules. I thought it would be lovely to go back to a place of shared memories.'

Chapter Twelve

'You two Stormy Petrels have lived up to your name this week, and then some,' Gideon said, looking from Linnet to India, his two favourite cousins.

Linnet frowned, repeated, '*Stormy Petrels*? Now where did that come from?' and stared at Gideon, then looked across at India quizzically.

India said, 'Don't look at me, I don't know what he means. But actually I do happen to know what a stormy petrel is . . . it's a rather beautiful bird that spends most of its life on the sea, and it follows ships quite a lot.'

Julian Kallinski began to laugh, shaking his head. 'What short memories you two have. And, Linnet, you also seem to have forgotten what your mother told us . . . the legend of the stormy petrel, that the name *petrel* is supposedly a diminutive of Peter. You see, when it's feeding the bird appears to flit and hover around, just above the water, and its feet look as if they're pattering on the surface of the sea. One gets a sense that it's actually *walking on water*, in the way that St Peter did in the Bible story, hence its name Petrel, for Peter.'

'Oh gosh, Jules, I think I do remember that now,' Linnet murmured. 'My mother *did* tell us about the stormy petrel. We were all very small, and we were staying at Heron's Nest in Scarborough for the summer, and there were stormy petrels flying around. And, very vaguely, I do remember you saying, Gideon, that the Harte girls were Stormy Petrels . . . but it's such a long time ago.'

'Yes, you're very ancient,' Julian remarked, chuckling as he spoke.

'*We're* not ancient. It's Tessa who's the Ancient One, at least that's what Lorne has always called her,' India reminded them.

Gideon smiled at India and remarked, 'Tessa's a stormy petrel too, and I'm paying you all a compliment . . . you see, I thought you were beautiful birds who could walk on water even when you were little girls. And I still think that.'

'Thank you, Gid,' India answered, smiling back at him. He had always been one of her favourites as a child, and he still was. He was there for her whenever she needed him, and devoted. 'It's a charming way of describing us,' she went on. 'From now on we'll call ourselves the stormy petrels, and remind the world we can indeed walk on water.'

'Tessa came through her ordeal very well, and Linnet, you were superb. What a good idea you had when you brought Jack in to help with the abduction. As for you, India, I think you're quite remarkable the way you handled the situation with

Dusty.' Gideon sat back, reached for his glass of wine and took a long swallow.

The four of them, best friends since childhood, were enjoying a drink before going out to dinner. It was something of a ritual, this weekly dinner, although sometimes there was one or other of them missing, because of business commitments or travels. But they endeavoured to get together even if they were not a full complement, because they cherished their lifelong relationships with each other.

Linnet began to fan herself with one hand, and remarked, 'It's terribly hot in here, Jules, are you certain the air conditioning is working?'

'I know it is, but, well, I'll check it, darling,' he murmured, and jumped up, went across to the unit, bent over and examined it and then straightened. 'It's okay,' he told her, looking across at her, his dark blue gaze full of love. 'Talking of Heron's Nest, I wouldn't mind being by the seaside in Scarborough right now. Oh, for a weekend on the beach, and the pleasure of a few salty sea breezes.'

India, who had been looking off into the distance somewhat pensively, exclaimed, 'Heron's Nest! Gosh, that's a good idea for Dusty, the perfect place for him to recuperate. What do you think? Would it be all right if I took him there?'

'I'm sure it's fine, but how will you manage?' Linnet asked, then reminded her, 'There's no real help there these days, India. Only Mrs Hodges keeping an eye on it and keeping it dust-free.'

'I'm a stormy petrel,' India shot back. 'I can

walk on water, remember? So I'll certainly be able to manage a house and a man who's recuperative, wouldn't you say?'

Linnet laughed good-naturedly, as always enjoying India and her pithy comments.

'How *is* Dusty?' Gideon asked, sitting up straighter, focusing on his cousin.

India sighed, bit her lip, and then her face suddenly clouded over. 'It's been worse than I expected, but he's going to be all right. To be very honest it was a lot more serious than he or I realized at first. The wound I mean. The brachial artery is where the pectoral muscle goes up into the shoulder, and that artery was almost severed completely. It was really touch and go for a while during surgery. And there was an enormous loss of blood. He could easily have bled to death –'

'It's thanks to you that he didn't!' Linnet pointed out swiftly. 'If you hadn't acted immediately, and driven him to Harrogate District Hospital, he'd be dead by now.'

India nodded, but remained silent, hardly able to countenance the idea of Dusty being dead. She loved him far too much to even contemplate such a catastrophe.

Julian leaned forward and asked, 'What's your feeling about the stabbing, India? Any new thoughts on it?'

She shook her head. 'Not really. But my common sense tells me that he must have known that woman at some time or other. A stranger is not going to find his studio, burst in unannounced, go berserk

213

at the sight of me, stab a portrait of me and then run away. For me to think the woman was unknown to Dusty would be pretty ridiculous, don't you think?'

'Yes, it would,' Gideon agreed. He knew a lot about Russell Rhodes now. He had had two of his crack investigative reporters on the story for the past week. Not that he intended to run anything in any of their newspapers, or tell India much of what he knew. But in order to properly protect her, and the family, he had needed to put top journalists to work at once.

Now he said, 'Your practicality serves you well. Dusty did know her. I'm not going to lie to you, India, I did have to put reporters on the story, but I'm not running anything in any of our papers. Let's hope the nationals don't either.'

India was sitting bolt upright on the sofa, staring at Gideon, and she exclaimed, 'Who is she? What did you find out?'

'Not as much as we'd like to know, you and I. She *was* his girlfriend for a while. A model and an actress. From what I gather she's had problems with drugs and has been hospitalized somewhere and for quite some time now. Trying to get de-toxed.'

'I see,' India murmured, looking suddenly morose, a little forlorn.

Picking up on her mood at once, Gideon added swiftly, 'From what I've been told by my reporters, their relationship had been over for a very long time. But seemingly she's been . . . well, a bit obsessed with him.'

'What's her name?' India asked softly.

'You don't really want to know . . . oh well, I can see you do. It's Melinda Caldwell.'

'I can't imagine why Dusty didn't tell me about her!'

'I think that's understandable under the circumstances, darling,' Julian interjected. 'If she's been bothersome to him he wouldn't want you to know and become upset. Also, men tend not to talk about old lovers to new ones.' Julian looked at Gideon for support, his eyes pleading. India was a favourite with them all.

Gideon said, 'Julian's right, there was no real reason for Dusty to talk about other women long gone. Now was there?'

'I suppose not,' she muttered, brushing her hair away from her face, which was suddenly much paler.

'Have you discussed anything with Dusty?' Julian asked. 'I suppose he's well enough by now to talk to you.'

'Actually, he's not been in top form,' India explained. 'So I haven't probed. I didn't want to upset him unduly, and so I decided to wait until he's better. Out of hospital.'

'I see. When is he going to be able to go home?' Julian continued.

'Next week. Either Monday or Tuesday. Hence my thought about Heron's Nest. If the heat keeps up it might be nice by the sea. On the other hand, I think perhaps it's wiser to take him back to Willows Hall, where there's a staff, and also it's only ten minutes away from the hospital. In case of any emergency.'

Linnet said, 'I'm glad you made that decision. I think Heron's Nest probably needs a thorough cleaning. None of us has been there for ages.'

'We should go though,' Gideon exclaimed, his eyes lighting up. 'I think I'd like to take Evan there for a weekend. Actually, we might all go and spend a weekend there. It would be like old times.'

'Why not. And I'm sorry Evan's not with us this evening,' Linnet murmured, standing up. 'But I suppose she felt obliged to take her parents to dinner. After all she hasn't seen them for eight months.'

'That's right,' Gideon replied. 'She booked a table at Rules. Apparently her grandparents used to take her there when she came to London with them years ago.'

'And where are we going?' India asked.

'I booked a table at The Ivy,' Gideon told her. 'Because I know how much you like it.'

'Thanks, Gid,' India said, and sighed as she, too, got to her feet. 'It's lovely to be with all of you. The last few days have been awful, worrying about Dusty, and when I think about last Saturday I go cold all over.'

'I can certainly understand why. It was the most bizarre thing I've ever heard of!' Linnet exclaimed, shaking her head. 'Incredible really.'

'It was surreal,' India announced. 'I still can't believe such a terrible thing happened.'

'It did, but let's forget it for tonight at least.'

Gideon took hold of India's arm, and walked with her to the door. 'I know the police now have the full picture, the right picture, and they won't be bothering you again, thank God.'

Things were better in the cab going through the park, The Mall and down The Strand to Rules Restaurant. For a few minutes, just before they had left the flat, Evan had decided her father was going to be grouchy and argumentative all evening. His expression was grim and discontented when they left; but suddenly he had grown lighter once the cab was on its way, and even made a bit of small talk.

And her father's mood improved once they were being welcomed at the restaurant by the head waiter and shown to a table. Rules was still one of Evan's favourite restaurants in London; she frequented it often and the staff knew her well, so the greetings were warm and friendly, the table the best in the house.

Evan ordered a bottle of Pouilly Fuissé, and they all had a glass of the dry white wine whilst they studied the menu. After much discussions about various dishes, those they had enjoyed most in the past, they ended up choosing the same – dressed crab to start, followed by grilled Dover sole and a mélange of summer vegetables.

As the three of them waited for their food, they chatted briefly about the restaurant and the fond memories it evoked in them of Glynnis and Richard. Her father had been close to his parents, on excellent terms with them, so there was much affection in his voice when he recalled the evenings they had enjoyed here with them at Rules.

Then both of her parents asked her probing questions about her job at Harte's Emporium in Knightsbridge, and she regaled them with details about her daily routine, and amusing stories, was doing so with such enthusiasm and joy in her voice there was no mistaking how much she loved her job. If there had been any doubt in her parents' minds about her sojourn in London being a happy experience so far, these doubts were now truly dispelled.

It was over the crab salad that Evan suddenly remarked, 'Dad, do you remember that you said you thought your mother had known Emma Harte during the Second World War, here in London?'

'Yes, I do, Evan. I mentioned that to you just before you left for London in January.'

'Is that all you know? That Grandma had been acquainted with Emma at that time?'

'Why yes, it is,' he answered swiftly, staring at her in puzzlement. 'Why?'

'Because the beautiful Glynnis Jenkins, as she was called then, the girl from the Rhondda Valley in Wales, was actually an employee at Harte's, just as I am today. Glynnis, your mother, was Emma Harte's private secretary, Dad, and very close to her lady boss.'

'Heavens to Betsy!' her father exclaimed, looking surprised. 'I never realized that.'

'Well, it's true,' Evan went on, 'and your mother

was quite a favourite with the whole family.' When her father remained silent Evan turned and glanced at her mother, and saw to her astonishment that there was the strangest expression on her mother's face. It was one she could not quite comprehend for a split second, and then she realized it was contempt in her mother's eyes she was seeing. And she knew, intuitively, that her father had just deliberately lied to her, and her mother knew that he had.

Clearing her throat, Evan changed the subject at once. 'I hope you'll come and have lunch with me at the store one day this week, the early part of the week if you can, Mom. And I'll give you a full tour as well.'

'Why, Evan honey, I'd love that. Of course I'll come.'

'Let's do it on Tuesday, Mom, because I have to go to Leeds on Wednesday. We're revamping some of the stores, and I'm in charge of the Leeds over-haul with India.'

'Who's India?' Marietta asked.

'She's Linnet O'Neill's other assistant, and her cousin. Lady India Standish is her full name, and she's a great girl.'

'I'm so happy you made some nice friends here,' Marietta murmured, smiling at Evan. There was a moment's hesitation and then she said slowly, 'It's an unusual name . . . *India*. I must admit, I've never heard it used as a first name before.'

'It's a Victorian name,' Owen announced, before Evan could answer, and explained, 'It came into popularity because of England's involvement in India, and its influence over the country for hundreds of years. During those years, the years of the Raj, the English loved so many things which were of Indian origin, and of course there were a lot of British troops stationed there, cavalry regiments and such, all part of the Indian army. Anyway, I suppose one day someone had the bright idea of calling a child after the country, and India became a favourite name for girls in the eighteen hundreds when Queen Victoria was on the throne and Empress of India as well. And it's still used today.'

'Gee, Dad, I didn't know you were so well versed in British history!' Evan exclaimed, glad they were now off the subject of Emma Harte and his mother. If he was reluctant to admit that he'd always known his mother actually worked for Emma Harte, then he would surely not like to hear that his *real* father was Robin Ainsley, Emma's favourite son. No way, José, she thought to herself, and looked up and nodded to the waiter to clear the plates away.

The conversation progressed normally from then on; they talked about her sisters, Elayne and Angharad, and her mother spoke rather proudly about their adopted daughters, who were having successes with their work and in their personal lives. Both of them had new boyfriends, and Marietta explained that she was quite certain Angharad would settle down with her current beau, that the relationship looked very serious indeed.

Evan listened, nodded and smiled, held herself very still and said very little, not wanting to become embroiled in a discussion about *her* love life and her future with Gideon Harte. And it seemed to her that her mother felt the same way, because within seconds Marietta had moved on, was talking about some of the day trips they planned to take whilst they were in London. And then her father launched himself on a long story about going to France to look for country antiques, and finally finished up asking her to join them on this jaunt.

'I just can't at the moment, Dad,' Evan told him, once he had finished, and then she filled him in about her work schedule. Mostly she talked about getting the Leeds store up to par; he appeared to accept this explanation with good grace, and, in fact, she decided he was in a wholly different mood by the time they were selecting desserts. He was certainly in a much better frame of mind than when they had set out from her flat.

He's calmed down, she thought, eyeing him over the top of her menu, thinking suddenly how handsome he looked tonight in his grey linen jacket, pale blue shirt and darker blue tie. God, he's the spitting image of Robin, at least the way Robin must have looked when he was the same age . . . fifty-seven. He's got Robin's elegance, his refinement. I wish I could tell him the truth. But she did not dare. At least not tonight. *And maybe never*.

'Do you think she's swimming in dangerous waters?'

Linnet looked up at Julian; a small sigh escaped before she settled back in his arms, leaning her head against his bare chest. 'I don't think so,' she answered at last, after thinking about his question for a moment. 'In any case, even if she were there's not much any of us could do about it. India's got a mind of her own, as you well know.'

'Yes, that's true, she does. But I've got to admit I'm a bit worried about her, darling. Russell Rhodes has quite a reputation.'

Pulling away from him, struggling up in the bed, Linnet looked into his face intently. 'Don't worry so much,' she murmured. 'India told me weeks ago that the reputation is somewhat phoney and self-manufactured. You know, all for the benefit of the press, for the publicity it gets him. She told me that the rabble-rousing is merely a great deal of noise about nothing, just boisterousness. And he hardly drinks at all. Nurses a vodka all night, she explained to me.'

Julian frowned. 'Gideon seems to think he's a bit of a womanizer, though.'

'But India says there are no other women around, and haven't been since she's known him, which is some months now. Also, she told me he had confided that he'd been on his own for quite a while before he took up with her.' When Julian was silent, Linnet continued, 'Listen, an artist who paints with the precision he does has to have a steady hand every morning, and his paintings are glorious, you know that.'

'They're *magnificent*. But I was talking about his *womanizing*, not his drinking.'

'I know. Gideon didn't seem to have much

information about that though, about women in his life. He only knew about this Melinda Caldwell,' she reminded him.

'He probably wouldn't want to talk about other women in front of India anyway.'

'Did Gideon confide something in you?' Linnet probed, searching her fiancé's face.

Julian shook his head. 'He didn't. All he did say, when you and India went to the ladies' room, was that the Harrogate police had seemingly buried the incident.'

'*Oh*.' She gaped at him, total surprise flickering on her face. 'That's strange. Why on earth would they do that?'

'Local-boy-made-good syndrome, that's what Gideon calls it. From what I understand, the police have wiped the slate clean and the hospital has done the same thing. Therefore the incident never happened. Also, Gideon's quite certain that Dusty's not bringing charges against the woman.'

'India does say it *was* an accident.'

'I suppose it was. And in a way, Linny, that's what I was getting at a moment ago. Is India swimming in dangerous waters because of Melinda Caldwell? This woman is apparently totally obsessed with Dusty, which probably means she's slightly bonkers. How do we know she won't pester him on a continuous basis, stalk him, make life hell for him, and for India as well? And there's another thing: how serious is their relationship?'

'It's serious as far as India's concerned, that I do know. She's very much in love with him.

Actually, she'd like to make it permanent. But he's not so keen about marriage.'

'What chap in his right mind would turn his nose up at India?' he exclaimed, sounding slightly irate.

'Dusty Rhodes, the poor boy from the back streets of Leeds.'

'But why?' Julian shook his head, his expression a mixture of puzzlement and disbelief.

'*Why*?' Linnet repeated, and she couldn't prevent a small smirk from settling on her mouth. 'Because she *is* India, because of *who* she is. He doesn't like her family, which is all of us as well as her parents, whom he's never met. And not any of us, either. He's against the Hartes because we're too posh and well-to-do, apparently, and even more against her parents Anthony and Sally because Anthony has a title. It's a kind of reverse snobbery, I suppose. For instance, he won't call his butler *the butler*, but instead insists on referring to him as *the house-manager*, if you can believe that one.'

'Oh, I can all right, I've met chaps like Dusty. But I suppose he'll come round when he's met us. We're not so bad.'

'I think *you're* wonderful, Julian Kallinski, husband-to-be, light of my life. Since we finally decided to get married on December the first I put the invitations into work earlier this week, by the way.'

Julian beamed. 'That's great.' He touched her face lightly with one hand. 'That'll please my grandfather.'

'It'll please mine, too.' She cocked her head on one side and said, 'The last ten days have been sort of . . . hellish, wouldn't you say? What with one thing and another, I sometimes think this family's cursed.'

'That's a silly thing to say!' Julian exclaimed, quickly looking at her. 'The Hartes are a big family and more things happen in a big family than they do in a small family . . . so it just seems overwhelming at times. But the Hartes are not cursed, neither are the O'Neills or the Kallinskis . . .' He shook his head. 'Very simply, life can be catastrophic at times –'

'For some families more than others, though,' she cut in. 'Currently there are two divorces pending, and one is going to be supremely unpleasant. There's been an abduction, failed, of course. But nonetheless it's put the fear of God in Tessa, changed her life to a certain extent. India's been involved in a stabbing, and let's face it, she could have been hurt –'

'That's what I was getting at when I mentioned *dangerous waters*,' he interrupted.

'I know that. And this Melinda Caldwell is a problem for Dusty. He's going to have to solve that one, Jules, because India won't put up with any nonsense. Which means her future with him is even more dubious than I thought.'

'I agree with you. Back to Tessa for a moment . . . do you think she means it when she says she wants to spend more time with Adele? And that her career must come second?'

225

'I'm not sure, but, well, yes, I suppose I do believe she means it . . . at the moment. It's hard to really know with Tessa, because she can change her mind so easily. But I believe she *is* afraid of Mark Longden, or rather, what he might pull next. Her solicitors met with his during the week, and there's now some sort of financial negotiation going on. But it doesn't make her feel any easier, from what she said to Mummy on the phone the other day.'

'Does your mother know you and I finally set the date for the wedding?'

Linnet smiled at him. 'Yes, and she's happy we've settled the matter. But to be honest, I'm wondering if we shouldn't have planned it for earlier, maybe for November.'

Julian nodded, understanding what she meant immediately; they had known each other since they were toddlers, had been involved with each other all of their lives. 'Because Grandfather's old, and not up to par,' he murmured, pulling her into his arms, stroking her hair. 'That's what you're getting at, isn't it?'

'Yes,' she murmured against his chest. 'And mine's getting on in years, too. Mind you, Grandfather Bryan's not showing his age.'

'Not at all, and it'll be fine, Linnet. The grand-fathers are not going to die on us before we're married.' He chuckled. 'You know they've always wanted us to tie the knot, because Emma loved the idea of the three clans being united in marriage. They're going to *will* themselves to stay alive until after the event.'

Linnet laughed with him. 'That's what Mummy said.'

'When is she coming back from New York?'

'The first week of September, as planned. Dad's going to the Bahamas for a few days, and flying back from there. Emily and Winston will be returning to London with Mums.'

'What did she say about the reception?'

'She wants to have it at Pennistone Royal, she's never changed her mind about that, nor will she.'

'I'm glad.'

Julian held her closer, his arms tightly wound around her and they lay together like this for a while. It was Linnet who broke the silence when she said, 'Two good things happened in the past week to counteract the bad. You and I finally set the date, and Evan and Gideon became engaged.'

'That's right! He's going to meet her parents on Sunday, make it official, then he plans to phone Emily and Winston in New York to tell them.'

'They'll be so happy, they love Evan.' There was a pause, and then Linnet said softly, 'I'd like us to have a baby straight away, Julian. I don't want us to wait to start a family. Is that all right with you?'

'Of course it is. I think it's best to have babies when we're young.'

'Especially women who work. A baby and a job are easier to handle when you're in your twenties.'

'Oh, you can handle anything, darling,' Julian pronounced in a confident voice. 'After all, Gideon has anointed you . . . you're a stormy petrel who can walk on water.'

There was a hint of laughter in her voice when she answered. 'Oh, Jules, darling, let's start practising now.'

'Walking on water?'

'No, silly! You know very well what I mean . . . making babies.'

'It'll be my pleasure,' he whispered against her hair, bent over her and began to kiss her passionately.

CHAPTER THIRTEEN

Evan sat at her desk in her office at Harte's on Saturday morning, staring at the simple sketches she had made for Linnet. She had started them last week, when she was at the Leeds store, and they showed her suggested changes for the various fashion departments. She was pleased with her ideas and hoped Linnet would be, too, because she knew the changes were good, could be made without the expenditure of a large amount of money.

When Linnet had given her the task of revamping three different fashion departments on two separate floors, Evan had been flattered by Linnet's confidence in her, as well as excited by the challenge the task posed. Now her eyes swept over the sketches, which were somewhat rough, but certainly they would help a draughtsman come up with more finished plans. What's more, they were absolutely accurate in their details and measurements.

Setting the drawings aside, Evan now turned on

her computer to check her e-mails, made a few notes about the Leeds project, then sat back in her chair and took a sip of coffee. All manner of things began to run through her head, but within seconds she was thinking about the dinner last night with her parents at Rules.

It had been successful in the end, but it had certainly started with a strange undertone. Her mind automatically veered to her father. He had seemed difficult when he had arrived with her mother for drinks. Her mother had been perfectly all right, though changed in her demeanour and looking wonderful. But her father was peculiar; it was almost as if he were spoiling for a fight.

Perhaps he had been nervous, and maybe he had imagined, perhaps even worried, that she had somehow changed in the eight months she had lived in London, that she was not the woman he had said goodbye to in New York.

In certain ways she had changed, Evan knew that, but not very drastically, and certainly not in her character or her personality. They were still intact. It seemed to her that once he had realized this he had calmed down, become his normal self again, the man she knew.

She had always been close to her father.

She loved him; no, adored him, really. And they had been a team of two when she was growing up. *Inseparable*. Grandma Glynnis had joked about that, the way they did everything together, like two old buddies, Grandma always said.

And then last night something truly odd had

happened, and it had thrown her off balance. She had spent the night tossing and turning, unable to sleep, thinking about Owen Hughes, who and what he was. He was still her father . . . but he had lied to her, she was positive of that, and suddenly he had become, in a flash, just like that, no longer the man she thought he was, had believed him to be.

In the end, in the early hours of the morning, she had convinced herself that it didn't matter. She still loved him, that was a given. You loved people despite their faults. After all, no one was perfect, everyone had human frailties. He had told her a lie, but it *was* a white lie, and perhaps there had been a reason for it.

Actually, Evan wouldn't have known he'd lied if she had not happened to glance at her mother at that precise moment. Her face had told the story; her mother's expression had been one of contempt. Or had it been disgust? Whichever, it had telegraphed the truth to Evan, had announced in no uncertain terms that Owen was lying.

There was a sudden knock, and before Evan could say anything the door flew open. Linnet came hurrying in, looking disturbed, Evan thought, and instantly straightened in the chair, automatically bracing herself for trouble of some kind.

'Do you have a minute, Evan?' Linnet asked.

'Of course. What's wrong? You look upset.'

'Perplexed is a better word,' Linnet sat down heavily in the chair near Evan's desk, and continued, 'I just had the strangest conversation with Tessa, and I've got to admit it took me completely by surprise. In fact, I'm still taken aback.'

'What was it about?'

Leaning forward, Linnet said in a low voice, 'She asked me to look after Adele while she goes to Paris with Lorne.'

Evan herself was momentarily startled by this, and then she exclaimed, 'But why wouldn't she ask *you*, Linnet? You're her sister, she trusts you, and has confidence in you. She's very nervous about Adele's welfare right now, concerned for her.'

'I know, but on the other hand I was a bit surprised she didn't ask our grandmother, Daisy Rickards. They're actually rather close, and Daisy would be much better looking after little Adele than me.'

'Obviously Tessa thinks *you're* the best choice, while your mother is still in New York. I'm sure she would have asked Paula to babysit Adele if she'd been here.'

Linnet puffed her cheeks, blew out air. 'Gosh, that's one tremendous responsibility, looking after another person's child, and especially Adele, under the present circumstances. Mind you, Elvira's going to be with us, and it is only for a long weekend,' Linnet explained. 'At Pennistone Royal, because Tessa's very insistent about that. Anyway,' Linnet paused, gave Evan a small smile, and asked, 'I was wondering if you'd come with us, spend the weekend in Yorkshire? It would be fun if our chaps were with us. Please say yes.'

'Yes.' Evan laughed, added, 'I'd be happy to be

with you and Adele at Pennistone Royal, it's one of my favourite places. And you're right, it would be great if Gideon and Julian joined us.'

'Thank you so much, I do appreciate it, Evan. Anyway, before I accepted to do this for Tessa, I did suggest she took Elvira and Adele to Paris with her, but she dismissed the idea out of hand. I can't say I blame her. I happen to agree that it's better if Adele remains in England with some member of the family, that she doesn't travel abroad until this nasty divorce is over and everything is settled. I fully understand Tessa's worry about Mark Longden. I don't trust him either.'

Evan said, 'And I have my suspicions about him, and his friend and client Jonathan Ainsley. I think *he's* a rotten piece of work, from everything I know about him. He's been a lousy son to Robin.'

'Jack Figg's on top of Jonathan,' Linnet told her, 'breathing down his neck. At least Jack's operatives in Hong Kong are, and we'll know exactly where he is from now on. By the way, Tessa's become a convert to the religion of Jack Figg, his religion of total security.'

Evan burst out laughing. 'You say that in such a droll way, Linnet, and I think Jack's a pretty terrific guy.'

'He is, and he's turned Pennistone Royal into the most secure house in the British Isles. Want to bet?'

'Oh, no way! I think you're correct.'

'There's one thing that does puzzle me,' Linnet suddenly announced, getting up, walking over to the window, glancing down into Knightsbridge. Without turning around, she went on, 'I just can't get over the fact that Tessa asked me to look after her child. I mean . . . she's always been so competitive with me, calling herself the Dauphine, the heiress apparent, wanting to take over from Mummy *now*. And Mummy doesn't even want to retire, for heaven's sake, won't retire until she's old and decrepit. Not that I think she'll ever be that. Oh well, I guess times have changed.'

'Or Tessa has changed,' Evan suggested softly.

Linnet swung to face Evan, gave her a hard stare. There was a quickening in her green eyes when she said, 'There's a certain truth there. I do believe that the abduction frightened her, made her truly aware how much she loves Adele. And perhaps she does put Adele first, before anything else. *At the moment*.'

'I wouldn't be surprised if she did retire and sooner than you think.'

'I'm not so sure she'd do that, Evan. You see, Tessa's far too ambitious. She wants to run the stores, because she's the eldest and thinks it's her right. But she wants to manage them in her way, on her terms, not the way Mummy has run them for over thirty years.' Linnet laughed lightly. 'You know what, Evan, Tessa would love *me* to retire, and that's the truth.'

'I know how she is, but it's a bit silly to discuss all this, since nothing's going to change as long as Paula is in charge.'

'Agreed.'

'Why is Tessa going to Paris with Lorne?' Evan asked, her curiosity getting the better of her.

'Because he's making a film there, starting in about another week. The whole cast and crew are going over, according to Tessa, and they'll be in Paris for about six weeks. Then they come back to work for two months at Shepperton Studios. He invited Tessa for the first weekend he's there, because he thought the change would do her good.'

'He's a really lovely man,' Evan said, and then glanced down at the sketches. 'I was just going over these before you came in, and was about to bring them to your office. My ideas for the Leeds store.' She handed Linnet the sketches.

Linnet looked at all of them quickly, and then started at the beginning again, studying the six sketches more carefully. Eventually she looked up. 'How clever you've been. Bringing all of the fashion departments onto one floor, and designing an open-floor plan so that they flow into each other.'

'With the small boutiques for accessories, in various corners and smaller areas,' Evan pointed out, 'there is a wonderful flow, as you just said. And the customer doesn't have to go to another floor for shoes or bags and other accessories. Everything is *there*.'

'I think it'll work perfectly. You've done a good job, Evan.'

'Thank you,' she answered, pleased by Linnet's reaction. Evan then explained, 'Actually, what I've done is borrow from your mother's idea on the fifth floor here, the way she has put lingerie, sleepwear, at-home clothes, casual and exercise clothes, hosiery, and casual footwear in different boutiques next to each other.'

'That's right, I see that now. But I think this open-floor plan works much better, Evan. Let's go to the fifth floor and take a look, shall we?'

One of the things Evan loved most about her job at Harte's was the store itself. Many a morning she came in early, long before its doors opened to the public, so that she could walk the floors. Being out on the floor was thrilling to her, especially when she was alone except for the odd maintenance person, or another early bird like herself. The store impressed her, gave her a great sense of satisfaction.

Linnet felt the same way about it; they often compared notes, and now as they walked through Lingerie together, Evan confided, 'I love all the floors, all the departments, but my favourite is cosmetics. What's yours, Linnet?'

'Cosmetics, too, but I'm also crazy about the Food Halls. You know when my great-grandmother, I should say *our* great-grandmother, first started she had a little shop in Upper Armley, on the outskirts of Leeds, and her mainstay was her food products. My mother told me that Emma Harte also loved the Food Halls here, too, and perhaps I inherited that inclination from her.'

'Maybe you did, and who wouldn't love our Food Halls: they're fantastic. I often see Tessa browsing around, buying there, but then she's very much into food, such a great chef. Gideon says she missed her calling, that she ought to be cooking for the world.'

'I bet he said "just like Paula", because my mother thinks she has to feed the starving multitudes, truly believes she's Mother Earth.'

'I know she does, and yes he did say that. Nicely.'

'Oh, I know. Gideon adores my mother.'

'Who doesn't? Anyway, getting back to my sketches, in particular I took this area as my model, Linnet, but instead of small, self-contained boutiques I made an open-floor plan . . .' Evan glanced around, and added, 'That way, with no real walls, or entrances into boutiques, the customer feels no constraints, can see everything, well almost. Oh goodness, there's my mother!'

'Where?' Linnet asked, glancing around, a look of expectancy on her face. 'I don't see anyone who could possibly be your mother, Evan.'

'Over there, the woman looking at the négligées. The blonde.'

'The blonde! That's your mother? Gosh, I can hardly believe it. She looks like your sister.'

'Not quite.' Evan giggled, and then taking hold of Linnet's arm she purposefully hurried her across the floor, exclaiming, 'Hello, Mom! Fancy seeing you here!' as Marietta Hughes swung around.

Her face lit up at the sight of her daughter. 'Hi, Evan honey. I was going to call you when I'd finished here.'

'Mom, I'd like you to meet Linnet O'Neill. And Linnet, this is my mother.'

The two women, both beaming, shook hands, and then Marietta said, 'You look very young to be the boss.'

Linnet began to laugh. 'I am too young to be the boss, and anyway, I'm not. My mother runs Harte's, Mrs Hughes.'

'Oh, I know that. I mean Evan's boss. That's what she always says, Linnet's my boss.'

'I bet I know why you're browsing through all these gorgeous nightgowns, Mom. You're looking for something special for Angharad, who you're convinced is going to be a bride soon.'

Marietta gave her daughter a bright smile and shook her head slowly. 'Why no, I wasn't looking for something for your sister. I was browsing for myself.'

This comment startled Evan, but she managed to keep a neutral look on her face and answered, 'Oh, well, there are some lovely things here, Mom. Linnet does a lot of the buying.' She turned to Linnet, and went on, 'What do *you* think would be suitable for my mother?'

'Let's go down to the other end, Mrs Hughes, I know just the designer for you. I think you'll love her nightgowns and négligées.'

'Thanks, Linnet, and please call me Marietta.'

Linnet inclined her head, smiled, and taking hold of Marietta's arm she led her to the other end of the nightgown section and a series of well-stocked racks.

Evan followed, walking behind Linnet and her mother. Today Marietta was wearing a pale-blue cotton skirt, matching cotton shirt, and high-heeled blue sandals. Evan couldn't help thinking what great legs her mother had. Funny, but she'd never noticed her legs before. Of course not. Her mother had been in a dressing gown or trousers for most of her life.

Once more, innumerable questions ran through Evan's head. What had wrought this extraordinary change in her mother? She had no idea and she was riddled with curiosity. She made up her mind to find out. As soon as she possibly could.

Tessa sat at her desk staring into space, thinking about her impending trip to Paris, feeling suddenly ambivalent about it. She wondered if she'd made a mistake, agreeing to go with her twin when he went to start the movie.

The thought of leaving Adele alone with Elvira worried her, even though they would be at Pennistone Royal, which was now a fortress, thanks to Jack Figg and his security systems. When she had voiced her worries to Lorne yesterday, he had suggested she ask Linnet to spend the weekend at Pennistone Royal in order to keep an eye on Adele. 'She'll never refuse you, Tess,' Lorne had said, had reminded her how much Linnet loved the little girl. 'Go on, ask Linny, you'll see, she'll say yes.'

And so this morning she had approached Linnet, admittedly a little tentatively, and had been happily surprised when her half-sister had so readily agreed. *Half*-sister. That's the way she always thought of Linnet. Just as she thought of Shane as her *step*-father, which he was, but he had treated her like his own, and she knew how much he loved her. But they were O'Neills and she was a Fairley, and somehow she could never forget that. On the other hand, Linnet had behaved like a true sister when Adele was stolen by Mark. She had taken charge, done all the right things, and because of Linnet everything had been handled with the minimum of fuss for the maximum of success . . .

The shrilling phone on her desk interrupted her thoughts, and she reached for it. 'Hello?'

'Is that you, Tessa?' a woman's voice asked.

'Yes, it is. Who am I speaking to?'

'It's Great-Aunt Edwina,' the Dowager Countess of Dunvale announced, bellowing down the phone like a bustling British general about to lead his troops into battle. 'Have you forgotten me, Tessa Fairley?' she went on. 'I certainly think so! I haven't heard from you in the longest time.'

'I haven't forgotten you at all, Great-Aunt Edwina. In fact, I was talking to India about you the other day, and we –'

'How is that granddaughter of mine? It strikes me she's become decidedly elusive lately. Haven't heard from her either. Never mind, you're both very young, no time for an old lady like me, what?'

'Please don't say that!' Tessa exclaimed, feeling guilty about neglecting her great-aunt, and also wondering why Edwina was phoning her. There was always a reason when she made a call. Suddenly Tessa thought of Dusty Rhodes and the stabbing, wondering if Edwina had got wind of it. But how? *Easily*. She lived near Harrogate, just outside Knaresborough, and news travelled fast, bad news travelled faster. And there was also Uncle Robin who lived nearby at Lackland Priory, and spoke to Evan all the time, who no doubt filled him in about everything.

Clearing her throat, Tess said, 'India and I were talking about giving a dinner party for you, Great-Aunt Edwina, and the only reason I haven't phoned you is because –'

'Adele was abducted,' Edwina interrupted. 'I'm glad Linnet managed to foil that terrible husband of yours. And that the child is safe. Now, what's this about a dinner party? Why would you and India give a dinner party for an old lady like me? And who would come, eh? Now answer that one, Tessa Fairley.'

'Your son and daughter-in-law would certainly come –'

'Bah! Rubbish. All the way from Ireland. Forget it. Anthony never moves too far from those damned bogs of his.'

'They *would* come, Great-Aunt, and so would your grandchildren, and Mummy and Shane, and I'd come, and what about your brother and sister, Robin and Elizabeth? And there's Emily and Winston. The whole family would come, I'm sure of it.'

'And would my darling India bring her new boyfriend, do you think? The famous artist.'

'You'd have to ask her,' Tessa murmured, non-committally, afraid to be drawn into a discussion about Russell Rhodes, unaware of how much the old countess knew. Probably everything, she thought to herself, groaning inside.

'I want to see you and India. And as soon as possible,' Edwina said.

'*Oh.* Is something wrong, Great-Aunt?'

'No. Well, not that I know of, but I am ninety-five, you know. Still in fine fettle, mind you, ready to tackle anything or anyone. So, how about it? When are you two likely to be in Yorkshire?'

'We both have to be there this coming week. We're revamping the Harrogate and Leeds stores,' Tessa explained quietly, more than ever worried now.

'Then I'd better see you then. You'll come to dinner at Niddersley House. Please be good enough to inform India. *I* can't reach her on the phone. And let me know tomorrow at the latest which evening you'll come to supper.'

'Yes, Great-Aunt Edwina. What about our dinner –'

'We'll discuss *that* when I see you next week.'

'I'll try to find India. She must be somewhere in the store, out on the floor.'

'When you *do* find her, please have her telephone me. And thank you, Tessa. Goodbye.'

''Bye, Great-Aunt. I'll tell India to give you a buzz, and we'll see you next week.'

Tessa hung up, sat back in the chair, and wondered what this was all about. She couldn't help asking herself if Edwina knew about the stabbing, that question rearing up again as it had a few minutes ago. How could she know? *Robin could have told her*. After all, they were siblings.

My God, she's the oldest of the lot, Tessa suddenly thought. Emma Harte's first child, born when Emma was only sixteen, out of wedlock. Only daughter of Edwin Fairley. And a true Fairley right down to her boots, even though she was illegitimate. Aunt of *her* father, Jim Fairley, who had been Edwin's grandson. God, what complications in this family, she thought.

Opening her engagement book, Tessa turned to the coming week, flipped the pages, looking for a night to go over to Niddersley House. And she noticed at once that she was due to fly to Paris on Thursday evening with Lorne. Thursday August 30th, 2001. And her mother was coming back from New York on September 5th.

We'll have to go to dinner with Edwina on Monday or Tuesday, Tessa decided, because she would have to return to London on Wednesday afternoon.

Closing the book, she stood up, grabbed her mobile, slipped it in her jacket pocket and went out into the store, looking for her cousin India, knowing she must relay the messages from her grandmother.

CHAPTER FOURTEEN

'I'm pleased we bumped into each other the way we did,' Marietta Hughes said, smiling across at Evan. Mother and daughter were having lunch together in The Birdcage, one of the restaurants in the store. Chatting away easily, sipping their water as they waited for their food, they were completely relaxed with each other.

'So am I, Mom,' Evan responded, 'and Saturday is always a good day for me. I'm usually working on my computer, catching up on paperwork. It gets really hectic during the week.'

'I was going to call you after I'd strolled around the store, but I'm afraid I got caught up admiring the beautiful nightgowns,' Marietta explained with a girlish laugh. 'Imagine that, at my age.'

Evan merely nodded, sat gazing at her mother, thinking that Linnet's words of an hour ago had been so true; Marietta didn't look old enough to be her mother. She was forty-nine, soon to be fifty, yet she appeared much younger. Did she look suddenly youthful because she was obviously not suffering from depression? Was she happier and less burdened down with the problems of her illness? Or was it something else as well as better health? A face job maybe? No, her father didn't have that kind of disposable income to pay for plastic surgery. Well, yes, he did actually, since his mother's death; Glynnis Hughes had left both her and her father small legacies.

'You're staring at me, Evan. Have I got dirt on my face? Or don't you like the way I'm dressed?'

Evan blinked, swiftly exclaimed, 'Don't be silly, Mom, of course you don't have dirt on your face! And to be honest, I think you look great. Just as you did last night. If you want to know the truth that's why I'm staring at you like this. You've undergone such a change it's fantastic. You're such a different woman I can hardly believe it.'

'Sure you can, you're seeing it and seeing is believing, isn't it, Evan Hughes? Remember when I used to say that to you when you were little . . .' Her mother's voice trailed off when she saw the sudden puzzlement on Evan's face.

Then Evan cried, 'Of course, I remember! When I doubted there was a Santa Claus you said, "Seeing is believing," and you and Grandma took me to the local department store to meet him one Christmas.'

Pleased that she had remembered Marietta broke into smiles, took a sip of her water, and remarked, 'You were such a lovely child.'

Evan leaned across the table and said in a conspiratorial whisper, 'Come on, Mommy, 'fess up, tell me what's happened?' When Marietta remained silent, Evan volunteered, 'You're on a new medication, aren't you? And it's changed your life, hasn't it?'

Marietta still didn't say anything and after a moment Evan sat back in the chair and waited. As the silence dragged on she wondered if her mother was upset, resented her probing, and she reached out, took hold of her hand, squeezed it. 'I'm sorry, I shouldn't pry this way. It's just that I'm thrilled you look so great, that you seem a bit better in health.'

'I'm a *lot* better, and you're not prying. And I do want to talk to you, Evan, but I don't know where to begin.'

'Begin at the beginning,' Evan suggested, 'and take as long as you want. I'm pretty much finished for the day, so I've plenty of time. And naturally I'm all ears.'

'The beginning, yes . . . it started last February, just after you left. I don't know whether you remember Auntie Dottie. She was my mother's sister and she lived in LA, not far from my mother. They were very close until Mom died.'

'I remember her vaguely; you used to talk about her sometimes. She'd worked as an actress in films when she was young, in the forties.'

'That's correct,' Marietta said, looking surprised. 'I can't believe you even remember that, you only met her a couple of times when she came East with her husband on business. You were very small at the time. I was her only niece and she usually made a big effort to see me. Auntie Dottie was married to Howard Kempson. He was head of publicity at Ardent Pictures until his death about ten years ago.'

'Do you know, I recall his death. You were upset, and that must have made an impression on me. Or you did, telling me stories about her working in pictures, and how she and Howard met.'

Marietta laughed. 'She was only ever a bit-actress, but the family loved to boast about her movie career.'

The waitress arrived with their tomato salads, refilled their glasses with iced tea, and hurried away.

After a forkful of tomato salad, Evan urged, 'So continue the story.'

'In February, Auntie Dottie came to New York, to attend the fiftieth wedding anniversary of an old girlfriend from her Hollywood days. And we got together. She was pleased I was doing relatively well, but thought I should really be doing much better. She told me about her friend, Dr Anna Marcello, and insisted I make an appointment to see her.' Marietta put down her fork, and leaned towards Evan. 'I'll never forget Auntie Dottie's parting shot. She said, "Get up, get going and get a life. Before it's too late, Mari." I guess her words . . . just galvanized me.'

'Sometimes we all need that kind of push from someone we trust.'

'I went to see Dr Marcello, who did take me in hand,' Marietta said. 'She gave me new medication and superior health care. But it wasn't only *that* which helped me to change for the better. Something else occurred.'

'Tell me,' Evan urged, her attention riveted on her mother.

'Not long after Auntie Dottie's visit to New York she died. She was in her eighties but seemed very fit to me, and she wasn't a bit senile. She'd only been back on the West Coast a week or so when she had a fatal heart attack. To cut to the chase, as she would've said, she left me everything. Her apartment in Brentwood, some stocks, and her jewellery. It's mostly costume but some of it is vintage and it's very nice. Anyway, as it said in her will, I received all her worldly possessions.'

'Just imagine you becoming an heiress, and all of a sudden, Mom. So unexpectedly.'

'I didn't inherit a fortune,' Marietta laughed, 'far from it.'

'What did Dad say?'

'Not much.'

'Wasn't he pleased?' Evan asked, looking nonplussed for a moment.

'Not really.'

'But why not, Mom?'

'Because by dying and leaving me her money and all, Auntie Dottie had changed the circumstances of my life. She'd made me independent.'

Evan gaped at her mother, flabbergasted. 'Dad didn't like it? Because you didn't need him anymore? Financially, that is. You're saying that, aren't you?'

'Yes, I am.'

'How awful. But you've been married to each other all of your lives. Since you were twenty-one, Mommy! He couldn't possibly think you were going to walk out on him *now*, because your aunt left you money. Or could he?'

'I don't know what he thought then, or thinks now, Evan. Your father never discusses it with me,' Marietta answered, and drank some of her iced tea. 'You know, I did take Auntie Dottie's advice last February and went to Dr Marcello. And I was glad I had listened to her. So after her death and receiving the inheritance, I decided I must absolutely take charge of my life. And my inheritance as well.'

'Because you know that's what your aunt wanted you to do, right?'

'Exactly. I contacted a real-estate broker on the Coast and put Auntie Dottie's apartment up for rent. Furnished, of course. The broker had a deal for me within the week, and I now have a regular income from that. I didn't sell the stocks, I kept them, and what money my aunt had in her bank account when she died I transferred to a bank in Manhattan. Where I had opened an account.'

'Mom, I'm so proud of you! Congratulations!'

'Thanks, that's praise indeed, Evan, coming from you.'

'I mean every word.'

'I just want to say this, I haven't gone mad with the money, you know. I've just bought a couple of new things. It's nice to have some pretty clothes to wear. For a change.'

Marietta sounded so wistful when she said this, Evan looked up and stared at her mother. Hadn't her mother ever had any nice things in the past? Not really, not that she could remember. Was that her father's fault? Hadn't he given her mother money to buy pretty things? Maybe he hadn't been able to afford it then, in those days. Don't blame him, Evan cautioned herself. Mom was very *sick*, always so sad, down in the dumps, depressed. Yes, Dad did his best, I'm sure of it, but he was awfully discouraged at times.

Evan concentrated on her salad for a few minutes, staring down at her plate, but looking at it more than eating. Suddenly she didn't feel very hungry, and she put her fork down and straightened in the chair.

A silence fell between Evan and her mother, but it was an easy silence, and there was affection flowing between the two of them. And Evan began to wonder about something . . . wonder if she had been unfair to her mother all these years, always blaming her, applauding her father. Perhaps her mother had needed a bit of praise, too, and applause at times. And love from *her*. Guilt settled on her.

The waitress arrived, removed their plates, said she'd be back in a moment with their crab cakes, and hurried off once more.

Evan said quietly, her eyes on her mother's face, 'I want to tell you something, Mother. You really looked lovely last night, just as you do today. Dad must be pleased that you're so much better, in every way. And looking so beautiful.'

'I don't know . . . I hope so, honey. But he doesn't really pay much attention.'

Evan shook her head. 'I can't figure him out, Mom,' she muttered, feeling suddenly annoyed by him and his behaviour.

Oh, I can, Marietta thought, but murmured, 'The money's not that important to me, as I said. I'm not going to rush out and buy lots of things. But I do like the feeling of independence it gives me, I like knowing that if I had to, I could support myself.'

For a moment Evan was at a loss for words. She understood what her mother was saying. What she couldn't understand was her father's attitude, one which was apparently grudging to say the least, by the sound of it. Was he jealous? Threatened? Did he really think her mother would leave him? But why would she do that? Suddenly, and with a small shock, Evan realized that she didn't know much about their marriage. After all, she had left home nine years ago and gone to live with her grandparents Glynnis and Richard in Manhattan. Did they have a bad marriage? Had her mother been too ill for too long? Did he resent the lost years?

On the other hand, her father had become a success as an antiques dealer in recent years. He enjoyed his home, enjoyed living in a lovely old farmhouse in Connecticut. How out of touch I am, she thought. Do I know either of my parents anymore?

'Please don't judge your father too harshly,' Marietta was saying.

Rousing herself from her racing thoughts, Evan replied, 'I don't judge him at all. However, I do want to ask you something. Last night you had a strange look on your face, when Dad said he hadn't known that his mother had worked for Emma Harte.' She took a deep breath and plunged. 'It was contempt I saw, Mother, wasn't it? Contempt on your face.'

'Not contempt, Evan honey. Merely dismay.'

'He lied to me, didn't he?'

Marietta couldn't bring herself to confirm this verbally, and so she simply nodded.

'But *why*, Mom? Why does it matter that she worked for Emma? And why does Dad hate the Hartes?'

'You've asked me three questions all at once, and I will answer them in three words . . . *I don't know*.'

'Let me ask you another question. If Dad knew Glynnis had worked for Emma Harte at the store, and he disliked the Hartes so much, why did he encourage me to go to London in January?'

'Because he didn't know about Glynnis and Emma then. Oh yes, he did remember that his mother had met Emma in the war years, and that they'd stayed in touch for a bit after the war. But he had no idea she'd been Emma's secretary.'

'He found that out after Grandma Glynnis died last November, didn't he?'

Her mother nodded.

'Did he discover some of his mother's papers?'

'A reference Emma had given Glynnis all those years ago, singing her praises as a secretary.'

'And that's all he found?'

'Oh, yes.'

'It still doesn't explain why he's taken this attitude with me.'

'No. Unless –'

'Unless what?' Evan interrupted.

'Unless he's just terribly upset. From the moment you walked into this store you've been madly in love – with the store, with Linnet O'Neill, with Paula O'Neill and India Standish. And Gideon Harte, as well. Maybe your father feels abandoned by you, Evan. Threatened by them all, fearful of losing you. Perhaps he thinks you'll never come home.'

'Oh Mom,' she said softly.

'I know you're not coming home, at least not coming home to live. I know you're going to stay in England. You see, women are intuitive and also so much more practical than men, and we see things differently. We see them as they really are, and not as we'd like them to be, the way men do.' Marietta sighed. 'I know you're very much in love with Gideon, and I'm happy for you, honey. You certainly have my blessing.'

'And not Dad's, is that what you're saying?'

'No, not at all. It's as I said, he doesn't want to lose you completely. You were always – the favourite, let's face it.'

Changing the subject for a moment, Evan asked, 'Why did you and Dad adopt Elayne and Angharad?'

'I couldn't have more children.'

'But you were a manic depressive, you found it hard to look after *me*, never mind two more.'

'Your father wanted a bigger family, Evan.'

Evan reached out, took hold of her mother's hand and held it very tightly. Intently, searchingly, she looked into her face, saw its loveliness, its calmness, the curved contours, the wide brow; her face was unlined; it had always been unlined and calm, full of repose. She had unique eyes, not blue, not green, but a subtle turquoise. Her mother's hair was a shining, blonde halo around her face, and Evan suddenly realized that Marietta had always looked like this, untroubled, calm, and perfectly beautiful in a quiet, very soft way.

Evan said, carefully, slowly, 'It was *you*, Mommy . . . you who wanted another child . . . because he took me away from you. He made me his, didn't he? He pushed you out, took me for himself.'

Marietta blinked and turned her head, swallowed the tears, made no response.

'I love you, Mom. I really do love you. I always have,' Evan whispered in a gentle voice.

'And I love you, Evan,' her mother answered, choked, and Evan saw the tears glistening in those extraordinary eyes.

The sudden arrival of the waitress with their crab cakes interrupted this conversation, and once they were alone again, had recovered their composure to a degree, Evan said, 'I didn't mean to upset you.'

'I know that. And after lunch I'd like us to go to your office for a moment or two. There's something I need to tell you, explain to you.'

Wisely Evan didn't ask what it was; she just nodded her acquiescence.

'I want to tell you something about your grand-mother,' Marietta said to Evan an hour later, after they had settled themselves in her office.

'Tell me then. Will it make me understand things better?'

'I hope so, honey. Last summer, before she got really sick, Glynnis asked me to come into New York to have lunch with her. I was happy to go because I knew she cared about me, and I loved her. Actually, I thought she wanted to discuss my health or hers, I wasn't sure which.' Marietta stopped, wondering for a moment if she should continue. Was she not opening Pandora's box, releasing terrible secrets?

Evan, sitting waiting, her eyes on her mother, cleared her throat several times, and pressed, 'And why did Grandma want to talk to you?' When Marietta remained totally silent, Evan exclaimed, 'I bet it was about your *health*. She was always concerned about you. Glynnis loved you, you know.'

'Yes, she did. However, that day she didn't want to talk about me. Or even about herself. It was *you* she was fretting about.'

'She was?' Evan seemed taken aback by this revelation, and looked at her mother intently.

'Yes, your grandma thought you were in a rut, going nowhere. Therefore, she told me, you must go to London. She was going to give you money and ship you off there. When I argued against this, asked her what you'd do there all on your own, she said you could work at Harte's. She explained that she'd been close to Emma Harte once, knew the store because she herself had worked there during the Second World War. She told me that Harte's in Knightsbridge was the perfect place for you.'

'My God, Mom, she was planning it then! Didn't she know Emma Harte was dead?'

'I'm fairly certain she did, Evan, but she didn't mention it to me that day. Glynnis said she wanted to put you amongst the Harte family, in their orbit, because that's where you belonged. When I asked her what she meant, she became rather quiet, almost withdrawn. After a moment, she did start to talk about them once again, told me that she had a long history with the Hartes and that I should trust her. When I still opposed the idea of you leaving New York, she said that children were only ever lent to us for a short time, and then they must leave, have a life of their own. "Let her go", she said, "send her to London. She's irresistible." Those were her exact words.'

'She meant I was irresistible to the Hartes?'

'Yes.'

'What did Dad say?'

'I never told him about the conversation. Your grandmother made me promise not to tell him. She put me on my honour.'

Evan leaned back in her chair, stared at her mother sitting on the other side of the desk, wondering just how much Marietta really knew. It was on the tip of her tongue to ask her mother if she knew that Glynnis and Robin had had an affair during the war, and then changed her mind immediately. It would be much wiser to probe a little more, rather than reveal the secret of her father's parentage. She was still ambivalent, uncertain about telling him the truth. And so she said quietly, with a little smile, 'Well, Grandma got her way in the end, didn't she?'

'That's right, on her deathbed,' Marietta murmured. 'When she told you to go to London to find Emma Harte, because she held the key to your future, Glynnis surely knew exactly what she was doing.'

'That's true. Because she was absolutely certain I would do what she said, that I wouldn't be able to resist going to London.'

'I know you don't have any regrets,' her mother said, her eyes not leaving Evan's face.

'That's true, Mom, I don't. Did Grandma tell you anything else about her connection to the Hartes? Whether she knew all the family?'

'No, she didn't,' Marietta answered, asking herself if she was doing the right thing by lying to her daughter. Well, she had no choice, at least for the moment. Perhaps later she would tell Evan everything, come clean with her, confide the truth.

Evan, scrutinizing her mother intently, exclaimed, 'Mom, you look worried. Is there something you're not telling me?'

'No, of course not,' Marietta lied.

'If there is something on your mind, you could tell me, you know. I wouldn't tell Dad.'

'Good God, you mustn't tell him what I've just revealed to you, Evan! I never said anything to him, not even after Glynnis died and you came to London. I promised his mother *on my honour*, and you must promise me now . . . promise the same thing.'

'I do. I won't tell Dad about your conversation with Grandma, I promise. *On my honour*.'

Marietta relaxed her body, let the tension ease out of it. She smiled at her daughter, and said in a low voice, 'Thank you for today, honey, I've so enjoyed being with you . . . sharing . . . and I'm sorry.'

'Sorry for what?'

'Being *absent* in your life when you were growing up. We missed so much, you and I . . .'

'You were sick such a lot. But there were times when you were there for me . . . I remember them all, Mom.'

'I'm glad. About lunch tomorrow with Gideon, your father and I are *both* coming after all. I think he's now quite looking forward to meeting Gideon.'

'And George wasn't upset that you can't keep the date with him and Arlette?'

'Of course not. That was just something floating around in your father's head. Now, where shall we meet, and at what time?'

'At the Dorchester at one o'clock. I'll be waiting for you in the lobby,' Evan replied, filled with happiness and relief that her parents were finally going to meet the man she loved and whom she had promised to marry.

It was two-thirty when India hurried into Tessa's office at the store, exclaiming, 'I'm sorry you couldn't reach me. I got your message about my grandmother. Is she all right?'

'She's fine, India, in fact she sounds like a British general at the head of an army about to quell the natives, as she usually does. Great-Aunt Edwina must be made of cast iron.'

India burst out laughing. 'I agree with you. Did she tell you what she wanted?'

'Yes, you're to phone her. But she also wants us to go to supper with her next week at Niddersley House. I said we would. But it will have to be Monday or Tuesday, because I have to come back to London on Wednesday afternoon. I'm going to Paris the next day with Lorne.'

'That should cheer you up a bit,' India said. 'I wonder why Grandmother wants us to go to dinner with her? Did she give you a clue?'

'None, but she sounded determined, feisty and, in a funny way, rather nice. I've often thought she was kind of – *cool*. Especially for a very old lady.'

'I know what you mean,' India concurred. 'She doesn't seem old, nor does she act it. Bustling around hither and yon like a youngster.'

Tessa smiled. 'I'm to let her know tomorrow which evening we're free.'

'I'd like to make it Monday, if you don't mind, Tessa, mainly because I'm hoping to take Dusty back to Willows Hall on Tuesday afternoon, and I'd be spending the evening there. Thankfully he's very much on the mend, and the hospital's going to discharge him at long last.'

'I'm happy to hear he's better, and Monday's fine with me. When are you going to Yorkshire? Tomorrow afternoon?'

'Yes. And you?'

'The same. I'm taking Adele and Elvira with me. I want to get them settled before I leave on Wednesday. Linnet's arriving at Pennistone Royal on Wednesday evening, to take charge, keep an eye on everything.'

'I understand,' India murmured, finally flopping down in a chair. She was convinced there was nothing to worry about now, since Jack Figg had turned the house and grounds into something akin to Fort Knox. India said, 'They'll be perfectly safe, to be sure they will. Any news of the dreaded Mark?'

'Ugh, no,' Tessa responded with an involuntary shudder. 'Thank God. His solicitors are talking to mine, but it seems to be slow going. Mummy says it won't be for much longer since once she gets back to London she's going to light a fuse under them all.'

'Knowing Aunt Paula, that's *exactly* what she'll do.' India stood up again, moved over to Tessa's desk and said, 'Do you mind if I call my grandmother from here? And you can tell her a day early that we'll see her on Monday.'

'Be my guest,' Tessa answered, indicating the phone.

India dialled, waited for the number to ring

through, and when it was answered she said, 'May I speak to the Dowager Countess, please.'

'You're speaking to her, India, dear. It's me.'

'Hello, Grandma. I'm with Tessa, she tells me you've been trying to reach me.'

'Correct. I wanted to talk to you about your boyfriend. How's he doing? Is he out of the hospital yet?'

India stared at Tessa, rolling her eyes and looking very surprised. 'He's better, Grandmother, and coming out of the hospital on Tuesday.'

'Glad to hear it. You'd better bring him over to Niddersley House to meet me when he's up to it. All right?'

'Yes, that's fine.'

'He has a giant-sized talent. Correction, it's more than great talent. The man's a genius.'

'Oh yes, he is,' India exclaimed, relieved that her grandmother was sounding positive about Dusty, obviously had no objections to him. 'Tessa wants to talk to you, today instead of tomorrow.'

'You've settled on a date for supper, have you?'

'Yes, Grandmother.'

'When?' Edwina barked.

'Monday evening, if that's all right with you?'

'Naturally it is. I'm hardly leading the social life of a debutante in demand, India. Oh, and by the way, what's all this nonsense about you and Tessa giving a dinner for me?'

'She mentioned it then? We just thought it would be nice to . . . *honour* you, as the oldest living member of the Harte family.'

'Don't remind me of that!' Edwina exclaimed, and then she chuckled. 'Since you're both part Fairley, as indeed I am, I'll consider the idea. Do you think you can drag your father out of the bogs of Ireland? Will he come?'

'I'm certain of it, Grandma.'

'Let us discuss it on Monday. Seven o'clock sharp, India. Goodbye.'

''Bye,' India said but Edwina had already slammed the phone down. India stared at Tessa and said in a puzzled tone, 'She knew about Dusty? Who could have told her?'

'You didn't?' Tessa asked.

'No. I hadn't told anyone except Linnet, and even then she didn't know his name, only that I was involved with someone. It was after the stabbing that it all came out in the open.'

'Then there's your answer. The whole family suddenly knew,' Tessa pointed out.

'She probably got it from Uncle Robin, because Evan chats to him every day, well, practically,' India remarked, making a good guess.

'Do you care she knows? Anyway, what was her reaction?'

'She says he's a genius . . . she wants to meet him.' India returned to the chair, leaned back against the cushions and muttered, 'The problem is, *he* won't want to meet her.'

'Why ever not?'

'Because he thinks the family's stuck up, snobbish, all that silly stuff, just because Daddy has a title.'

'I bet he will meet her if you paint the right

picture, oh, do excuse the pun. You must make her sound like a real eccentric, which she is.' As she was speaking Tessa turned off her computer, reached for her handbag and said, 'I'll meet you at Niddersley House on Monday evening, and now I'm going home to be with my child.'

India jumped up, saying, 'I'm going to call it a day, too. Do you have your car, or can I give you a lift to your mother's house?'

'I was going to walk, but that'd be great, India, thanks.'

Within minutes the cousins were strolling to the carpark not far from the store. As they turned into the small parking lot, Tessa said, 'I'm surprised you still use this place, after what happened to Evan, the way she was mugged around here in June.'

'It's all right in the summer months,' India explained, 'when it's still light. I'll have to make other arrangements in winter, probably use a car service, or a driver, like you do.'

'I think that would be extremely wise on your part,' Tessa remarked as they came to a stop next to India's Aston Martin. 'It's so dangerous in London lately . . . even in daylight.'

On the way to Paula's house in Belgrave Square, India spoke for a few minutes about Dusty and the portrait he was painting of her, and then she suddenly asked, 'How long are you going to live with your mother and father, Tessa?'

Glancing at her swiftly, Tessa replied, 'Until the divorce is final and everything's settled with Mark.

Then I'll find a flat. I don't want to live at the Hampstead house, even though it's actually mine. I can't bear the place, Mark turned it into something so ugly, cold and grim. He can have it and he's welcome.'

'I know he wants a lot.'

'He does. My mother seems to have some sort of plan, but I won't know about it until she gets back at the beginning of September. In the meantime, the Belgrave house is rather large, and there's the downstairs flat, Paul McGill's old quarters. I have a bit of privacy down there, if I need it.'

As they turned into Belgrave Square, India said, 'Can I pop in for a minute? I'd love to see Adele, give her a hug.'

'Of course. Oh, my God, India! That's Mark on the doorstep, ringing the bell. Oh God, what does *he* want?'

India said firmly, 'Don't panic. *We* can deal with him,' and a moment later she brought the car to a standstill outside the house, pulled on the brake. 'Keep calm,' she murmured as Tessa made to get out of the Aston Martin.

'I will.' Alighting, Tessa hurried across the pavement, exclaiming, 'Mark, what do you want?'

He swung around on hearing her voice. 'I want to see my daughter, that's what. You're keeping her from me and that's not fair,' he said in a belligerent voice, his face turning red, filled with anger.

'You know you're supposed to make an appointment, you can't just show up like this,'

Tessa cried, drawing to a stop at the bottom of the steps, staring up at him, trying to hold her emotions in check.

'Well, here I am, Mrs Longden. It's my right to see Adele, she's my child. I love her and she loves me.'

'You forfeited the right to see her the day you abducted her,' Tessa told him.

'I didn't abduct her, I just took her out for a drive and lunch. I brought her back unharmed, I would never harm her, whatever you might think, and I have said so to your solicitors. You're unconscionable, the way you've badmouthed me.'

'You cannot see her until we have an iron-clad agreement,' Tessa announced coldly, glaring at him. 'You're the one slowing it down.'

'You're such a bitch, and —'

At this moment the door flew open and Harriet, the housekeeper, stood on the threshold, having just responded to the ringing doorbell.

'Oh, it's you, Miss Tessa,' she said, and waited for instructions, since, like the rest of the staff, she knew the situation.

India hurried to join Tessa and took hold of her arm. 'I think it might be better if we let him come in for tea. You can't stand here, having a shouting match, it'll be much easier in the end.'

Tessa walked up the steps with India at her side, and said to him in a lowered voice, 'Come in then, Mark. We'll have tea with Adele.'

Harriet was hesitant for a split second, and then opened the door wider for Tessa. 'It's all right,'

Tessa murmured. 'There's no problem, Harriet. Is Ben here?'

'Yes, thank God,' Harriet muttered, relieved that her husband was in the house watching TV.

Once they were inside the hall, Tessa turned to Mark and said in a voice dripping ice, 'Just this once I'll overlook the rules you agreed to last week. But this is it until we have the settlement worked out. Do you understand?'

He nodded, and quietly followed her up the stairs to the playroom which had been used by the rest of the family when they were young. Now it was Adele's favourite place, her haven.

When they walked inside and Adele saw her father she smiled and waved, but it was Tessa to whom she ran, crying, 'Mumma, Mumma, I'm glad you're home.'

Tessa bent down, caught the running child, hugged her to her, kissed her cheek, and hugged her again. Then straightening, she said, 'Here's Daddy and Aunt India. We're going to have a tea party. With you, Elvira and your dolls.'

'Oh, that's lovely, Mumma. And Reggi has just put the kettle on,' she said inventively, in her usual imaginative way, pointing to the favoured rag doll.

'Well then, let's all sit down and wait for Harriet to make the tea,' Tessa murmured lovingly.

An hour and a half later Tessa escorted Mark down the stairs to the marble entrance foyer. 'Thanks,' he said softly, and before she could stop him he had pulled her into his arms, began to kiss her face, stroke her silver-blonde hair. She struggled with him, finally managed to push him away, and exclaimed, 'Don't ever do that again! *Ever*, do you hear me?'

'I'm sorry, I didn't mean to grab you so hard.'

'Just don't ever touch me. Not ever,' she cried, her voice shrill.

'Tessa, I'm sorry. I know I surprised you, I surprised myself. Look, I love you. Let's try again, let's start over, forget this divorce. Let's be a family again. The three of us.'

Tessa stood in the middle of the hall gaping at him in fury, finding it hard to believe what she was hearing. The gall of him. He was preposterous. Suddenly, something in her snapped, and she cried, 'Start again! You've got to be out of your mind. After all you've done to me – humiliated me, abused me, mentally *and* physically, stolen Adele. You're insane to think I'd even consider it!'

'Tessa, please, you're exaggerating as usual.'

'Please leave,' she said, her tone icier than ever; she walked over to the front door and opened it. 'Leave, Mark. *Now*.'

He threw her a sour look and left without uttering another word, the set of his mouth mean and ugly, his eyes filled with anger.

She slammed the door behind him and slid the bolt, then turned and ran upstairs. She was shaking inside, and still furious, but she managed to push the bland expression onto her face before she went back into the playroom.

India rose when she saw her, and hurried across the floor. 'Is something wrong?' she asked, knowing there was. Her eyes gave her away.

'He just suggested we get back together. Can you believe that bastard? He tried to pretend *he* didn't do anything to ruin our marriage.'

CHAPTER FIFTEEN

Gideon Harte stood in the lobby of the Dorchester Hotel waiting for Evan.

Glancing at the clock above the revolving door, he saw that it was ten minutes to one, and he knew that she would come rushing in at any moment. Evan was punctual. It was another characteristic they had in common, and it was one which pleased him.

He wished they were having lunch alone. The idea of meeting her parents had suddenly lost its appeal, perhaps because it had assumed such enormous proportions in the past few days. In fact, he wished they hadn't come to London at all. Their presence was making her nervous and distracted; she hadn't been herself since their arrival, and she was growing more ambivalent about telling her father the truth about Robin Ainsley.

Initially he had said whatever decision she made about that was all right with him. But he had come to realize how much the truth really mattered. He felt it was important her father knew he was part Harte, as she herself was.

This train of thought dissipated as she came whirling through the revolving door, a smile illuminating her face when she saw him. He thought how pretty she looked in a loose, rather floaty frock made of pale-blue cotton. She had on very high-heeled blue sandals, which made her appear even more willowy; there were smokey-blue beads at her neck and on her ears and these echoed the colour of her large, wide-set eyes.

'I'm not late, Gid, am I?' she asked, her smile wide and warm.

He shook his head. 'Early, in fact. But where are your parents?'

'I told them to meet us here at one-fifteen. I just wanted a few minutes alone with you. I haven't seen you since Thursday night and I've missed you.'

'Me too, you.' Taking her arm he went on, 'Let's go and sit over there on the sofa, shall we?'

'I told Mom that we'd be in the Grill, so we might as well go in.'

After being seated at Gideon's favourite table in a corner, he ordered a bottle of Veuve Clicquot and then sat back and looked at her, a smile on his face. 'You look wonderful, Evan,' he began, and then stopped abruptly. The smile slipped. 'You're not wearing your ring,' he said, staring at her left hand.

She stared back at him, her face suddenly colouring a bright pink.

'Evan, you haven't told them, have you?'

'Look, Gideon, please don't be angry, but I just didn't dare say anything on Friday night. I hadn't seen them for months, and Dad was definitely in a peculiar mood, to say the least, and I didn't want to hit them with that straight away. I wanted to wait until after they met you.'

'Oh, and does that make a difference to you? What they think of me? Will you change your mind about me if they don't approve?'

'Don't be silly, of course I won't,' she said in a low voice, leaning closer to him. 'You know I love you, that I want to spend the rest of my life with you. But my father's always been a bit . . . well, possessive of me, and he's got to adjust to the fact that I'm not going home, that I'm going to be living in London. He'll have to come to terms with that.'

'Yes, he certainly will.' His green eyes narrowed darkly.

'Please try and see it from my point of view, Gideon. Please, darling.'

He sighed. 'I suppose I understand . . . well, a little bit. And what about Robin? Have you told him about Robin Ainsley, have you told your father he's actually a Harte, a member of the family he loves to hate?'

She bit her lip. 'No, I haven't. I just felt it was better, kinder, not to bring up all of this stuff when he'd just seen me for the first time in eight months. Mom was great, of course, and I had lunch with her yesterday. She knows how much I care for you. I know she's expecting me to marry you, Gid, and she gives us her blessing. She said so.'

'That's good to know,' he muttered, the tension in his shoulders relaxing. 'I'm not being difficult, Evan, I simply want them to know about our engagement so that I can tell my parents before someone else does. After all, the cousins are in on our secret which of course isn't one anymore.'

Always cued in to his moods, she was sorry his voice wasn't calmer. 'I promise I'll tell them soon, and that I'll talk to my father about Robin as well –'

The arrival of a waiter with the champagne interrupted this conversation, and once it had been poured and they had clinked glasses, taken a sip, she said, 'I hope he understands about Glynnis and Robin . . . I hope he won't be terribly upset.'

'I suppose it will be a shock,' Gideon murmured a little grudgingly, and then he deftly changed the subject when he started to talk about the newspapers he ran, and his plans for the next few months.

Gideon was surprised. Owen and Marietta Hughes were pleasant, and certainly her father didn't seem to be quite the curmudgeon Evan had made him out to be.

Gideon had done a double-take when they had first arrived at the table and Evan was introducing them. Her father was the spitting image of Gideon's great-uncle, Robin Ainsley, and it was something of a shock to see the strong family resemblance. It was much more pronounced in her father than it was in Evan. There was no doubt that Owen

Hughes was actually a Harte. Tall, slender, good-looking, he had Robin's aquiline features and dark hair flecked with grey. It took Gideon only a moment to recognize that he had a very strong likeness to his own great-grandfather, Winston Harte the first, the brother of Emma.

Her mother was a bit of a surprise, too. A pretty woman in a soft and feminine way, she looked very young, and there was no hint of the manic depressive about her. In fact, she was full of smiles and genial good humour. That was the medication kicking in, no doubt about that, Gideon decided.

After the waiter had served them champagne, and they had all toasted each other, there was a bit of small talk about the weather and such, which suddenly seemed endless to him.

Eventually Gideon managed to get all of that out of the way, and he said, 'I had hoped to take you out to the Waterside Inn at Bray for lunch, but unfortunately, I'm working today. I have to get back to the papers fairly early, and it's a bit of a drive there and back. But another time perhaps, I know how much you like the water and sailing, Mr Hughes.'

'I do, yes,' Owen Hughes said, 'and it would've been great on a hot day like this. On the other hand, I've always had a soft spot for the Grill here at the Dorchester. My mother brought me here when I was a little boy.'

'Did she really!' Gideon exclaimed, and threw a pointed look at Evan, who glanced away, not wanting to have prolonged eye contact. Also, she was truly startled. She hadn't known her father had come back to London as a child; what else didn't she know, she wondered.

'I came to England with her several times in the fifties,' her father was telling Gideon, and Evan pricked up her ears alertly; her mother, who was staring at her intently, gave her a knowing look.

Evan ignored this, and said, 'I was telling Gideon you were planning a trip to France, Dad, and he wondered if you were intending to go to the south at all?'

'Probably. I'd like to take your mother to Monte Carlo, she's never been there.'

'It's very built-up these days,' Gideon murmured, 'a pile of concrete, to be exact. But if you do go, perhaps Evan and I could join you for a couple of days.'

'That'd be nice,' Owen responded, in a voice so low it was almost inaudible. It was obvious he was taken aback by Gideon's suggestion.

'It would be absolutely lovely,' Marietta jumped in, smiling hugely. 'We haven't had a vacation together for years, have we, Evan?'

'No, Mom.'

'I thought you couldn't get away from work,' her father said, his eyes on her.

'I can't, at least not when you're planning to be in Paris, when you're touring around, visiting Normandy and such. But later on I think I can swing a long weekend.'

'Sounds good,' her father answered in a clipped fashion.

Gideon said, 'Shall we order? I'm not rushing you, but I do like to have a leisurely lunch on Sunday, don't you, Mrs Hughes?'

'I certainly do, Gideon, and please call me Marietta.'

'I will, thank you very much.'

'I know this is one of your favourite places, Gideon, Evan told me that. So what do you recommend?' Marietta asked, looking at her daughter's boyfriend, liking him a lot, liking his clean-cut good looks, his direct approach, his straightforwardness. She prayed Owen wouldn't spoil things today by being grumpy and grudging with Evan, because she intuitively knew that these two were very much a couple, and that the relationship was extremely serious. But had Owen picked that up? She wasn't sure.

Gideon, studying the menu, looked up and smiled at Marietta. 'I tend to have the same things all the time,' he explained. 'Usually smoked salmon or potted shrimps, something like that to start with, and then I'm afraid I always fall for what's on the trolley, either roast lamb or roast beef.'

'And Yorkshire pudding,' Evan interjected. 'However, Gideon says there's only one place where they make real Yorkshire pudding and that's Yorkshire.'

Gideon laughed. 'I'm prejudiced, I'm afraid, being a Yorkshireman born and bred. They do a sort of popover here and it's very good, really it's very good.'

'I think I'll have the roast beef,' Evan said. 'What about you, Mom? And Dad?'

'The same,' her mother answered.

Owen nodded. 'That's my choice, too, and I'll start with the Morecambe Bay potted shrimps.' Looking at Marietta he murmured, 'Why don't you try them, dear?'

'Thanks, Owen, but I'd prefer the asparagus. Cold with vinaigrette.'

Once all of the orders had been taken, Gideon said, 'Talking about Yorkshire pudding, I do hope you'll come up to stay with my parents at Allington Hall, or perhaps at Pennistone Royal with my aunt, Paula O'Neill and her husband Shane. I know they'd love it.' When there was no response from anyone, Gideon pressed on undeterred. 'It's such beautiful country, most especially the Dales where we all live. Have you ever been to Yorkshire?'

'Yes, I have,' Owen said without thinking, startling himself as well as everyone else. In order to cover his embarrassment at blurting this out, and wanting to cut off any further discussions about Yorkshire, he swiftly added, 'I did quite a lot of touring around with my mother when I was a little boy. She wanted me to know her country. And so she took me up to Scotland, and also to Wales. She was Welsh, you know.'

'So I'd heard,' Gideon murmured, and gave Evan a sly look.

Evan ignored Gideon; she was almost afraid to look at him in case she began to laugh. So instead she said to her father, 'Fancy that, Dad, you *are* secretive! You never told me you'd toured the length and breadth of Great Britain. Did he tell you, Mom?'

'No, he didn't,' Marietta said, and she spoke the truth.

'You'd like Pennistone Royal,' Gideon went on, determined to catch Owen out if he could, to make him say something about the Hartes. 'It's a wonderful house, very old, and one of England's great stately homes. But what you'd love about it, I think, is the furniture. My great-grandmother, Emma Harte, was an expert on Georgian furniture, and she collected it. I understand from Evan that you're also an expert on this period.'

'Yes, I am considered such,' Owen said, afraid to say too much in case he let something slip that he shouldn't.

During the first course, as she cut into her thinly-sliced smoked salmon, Evan looked first at her mother, then at her father, and said, 'It would be nice if you could visit Yorkshire. We could have a weekend there together.'

'I'm not sure,' her father murmured in that very low voice again.

'I think it would be wonderful,' Marietta exclaimed, flashing a bright smile at Gideon and Evan who sat opposite her. 'And you know, Owen, you could do a bit of business up there perhaps, go to a few antique shops. I've heard they're very good. You might find some Georgian pieces.'

'Oh yes, especially in Harrogate,' Evan interjected. 'Think about it, Dad.'

'I will,' he muttered and concentrated on his potted shrimps.

Halfway through the first course, Gideon asked,

'Would anyone like wine? Since we're all having the roast beef I think a full-bodied red would be excellent.'

'Thank you,' Marietta said, once more taking the lead, wanting to put this nice young man at ease.

Gideon motioned for the wine waiter, and after studying the wine list he finally ordered a Château Duhart-Milon, one of his father's favourites. To Owen he explained, 'Dad likes this wine very much, and I'm sure you will, Mr Hughes. It's from the Domaines Barons de Rothschild, and it's superb.'

Owen merely nodded. He had a sinking feeling that this young man, with his looks, magnetism, self-confidence and personal charm, had undoubtedly conquered his daughter. It made him sad that she was lost to him, and in a funny way he resented Gideon for being who and what he was: a Harte and a superior Harte at that. The chatting went on around him; he was lost in his morose thoughts.

It was towards the end of the lunch that Gideon suddenly lifted his glass and, looking at Owen and Marietta, he said slowly, 'I would like you to join me in a toast to Evan.'

All three of them were startled, especially Evan, but they picked up their glasses and stared back at Gideon.

He said softly, in a loving voice, 'Here's to you, Evan, the most unique woman I've ever met, and my future wife.'

There was a stunned silence.

Gideon, fully aware that he had dropped a bombshell, glanced at Owen and Marietta and said, 'One of the reasons I wanted to have lunch with you both today is to tell you that Evan and I are engaged. I do hope you approve.'

Owen, totally astonished, looked at Evan furiously, then cleared his throat several times. Finally he said in an uptight tone, 'Why yes, if that's what Evan wants.'

He scrutinized his daughter with a degree of intensity, and so did Gideon, turning to face her. Gideon noticed at once how pale her face had become, but otherwise her expression was unreadable.

Marietta, aware of the enormous discomfort between her husband and her daughter, jumped to the rescue yet again. 'Congratulations to the two of you, Evan, Gideon! You have our blessing. We're delighted for you.' Disregarding her husband's obvious anger and disgruntlement, the dark look on Owen's face, she asked, 'And when will you make it official?'

'Why right now, Marietta,' Gideon responded, and then turning once more to look at Evan, he said in a light, bland voice, 'What a pity you're not wearing your ring, darling.'

Swallowing, knowing that there was no use fighting him, she murmured, 'Oh, but I have it with me, Gideon,' and she fumbled in her handbag as she spoke.

A moment later it was gleaming on the third finger of her left hand, and being admired by her mother, who was duly impressed by the size of the

sapphire and the surrounding diamonds. 'It's beautiful, Evan,' she said. 'You're a very lucky girl.'

Done, Gideon thought with a spurt of satisfaction. And done in the best Harte style.

Gideon was just leaving his office for the late afternoon editorial meeting when his cell-phone began
to shrill. Realizing he had forgotten to put it in his
pocket, he rushed back to his desk and grabbed it.
'Hello?'

'It's me,' Evan said.

'Hi, sweetheart, I can't really talk now. I'm
running late for the editorial meeting. The traffic
was lousy from the Dorchester. Is it important?'

'I think so. Gideon, how *could* you?'

'How could I what?' he asked mildly, although
he knew exactly what she meant and he could tell
she was annoyed.

'Just announce it like that, so unexpectedly and
so bluntly, that we were engaged. I'm really upset
about the way you handled this.'

'Well, you shouldn't be. Your mother is thrilled
and your father didn't look all that unhappy.
Anyway, be —'

'He was really upset that I'd been what he called
sneaky, that I hadn't told him anything in advance.
Actually, the afternoon fell apart and he went off
in a snit.'

'Really. What a sudden change of mood. He
was actually very cordial with me when I left. In
any case, it's over and done with, so now let's
move on.'

'It's hard for me to do that. You didn't even give me a hint you were going to pull this –'

'I didn't pull anything, Evan, I simply spoke the truth,' he snapped, and then softening his voice, he added, 'I think you *must* move on, darling, and push your father's resentment to one side. Look, in a few days you should tell him about Robin Ainsley being his father, get that out of the way once and for all, as well. Wipe this slate clean, so there are no secrets, and I think we'll all be the better for it.'

'I can't tell him about Robin now!' she cried, her voice rising shrilly. 'It'll be all too much for him.'

'I doubt it,' Gideon said coldly. 'I have to go, I'm late for the meeting. They can't start without me. Talk to you later, darling.' He clicked the phone off, slipped it in his pocket and left his office, wondering how a woman as bright and intelligent as Evan could be so wishy-washy and weak-kneed when it came to her father.

He couldn't help wishing she'd behave like a true Harte. He wanted her to be bold and strong like his female cousins. But then she hadn't been brought up a Harte, had she?

This unexpected and troubling thought did not hinder his rush to the editorial meeting. But later that night it did give him reason to pause, and ponder long and hard on his relationship with Evan Hughes.

Tessa stood in the entrance foyer of Niddersley Hall watching Great-Aunt Edwina walk slowly down the grand staircase. She wore a dress of purple silk, her favourite colour, a royal colour, very regal, and she looked both regal and royal, Tessa thought. Her silver hair was swept up in an elegant style, and as usual she was carefully made up and well turned out, looked twenty years younger than her age.

'There you are, Tessa!' she exclaimed as she glided towards her great-niece, who came to meet her. 'You're looking much better than I expected after all you've been through lately. Such an ordeal.'

'Thank you, Great-Aunt Edwina, and *you* look fantastic!' After kissing her aunt on the cheek, Tessa stepped back and eyeing Edwina she couldn't help asking, 'Are those pearls *real*?'

'My dear girl, the whole world knows I never wear anything that's artificial. Of course they're real. I just bought them a few weeks ago. South Sea pearls, perfectly matched. I thought I'd give myself a treat, you see.'

Tessa and her aunt walked into the drawing room; a relatively small room, it was nevertheless elegant with a beautiful Adam fireplace and several tall windows which overlooked the garden.

'Shall we sit over there,' Tessa suggested, indicating an arrangement of chairs near an open window. It had been another hot day, and even though it was now early evening and the sun had set, it was still balmy; Tessa preferred to sit in a cool spot like this.

'Certainly,' Edwina answered, making her way to the chairs grouped around a low coffee table.

'I told Frome to bring us champagne. Or do you prefer something else?'

'That's lovely, thank you.' Tessa seated herself opposite her great-aunt, and said, 'India will be here in a moment. I only had to come from the Harrogate store, she's driving over from Leeds.'

'Yes, she phoned me and said she'd be a bit late, but that's all right, my dear, we can have a little chat while we wait. Ah, there you are, Frome,' she continued as the butler came in carrying an ice bucket and bottle of champagne on a tray. 'We'll both have the champagne, thank you.'

'Yes, m'lady,' Frome answered, and within seconds he was carrying two crystal glasses on a tray across the room to them. They each took a flute and thanked him.

Edwina lifted her glass and, smiling at Tessa, she said, 'Here's to you, Tessa, and a sparkling future.'

Smiling back, Tessa clinked her glass to her aunt's. 'And to your sparkling future, too, Great-Aunt.'

Edwina burst out laughing. 'Well said, little Tessa, well said. Thank you. I certainly don't intend going anywhere just yet, so I'll be around.'

'Obviously,' Tessa shot back, laughing with her. 'When you buy yourself a string of pearls like those, you plan to wear them. I think it's marvellous that you treated yourself, it shows a most positive attitude on your part.'

'I suppose it does.' After taking a sip of the

champagne, Edwina settled herself against the needlepoint cushions in the French armchair, and went on, 'Now what's afoot with that ridiculous fool of a husband of yours? He's got a few screws loose, in my considered opinion.'

'He's very difficult, Great-Aunt, and I agree with you, I think he is a bit off the wall, and –'

'He must be to treat a wonderful girl like you so shabbily. I'm appalled at his behaviour towards you and extremely glad you've taken the steps you have to get a divorce,' Edwina told her rather forcefully.

Tessa explained, 'He'll soon be my ex.'

'Whatever it costs, just get rid of him. He's caused you far too much heartache already. I'm a great believer in divorce, you know. It's ridiculous for a couple to stay together if they're making each other unhappy. I understand he wants a lot.'

Tessa nodded. 'Yes, he does. Mummy's going to get things moving along a bit quicker once she returns from New York next week.'

'Well, as I said, just pay him off, get him out of the way.' Edwina took a sip of champagne, and continued, 'You know, Tessa, everybody has their price and it isn't always money –'

'As your mother always said,' Tessa cut in. 'I know Emma Harte's credo, too.'

'I'm glad to hear it. She was the most remarkable woman, a legend in her own time. You can't go wrong, following her rules. Anyway, I was going to say that there are often other considerations, and several ways to skin a cat.'

'Not with Mark, Great-Aunt Edwina, all he's interested in is money.'

'And a few other things, from what I've heard. Such as wine, women and song, to put it in a polite way.'

'That's true. But I don't care about him anymore. I just want him out of my life.'

'It was rather foolhardy of him to kidnap Adele in that way, asking for trouble.'

'It hasn't done him any good in the eyes of my lawyers – or his own, I might add.'

'I'm sure not.' There was a small pause. Edwina stared at Tessa intently and finally said in a kindly voice, 'I hope he hasn't made you afraid to have another relationship with a man, Tessa. You're young, a very beautiful woman, so you must get over this hurdle as quickly as possible, put it behind you. You must find a way to quell your fears about him taking Adele again, and move on to greener fields.'

'How did you know I fear that?' Tessa asked, studying the older woman, thinking how extraordinary she was for her age. A handsome woman, beautifully dressed and groomed, obviously completely competent and with all of her faculties intact.

'Because it would be natural for any mother to fear another kidnapping when she's dealing with a fool like Mark Longden. But I doubt he'll do it again, once he's been paid off by Paula.'

'I do hope you're right.'

At this moment India came hurrying into the

drawing room, looking flushed and a little out of breath. 'Sorry, Grandma, but the traffic from Leeds was quite impossible tonight.'

'We're not going anywhere,' Edwina murmured, and lifted her face to be kissed. 'Now relax, India dear,' Edwina continued, 'and pour yourself a glass of champagne, it'll be quicker than if we ring for Frome. He's getting a bit old.'

India laughed hilariously. 'Grandma, he's all of fifty if he's a day! Much younger than you.'

'Maybe, but he's a bit of a slowcoach. I'm a lot more sprightly, fast on my feet. Do you prefer something else? Other than a drop of bubbly?'

'Champagne's great, thanks,' India told her and walked over to the chest where the drinks tray stood and poured herself a glass, still laughing. Her grandmother was a hoot: outspoken, blunt to the point of rudeness at times, and something of a character, a true eccentric, in fact. But she was very special, unique, and India adored her. Her father always said they'd thrown the mould away after making his mother.

Returning to the group of chairs, India sat down next to Tessa, lifted her glass, said, 'Cheers,' and took a sip. Then she leaned forward and said to her grandmother, 'Who told you about Russell Rhodes, about my involvement with him, and the stabbing, Grandma?'

'As a matter of fact it was someone who works at Harrogate District Hospital, India, but I did promise to keep a confidence and so I must, my dear.'

India was taken aback and she exclaimed, 'So it wasn't anyone in the family?'

'Not at all. I haven't spoken to Robin or Elizabeth for weeks, and you younger lot don't bother too much with me these days.'

'Oh, Grandma, don't say that, it makes me feel awful.'

'Well, it shouldn't, because I don't mind really, except for you and Tessa, India. You two are my best girls, part Fairley like I am, and I do miss hearing from you both. I feel left out of your lives.'

India looked at Tessa, knowing her cousin felt as guilty as she did.

Before India could say anything, Edwina went on, 'I know he's recovered and that he's going home to Willows Hall tomorrow. Perhaps later this week, if he's up to it, you'll bring Dusty here to meet me. Lunch, tea or dinner, whichever you prefer, my dear.'

'I'll try for dinner, Grandmother, but he's not an easy man.'

'Do your best. I know I bluster a lot, and boast that I'm not going anywhere, but you never know what can happen. Life has a funny way of coming and hitting you in the face when you least expect it.'

'Don't say that!' India cried. 'You'll be here for a long time yet.'

'Let's hope so. Now, do you love this man enough to want to spend the rest of your life with him?' Edwina asked briskly.

India nodded and opened her mouth to say

something but changed her mind and sat very still in the chair, staring at her grandmother silently.

Edwina nodded. 'Not sure about his intentions, eh?'

'You're right as usual, Grandmother,' India admitted ruefully.

'If you want him then it's up to you to get him! That's the way it always is, most men can't make up their minds about women, or about a long-term commitment. Anyway, my dear, if you love him then I trust your judgement. I know he must be a decent man, a man of honour, if you have set your sights on him.'

'Yes, he is. At least, *I* believe he is.'

'Now . . . one of the reasons I wanted to see you, invited you to dinner, is to give you both a gift.' Pushing herself to her feet, Edwina added, 'Follow me, girls,' and marched forward purposefully towards the hall. She crossed it in the same majestic way and went into the library; India and Tessa, both somewhat mystified, followed behind her, exchanging baffled glances.

Taking a key out of her pocket, Edwina sat down behind the huge Georgian partners' desk in front of the bay window and unlocked one of the drawers.

'Don't stand around like that, like a couple of clucking ducks,' she instructed sharply. 'Sit down both of you. On the sofa.'

They did as she asked without uttering a word; they knew it was wise to remain silent, to leave the floor to the Dowager Countess of Dunvale, who obviously was in cracking form tonight.

A moment or two later, after taking various items out of the drawer, Edwina beckoned to India and Tessa. 'Come and help me to carry these things to the coffee table,' she said, rising, picking up one of the items herself.

The two young women joined her and helped to bring them over to the coffee table, and then they all three of them sat down. Edwina was quite certain her granddaughter and great-niece were riddled with curiosity, and she smiled to herself, thinking of the shock they were in for.

Well, it's a nice shock, she said under her breath, knowing she would enjoy these next few moments. This pleased her, since she hadn't enjoyed much lately, in actuality; she had been troubled and disconcerted when she had heard about the abduction of Adele, and, so soon after that, the stabbing of Russell Rhodes, who happened to be her favourite living painter.

Her lovely girls had been at the receiving end of some bad goings on, much to her dismay. She loved them both very much and was exceedingly protective of them; now she wanted to show them her love in a very real way.

Sitting up a little straighter in the chair, Edwina ran her hands over her knees, smoothing the purple silk dress. And then she looked at Tessa.

Slowly, Edwina said, 'You are a few years older than India and therefore I shall talk to you first. Your great-grandmother, Emma Harte, was the most extraordinary woman, and everything you are, everything you have in this world, you truly owe to her, to her brilliance as a businesswoman and entrepreneur, to her doggedness, stamina, hard work, and determination to succeed. And her foresight, of course. You must never forget that, Tessa. Well, let me proceed on another matter . . . many, many years ago my mother gave me a gift. She knew it would be very meaningful to me because I thought of myself as a fully-fledged Fairley, rather than an illegitimate one, which I was. I was also a Harte, but I was a bit of a snob in those days, and liked to think of myself as an aristocratic Fairley, as if such a thing really matters in the long run. Who cares these days?'

Edwina glanced at the items on the coffee table, let out a long sigh, as if remembering something from long ago, and then continued softly: 'The gift my mother gave me many years ago was for Christmas. She knew its meaning would not be lost on me, because it had once belonged to my grandmother Adele Fairley.'

Reaching for one of the items, an extremely old black leather case of a circular shape, Edwina opened it and then placed it on the coffee table again.

Both Tessa and India gasped, then leaned forward to get a better look.

Placed on the black velvet inside the worn leather box was the most beautiful diamond necklace either of them had ever seen. It was in a lacey pattern, fell almost like a bib, and was composed of hundreds of diamonds. It was full of bright white fire, glittering in the lamplight, and it was a magnificent thing to behold.

Both young women looked up at Edwina, who was scrutinizing them in the most thoughtful way. It was India who spoke first, when she said, 'It's simply gorgeous, Grandma, but how did Emma come by it, if it belonged to Adele Fairley?'

'Many years before my mother actually gave the necklace to me, she had bought it at an auction of Adele's jewellery in London. In fact, she bought the entire collection of Adele's jewels.'

'Why was it being sold at auction?' India wondered aloud.

'Because Gerald Fairley needed money to keep his businesses running, and he had inherited his mother's jewellery collection from his father.'

'So Gerald put it up for sale and Emma bought it,' Tessa murmured.

'Yes. I think she saw the irony of it all, as only she could. This necklace,' Edwina indicated it with a finger, 'was Adele's favourite, and when Emma was a little servant girl at Fairley Hall she used to fasten the necklace around her mistress's neck. Years later, she was the owner. What an ironic reversal, eh girls?'

'Yes, indeed,' India said. 'And did Emma enjoy wearing it, too?'

'Oh, she never wore it. Oddly enough, it was never worn by anybody after Adele, until my mother gave it to me. I wore it a few times, and now, Tessa, I am giving it to you.'

'Oh, Great-Aunt Edwina, I can't take it! The necklace should go to India, she's your granddaughter. Thank you, but –'

'No thank you, is that what you're saying?' Edwina asked.

'Absolutely.'

'No, Tessa!' India exclaimed. 'Grandmother should do as she wishes, and she wants you to have it.' Looking at Edwina she added in the most genuine way, 'You must do what you want.'

'There's a real reason why Tessa should have it,' Edwina replied, looking from India to Tessa. 'Jim Fairley was a *legitimate* Fairley, grandson of Edwin, and he was your father, Tess. I think Adele's necklace should therefore be yours. And there's another reason . . . Your mother was very close to Emma. Since Emma ultimately owned the necklace, she might easily have given it to Paula one day, rather than to me.'

'But I –'

Edwina held up her hand. 'Please don't argue with me, Tessa dear. This is my gift to you, because of who you are, a true Fairley through your father. But you must never forget that you are also a Harte, Tessa. Never. I did once and I lived to regret it. I love you, and it's yours.'

'Thank you,' Tessa said a little tremulously, her eyes filling up. She tried to swallow but her throat suddenly ached and she flicked the tears from her lashes, feeling unexpectedly emotional.

'Now to you, my beauty,' Edwina went on, looking over at her granddaughter. 'The rest of the jewellery in those old boxes belonged to Adele, too, it's the collection Emma bought at that auction long ago, and she left everything to me in her will. You can choose anything you want, India, but I thought you might like this.' Bending over the coffee table, Edwina picked up a tall red-leather case and opened it.

Again the two young women gasped in surprise and stared at each other and then at the old dowager countess.

'It's for me, Grandma?' India whispered, her eyes wide, full of astonishment.

'If you want it, my dear.'

India was silent. She simply bent over the coffee table and picked up the choker. It was made entirely of pearls and it was very wide, in the Edwardian style. At its centre was a huge sapphire surrounded by five rows of large rose-cut diamonds; the whole centrepiece was oval in shape, and, like the diamond necklace, it was a truly magnificent piece.

'I thought it would suit you, India, since you have a long, swanlike neck. There's another box there, containing the matching sapphire earrings. Oh, and Tessa, there are diamond drop earrings to match your necklace. Now why don't you rummage among the smaller cases and find them.' Edwina sat back, smiling.

'Is this really for me, Grandma?' India asked, her voice quavering ever so slightly. She was awed by the choker.

'It is, my darling, because I love you very much. You, too, are a Fairley through me, and you should also have something that belonged to your great-great-grandmother.'

'Thank you, thank you so much,' India said, and putting the necklace down in its box she went to her grandmother and embraced her, her eyes damp, so touched was she.

Tessa followed her, and kissed her aunt, and then Edwina began to laugh, delighted to witness their shock, their pleasure, and their obvious gratitude. 'There's a mirror over there. Why don't you girls try them on?'

India, who was wearing a black dress with a scooped-out neckline, found that the choker went on easily, and she turned and said to her grandmother, 'How does it look? It's so beautiful, isn't it?'

'It suits you perfectly, India. I was absolutely right, choosing it for you. Come here, let me look at you properly.'

Hurrying over, India stood in front of Edwina, who nodded her approval. 'It's absolutely perfect on that long neck of yours, my dear.'

'Thank you again, Grandmother, it's so generous of you.'

'I'm having trouble with this necklace,' Tessa said, over her shoulder. 'It doesn't seem to fall properly.'

India ran across the room, and unzipped the back of Tessa's white dress. 'Slide the dress down a little bit, off your shoulders, then the necklace should sit properly.' Tessa did as her cousin told her, and then went to show Edwina.

'What do you think, Great-Aunt Edwina? Does it suit me?'

Edwina nodded, and unexpectedly her eyes welled. 'Why, the two of you suddenly look like beautiful ethereal beings from another age, a long age ago, and you know something, you both look more like Adele than ever. It's your blonde hair and silvery eyes . . .' Edwina groped in her pocket for a handkerchief and blew her nose. Recouping quickly, she said in a more businesslike tone, 'The jewellery is my legacy to the two of you, and the rest of Adele's collection I will give to your mother, India, and to Paula.'

Now Edwina stood up. 'Let's go in for supper,' she said in a quiet voice. 'I think I'm really quite hungry.'

'Yes, let's do that, Grandmother,' India agreed, 'but perhaps we ought to lock the other leather cases away, don't you think?'

'Good idea,' Tessa said, taking off the diamond bib, placing it in the box and then fastening her dress. She suddenly threw a pointed look at India, and turned to Edwina, 'Don't you have a safe here, Great-Aunt?'

'You don't think I keep all of this priceless stuff lying around, do you, you silly girl? Jack Figg would have my guts for garters, if I did.'

Tessa and India burst out laughing at the same time, and India asked, 'So who sent Jack to see you?'

'Gideon Harte. Who else? He's got a soft spot for me. And Jack was very pleased to see I had three safes. One for documents, one for jewellery and one for the silver. He was most impressed.'

'I bet he was,' Tessa laughed.

'Oh, Grandma, you're such a scream.' As she spoke India began to carry the cases over to the desk, and Tessa helped.

Edwina watched them, her face glowing with pleasure.

CHAPTER SIXTEEN

The paintings were beautiful, landscapes which Dusty had painted earlier in his career, dominating the walls of the drawing room at Willows Hall.

India stood in front of each one for several minutes, studying the scenes intently before moving on to the next. There were four altogether, one on each end wall and two hanging on the long back wall, which was intersected by French windows leading out to the terrace and the gardens.

She loved these landscapes, with their lush dark greens and pale-blue skies, light-filled and luminous. His skies reminded her of the sky in the Turner painting that hung at Pennistone Royal. She knew how hard it was to capture light on canvas, and how brilliantly Dusty had achieved it here. She admired the style he painted in, Classical Realism, and he had once mentioned to her that it was hard to master. 'Painting landscapes and people as they are exactly seen by the world is not an easy thing to do,' he had pointed out. She had nodded her understanding, had wanted to tell him how his landscapes of the English countryside resembled the great classical paintings of Constable. But she hadn't dared for fear he thought she was saying he had copied Constable, which he hadn't, of course. He could be touchy.

Over the beautifully-carved white marble fireplace hung a fifth painting. This was a portrait of a beautiful woman dressed in the clothes of the Georgian period. It looked as if it had been painted in the 1700s, but there was Dusty's small signature in the right-hand corner to prove otherwise. It brought to mind George Romney's famous portrait of Lady Hamilton that hung in the Frick Museum in New York. Her maiden name had been Emily Hart, and she had later changed her first name to Emma, and so became Emma Hart, oddly enough, but without the *e* at the end. For that reason, that odd coincidence, Lady Hamilton, Lord Nelson's mistress, had always been of interest to India.

Walking across the floor she went and sat down on the sofa facing the fireplace, gazing up at the portrait of the young woman, but her mind was filled with thoughts of the artist, not the subject.

She had driven to the hospital in Harrogate this morning, picked him up and brought him home to Willows Hall, and after a light lunch, which the housekeeper Angelina had prepared, Dusty had gone to the studio. 'To re-acquaint myself with it,' he had explained, 'to banish the hobgoblins.'

He had not had to tell her he wanted to go there alone; she understood that. This was one of India's great assets, her awareness of another person's moods, her ability to understand them, even to second guess them, to empathize: reasons everyone in the family loved her.

She heard footsteps in the marble hall, and she turned her head towards the handsome walnut doors, which stood open. Her face lit up at the thought that it was Dusty, but the smile faltered slightly as Paddy Whitaker hove into view.

'I'm not disturbing you, am I, Lady India?' he asked from the entrance to the room, his manners scrupulous, as usual.

'No, you're not, Paddy,' she answered, 'I was just sitting here admiring the portrait over the fireplace.'

'Yes, it is rather lovely,' he agreed, now stepping into the room. 'Mr Rhodes was wondering if you could come over to the studio . . . he just buzzed me on the intercom in the butler's pantry. There isn't one in here, you see.'

'Of course,' she replied and jumped up, walked around the sofa towards the double doors.

'This is the first opportunity I've had to thank you for putting me in touch with Jack Figg,' Paddy said. 'He came over to look at Willows Hall, and then sent in a team of specialists. Remarkable blokes. You know, I've long been after Mr Rhodes to spruce up the security here. Anybody can wander in whenever they want. At least they could. Things have already improved.' The house-manager looked directly at her, and added, 'You saved Mr Rhodes's life, Lady India, and for that we are all grateful, very grateful indeed.'

Dusty Rhodes was standing near the easel when she walked into the studio, and he stepped forward, stretched out his hands to her, smiling broadly. 'It's all right in here, India, after all. Perfectly all right. No hobgoblins, no bad vibes.'

She took hold of his hands, smiling back, allowed herself to be pulled forward, closer to him. Dusty leaned into her and said against her cheek, 'Thank you.' Then he moved away, looked into her face, and added softly, 'It's been such a difficult time for you. I'm sorry.'

'Dusty, there's nothing to be sorry about! It happened. Thank God you're all right. You *are* all right?'

'Yes. Are you?' he asked carefully.

'*Absolutely.* I'm fine . . . as long as you're fine.'

'I thought I might feel uneasy in here, but I don't. So I can happily go back to work tomorrow, India my sweet.'

'Are you sure of that?'

'Oh, yes, very sure. Anyway, I paint with my right hand, not my left.'

She nodded, and walked across the studio, sat down in one of the armchairs.

After a moment or two loitering near the easel, Dusty came and joined her, took the other chair and stretched out his legs. There was a small silence before he said, 'I haven't felt up to talking about the stabbing before now, even though I know you've been anxious to discuss it.'

'Yes, I have needed to talk it through with you, Dusty.'

'The day it happened it wasn't possible, and since then I haven't been in the right frame of mind to explain, but it's okay now. There's one thing I must make clear, India. I *do* know her . . . the woman who stabbed me.'

India simply nodded.

He said: 'We were involved once, a few years ago now, but only for a short while. We split up about a year and a half ago. She's a drug-addict, very self-destructive, and, to be honest, try though I did to help her, she just couldn't stay away from smack-heroin. I hadn't seen her for a year, until about six months ago, when her mother phoned me up. Melinda, that's her name, was really bad, and her mother needed help to get her into a clinic. I did my best to find the right place, and fortunately she agreed to go into detoxification. I thought it was all going well until she showed up here, then went berserk when she saw you.'

'She must be still involved with you,' India suggested, her eyes on his.

'I dunno, maybe. And how she ever got out of the clinic I'll never know,' he answered, slightly embarrassed.

'Is she back there now?' India probed.

'Yes. Her mother's a good woman and she found Melinda within a day, convinced her to go back to the clinic. She put herself under the care of Dr Jeffers again.'

'Can she get better, Dusty?'

'If she wants to, and if she works at it. I hope she can, for her sake.'

'Well so do I.' India cleared her throat, gave him a very direct look and asked, 'You didn't press charges did you?'

'How could I, India? She was off her head that day! I'm convinced she had access to drugs of some kind, and you know full well she was going for the painting, not me.'

'Yes, I do,' she replied softly. Biting her lip, she added in a low voice, 'I think you did the right thing, actually.'

He looked at her alertly and held himself still, conscious of the worried expression on her face, the lack of energy when she spoke. He hoped she wasn't going to tell him that she was going her own way. He wanted her to stick around, to be part of his life; he had known that in the hospital, and now he truly understood that she had become important to him. He leaned across the space between the chairs, took hold of her hand. 'It wouldn't have been a good idea to bring a case against her, darling.'

'I know that, and I also know that stabbing you was an accident.' India swallowed hard before asking, 'Do you think she's going to be a pest, though? She could make your life miserable.'

'And yours, too, that's what you're getting at, isn't it?'

'Yes, it is. I'm concerned for both of us, Dusty.'

'She's going to be in the clinic for a long time. Also, thanks to your bloke, Jack Figg, there's no way she, or anyone else, can get onto the estate without being spotted. Security's tight.'

India began to laugh. 'Poor Jack undertook to do something for Linnet, and now he's become the security expert for the entire family, and you, too. Oh dear, Jack must be cursing us all.'

Hearing the laughter, seeing the sudden cheery smile, Dusty immediately felt a lightening of his spirit. Everything was going to be all right with India and him, he felt certain of that. Wanting now to please her, he said, 'What was it you told me earlier? About going to have dinner with your grandmother?'

India exclaimed, 'Would you go?'

'She sounds like a gutsy lady, just my type, don't you think?'

'She is. And she'll be thrilled. Whenever you feel up to it, she'd love us to go to supper. She's not far away, between Harrogate and Knaresborough. Can I tell her yes? Maybe over the weekend?'

'You can tell her yes,' he responded, smiling and then standing up. 'Come on, let's go back to the house.'

They left the studio hand in hand and walked in the direction of the back terrace. India was thinking how pleased her grandmother would be to meet Dusty.

And he was thinking how cowardly he had been not to tell India he had a child by Melinda. He hoped to God the press wouldn't find out and make splashy headlines out of the story.

Fingers crossed, he said to himself. *Fingers crossed.*

'I do like this suite,' Lorne announced in his mellifluous voice, walking through the large sitting room and opening the door at the other end. 'Oh, Tessa, *look*, here's another bedroom. Well, my darling, this is a treat.' He swung around to face his twin sister, and added, 'When I spoke to Dad in New York the other day he said he'd made sure we had a large suite we could share, and he's done us proud.'

'And then some,' Tessa agreed, glancing around the beautifully-furnished sitting room of the Paris O'Neill Hotel at the very end of Avenue Montaigne. 'And it's nice to have that bird's eye view of the Eiffel Tower.'

Hurrying to her brother, she hugged him. 'I'm glad I came with you, Lorne. Thanks for making me. I've been very down, so I think this trip *will* cheer me up, like you said.'

'Just as long as you're going to relax and not worry about Adele. She's absolutely as safe as houses with Elvira and Linnet at Pennistone Royal, and Evan's there as well, isn't she?'

'Yes, she's been working at the Leeds store with India, but I suppose India's staying with Dusty Rhodes at the moment, and not at Pennistone Royal. Gideon and Julian will be spending the weekend with Evan and Linnet, they're arriving tomorrow night, Linnet told me. So I'm fine with it, honestly. Now, which bedroom do you want?'

Lorne glanced over his shoulder, looking into the room he'd just discovered, and said, 'I think this is the more feminine of the two, and the larger. Why don't you take this one, Tessa, and I'll use the one at the other end of the sitting room.'

The doorbell rang and Lorne went to answer it. He ushered in the bellboy with the bags, directed him on the placement of the luggage, and tipped him.

Alone again with Tessa, Lorne said, 'Now, Tessa my darling, I want you to get all spruced up. We've got a special evening ahead of us.'

'We do? Where are we going? You didn't mention anything before on the plane coming to Paris.'

'I thought it would be a nice surprise. First we're going to a book party – a sort of cocktail party and book-signing combined – and after that we're going on to dinner as guests of the author.'

'Who's the author? I suppose it's a beautiful woman, knowing you, brother of mine,' Tessa murmured, throwing him a pointed look.

'No,' Lorne said, shaking his head, smiling at her, his eyes full of mischief. 'It's Jean-Claude Deléon.'

Staring hard at him, Tessa frowned. 'You say his name as if I should know him. Do I?'

'You did meet him once. Briefly. At an opening of mine. But I don't know that he registered on you that night. However, you should know him,

Tessa, since he's the most famous intellectual in France after Bernard-Henri Lévy.'

'I've never heard of him either. Who's Bernard-Henri Lévy?'

'Oh, Tess, don't be such a dunce. Lévy is the *first* most famous intellectual in France, and look, both men are renowned, they're celebrities.'

'I don't think I want to go. This party's *pas ma tasse de thé.*'

'It *is* your cup of tea, don't be so silly. Anyway, the party's seven to nine. So we'll go at eight-fifteen for forty-five minutes, then go on to dinner with him and a small group of his friends.'

'Even forty-five minutes sounds too long to me. Can't I come for the last ten minutes?'

'No, you can't,' he exclaimed sharply. 'It's about time you got out and about. We're in Paris, you agreed to do whatever I wanted before we came, so we're going to the book-signing. At eight-fifteen.'

'All right, all right, don't get your knickers in a twist!' she exclaimed, and glanced at her watch. 'It's six-thirty, an hour earlier in England, so I'm going to phone Elvira and Adele, and then I'll get ready.'

'I want you to look gorgeous and glamorous,' Lorne instructed, and hurried to his bedroom to get ready himself.

An hour later Tessa stood staring at herself in the bathroom, the walls of which were entirely mirrored. Turning this side and that, she was wondering if she had chosen the right outfit.

Perhaps she should have worn something a little more dressy for the book party. Lorne had told her that Jean-Claude Deléon was a national celebrity, and a special favourite amongst the chic in the worlds of literature, theatre and society. Therefore it would be full of sophisticated writers and intellectuals and the beau monde of Paris, as well as actors. And certainly this outfit was simple, to say the least.

And yet her reflection now told her that she looked pretty, and this pleased her. She hadn't felt pretty in the longest time, weighed down by worries about the divorce, her sense of failure that the marriage had ended. And then there had been the dreadful experience of Adele's abduction; she could not deny that the fear had taken its toll, rendered her helpless at times.

One of the reasons she had chosen the outfit she was wearing was the weather. It was as hot here as it was in London, and a short while ago, as she had looked over the clothes she had brought with her, she had settled on this skirt and top made of white voile. The voile was gauzy and light as air, the three-quarter-length skirt, that fell to just above her ankles, was relatively full and intersected with bands of narrow lace. Each band was set into the voile at intervals from the hip down, and the same narrow lace trimmed the hemline. The matching top was sleeveless and had a draped neck line that was flattering to her, very becoming, she thought. A white leather belt clinched her waist and matched her high-heeled sandals, and her only jewellery was a watch and chandelier earrings made of pearls.

Glancing at herself one more time, she nodded, decided she'd done the best she could, and went back into the bedroom. Picking up a small white leather purse, she opened the door to the sitting room and walked in.

Lorne was speaking on the phone, and he looked across the room as he heard the door opening. 'Got to go, Phil. My date's arrived. See you tomorrow,' he murmured and hung up.

Coming towards her in long strides, her brother let out a low wolf-whistle, and exclaimed, 'You've done me proud, Ancient One! You look absolutely bloody wonderful!'

Tessa laughed. 'And you don't look so bad yourself, Lorne Fairley. Now isn't it great that you're wearing black. We blend very well, wouldn't you say?'

'I would. And thank God I didn't wear my white shirt and trousers, we'd have looked like some awful double act, the *two* of us in white.'

'Never,' she shot back. 'We could never look *awful*, Lorne. I might, but not you, sweetie pie.'

'Oh, you're just prejudiced because you're related to me. Little *me*, a famous actor,' he said in his self-deprecating way, laughing. 'Now, come on, let's get a move on, I don't want to get there any later than eight-fifteen.'

'But it's early, only twenty to eight –'

'Ah, but the traffic is worse here than London,' he cut in. 'And we have to get to the Faubourg Saint-Germain.'

'So come on then, slowcoach, let's get going,' Tessa replied, and hurried towards the door of the suite. 'I'm assuming you arranged for us to have a car.'

'Of course we've got wheels, silly girl,' he exclaimed, taking hold of her arm and opening the door at the same time. 'I'm very well organized. The Harte training, you know.'

She looked up at him and began to laugh, suddenly feeling happy for the first time in ages, happy to be with someone who cared about her, loved her as Lorne did, and to be in Paris, a city she had a very soft spot for. Their mother had brought them to Paris when they were quite young, and they had been coming here ever since, often on their way to the south of France and the Villa Faviola, which they visited several times a year. As they went down in the lift she felt a sudden sense of anticipation, and wondered why.

Once they were settled in the car and the driver was edging away from the hotel, Tessa said, 'I like the seventh arrondissement, in fact I've often thought I'd like to have an apartment in that district. Actually, anywhere on the Left Bank would be fine by me, I've always enjoyed it, felt at home there.'

Lorne was taken aback, and he looked at her in surprise, and exclaimed, 'Anywhere around the Faubourg Saint-Germain costs an arm and a leg, but those private houses are quite beautiful.'

'I wasn't talking about a private house, just a

little garret for me and my child. It might be a nice escape from time to time.'

'Well, why not,' he murmured, wondering if she was serious. Then he said, 'I like the area, too, because it's such a great mix, an enclave for aristocrats and a haven for students, artists and writers. And aside from all the historic buildings such as Napoleon's tomb, the French Academy and the Rodin Museum, there are two of the most famous hangouts for writers and artists, the Café des Deux Magots and the Café de Flore. Both of which I love.'

'I know, and what about all the little antique shops, and bistros and art galleries? It'd be a wonderful place to have a little hideaway around there – it's charming.'

'If you really mean it, we can look at some real estate in the next few days. Actually, I'd enjoy it,' Lorne remarked, deciding to call her bluff, still wondering if she was merely daydreaming.

'Maybe we can do that; it would be fun, a little adventure,' Tessa murmured, then said, 'When actually do you have to check in for work?'

'Shooting starts on Monday, but I'm not on call until Wednesday morning. Why?'

'No reason, you hadn't really said and I just wondered. Anyway, Lorne, tell me about Jean-Claude Deléon.'

'I've told you.'

'No, you haven't. All you said is that he's famous, a celebrity, an intellectual, and a good friend of yours. Tell me a bit more about him, so I don't feel a total fool when I meet him.'

'Let me see . . . he's a journalist as well as an author of books, and he also lectures. He's considered to be one of the great modern thinkers in France today, and he's certainly thought of as a philosopher, ranks second to Lévy. He's genial, charming, a great bloke. You'll like him, and I think you'll enjoy the evening.'

'How do you know him?'

'I met him in the south of France a few years ago, when I was staying at Villa Faviola with Gideon, Toby, Uncle Winston and Dad. If you remember, we had that all-male weekend together. Jean-Claude came over with one of Toby's friends, and we hit it off. Spent a lot of time talking about the theatre and films. And then whenever he was in London he called me, and we got together if we could.'

'And is there a Madame Deléon?'

'No, there isn't. And I don't think there ever has been. To my knowledge Jean-Claude has never been married. Mind you, he does have quite a reputation . . . as being something of a ladies' man.'

'Oh, so he's young then?' Tessa asked.

'Maybe he's forty-nine, fifty, I'm not sure.'

'And where are we going to dinner after the party?'

'Tessa, darling, I've no idea. He simply said, "Bring your sister to the book party and afterwards you'll both join me for dinner with a few friends." So your guess is as good as mine. We'll just have to wait and see.'

CHAPTER SEVENTEEN

He saw her the moment she walked in. A vision in white. Ethereal, almost otherworldly. He moved his head slightly, to see her better. He knew at once who she was: Tessa Fairley, Lorne's twin sister. Lorne was holding her elbow, moving her through the group clustered near the door, moving her towards him, bringing her to him.

He was sitting at a *bureau plat* at the far end of the grand entrance foyer, in one of the great private homes on the Faubourg Saint-Germain, signing his latest book. Except that he wasn't signing at this moment. He was sitting waiting for the woman in white, the most beautiful woman he had ever seen, breathtaking in her beauty.

As she drew nearer her eyes met his, registered his concentrated stare, and she blinked, appeared to recoil for a split second, but she continued to walk towards him and her eyes never left his.

The chattering around him became just a dim noise in the background; no other person present interested him any longer. Only this girl, for that is how he saw her, so young, so fresh, so innocent-looking, a little unworldly even.

He was suddenly on his feet, walking around the writing table, waiting for her to come to him.

'Jean-Claude, good evening,' Lorne said, as they drew to a stop.

'Ah, Lorne, *quel plaisir de vous voir.*'

The two men shook hands, and then Lorne went on, 'This is my sister, Tessa.' As he spoke Lorne moved her forward slightly, closer to Jean-Claude.

'*Enchanté,*' he said, and switching to English he added, 'I am happy you could come.' To Jean-Claude his voice sounded gruff, even hoarse.

'I'm pleased to meet you, too, Monsieur Deléon,' Tessa answered in a clear light voice, offering her hand to him.

He took it in his, held it tightly.

She smiled at him. The smile, her silvery eyes, that pale, silken hair were heartstopping. His gaze fastened on hers. They were mesmerized by each other, stood staring.

He forgot where he was for a moment. She seemed like a dream . . . Inside him was a mystery he'd never been able to fathom, to solve. In her were all of the answers to those innumerable questions in his mind and heart . . . answers that suddenly seemed just within his grasp. He knew she held the secret to so much, to many things, things which he had been searching for . . .

'I think I've got to break this up, people are staring at the two of you,' Lorne said softly, with a slightly embarrassed laugh.

313

Jean-Claude blinked and murmured, 'Excuse me, I must continue with the signing.' Reluctantly he let go of her hand, smiled at her, and walked around the desk, where he sat down once again. To Lorne he said, 'I shall now sign books for the two of you, *mon ami*.' As he spoke he pulled one towards him, signed it, handed it to Tessa and then signed one for Lorne.

'Thank you,' Tessa said as she opened her book. After reading the inscription she stared at him, her expression puzzled, her eyes questioning.

Jean-Claude looked at her intently. A small smile struck his mouth when he saw the bafflement on her face, and then he looked at Lorne, gave him his signed book. 'Take Tessa to meet our hostess, Marie-Hélène. You've met her with me before. She's in the salon. I have more books to sign. After, we go to dinner.'

'Thanks for the book, Jean-Claude, that sounds great,' Lorne murmured.

Jean-Claude nodded and glanced around. It seemed to him that all those who had crowded around him had dispersed, drifted away, and he shrugged and wondered if he could bring the book-signing to a close sooner rather than later. But no . . . here they came again, once they saw he was alone. His friends and acquaintances flooded around the desk once more, wanting the book, his signature, and so he smiled and signed, and wished he were alone with the young woman who had disappeared from his sight. Later, he thought, I will be with her later.

Lorne had propelled Tessa through the vast and handsome marble foyer with its wall-hung tapestries, crystal chandeliers and elegant furniture, and, once there was enough distance between them and Jean-Claude, he whispered, 'My God, what was that all about? What happened back there?'

'I don't know,' Tessa muttered, and thought: I met Destiny. I met the man who is my destiny. As bizarre as she knew this thought was, she also knew she was right. Unexpectedly a strange calmness settled over her, like a soft transparent veil. And her heart was suddenly perfectly still. Tessa thought of the words he had written in the book and suddenly knew what they meant. He felt the same as she did. *Of course.* But hadn't she known that before reading his words? She had seen it on his face . . . and in his eyes. They had reflected what she was feeling exactly.

'You've suddenly gone very quiet,' Lorne murmured, searching her face. 'Are you all right?'

'I'm perfect,' she replied, and gave him a small smile.

'Then let me take you to meet the hostess of this event.'

'Who *is* Marie-Hélène?'

'She's a socialite, married to a French industrialist, Alain Charpentier, and they're old friends of Jean-Claude's. I think they're coming to dinner, along with another couple, and Jean-Claude has invited his editor as well as us. We're eight.'

'He said you'd met Marie-Hélène before, but do you know any of the others?'

'I've met Alain, her husband, and Jean-Claude's editor, Michel Longeval, several times before, but I don't know who the other couple are. Anyway, we'll soon find out. In the meantime, there's Marie-Hélène over there near the fireplace, let's go and say hello.'

A moment later Tessa was shaking hands with one of the chicest women she had ever seen, including her mother. It was the kind of elegance that only a French woman knew how to achieve. Marie-Hélène, a slender blonde of medium height and indeterminate age, wore a simple black linen sheath with a round neckline and no sleeves, which was obviously haute couture. On her ears were pearl-and-diamond studs, and around her neck a single strand of large pearls – South Sea pearls. They're not as beautiful as Great-Aunt Edwina's, Tessa thought, and this made her smile to herself. She couldn't help wondering, all of a sudden, what Edwina would make of Jean-Claude Deléon.

Their hostess was charm personified and chatted away to Lorne and Tessa in the most entertaining way, while they sipped from their flutes of Dom Pérignon. Lorne was the one who mostly chatted back and, Tessa vaguely noticed, flirted in a mild way with the older woman, who on close inspection looked to be in her late fifties.

She herself nodded occasionally and said only a few words because her concentration was elsewhere. Her mind was on the man in the entrance foyer signing his latest book.

* * *

He elected to sit in the front seat with the driver, whilst Lorne, the editor Michel, and she sat in the back of the car.

Alain and Marie-Hélène had taken the other couple to the restaurant with them. They were called Natalie and Arnaud; she hadn't caught their last name, but they had seemed very pleasant when they were introduced in the house.

Tessa sat staring at Jean-Claude's head, thinking it was very shapely and that he had good hair. Suddenly, as if her eyes had bored into him, he glanced over his shoulder and stared at her. And she stared back. Then without saying a word he swung his head rather abruptly and looked straight ahead through the windscreen, remained totally silent as they drove to the restaurant.

Tessa sat very still, not moving at all, saying nothing, just thinking about him, asking herself what was happening to her? And why now? She half-listened to Lorne and Michel discussing an old French movie they both loved, *Belle de Jour*, but mostly she was thinking about Jean-Claude Deléon, replaying in her head their meeting just over an hour ago. Was that all it was? Only an hour? She felt as if she'd known him always . . . how curious to feel that . . .

Quite innocently she had gone with Lorne to that grand private house on the Faubourg Saint-Germain; a *hôtel particulier* it was called, as were all these grand private homes in Paris, each one hidden behind forbiddingly high stone walls. They had entered the inner courtyard through a black-painted door set in a narrow side wall, crossed the large cobblestone yard, gone through the front door of the house and mounted an imposing staircase which led to the handsome foyer.

Since Lorne had not told her very much about his old friend, she had not known what to expect; much to her astonishment she had found herself mesmerized by him the instant she set eyes on him.

He had been sitting behind the flat-topped writing desk, books stacked in front of him, people clamouring at his shoulder for his attention and his signature. It seemed to her they were full of adulation.

And then he had moved slightly when he had caught sight of her walking towards him with Lorne, and their eyes had locked and held. Immediately she had been drawn to him, pulled closer. Perhaps it was his eyes, which were magnetic, amber-brown and deep set below shapely dark brows that matched his dark hair. His face was well-defined with a strong jaw, broad brow, aquiline nose, generous mouth and a full lower lip. She wasn't sure how old he was, a lot older than her certainly but she didn't care; it was instantly apparent to her that he was all male, masculinity personified, in fact. A man's man.

Suddenly her legs had felt weak and she had trembled inside as he had risen, walked around the desk, stood waiting for her. She had met his intense gaze head on and had found it impossible to look away. They had shaken hands but he had not let go of her fingers, and she hadn't minded that. And they had just stood there oblivious to everyone, gazing at each other. She had realized at that moment how irresistibly drawn to him she was, had felt the strong pull of sexual attraction and desire. And yet it was so much more than a purely physical thing. It was spiritual also. She felt as if he were looking deep into her soul, seeing her innermost self, and she had understood something else . . . understood that they were making a pact with each other, albeit unspoken. At that moment, in that grand entrance foyer, something profound had happened, had connected between them, and she was aware there was already an undercurrent of intimacy even though they had only just met.

Now as she sat in the back of the car, being driven through the busy streets of Paris, an involuntary shiver ran through her. Automatically she straightened on the seat as she admitted to herself that there was something inevitable about them.

Matters were out of her hands. The fates had brought them together. Other forces were at work.

He took them to Taillevent on the rue Laminnais, a restaurant she was familiar with but did not know well. It had been closed for a month's summer vacation since mid-July, had only just re-opened, so there was a flurry of greetings and friendly chatter when they arrived. And he was treated with such deference and awe, as though he were a king, that Tessa was startled. Yet there was a warm familiarity between him and the staff which he appeared to encourage, and she realized there was a sense of humility in him despite his fame. This pleased her, gave her pause for thought.

Once they were shown to the table, Jean-Claude began to seat them, just as Marie-Hélène, her husband, and the other couple arrived. All of a sudden Tessa noticed she would not be sitting next to him; he had placed her at one end of the table, flanked by Alain and Michel, whilst he took the other end, between Marie-Hélène and Natalie.

This meant he was looking directly at her down the stretch of the table, and although he was the perfect host, cosseting them all, talking to everyone, motioning to waiters, being the bon vivant, his eyes inevitably came back to her face every few minutes.

It seemed to Tessa that the evening passed in a foggy blur. She did everything by rote, ordered food, played around with it whilst barely tasting it or enjoying it. Occasionally she sipped her wine, and made conversation with the two men seated on either side.

Sometimes she looked across at Lorne, half smiled or spoke a few words to him, but mostly she remained quiet, attentive, listening, trying to glean as much as she could about Jean-Claude. And she rarely took her eyes off him. Once or twice he asked her if she liked the food, or gave her a faint smile, but mostly he spoke eloquently about the things which interested him and the others at the table – theatre and film, literature, and politics. Endlessly they all chattered about international politics, world conditions and the future.

As he talked she began to understand more about him. She knew he was considered a great thinker and philosopher in France, but she hadn't realized he had covered wars – in Bosnia, Kosovo and Afghanistan. That he was a journalist of some standing and repute quickly became apparent to her; she also learned he was a protégé and favourite of President Mitterrand; that the French elite thought of him as another André Malraux; and that he had made documentaries, and written a play that had run at the Comédie Française, one of the great theatres of Paris.

The only thing she didn't know was his exact age. Lorne had said he was about forty-nine, but she thought he was wrong. Jean-Claude looked to be in his fifties to her, although she had to admit to herself she'd never been very good at guessing people's ages.

And so the evening went until it was time for them to leave the restaurant. Once more he came with them in the car, but insisted that she and Lorne were dropped off first at the hotel. When they arrived there, Jean-Claude got out, came to say goodnight to her on the steps. He took one of her hands, brought it to his lips and kissed it. Then he stepped back, gave her a long penetrating look as if committing her face to memory.

'*À bientôt*,' he murmured and stepped to one side, shook Lorne's hand and said goodnight. A moment later he was gone, the car driving off down the street.

As she and Lorne walked through the lobby to the lift, her brother said, 'That was an abrupt departure. I was about to ask him to come in for a nightcap. I know he likes a good Calvados.'

'Obviously he wants to get home,' she responded softly.

'He's very taken with you, Tess.'

'Is he?'

Lorne gave her a swift, peculiar look and exclaimed, 'Come on, you know he is!' When she was silent, he asked, 'What about you?'

'What about me?'

'You know what I mean. Are you interested in him? Stupid question, isn't it, when you were practically swooning at his feet.'

'Is that what I was doing?' She looked up at her brother, her silvery eyes questioning.

'Yes, you were. I've never seen you like that ever before. But then I've never seen him behave like that either.'

'So you've seen him with women have you, Lorne?'

'Occasionally.'

'And how did he seem then?'

'Laid back. Cool.'

'And how was he with me? At the actual book-signing, I mean?'

'Bowled over. Very taken. Suddenly smitten. Actually, I think the word I'm looking for is *intent*. He was very intent and intense.'

322

Tessa sighed but said nothing as they got into the lift and went up to their suite. Once they were inside, she swung around and said to her brother: 'I'm going to say goodnight, darling. I'm tired. I want to go to bed. You don't mind, do you?'

'No, of course not, Tess.' He kissed her cheek, watched her as she walked down the sitting room to her bedroom. He thought: She'll be all right.

Once she was in her bedroom, Tessa sat down in the chair near the bed and looked at the book in her hands, which she had clutched all evening. It had an arresting cover, showed a collapsed suit of medieval armour. *His* name blazed across the top and at the bottom was the title. One word. *WARRIORS*. She turned to the inside back flap, studied his photograph for a moment, started to read about him.

The phone began to ring, and she reached for it. 'Hello?' she said.

'*C'est moi.*'

'I know.'

'When can I see you?'

'Tomorrow?'

'That's good. For lunch?'

'Yes,' she said, her heart beginning to clatter against her ribcage.

'I hope Lorne will not feel – how shall I say? Left out.'

'He has other plans tomorrow,' she improvised.

'*Bien. Je vous envoi une voiture.* At noon.'

'Thank you.'

'*À demain,*' he said and was gone.

Tessa stared at the phone for a moment, put the book down on the bed, and went out into the sitting room. Lorne was nursing a balloon of Calvados and watching a political show on CNN, but swung his head as she came in. 'Do you want one of these?' he asked, lifting his glass.

'I don't know . . .' She paused when she came to the sofa and stared at her brother. 'Jean-Claude just phoned.'

'I guessed it was him.'

'I'm having lunch with him tomorrow.'

Lorne nodded. 'He told me he was going to phone you about lunch.'

Seating herself on the arm of the sofa she exclaimed, 'He did! Was he asking your permission? I hope not. I'm thirty-two, for heaven's sake, a mother, and about to become a divorcee.'

Lorne threw back his head and laughed. 'Don't sound so indignant. Of course he wasn't asking my permission. He's not like that. When we were leaving Taillevent he told me he intended to call you when he got home, that he wanted to take you to lunch. And I suppose he wanted me to know that, since I'm your brother and we are here in Paris together. Also, he and I are good friends.'

When she remained silent, biting her lip, and looking worried, Lorne added, 'He's a grown man, Tessa. He'd never ask my permission to take you out. He was simply being courteous. He's very gentlemanly, well mannered, always has been, about everything.'

She merely nodded, murmured, 'I understand,' and walked over to the bar, where she poured herself a small glass of Calvados.

As she returned to the sofa, Lorne lowered the volume of the television set, raised his glass and with a smile said, 'Cheers.'

'Cheers.' Tessa sat down opposite him and asked, 'What did he write in your book?'

'He said he admired my talent as an actor, called me his *bien ami*, and wished me luck with the film. What did he put in yours?'

'Something rather odd.'

'What?'

'He wrote my name, and then *Je suis là*.'

'I am here. That's what he wrote? It does sound a bit odd. I am here *what*?'

Tessa shook her head. 'I am here . . . *waiting*. I am here . . . *for you*. That's how I interpreted it.'

'I think you're correct. And I was right, he is full of *intent*.'

'I find him very compelling.'

'Yes, he's extremely charismatic.'

'And you don't mind that I'm having lunch with him? You're not warning me about him?'

'No. I wouldn't warn you about a man like Jean-Claude Deléon. He's . . . a giant of a man, very serious, very responsible. He's what Uncle Ronnie would call a *mensch*.'

'But *you* said he was a ladies' man,' she reminded him.

'I did, but I didn't mean he was a *womanizer*, because I don't believe he is. Oh, there've been lots of women in his life, I know that. But he's not a philanderer. What I meant when I said he was a ladies' man is that he likes women, *admires* women. He's not a misogynist like some men I know who are red-blooded but don't *like* women.'

'I see.' She leaned back in the chair, and sipped her drink. After a moment she said, 'He's sending a car for me tomorrow at noon.'

'I told you he was a gentleman. Anyway, my Tess, you should be flattered. Before he meets you for lunch he's going to be at the Élysées Palace with the President of France.'

Not far away from the Paris O'Neill Hotel, Jonathan Ainsley sat in a small bar on a narrow street just off the Champs-Élysées.

He was waiting for Mark Longden, wondering where he was and sipping a glass of Napoleon brandy. He kept glancing at his watch, cursing the other man under his breath. He was a stickler about time, loathed unpunctuality in others.

Lately, he had come to wonder if Mark had become something of a liability, a hindrance. He had expected more from him, had expected the man to have done much more to destroy Paula through her children.

Whilst it was true that Mark had managed to bring Tessa to her knees, there was still Linnet to take care of, and then Emsie. Jonathan wanted these three Harte women ruined, along with Paula. He hated all Harte women, except for his cousin Sarah; she was the exception to his rule.

Paula and her three daughters reminded him far too much of his grandmother, Emma Harte, whom he had detested throughout her life. He continued to harbour hatred for her, even in death. He believed that she had cheated him out of his inheritance, favouring Paula.

Mark suddenly pushed through the door, came hurrying into the bar, making for the table.

Watching him cross the floor, Jonathan was instantly struck by Mark's ghastly pallor, his strained look, the tired eyes. After they greeted each other, Mark sat down and motioned to a waiter standing near the bar. When he came over to the table, Mark ordered a Napoleon, a cup of black coffee and a packet of Gauloise cigarettes.

'Started smoking again, have you, Mark?' Jonathan asked, a brow lifting sardonically. 'I thought you were one of the true believers, that you condemned out of hand second-hand smoke.'

'I still do, but I *need* a smoke tonight. I suppose you could say I need to indulge myself a little bit after a hard week.'

'My dear Mark, I've plenty of things available which you can indulge yourself in, you just have to say the word. And certainly things that are much more pleasurable than a mere cigarette.'

Mark looked at him sideways and shook his head. 'No women tonight, my friend. Or anything else. I'm too damned tired. It was a rough trip down from Thirsk to London, and I just made the plane to Paris.'

'I told you to fly from Manchester. You could

even have taken a flight from Yeadon. Well, never mind. How's my house coming along?' He asked this in a warm voice even though it was of no real interest to him. The last thing he wanted was a house in the north.

'Even though I say it myself, it's looking wonderful. I know you're going to like it, Jonathan,' Mark said. 'More than that, you're going to love it. You won't want to leave. *Ever*.'

Now Jonathan merely smiled, inclined his head, knowing very well he would want to leave it and leave it a lot. There was his luxurious apartment here in Paris, and his palatial house on a hill over-looking the harbour in Hong Kong, not to mention his farm in Provence, the latest acquisi-tion. Of course he would continue to travel to these homes, which were much more splendid than the country house in Yorkshire. The building at Thirsk was really only a ruse, wasn't it? A ruse to delude Mark into thinking he needed an archi-tect, when he had only needed a man to do his dirty work . . . which was ruining those ghastly women. With his inferiority complex, his desire for fame and money, Mark had been an easy target, particularly since he had innumerable weak spots. He was lustful and loved tarty women, and he couldn't get enough of Ecstasy, even smack at times, although he was a bit more cautious when it came to heroin. And he liked to booze it up.

He is my creature, Jonathan thought, looking across the table at the younger man. He will do my bidding because I have him totally in my control. He needs all the things I can offer. Jonathan sat back, a satisfied smile playing around his mouth.

Mark drank the coffee, took a gulp of the cognac and then lit a cigarette, inhaling deeply, and once he had smoked for a few seconds, he said, 'I heard on the grapevine up in Yorkshire that your father's other son is in London . . . Owen Hughes. Staying at that Welshman's hotel in Belgravia. Brought his wife with him from New York. Is seeing his daughter Evan, your father's only grandchild, and has even had lunch with Gideon and Evan. It seems like there's a family gathering going on. How about that?'

Jonathan was furious when he thought of Evan Hughes. The grandchild his father had always craved. *She would have to be dealt with as well as the Harte women.* He laughed silently. But *she* was a Harte, too, an offspring of the dreaded Emma. He would deal with *her* himself.

Before he could stop himself, Jonathan said, in a boastful voice, 'I have a son, you know.'

Mark was flabbergasted and he gaped at Jonathan. 'You have a son! Jesus Christ, man, why isn't he with you, visiting your father with you in Yorkshire? That would certainly put Evan Hughes's nose out of joint.'

'My son lives in another country,' Jonathan answered, which was the truth, and then realizing that more of an explanation was required, he added, 'He has not been well for some time. He has to be protected, has to live in a warm climate, a special environment.' This was not true. The truth was the son his wife had presented him with some years earlier had actually not been his, but that of his Chinese partner Tony Chui. It was his eyes that had given *her* game away, telegraphed to Jonathan the baby was not his. Damn and blast *her*, too.

'Who told you all this about Owen Hughes, Mark?'

'I picked it up here and there. I have my sources. I nosed around. Anyway, how long are you staying in Paris?'

'I'm not exactly sure. That's why I needed you to come to see me, rather than meeting you in London. I have to pop down to the south of France. I've bought a Provençal property, a rather nice old farm . . . I'm going to need you for that you know, Mark, as well, need your input for which, of course, you will be very well paid. But we'll get to that later. Right now I'd like to know how your divorce is coming along? You know how much your separation from that dreadful girl has meant to me. We can't have you, such a talented architect, hampered in your rise by a mere Harte, now can we? And she is something of a bitch, isn't she?'

'Bitch is not a strong enough word to describe Tessa Fairley. She's impossible. I wish I could get Adele away from her,' Mark cried passionately.

'Well, my dear boy, why don't we try? Money's no object as far as you're concerned. I'll give you anything you need in this fight to . . . the death, shall we say.'

Mark glanced at him swiftly, and exclaimed in a low voice, 'I don't mind bashing her around a bit, but I'd never kill her, Jonathan. I'm not a murderer and I'm not going to swing for any woman.'

'Listen here, my friend, I have a few ideas.' As Jonathan spoke Mark leaned closer to him, listening carefully, and slowly a smile spread itself across his face.

The two of them sat talking and drinking for another hour or so, and then finally Jonathan paid the bill and he and Mark left the bar together.

In their merriment, and still embroiled in their plotting, they did not notice a nondescript couple sitting in a corner of the bar, who had been watching them for the entire time they had been there. The couple, a man and a woman, quickly followed them out into the street and kept them under surveillance until Jonathan located his car and chauffeur. Once he and Mark were being driven off the couple followed in their own vehicle, both bracing themselves for a long night.

It was noon on Friday and Lorne was alone in the hotel suite, studying his lines. Next week he had to report to the studios outside Paris and he wanted to be word perfect.

He was on his fifth reading of the first few pages of his part when the ringing of the phone on the desk cut into his concentration. Putting the script on the coffee table, he went to answer it.

He had barely said 'Hello,' when his half-sister Linnet exclaimed, 'Hello, Lorne, it's me.'

'Little Bird, how lovely to hear your chirps. Where –'

'I do think our mother should have known better, not named me after a bird, of all things! And I'm here, at Pennistone Royal.'

'How's the weather?' he asked.

'It's cooler; in fact it's very pleasant, and I'm sitting here on the terrace, taking it easy for once in my life.'

'You taking it easy! Balderdash. I'll believe that when I see it.' He laughed, full of affection for Linnet. 'All is well there, I presume?'

'Yes, nothing untoward is happening. I can see Adele, playing with her dolls, Elvira is with her, and Evan is due here for lunch. She, too, is taking the afternoon off. It's been quite a week for her at the Leeds store. Anyway, how's Tessa? I hope she's not worrying too much.'

'No, she's not, and I'd put her on, but she just left a few minutes ago for lunch with a friend.'

'No, no, I didn't want to speak to her, it was you I was looking for, Lorne.'

'What's the matter? You suddenly sound strange.'

'Everything's okay, more or less. But I wanted to alert you to the fact that Jonathan Ainsley's left Hong Kong. He's in Paris –'

'How do you know?' he cut in quickly, his hackles rising.

'Jack Figg just phoned me a short while ago. His operatives are all over the place, have their sights on Mr Ainsley. Anyway, he was spotted in Paris last night, with the dreaded Mark Longden. They were in a bar drinking together, looking very cosy indeed.'

'Oh, hell, that's the pits.'

'Lorne, don't worry, and please don't tell Tessa. I don't want to ruin her trip. There's no need for her to know about them being there together, you can say I called to tell her all is well here, which it is.'

'I hope those two buggers are not plotting something nasty,' Lorne muttered, 'I don't trust either of them.'

'Neither do I,' Linnet agreed. 'But it could be just a meeting about the house Mark Longden designed for Ainsley in Thirsk. He was up in Yorkshire for a couple of days. So Jack tells me. Try not to be alarmed, and as Dad would say, keep your eyes peeled.'

'I will, and thanks for alerting me. When is Mums actually coming back? Tessa said she would be back next week, Dad a few days later.'

'That's right, Mummy's coming with Winston and Emily, around the sixth, but Dad has some more meetings in the Bahamas or Barbados, and another in New York. From what she said, Mummy wants to get the divorce moving for Tessa, and she feels her presence is required.'

'I think it probably is, so listen, chickadee –'

'Hey, stop all this bird stuff, dearest brother of mine, I had enough of it as a child.'

He smiled into the phone, and said, 'Sorry, but old habits die hard, you know. Big kiss, Linnet.'

'Big kiss to you, big brother. And break a leg next week.'

Chapter Eighteen

After helping her into the back of the car, the driver gave her an envelope. Sitting comfortably against the leather seat, Tessa looked at the envelope on which Jean-Claude had written: *Madame Tessa Fairley.*

She gazed for a moment at the handwriting, admiring it. His penmanship was beautiful, she thought – bold and flowing. Opening it, she took out the note. *Dear Tessa:* he had written, *The chauffeur will take you to my home. If I am a few minutes late my houseman Hakim will serve you refreshment. JCD.*

After reading the note again, she put it in her handbag and glanced out of the window, wondering where he lived. But the driver had not volunteered any information and she decided not to ask. There had been many questions on the tip of her tongue this morning, when she had had breakfast with Lorne, but she had resisted asking them. She wanted to find out about this man herself; the opinions of others were not important, not even Lorne's. In any case, she knew her brother would not say anything about the writer that was not laudatory because he was an old friend, a man Lorne much admired.

Tessa straightened the black linen tunic she was wearing over matching narrow trousers, and settled herself comfortably in the corner of the car seat. Uncertain of where they would be going to lunch, she had chosen this simple tailored outfit because it could go *anywhere* – to a bistro or a much more elegant restaurant. A pair of pearl studs and a pearl-and-gold flower pin on the shoulder added a certain chic, and yet all could be removed and put in her bag if it was necessary to play down the outfit.

The heat had hit her when she had come out of the hotel, and now she was glad she was wearing the sleeveless linen top and strappy sandals on her bare feet. It was obviously going to be a sizzler, this last day of August, and the black linen was cool and comfortable.

As the car pushed through the traffic, Tessa began to realize that they were more than likely heading to her favourite part of Paris, the seventh arrondissement, and sure enough it was not very long before the driver was turning onto the rue de Babylone. He eventually came to a stop in front of an old, turn-of-the-century building with a massive *porte-cochère*, those huge wooden doors where horse-drawn carriages used to pass through into the courtyard in days gone by.

After helping her out of the car, the driver indicated the small door cut into one side of the *porte-cochère*, and bid her goodbye. She smiled, thanked him and went through the door into the cobbled courtyard of the building, which obviously had once been a *hôtel particulier*, a grand house in the past before it became apartments.

The concierge of the building immediately stepped out of his small office, greeted her pleasantly and asked how he could help her. She told him that Monsieur Deléon was expecting her, and he nodded, led her into the apartment building and showed her to a pair of double-mahogany doors to the right of the small cage-like lift that went up to apartments on other floors.

Thanking him, she walked over to the doors, rang the bell and waited; a moment later one side of the double doors was opened by a smiling middle-aged man in a white butler's jacket. From his olive skin and dark hair she thought that he was probably North African.

'*Madame, bonjour,*' he said at once, opening the door wider, ushering her into the apartment. 'I am Hakim,' he added in accented English.

'*Bonjour*, Hakim,' Tessa replied, her high heels clicking rat-a-tat as she followed him across the marble floor of the entrance foyer.

Showing her into a large room that was obviously a library, Hakim said, '*Madame . . . un apéritif?*' and added, by way of explanation, '*Monsieur sera de retour dans dix minutes.*'

'*Un verre d'eau, s'il vous plaît,*' Tessa murmured.

Left alone, Tessa surveyed the library from the doorway, not moving for a moment, taking everything in eagerly, wanting to know as much as possible about Jean-Claude Deléon, and his home would certainly tell her much, she knew that.

The library was unlike any room she had ever seen, and quite extraordinary, very beautiful in an understated, rather masculine way. It had enormous elegance and bespoke great taste, especially evident in the antiques, which looked like museum pieces to her.

Basically, it was a monochromatic room based on a play of soft creams and beiges, and this mix of pale colours made a subtle background for the ripe and mellow wood tones of the various antique pieces.

The creamy walls matched the full-length cream-wool draperies at the windows and the cream-and-beige upholstered sofas and chairs, while the highly polished wood floor shone like glass and was totally devoid of rugs, which added to the lustre of the room, not to mention its elegance.

From where she was standing in the entrance Tessa faced two tall windows at the far end. A large mahogany antique desk stood in front of the windows and it was partnered with a mahogany chair which she thought was from the French Empire period. On the desk were a pair of gilded-wood column lamps with square black shades, and various other things she couldn't quite make out from this distance, except for the back of a tall clock.

Glancing to her left, Tessa saw that this wall was dominated by an imposing white marble fireplace over which hung a *trumeau*, an antique mirror. The main seating arrangement was grouped in front of the fireplace and was composed of four Louis XV *bergères* and two matching sofas. They surrounded a glass coffee table, which did not seem out of place to her at all amongst the antique furniture.

On the opposite wall were floor-to-ceiling bookcases made of dark polished wood; these ran the entire length of the room, and were filled to overflowing with hundreds and hundreds of volumes. Just in front of the bookshelves was a lovely eighteenth-century library table, and in one corner, to her right, stood a guéridon, an antique pedestal table, and next to it a straight-backed chair and a standing lamp.

At this moment Hakim reappeared, arriving on silent feet with her glass of water, and after taking it and thanking him she walked down to the windows and stood looking out.

Much to her surprise there was a wide terrace immediately outside the windows, and, beyond, a lawn and flower beds filled with white flowers; growing against a high stone wall were a variety of large trees, shrubs and bushes, all creating a lovely green bower, welcome shade on a hot day like this. Underneath the trees were several metal garden chairs, and she couldn't help thinking what a lovely spot this was in the very heart of Paris. Such a luxury, a garden in the city.

Hakim now came out onto the terrace and began to set the table, and she suddenly understood that she and Jean-Claude were going to have lunch here and not in a restaurant, and this pleased her.

Turning around she glanced at the desk. The antique clock was by the famous Paris clockmaker, Le Roy et Fils; there was an elaborate gilded-bronze box close to it, two crystal paper knives with bronze-filigree decoration on the handles, and a black leather desk blotter with white blotting paper untouched by ink. And that was it. There was a paucity of clutter on the desk, which looked elegant and masculine in its pristine state.

Walking down the room, she went to look at the books on the shelves. So many philosophers . . . Descartes, Aristotle, Plato, Sophocles; books by such French writers as Victor Hugo, Celine, André Malraux, Jean-Paul Sartre, Emile Zola and Colette; volumes of French, English and American history; some of her own favourite novels by Dickens, the Brontë sisters and Jane Austen. Politics were covered from all aspects, as the different books by Charles de Gaulle, Winston Churchill, and others attested. There were a variety of political biographies about Churchill, John Major, De Gaulle, John Kennedy, Ronald Reagan and Roosevelt, and histories of Napoleon, Talleyrand, Nelson, the Duke of Marlborough, and Cromwell, as well as Elizabeth Tudor and Charles II. And, she noticed, a collection of Churchill's famous rhetorical speeches from the Second World War years, plus his *History of the English Speaking Peoples* in its many volumes.

Every religion was represented, with books on Christianity, Judaism, Buddhism and Islam. In fact, she realized there were a lot of volumes on Islam lined up alongside a collection of newer books on terrorism. Next to these were volume after volume covering the hundreds of wars which had been fought over the centuries. Conversely, on yet another shelf, there were many novels which had been published recently, and she recognized a number of English titles with colourful jackets by well-known British authors.

Stepping further along, she stared at a number of art books stacked on a shelf, which featured the work of Renoir, Picasso, Manet, Monet, Degas, Gauguin, Turner, Constable, Gainsborough, Bernard Buffet, and Rodin. Resting on another shelf were books on the music of Massenet, Bizet, Ravel, Bach, Beethoven, Mozart, Puccini, and the operas of Wagner.

She couldn't help wondering if he had read all of these books and decided it was more than likely that he had. She could not fail to understand that he had wide-ranging tastes as well as an interest in art and music.

Having sipped most of the water, Tessa looked about and finally went and put the half-empty tumbler on the glass coffee table, deeming it to be the safest place in a room full of valuable antiques.

Now she began to wander around, looking at the art on the walls. An arresting portrait of Napoleon, and another of Napoleon and Josephine together, were hanging side by side to the right of the mirror over the fireplace, and on the other side there was a lovely painting of an elegant woman in a blue dress that appeared to be very old, and she wondered if it was by Ingres. It looked as if it might be. On either side of the door leading to the foyer were framed antique panels, each one of a man and a woman in seventeenth-century clothing, depicting autumn and winter, she thought. Old, and unusual, in the style of Fragonard.

Finally, she returned to the fireplace and allowed her eyes to roam, assessing the overall effects as they ranged around the entire room. Taking in everything once more, she acknowledged that this library was a room not only of taste and refinement, but a reflection of the extraordinary man who occupied it. A brilliant man who was highly educated, cultured, an intellectual and a philosopher, a man of immense accomplishment.

Suddenly she heard his footsteps coming across the foyer. A second later he was standing in the doorway, regarding her. He wore a dark suit and a white shirt, and as he stood there looking at her so intently he struggled with his tie, loosened it, as if it were too tight for him. And then he walked towards her.

An unexpected attack of nerves made her tremble inside, and she was frozen to the spot, unable to move. She was taken by surprise when she realized she was curiously intimidated.

He came to a standstill in front of her and stretched out his hand. She took it. He brought her hand up to his mouth, barely brushed his lips against it, and let it go.

'My apologies. I kept you waiting,' he said.

'That's all right,' she answered, swallowing, wondering why her mouth was so dry.

Jean-Claude stepped away from her, explaining, as he did, 'Would you excuse me, please. I want to put on different clothes . . . more comfortable. *Je reviens tout de suite.*'

And then he was gone again, and she was alone once more, and she sat down heavily on one of the *bergères*, feeling slightly weak at the knees as she waited for him to return.

Jean-Claude moved rapidly across the foyer, went up the staircase to the next floor, taking the steps two at a time, and hurried into his bedroom. After quickly shedding his clothes, he put on a clean white cotton shirt, rolled up the sleeves, went into a walk-in closet and found a pair of beige cotton trousers. Once he was dressed, he slipped his bare feet into a pair of brown loafers, feeling much better already. The attire he had worn for the meeting at the presidential palace had been stifling on this hot morning, and he was glad to be rid of it.

Walking across his bedroom, he picked up the phone and dialled Lorne Fairley on his cell-phone number.

Lorne answered it almost immediately with a brisk, 'Hello?'

'*C'est moi*,' Jean-Claude said. 'I am now at my home. Tessa is here, and we shall take lunch in the garden.'

'That's a good idea, Jean-Claude, I don't think it would be wise for her to be seen in Paris with another man, although I'm sure two Englishmen wouldn't stray into your world, but you never know.'

'I have a question. I forgot to ask you earlier.'

'Ask me now.'

'Is the presence of her husband a coincidence? Or is he stalking her, perhaps? Should I get security for Tessa, to be sure she is safe?'

'That's not necessary, but thanks for thinking of it. I'm pretty certain Mark Longden's in Paris to report in. Actually, he's probably been summoned by Ainsley.'

'*Bien*. I understand. And be relaxed, Lorne, she is safe with me. I will stay in touch with you . . . and you must do the same.'

'I will, and thanks, Jean-Claude. Remember, don't say a thing to Tessa. If she knows Longden's in Paris she'll be upset.'

'Not a single word. *Au revoir, mon ami*.' Once he had hung up Jean-Claude crossed to the chair where he had thrown his jacket, retrieved his cellphone, and slipped it into his trousers' pocket, then proceeded into the bathroom.

After washing his hands, he slapped cold water onto his face, patted it dry, added cologne, and ran a comb through his hair. Once he had refreshed himself he turned away from the basin, but instantly turned back, stared at himself in the mirror. It struck him that he looked tired, a little weary today.

Am I too old for her? he asked himself, pausing to ponder this for a moment, seeing Tessa Fairley in his mind's eye. He sighed deeply. He had long understood that the question of age did not play in matters like this – matters of the heart.

He felt as if his life had been turned upside down since meeting her last night. Nothing was the same anymore. Even though he had been very concentrated at the meeting at the Élysées Palace earlier, there had been a moment when his thoughts had strayed to her and, embarrassed, he had had to pull himself up short.

What to do about her? How to handle this whole situation? He who was always so adept at handling every kind of problem was suddenly at a total loss.

I will let it handle itself . . . I will simply let it come at me like a speeding train. What else is there to do?

Striding through the bedroom he did not pause, but went into the corridor and down the stairs. And as he walked back into the library a moment later he acknowledged that matters were out of his hands. He was a man and she was a woman and something intimate, profound and deeply moving had passed between them last night . He must let things take their course.

CHAPTER NINETEEN

Tessa was standing at the window, looking out at the garden, thinking about Jean-Claude and still wondering how old he was, when he came walking back into the library. At the sound of his determined steps on the parquet floor she swung around to face him.

He came to a stop at the glass coffee table and his eyes met hers; he studied her for a moment and a smile began to play around his mouth.

She returned his smile and felt impelled to walk over to him.

'Champagne, I think,' he murmured, lifting the bottle out of the silver bucket which Hakim had brought into the library a few seconds before. 'It's Rosé Billecart-Salmon, a favourite of mine,' he told her. 'I find it smooth . . . I hope you like it.'

'I love pink champagne,' she answered, speaking the truth; it was her favourite even though she was not a big drinker. As she stood there watching him open the champagne, Tessa swallowed several times, discovering that she was feeling intimidated again. But then who wouldn't be intimidated by him? she asked herself. He was an accomplished, celebrated man, the darling of the French elite and seemingly the favourite of presidents.

This aside, Tessa also realized that a mixture of other emotions were swirling around inside her. For one thing she felt awkward, even slightly nervous being in such close proximity to him. She wanted to reach out to touch him, wanted *him* to touch *her*, wanted his arms around her. Strong-looking arms, she thought, and with a quick intake of breath stepped away from him, moved around the coffee table to the other side before she made a fool of herself.

But he was standing next to her again within a split second, handing her the glass of champagne. His hand brushed against hers as he did so, and it was like an electric shock. She sat down in the chair without a word. And she did not fail to notice an amused smile on his face as he went to fill his own glass.

A moment later he raised the flute to her across the coffee table. 'Santé,' he said.

'Santé,' she answered and took a very long swallow, found it refreshing.

There was a silence, and then he asked, 'And so, Tessa . . . how are you?' His dark, mesmeric eyes rested on her reflectively as he waited for her answer.

His question had startled her and she did not answer immediately. She stared at him, frowning, and before she could stop herself she said, 'Intimidated.'

'By me?' He sounded taken aback, and now his brows drew together in a frown.

Somewhat thrown by her own honesty, Tessa shook her head, and replied, 'Yes, well, by your accomplishments and achievements, your importance and standing in this world. I'm not used to famous men like you.'

'But I *am* just that . . . *a man*, Tessa. Like other men.'

'No, you're not. You're very celebrated.'

'Fame is meaningless to me.' He sat back in the chair, and once more looked at her thoughtfully before continuing, 'You are nervous perhaps, you even feel awkward. Yes, that I think you are. Because I am.'

'*Oh*,' she said, sounding surprised, looking across at him over the rim of her glass.

'It is natural. Of course we feel this way. Suddenly we are alone together. We do not know how to handle ourselves with each other.'

'Perhaps . . .' Her voice trailed off.

Leaning forward in the chair, Jean-Claude pinned his eyes on her, and began to speak to her softly, almost gently. 'Last night something happened between us. I looked at you in that grand foyer in Marie-Hélène's house and you looked back, and we made a connection. The most intimate connection there is between a man and a woman. We understood each other *exactly*. Moreover, if we had been alone I would have done something about it.'

'What do you mean?' Her gaze was riveted on him.

'I would have said . . . *come home with me.*'

'You should have asked,' she murmured. 'I would have come.'

'*C'est dommage.*' Jean-Claude lifted his hands in the Gallic manner, lightly shrugged, smiled at her rather ruefully.

'So why didn't you ask me?' she pressed, her eyes still on his face.

He did not respond.

'Was it because your friends were with you?' she ventured, questioningly.

'*Non, non,*' he replied. 'Not that at all. I do not live my life by or for the world. It was because of Lorne.'

'But he wouldn't have minded! He adores you!' she exclaimed.

'That is a strange word to use, no?' He gave her an odd look.

She shook her head. 'He idolizes you, looks up to you, he thinks there's no one like you in this world. You can do no wrong with my brother.'

'I am flattered. *Naturellement.* You must understand how much I value his friendship. I would never do anything to undermine it.'

'He says you are a true gentleman,' Tessa thought to add, and took several quick sips of the pink champagne. She wondered if she was getting a bit tipsy.

'I am not sure if that comes into this equation,' was his quiet response.

Tessa gazed at him but said nothing.

There was a silence, although it was not at all

awkward. Talking to each other in such an open way had eased the tremendous tension between them. Tessa was fully aware that she had never had this kind of honesty with Mark. The very thought of *him* made her cringe inside, and she pushed the thought away. There was no place for memories of *him* here in this apartment with this man, who was a real man and not a poor excuse for one. A giant of a man . . . Jean-Claude Deléon.

On his part, Jean-Claude was glad that he had encouraged her to speak about her feelings. It had somehow brought them closer together very quickly. He hated long drawn-out games between men and women. He found them childish, ridiculous and distasteful. Only honesty and the truth were acceptable to him.

Suddenly standing up, he took the bottle of champagne and went to fill her glass, and returning to the other side of the table he topped up his own flute.

Settling back in the bergère, he savoured the champagne before saying, 'Are you afraid?'

'A little bit,' she was quick to respond.

'Not of me? Surely not?'

'No, not really . . . of what might happen though. Between us.'

'Ah, yes, embarking on a love affair *is* risky.'

She was quiet; her silver-grey eyes were suddenly pensive.

He said in a warm tone, a hint of laughter in his voice, 'A centime for your thoughts, Tessa Fairley.'

'How old are you?' Her words fell into the middle of the room like a huge lump of lead.

Jean-Claude stared at her. It was apparent he had not expected such a question.

Tessa could have bitten off her tongue. What she was thinking at that moment had just tumbled out carelessly. She was stricken, and she apologized. 'I'm so sorry. How could I be so *rude*? How terribly gauche of me.' She felt herself colouring. 'You don't have to answer that question because it –'

'Much too *old* for you,' he cut in, smiling at her, a look of regret striking his face momentarily.

'No, you're not.'

Ignoring her comment, he told her, 'Last night, here alone, contemplating the evening as I was, I asked myself why the sight of a woman should bring me up with a shock. That is something I must fathom out.' But he already knew the answer. It was the shock of recognition, of knowing this was the one woman in the world who could solve the riddle of his life. That was what had happened to him last night.

'It's your turn to look introspective,' Tessa said, cutting into his thoughts.

'Ah, yes. I was thinking of you. What are your plans?'

'Do you mean this weekend? Or in the future?'

'Both.'

'I have no plans for the weekend.'

'Would you spend it with me?'

'Yes.'

'What about Lorne? I cannot take you away from him. You came to Paris together. To abandon him would be . . . *unkind*.'

'My brother's so serious about his work, but you know that, Jean-Claude, and he'll be happy to study his lines. He always wants to be word perfect, totally prepared when he performs, he's something of a perfectionist.'

'*Mais oui*. That I do know. We must include him, however.'

'We can ask him, yes. Why not?'

'You sound more relaxed, Tessa.'

'I am. I think I do feel a bit better.'

'And what about the future? What are your plans?'

'I must push my divorce through. Once my mother gets back from New York next week I think everything will move much quicker. She's very good at dealing with problems, and especially good at dealing with lawyers. Have you met her with Lorne?'

'I have. She's an exceptional woman.' And I'm afraid she won't approve of me for you, but thought it wiser not to voice this.

Hakim appeared at the door of the library. '*Monsieur, s'il vous plaît*.'

'*Merci, Hakim*.' Pushing himself to his feet, Jean-Claude said, 'Come, Tessa. Lunch is ready. We shall go to the garden through the dining room.'

The dining room was next to the library and Jean-Claude managed to usher her through it without actually touching her. As they headed towards the French windows which opened onto the terrace, she was aware that he felt as she did . . . that any physical contact with each other would precipitate an explosion.

When they stepped out of the air-conditioned apartment onto the terrace the intense heat hit them with a blast and Jean-Claude paused, hesitating. 'I think this was a mistake. It's very hot out here.'

'I know. But look, the sun has moved over there.' Tessa indicated the far end of the garden. 'I'm fine with it if you are. And it's nice to eat outdoors sometimes.'

'Very well,' he agreed and led the way to the table. He pulled the garden chair out for her and once she was seated he moved the large umbrella closer, so that they would be completely in the shade. Sitting down opposite her, he picked up the bottle of water and filled their glasses. After taking a sip, he asked, 'Shall we finish the champagne, or would you prefer white wine with lunch?'

'I'd like the champagne, please,' she replied, knowing very well that the wine would go to her head, and that was the last thing she wanted.

'Excuse me, I will only be a moment,' he said, rose and strode across the terrace towards the French windows, obviously going to retrieve the champagne.

Tessa's eyes followed him, and she thought he looked very fit. He was tall, muscular and well built, with broad shoulders, but there was no fat on him and he appeared much younger wearing the white shirt and cotton trousers than he had in a suit. Perhaps he *is* still in his forties, just as Lorne said, she thought. On the other hand, he *had* said he was too old for her. But what exactly did that mean? How could anyone ever calculate something like that? It just wasn't possible. Some people were mature for their age, others rather juvenile; that was actually the reason age did not matter one iota in her opinion. Everyone was different; it was impossible to generalize. She was thirty-two but considered herself to be very mature for her age. On the other hand, would he? This was a man unlike any she had ever known; he was unique.

He returned to the terrace almost at once, carrying the silver bucket that contained the pink champagne, and fast on his heels followed Hakim, holding a tray with two clean champagne flutes on it.

'*Voilà!*' Jean-Claude exclaimed, putting the ice bucket down on the flagstones, while Hakim placed the flutes on the table, then hurried off. A few minutes later the houseman came back carrying a small metal table; he put the champagne and the water on this, nodded politely and disappeared once more.

Pouring champagne for her, Jean-Claude said, 'Lourdes, my cook, has prepared a simple lunch, rather light. It's far too hot to eat anything heavy.'

'Yes, it is,' she agreed, wondering whether she would be able to eat at all. She had no appetite, but, this aside, she was unexpectedly tense and nervous once again. She had begun to relax a short while ago, after their rather honest conversation, but now, suddenly she was oddly at a loss, ill at ease, inadequate, she who was normally so self-assured. In fact she felt like a schoolgirl as she sat here opposite this sophisticated man in his elegant garden in the middle of Paris . . . overwhelmed by him, the situation, and her reaction to him.

As if reading her mind, Jean-Claude suddenly said, 'It is very difficult . . . getting to know a person, feeling at ease with them. I understand that, I am part of this . . . but it will be all right . . . trust me.'

'How did you know?' she asked softly, staring at him. 'It's as if you read my mind.'

'I have no magical powers, I can assure you,' he murmured, shaking his head.

Oh, but you do, she thought, making me so nervous. I've never ever felt like this before. But she remained absolutely silent, picked up the crystal glass and sipped the pink champagne. Not wishing to speak about their feelings at this moment, she changed the subject. 'The library here is one of the most elegant and beautiful rooms I've ever seen. But you don't work in it, do you?'

'No. However, I often sit there and think.'

'So where *do* you write? Do you go to an office somewhere?'

'No, I don't. I work here in the apartment. I have an office upstairs, I'll show it to you later if you like.'

'I'd like that. Did you write *Warriors* up there?'

'I did –' he broke off, drank some of the champagne and then said rather rapidly, 'I gave you my book as a courtesy, because you were at the party, you don't have to read it, you know.'

'Oh, but I've started it already,' she answered, and then blurted out, 'I couldn't sleep last night.' Instantly embarrassed by this admission, Tessa sat back in the chair with a jerk, colour flooding her face. Then she went on, very quickly, 'Anyway, I picked up your book and discovered I couldn't put it down. I became terribly involved. You know a lot about wars and terrorism and politics, don't you?'

He nodded. 'Why couldn't you sleep?'

She swallowed several times and was about to tell him some ridiculous lie, then opted for honesty. 'I was thinking about you.'

Jean-Claude took a deep breath. 'I know. I had the same problem.' His piercing gaze rested on her unrelentingly until she finally blinked and looked away.

Wanting to draw her back to him at once, he said, 'I'm glad you understand French, it's important to me.'

She wanted to ask him why, but did not. 'Where did you learn to speak English?' she said instead and striving for normalcy, added redundantly, 'It's perfect.'

'I took lessons when I was very young, just a boy, and I studied, worked hard. When I was twelve or thirteen, thereabouts, I'd decided to be a writer, and I longed to travel, especially to America and England. For that reason I wanted to have total command of the English language.'

'Well, you do.' She wondered what was wrong with her. Why did she keep telling him what he knew?

The arrival of Hakim with the cold vichyssoise soup curtailed their conversation for a moment. When he had served her the soup she picked up her spoon, took a mouthful, but discovered she could hardly swallow it even though it was delicious. Food was the last thing on her mind at this moment.

Once Hakim went hurrying off, Tessa said, 'You've covered many wars as a writer, but surely that's dangerous.'

'Life is dangerous.'

She did not respond.

'*You* know that, Tessa.'

Her eyes narrowed slightly. 'Lorne has told you things about me,' she asserted.

'No, he has not. I saw him two weeks ago, when he was flying from Istanbul to London via Paris. We had dinner together, and it was then he told me about the abduction of your child. But that's all.'

'I see.'

'He was worried about you.'

'I know.' She sighed. 'But putting yourself in the middle of a war is like asking for trouble, isn't it?'

'No. I don't take risks . . . at least not in wars.'

There was a long pause. A suggestive look entered his eyes and they lingered on her face. He smiled at her, a warm, loving smile.

The magnetism of him reached out to her, was

a palpable thing, and in an effort to break the spell he had cast on her she picked up her flute of champagne. Much to her dismay her hand trembled so badly she was startled. Trying to stop the shaking she took a few deep breaths, and steadied herself finally, put the flute down without spilling the champagne.

Although he did not say anything she knew he had noticed. How could he not have?

Hakim came and cleared the table, returned with the omelettes and departed yet again. She tried to eat without much success, and after a few seconds she realized that Jean-Claude was not eating either.

Becoming aware of her rather fixed scrutiny, he said, 'I'm not hungry.'

'Neither am I.'

'I think we'd better get it out of the way, deal with it.'

'What?'

'The physical aspects . . . of this situation. Come, Tessa, come with me.' He stood up and so did she and together they left the garden.

In the entrance foyer he turned to her and said, 'I told you I would show you my office. It's up there.' He indicated the staircase and led the way to the second floor.

After opening the door for Tessa, Jean-Claude followed her into his office, and just as he was about to take her in his arms the phone rang. '*Merde*,' he muttered to himself, pushed the door closed with his foot and hurried down the room to his desk. Picking up the receiver, he discovered it was his sister Marie-Laure on the other end of the phone.

Speaking to her warmly, listening for a moment or two, his eyes came to settle on Tessa, who was looking at the photographs hanging on one of the walls: photographs of himself with other writers, politicians, actors, philosophers, painters, friends, the beau monde of Paris, of the world. Endeavouring to make the conversation with his sister very fast, he explained he was in a meeting and couldn't talk long; he had been on the phone for only a few seconds yet it seemed like a lifetime to him. At last he managed to hang up, and as he did so Tessa turned, stared at him. At once he saw the pent-up longing on her face, the yearning for him in her eyes, and he recognized she was as overwhelmed by desire and sexual tension as he himself was.

He came around the desk very quickly, found himself rushing towards her, and she fell, almost stumbled into his arms. A small cry escaped her as she clung to him, and then a second later she buried her face in his shoulder. She was trembling so much Jean-Claude was alarmed, and he tried to calm her, stroking her back, holding her tightly, very close to him, murmuring gently to her. 'Tessa, it's all right, relax, *chérie*, relax,' he whispered against her silver-gilt hair.

Finally, she looked up at him, raised her face to gaze into his face. He felt swamped by those unique silvery eyes. Looking down at her, being so close to her like this made him catch his breath, and yet again he was thunderstruck by her heart-stopping ethereal beauty. She parted her lips ever so slightly, then licked her lips with the tip of her tongue.

Inflamed by this, no longer able to resist her, he brought his mouth down on hers, crushing it, and then his tongue went into her mouth, and they savoured each other. This intense moment of absolute intimacy sent a thrill running through him, and he held her closer than before. They went on kissing, standing in the middle of the floor, lost in each other, lost to the world, oblivious to everything except themselves and their feelings.

A moment later, still clinging together, they sank onto the sofa, and he continued to kiss her passionately, just as he had wanted to the previous evening and every minute since then. At last she was exactly where he wanted her to be, in his arms, about to become part of him as he would make himself part of her. To be possessed by her, to possess her in return, that was what he craved.

After a short while he got up impatiently, began to unbutton his white shirt as he strode to the door and locked it. When he came back to her she was waiting on the sofa, having undressed, her long, lithe body stretched out for him. How beautiful she was, he thought.

A second later he, too, was undressed, his clothes thrown carelessly on the floor. He lay down next to her, overwhelmed by desire, and took her in his arms. He held her as close to him as possible, listening to his heart slamming against his ribcage in unison with hers.

Eventually, pushing himself up on one elbow, he looked into those extraordinary eyes again, and she returned his intense gaze, touched his face.

'Jean-Claude,' she said in a low voice.

'Yes, darling?'

'I want you so much.'

'No more than I want you.' He kissed her brow, her eyes, her small firm breasts, stroked her long body, and her stomach, caressed her languidly, taking his time. His hands fluttered over every part of her until she was moaning softly, her pleasure apparent as she responded to his touch, and touched him in return.

When his hands and mouth came to rest in the silky hair between her legs she could no longer restrain herself, and she cried out in pleasure. It was with tenderness and expertise that he brought her to a climax, felt her cresting on wave after wave. Moving onto her, positioning himself between her legs, he entered her swiftly, murmuring against her hair, 'Chérie. Ah my Tessa, my love . . .'

'Jean-Claude, Jean-Claude,' she sighed, and put her arms around him. She held onto him tightly, wanting all of him.

It seemed to him that they were rising and falling together in slow motion. Their bodies fit perfectly, and they moved in perfect rhythm, as though they were one entity. Passion spiralled upward and they began to move faster and faster, panting, gasping as they crested and came together in an explosive climax. He felt as though he were falling down into some silvery, light-filled space, taking her with him, knowing he could never ever let her go.

They lay together on the sofa in a soft haze of pleasure, both of them slightly dazed. Pent-up desire and longing for each other had been assuaged, all tension had fled, and there was only joy and fulfilment between them.

Against her hair, Jean-Claude said, 'Are you all right?'

'Very all right. Except I'm thirsty.'

He kissed the tip of her nose, pushed himself up off the sofa and crossed the room.

She watched him, thinking how well he moved, and in such a positive, determined way. At one moment last night Lorne had called him a man of action, because he was always rushing off on assignments, covering wars, taking on foreign projects, and she noted how fit he was, what good shape he was in.

He had gone through a door into another room, and when he came back out carrying a bottle of water and two glasses, she asked, 'Do you have a kitchen up here?'

He laughed. 'No, it's the bathroom. But I put in a refrigerator for water and soft drinks, and there's a coffee pot.' Placing the glasses on his desk, he fiddled with the bottle, poured the water and carried the two glasses over to the sofa.

Tessa sat up, swung her long legs to the floor

and took the glass from him. 'Thank you. I'm very dry, it must be all that champagne you gave me.'

Sitting down next to her, glancing at her quickly, he exclaimed, 'I suppose you're now going to say I got you drunk and seduced you.'

'No, I'm not. You did that last night, in Marie-Hélène's foyer. In front of half of Paris.'

He laughed out loud, enjoying her. '*Touché*.'

'Do you have a robe or a shirt I can put on? Oh look, I can wear this,' she said, reaching for his white shirt on the floor.

'Let me get you something else, that shirt's not clean, I've worn it.'

'That's why *I* want to wear it.' She buried her face in the shirt. 'It smells of your cologne.' Standing up, she slipped the shirt on, fastened a couple of buttons, added, 'And it smells of you.'

He chuckled as he went back to the bathroom and returned a moment later wearing a navy-blue silk robe. 'Are you hungry?'

'A little bit. But I don't think those omelettes will still be hot.'

Laughter tugged at his mouth again, and walking over to her he put his arms around her, held her close. 'I think I can rustle up some sandwiches. However, I want to talk to you first.'

'What about?' she asked, pulling away slightly as the seriousness of his tone registered. Staring up at him, she hesitated for a moment, then said quickly, 'Is there something the matter?'

'Sit there,' he said, sounding a little imperious,

indicating the sofa. She promptly did as he said, knowing he was serious.

He turned around, pulled a chair closer to the sofa, and sat down opposite her.

For a moment he remained silent, sat in the chair pondering, looking contemplative.

She studied him surreptitiously, thinking what a good-looking man he was. No wonder women fell at his feet. Well, hadn't she also? He was handsome, with a strong hard body, long legs and broad shoulders. His dark-brown eyes were soulful, and at times brooding as well as mesmeric, while his gaze could be piercing. There was a sensuality to his fine mouth and yet it was kind as well. Yes, that was it. That elusive thing about him was the kindness reflected in his face. But now, as he stared back at her and very intently so, she saw a graveness settling over him, and once more she asked rather worriedly, '*Is* there something wrong?'

'No.' He took a long swallow of the water, put the glass on a nearby side table, settled himself in the chair. 'I'm a fifty-three-year-old man, a grown-up man. This –' he paused, waved his hand between them airily – 'is not a sport for me. This is not a game I'm playing.'

'I think I know that, Jean-Claude.'

'I've seen too much, done too much, lived too hard in many different ways. Pain, heartache . . . they're old familiars. I have grappled with disillusionment and despair, I have borne many sorrows and I suppose you could say I've experienced most things. There are those in Paris who think I am weary, jaded even, and in some ways perhaps I am.' He reached for the water again, obviously as thirsty as she had been.

'And so now, at my age,' he went on, 'I cannot afford to squander my time because I still have much to write, to study, to achieve, and to do. Do you understand what I'm saying, Tessa?'

'I think so, yes.'

'Last night when I came home after dinner I felt *bludgeoned*. That's the only word I can think of . . . *bludgeoned*. And by you. By our meeting. You had an enormous impact on me. And I believe I had the same impact on you. Am I not right?'

'You are. And I feel exactly the same way you do. Haven't we just proved that to each other, Jean-Claude? But –' she cut herself off.

'But what?'

'I'm a bit frightened.'

He smiled at her. 'And I am *terrified*.'

Clearing her throat, she said, 'What you meant a moment ago is that you don't want *me* to waste your time, isn't it?'

'That is correct. I've managed to waste a lot of my time over the years, and quite often with women who turned out not to be the women I thought they were.'

'What about me then? What do you think I am?'

'The woman I've been searching for all of my life.'

'In your book, the one you inscribed for me, you wrote, "*Je suis là*." What did you mean when you wrote *I am here*? It's enigmatic.'

'What do you think I meant?'

'I am here for *you* . . . *waiting* for you.'

'That's very perceptive of you, Tessa.'

'Lorne said he'd never seen me behave like that. He told me I was swooning at your feet, and I was. At least that's how I felt.'

He nodded, but made no comment.

She went on, 'He said he'd never witnessed you behaving like that either.'

'Lorne is right, I don't think I ever have.' He suddenly chuckled as if amused by his behaviour of the night before. 'I just wanted to grab you, bring you here and take you in my arms, hold you close to me forever. And it was such an over-whelming feeling I was stunned.'

'You said you didn't want me to waste your time . . . What is it you expect of me?'

'A fair shake, as my American friends would say. At this moment, right now, I would like to know if you are ready to embark on a relation-ship with me? But there is one other thing . . . I must know that you will always be honest with me, always truthful.'

'I would never lie to you,' she exclaimed, and then said in a softer voice, 'As for a relationship with you, of course I want that. Haven't we just started one?'

'There are some who might consider it . . . a one-night stand.'

'A one-afternoon stand,' she corrected and began to laugh.

He had the good grace to laugh with her, shaking his head, amused.

Tessa adopted a very low voice, when she pointed out, 'We live in different cities. I have a three-year-old child. And I also have a career, responsibilities.'

'I know all of those things, Tessa. But let us try, shall we?'

When she did not answer, he pressed. 'Are you willing?'

'I'm willing,' she answered.

CHAPTER TWENTY

Brushing the hair away from her face with her hand, Tessa remained seated on the sofa, staring at the door. Jean-Claude had gone downstairs to get sandwiches. She was wondering why she felt suddenly out of sorts. Within the space of a few seconds it hit her . . . she missed Jean-Claude's presence most acutely. His absence made her feel deprived. And he had only been gone for a few moments.

This knowledge amazed her, and then instantly she remembered last night, how she had not been able to sleep, how thoughts of him had crowded out everything else in her head. And because she had been restless she had finally turned on the light, picked up his book and begun to read it. Apart from making her feel closer to him, it told her a great deal about him, gave her an insight into his mind; the brilliance of his writing had amazed her. He was a remarkable thinker, philosopher and writer, and she had been bowled over by the first few chapters she had read.

Last night she had silently thanked her mother for insisting she learn to speak French and making her stick at it. Once again she felt a sense of gratitude to Paula, because if she couldn't understand his language she wouldn't be able to read his books, and that, it seemed to her, was imperative.

He's larger than life, she thought, clever and accomplished, not to mention charismatic. It struck her that when he was in a room he dominated it with his physical presence and personality, and that was why she missed him now. His office was quiet, lifeless without him in it.

It was the same in a public place; she had noticed that last night. He took over the space when he walked in, and without doing anything spectacular. Of course, *he* was spectacular. He displaced the air around him, made gigantic waves.

He also made love in a way she was not accustomed to, had never experienced before. There had only been one other man before she had married Mark, and he had been a disaster in bed. As for Mark, he was a bit rough, always in a hurry: never considering her, never satisfying her. And then he had turned violent, had actually hurt her during sex, and had finally raped her in such an ugly and violent manner she had left him, lucky to have escaped with her life.

Don't think about Mark, she instructed herself, and immediately blocked him out. Think about Jean-Claude Deléon instead. She lay back on the sofa and closed her eyes, relived their lovemaking . . . an hour of such bliss . . . and he was bliss . . .

She knew how serious he was about her, he had made that perfectly clear, had spoken to her in the most open and honest way, and with enormous clarity. Well, he *was* a communicator, wasn't he? He wanted a long-term relationship. And so did she, she understood that already. Did that mean marriage? She wasn't sure. How could they make it work? He lived in Paris; this was his domain where he was one of the philosopher kings. He rushed off to cover wars and uprisings, to interview politicians and presidents all over the world . . . he put himself in danger. Could she handle *that*? His being in constant danger?

And then there was *her* life . . . and her darling sweet Adele. Wherever she went, Adele came too, but that did not present a problem. Jean-Claude would immediately fall in love with Adele, everyone did. Her child was irresistible.

But there was her career to consider, her job at Harte's, her responsibilities. How could she work in London and live in Paris? And she would have to live here if their love affair progressed the way he wanted – no, actually expected it to. Certainly he would never move to London, at least not on a permanent basis.

After Mark had abducted Adele a couple of weeks ago she had suffered so much pain she had truly understood that her daughter came before everything else in her life. And she still felt the same way. Her career had been moved to second place in her own mind. Might it now take third place because of Jean-Claude?

She sat up.

She had fallen in love with him.

Instantly, last night.

She had looked into that face, so handsome yet full of character and kindness and gravity, and she had fallen heavily. Just like India fell for Dusty Rhodes, she suddenly thought, and with a rush of clarity she understood about her cousin and the artist.

Jean-Claude said he had felt bludgeoned; she had been dumbstruck. And the emotions he had aroused in her were manifold. There was no question that she had never felt like this before, and she acknowledged that this was because of Jean-Claude and all the things he was as a man.

Once again needing to understand more about him, she got up and began to wander around his office, looking at a selection of photographs on another wall, finding a long line of books on a shelf, books bearing his name as the author. Twenty-five in all. Then she noticed that some of them had been translated into English, and other languages as well, and this pleased her. She laughed to herself. Why had she felt that sudden stab of pride? After all, she had only met him last night. It didn't seem possible . . . *only last night.* Yet her life had been turned upside down, changed irrevocably. It would never be the same, nor would she.

Unexpectedly, Tessa experienced a rush of panic. What was she going to *do*? How was she going to *handle* all of this? For a moment she felt overwhelmed, and then she took a deep breath and forced herself to relax. The only possible thing she could do was to let it happen and deal with everything one day at a time.

Now her eyes swept around his office, and she understood why he had said it was unique. A gallery encircled the entire room and fronted bookshelves rising to the ceiling on several walls, and there was a polished steel-and-brass circular staircase that twisted up to the gallery.

It was a spacious airy room, with a high ceiling and a tall window at the far end, and the colours were warm and masculine, a deep brick-red and fir green mixed in an arresting combination. A brick-red woollen fabric upholstered the walls, a matching velvet covered the sofa, and the rug was a combination of red and green. His desk was spectacular, a huge slab of heavy glass set on thick polished steel-and-brass legs, and the two lamps on the desk were made of stainless steel with dark-green shades.

She glanced at the desk with enormous interest, saw that the surface was empty except for a blotter, an inkstand and several metal trays for papers. Instantly she knew he was a tidy man with a tidy mind, and she liked that. She was a neat person herself, and couldn't stand mess.

Along another wall, off to one side of the desk, there was a work table and on this stood his typewriter, computer and printer, and two steel lamps matching those on the desk. Serious work goes on here, she thought, nodding to herself. She had the feeling he was fast and efficient.

Tessa meandered back to the centre of the office and glanced at her watch as she did; to her amazement she saw that it was almost three o'clock.

At this moment the door opened and Jean-Claude was standing there. 'I am sorry it took so long,' he muttered, bending to pick up the tray on the floor. He came into the office, walked down to his desk and placed the tray in the middle.

Beckoning to her, he said, 'Come, Tessa, come here, sit in this chair behind the desk. You will be more comfortable.'

Bossy, as well, she thought, but gave him a wide smile and hurried to join him at his desk. He put his arms around her, hugged her to him. '*Chérie*,' he murmured, stroking her hair, and then releasing her, he went and brought a chair over, sat down facing her.

The tray had been beautifully set, she noted, obviously by Hakim. There was a sparkling white organdy cloth on it, matching napkins and pretty china. Tessa took a plate and a napkin, and sat back until Jean-Claude insisted she started to eat, which she did. He poured the tea, took a sandwich himself, and they were both silent until they had finished.

After drinking his tea, Jean-Claude looked across at Tessa and smiled. 'So preoccupied was I with you I didn't realize how ravenous I was.'

'I know, I was starving myself,' she replied. Then she cocked her head on one side thoughtfully, staring back at him intently.

'What is it?' he asked, alerted by her expression, putting his cup down.

'I've just had the most curious thought. Do you think my brother set us up?'

Jean-Claude was startled and his eyes narrowed slightly, and then he began to laugh, obviously highly amused by her suggestion. After a moment, he said, with another chuckle, '*Mon Dieu!* What a thought that is, and I must say this to you, if he did then I shall be eternally grateful to him.' He shook his head, still amused. 'What made you think this?'

'Well, I recently had a conversation with him, and I said I would probably never get married again after this débâcle with –'

'Lorne's response?' he asked peremptorily, cutting her sentence off.

'He said that was all right, but he wasn't going to allow me to lead a celibate life, that he was going to make sure I had lots of lovers.'

'Only one, *ma chérie.*' He reached out, put his hand over hers.

'*Oui, absolument.* Only one. *You.*'

His face was illuminated by a bright smile and his dark eyes were warm, loving as he said, 'You had this thought about your brother, and I had one too when I was downstairs getting the sandwiches. It occurred to me that it would be nice if he came to the country with us tomorrow.'

'We're going to the country?' she asked, sounding surprised.

'You did agree to spend the weekend with me, didn't you?'

'Yes, I did.'

'I have a house outside Paris, small but comfortable.' He made a gesture with his hand and continued, 'It is pleasant there, you would enjoy it. You will come, won't you, darling?'

I would go anywhere with you, she thought, and said, 'It would be nice. And perhaps we should speak to Lorne now. I'm not sure what his plans are.'

'I thought he was learning his lines,' Jean-Claude responded, picked up the phone on the desk and dialled the hotel number.

A moment later he was speaking to Lorne. '*C'est moi, mon ami. Comment tu va?*'

'Hello, Jean-Claude,' Lorne exclaimed. 'I'm fine, and you? Is everything all right with you and Tessa?'

'*Bien sûr.* Are you busy tomorrow?'

'No, just studying my part. Why do you ask?'

'I thought it would be a good idea to take Tessa out of Paris for the weekend, and it would be a great pleasure for me if you would come also. To my little house . . . you've been there.'

'Little house!' Lorne exclaimed, laughing. 'Haven't you told her it's a *château*?'

'Ah, my dear friend, you exaggerate always, it's hardly a *château*. But you *will* accompany us, won't you?'

'Thanks for your invitation, Jean-Claude, and I think it is a very good idea to get her out of Paris while those two scoundrels are skulking around.'

'That was my thought exactly,' Jean-Claude replied. 'And so you will join us?'

'If she wants me along.'

'Let me put her on,' Jean-Claude murmured, and handed the phone to Tessa.

'Hello, Lorne,' she said. 'You are going to come with us, aren't you? If not, I won't go either.'

'Of course I'm coming, I love that house of his. Are you all right, sweetheart?'

'More than that, I'm . . . *great*.'

'He's a fantastic man, a really wonderful person, Tessa. It makes me feel better knowing you are with him. You'll always be safe with Jean-Claude.'

'I realize that. I suppose Jean-Claude will call you later with the exact plans. No news?'

'None. Have you heard from Linnet?'

'No, but I didn't expect her to phone. I spoke to her this morning, before I left for lunch, and all was well. I have my mobile and it's on all the time.'

Jean-Claude took the tray back to the kitchen, and whilst he was gone Tessa put on her clothes. She was standing looking at a photograph of him on the wall when he walked back into his office, and she swung around to face him, puzzlement reflected in her eyes.

'Who's this child with you? It is *you*, isn't it?'

He came to join her, stood with his arms around her. 'Yes. And that's my son,' he said, looking down at her. 'When he was ten.'

'Oh,' was all she could manage, so startled was she.

'He's grown up now, he's almost your age. I told you I was too old for you. I'm old enough to be your father.'

'No, you're not! I didn't know you had been married.' She cleared her throat. 'You *were* married to his mother?'

'Very briefly. When I was young. It was a long time ago. I was twenty-one, and Philippe was born when I was twenty-two.'

'I see. Does he live in Paris?'

'No, the south of France, he's an artist,' Jean-Claude explained.

Tessa hesitated, and then she said, 'Are you still married?'

He burst out laughing. 'Of course not. I'm divorced and I have been for many years.'

'And you never got married again?'

'No . . . there have been plenty of women . . .'

'So I gather.'

Turning her towards him, he held her by her shoulders. 'I cannot erase the past,' he said, looking down into her upturned face. 'Neither can you, *ma chérie*. We both bring . . . a certain amount of baggage to this relationship. And we have to deal with that the best way we are able. I can say this to you in sincerity . . . I believe you are *right* for me. I think you can fill all the empty places in my heart, as I will fill those in yours. So don't ever dwell on my past. Or yours. The past is gone, we have the future.'

She laid her head against his shoulder and thought of Lorne's words a short while before . . . 'You will be safe with Jean-Claude,' he had said. And she knew her brother had spoken the truth.

* * *

Jonathan Ainsley sat at the Louis XVI desk in the study of his sumptuous apartment on Avenue Foch, one of the most elegant streets in Paris. The phone was pressed to his ear and he listened attentively to the woman on the other end of the line.

Once she had finished speaking, he said, 'But are you sure Tessa Fairley is in Paris?'

'Yes. With her brother, Lorne Fairley. And they are bound to be staying at the Paris O'Neill Hotel, where else but at their father's hotel?'

'Only too true, my dear,' Jonathan replied, playing with the piece of jade in his hand. 'When did they arrive?'

'Thursday evening, and she's not expected back in London until Wednesday of next week. Her brother is staying on, he's filming in Paris. She's coming back sooner, no doubt because her mother is returning from New York on September the sixth.'

'Well done, well done, there'll be a really nice surprise for you when I see you in London, a little gift, and of course a rendezvous, a reunion. You'd like that, wouldn't you, sweetie?'

'You know I would, Jonathan.'

'Very well, I'll let you know when I am coming over. In the meantime, thanks for the information, it's very useful.'

They said goodbye and hung up, and Jonathan immediately dialled the Ritz Hotel where Mark Longden was staying. But he was obviously not in his room. The phone rang and rang and nobody picked up. Slamming the receiver down, he next dialled the Paris O'Neill Hotel and asked for Mrs Tessa Longden.

A split-second later the operator was back on the line, and told him in slightly-accented English, 'Mrs Longden is not registered.'

'Perhaps her brother Mr Lorne Fairley is staying at the hotel and she is with him. Can you please try his suite?'

'Mr Fairley is not here, sir. None of the family is in residence at the hotel at this time.'

Irritated to the point of anger, Jonathan muttered his thanks and hung up, an ugly grimace clouding his face. Settling back in the chair, he brought his hand up to his chin and pondered for a moment or two. Obviously they were not at their father's hotel after all, but it was hardly likely they would be staying somewhere else. Since Fairley was filming in Paris, he could have rented an apartment for a few weeks, perhaps even a few months.

Jonathan wondered how to find out if that were the case. Mark Longden would have to do the dirty work, find out what was happening with the Fairley twins. He loathed to miss an opportunity to do Tessa harm; how easy it would be to arrange an accident of some sort if he knew where she was staying in Paris.

Since Longden had vanished for the moment, Jonathan decided to call his cousin Sarah Pascal. She probably wouldn't know anything at all, since she was on equally bad terms with the Hartes as he was. But occasionally he did get a little sadistic pleasure making digs at Sarah about their cousins.

His taunts always seemed to rile her, much to his amusement.

Once again he was out of luck. He telephoned Sarah at her office, only to be told she was not in Paris, that she had left for the weekend. Of course, it was Friday afternoon at four o'clock and she had no doubt gone to join her husband at their country home.

Too bad, he thought, and dialled his mistress, Yvette Duval. To his utter astonishment, when her housekeeper heard his voice she told him that Madame had gone to Rome. 'Rome!' he spluttered and banged the receiver into the cradle in fury and frustration.

What the hell was *she* playing at? He suddenly wondered if she was going to be as faithless a bitch as his wife had been. Suddenly he saw her in his mind's eye – *Arabella Sutton*. A woman he had loved to distraction, who had betrayed him, cuckolded him in the most foul way, by sleeping with his Chinese partner Tony Chui. How he loathed her. He had often thought of putting *her* on his hit list, along with the Harte women and Evan Hughes. Yet somehow he had balked at that. Maybe because he had once loved her. But what the hell, why not? She deserved to suffer after what she had done to him.

As for Yvette Duval, he was finished with her. Tonight he would resort to one of the high-priced whores from Madame Simone's for his pleasures of the flesh. And next week he would start courting Yvette's daughter Chantal. What better form of revenge? He would dump the mother and start up with the delectable, beddable daughter – only nineteen, but a hot number he believed.

The mere thought of all this intrigue brought a smile of delight to his face. Picking up the phone once more, he dialled the Ritz Hotel, asked for Mark Longden.

When there was still no answer, he left a message. Eventually he would hear from him. Weak, depraved, gasping for money, Mark would do his bidding. After all, the architect was his creature, at his beck and call. For as long as he needed him. When Longden was of no further use he would simply discard him, throw him to the wolves.

Jonathan was not at all surprised when Mark Longden telephoned him later and invited him to dinner. With nothing better to do, he decided to accept the invitation, and the two men met for cocktails at the Ritz Hotel in the Place Vendôme.

As they sat together in the bar drinking dry martinis, Jonathan couldn't resist telling Mark about the bit of gossip he had heard earlier in the day.

'That beautiful wife of yours, the delectable Tessa, is in Paris, Mark. Bet you didn't know that, did you?'

Mark was obviously startled, and he stared hard at Jonathan. 'How do you know?'

'A little dickey bird told me. She's here with her other half, her twin that is, the handsome actor, Lorne Fairley. He's going to be making a film here.'

Mark merely nodded, took a slow sip of the drink.

Irritated at the lack of response, wanting to goad Mark, Jonathan said, 'Pity you're not in England. You could have a visit with your *adorable* child.'

To Mark's ears this sounded sarcastic, and he stiffened and said, 'Adele *is* adorable, the most beautiful child in the world.'

Softening slightly, remembering one didn't catch flies with vinegar, Jonathan continued, 'She is *beautiful*, Mark, I'll grant you that. You must miss her.'

'I do,' Mark confided. 'She's such a little chatterbox, loves to tell me about the things she does. She's going to be a bridesmaid at Linnet O'Neill's wedding. She's very excited to be included along with the older girls.'

Jonathan pricked up his ears, leaned forward, his eyes alert and shining with glee. 'And when is the famous wedding? I've forgotten.' He lied, never having known the date; Eleanor was no longer forthcoming with information. She would have to go, no two ways about that, he decided.

'The first Saturday in December. It's the first, I think.'

'Really. And all the clans will be there, I've no doubt. All of the Hartes, the O'Neills and the Kallinskis. Imagine that, Mark. All of them in Yorkshire at the same time. And where is the wedding taking place?'

'The little church in Pennistone Royal village,

and the reception is at Pennistone Royal, at least that's what I've gathered.'

'I'd love to be there . . . as a fly on the wall, I mean. Wouldn't you?'

Mark made a face. 'Not on your life. Not with that snobby bunch.'

'Just imagine, all of the clans . . . what a pity we can't drop a bomb on the church. Blow it up. Or set fire to it. Oh my God, just imagine that!' He began to laugh hilariously.

'You're joking aren't you?' Mark said, eyeing Jonathan warily.

'Of course I am, dear boy. Do you think I'd put myself in that position . . . having to swing for a bunch of Hartes. Not on your life. But you know something, Mark, I wish I could upset the apple-cart a bit. You know, just for fun.'

'No, you don't,' Mark said swiftly. He laughed and added, 'You merely love to shock.'

'Yeah I do, that's true,' Jonathan agreed. 'I read a story recently in the *Daily Mail*, about a bunch of yobbos, you know skinheads, hooligans, who went in a van to one of those picturesque villages in Somerset, and camped on the village green. They claimed it was public land and they had squatters' rights. Just imagine, the police couldn't get them off that village green for months. It disturbed the life of the village no end. Just *imagine* that.'

Motioning to the waiter, Mark ordered two more dry martinis, and then said to Jonathan quietly, 'You shouldn't joke about such things,

Jonathan. At least not to anyone else. Someone might take you seriously.'

Jonathan simply smiled again, sipped the second drink which had suddenly materialized at his fingertips. But I am serious, he thought, smiling inside. Deadly serious. A nice little fire in that church will fry all of the Hartes, O'Neills and Kallinskis. I could kill three clans with one stone, or rather, one fire. Now all I need to do is hire a bunch of yobbos, get them a van and send them up to Pennistone Royal village to create chaos and mayhem on December the first. Well, what a good idea that is. A very good idea indeed.

Chapter Twenty-One

Lorne was packing a bag for the trip to the country when his mobile rang. He answered it immediately. 'Hello?'

'Mr Fairley, it's Vincent.'

On hearing the hotel manager's voice Lorne exclaimed, 'Hello, Vincent! I must have had some phone calls. Right? Or are you calling about something else?'

'About a phone call, Mr Fairley. A few minutes ago a man telephoned asking for Mrs Longden, then for you. As you instructed us earlier this afternoon, the operator said none of the family were in residence.'

'Good. And incidentally, that now happens to be the truth. My sister has left Paris, and I'm going away myself in half an hour. I'll be back after the weekend. However, keep our names off the register and the phone blocked. To all intents and purposes, we're not here.'

'I understand, Mr Fairley. Have a nice weekend.'

'Thanks. Oh, Vincent, I suppose the man who

called didn't leave a name, did he?'

'No, he didn't, but the operator who took the call said he was an Englishman.'

'I see. I'll check in with you over the weekend, and have the telephone operators monitor any calls for us. And keep a record, please.'

'I will, sir.'

The manager hung up, and Lorne finished packing his bag, then he went into Tessa's bedroom, took out a small suitcase, looked at the list she had given him over the phone: nightgown, dressing gown, underwear, flat shoes, sandals.

Within a few minutes he had gathered all of these items and laid them on the bed. Perusing the list again, he noted that she wanted the white outfit she had worn on Thursday, the white Manolo Blahniks, and the pearl chandelier earrings. He located everything, decided to add a couple of other pieces of clothing he liked on her, and finally began to pack the suitcase.

Going into the bathroom he found her make-up bag on the floor, scooped up certain cosmetics she had requested, plus her toothbrush and toothpaste, a few other essentials, and put all of these things in the make-up bag, along with her hairbrush.

Within half an hour he was finished with her bag and his own. Returning to the living room of the suite, he dialled Linnet at Pennistone Royal on his mobile.

'Pennistone Royal,' Margaret was saying a few seconds later.

'Hello, Margaret darling,' Lorne answered in the special voice he reserved for her. 'How're you feeling? Not overdoing it, I hope. You know you've got to take it easy these days.'

'Oh, Lorne, how luverly to hear your voice,' she said in a warm tone. 'How's Tessa?'

'We're both fine, Mags, enjoying Paris. I assume everything is all right at the house?'

'Not a blessed thing out of place,' Margaret reassured him. 'Now, I suppose you're looking for your sister.'

'Yes, I am. Thanks, Margaret.'

'I'll tell her you're on the phone, and give my love to Miss Tessa. Now don't be going away, I'll just put you on hold. Take care of yourself, luvy.'

It's funny how she veers between calling Tessa by her first name and sometimes adds a Miss in front, he thought, but she never does this with me, thank God. I'm always Lorne. Margaret had known them since they were toddlers, and she was part of the family. And yet there were odd moments when she became quite formal with them, as if she'd suddenly remembered she was the house-keeper.

'It's Linnet,' his sister said.

'Hi, Sis!' he replied. 'I'm just checking in.'

'Nothing to report here. All's quiet on the Western front. And I like this Sis bit, far better than all those chirpy names you dig up for me.'

He chuckled. 'Listen, I just wanted to tell you what's happening here.'

'Everything *is* all right, isn't it, Lorne?'

'Absolutely. I decided to take Tessa away for the weekend. We're going to stay with my friend Jean-Claude Deléon, you met him last year, if you remember. Here in Paris with Ma and Pa, en route to the south.'

'How could any woman forget *him*? He's rather dishy, to say the least. Okay, so you're going to spend the weekend at his country place. I think that's a splendid idea.'

'He'd invited us, and I hadn't actually accepted, but then when you alerted me to Mark Longden's presence in Paris, along with Ainsley's, I decided to take him up on his offer. We might never run into either of these two buggers, but you never know. Best to be on the safe side.'

'You don't think they'd try to do anything to you and Tessa?' she exclaimed. 'Or do you?'

'Who the hell knows, Linny. Jack has a bit of a bee in his bonnet about them right now, so I'm not going to take any chances. I can't tell you how glad I am that I accepted the invitation, because the hotel manager just told me an Englishman has been calling, asking for Tessa and then me. I know it's not anybody from the family, because everyone has my mobile number. Anyway, they would have left their name.'

'They would. And Tessa was happy to tag along?'

'Of course. She didn't want to reject the idea, because she didn't want to deprive me of the peace and quiet of the country. She knows I've got to study, learn my part.'

'I'm glad you're getting out of the city. Is it still hot?'

'Very. Anyway, my mobile's on all the time and so is hers – because of her worries about Adele.'

'I know that. Listen, this was a brilliant idea of yours, bundling her off to the country.'

'Yes. Big kiss. Talk to you soon, Linny.'

'Lots of love.'

Lorne sat for a moment staring into space after they had hung up, thinking of Jean-Claude. It had been his idea to cart them off to the country. Not long ago he had phoned again and said he thought they should leave that evening in order to have longer there. Jean-Claude had suggested he pack their bags before coming over to the apartment for a drink. When Lorne had hesitated, had pointed out that Tessa would wonder what was going on, his friend had persuaded him otherwise. A little later Tessa had phoned and had sounded perfectly normal when she had rattled off the items she needed for the weekend. So that was that.

Jumping up, Lorne put the script, his notes, a pad and a few other small items in a carry-all, then went to the desk. He dialled the concierge, asked for a bellboy to bring the luggage down, and hurried to the bedroom to grab a jacket.

Ten minutes later he was being driven across Paris to the seventh arrondissement and the rue de Babylone.

Clos-Fleuri was in a private park on the edge of the Forest of Fontainebleau, and as Jean-Claude drove in through the iron gates Tessa caught her breath in surprise.

The house stood at the end of a short driveway, and now at dusk, in the fading light of day, it looked perfectly beautiful, silhouetted as it was against a deep-pavonian blue sky. Lights had been turned on and the windows glittered brightly, inviting, beckoning to them. What a lovely welcoming sight, she thought.

She saw at once that it wasn't a *château* at all, just as Jean-Claude had insisted earlier on the way from Paris. Lorne had disagreed with him, teasing him, telling him he was far too modest about his country home.

But Jean-Claude had been accurate in calling his house just that – a house, she saw that now. It was of medium size, looked compact from the outside, and it had rounded towers at the four corners, each one topped with a conical-shaped, dark blue slate roof. There were four chimneys and all those tall slender windows . . . far too numerous to count. To the left of the house were buildings which Tessa thought were old stables, and to the right a copse of trees. It was an ancient property, she could see that from the time-worn stones, and pale-rose bricks, and possibly dated back to the eighteenth century.

As they drew closer, Tessa admitted to herself that she had never seen a house that was so appealing to her, and she knew she would never forget this first impression of that lovely, graceful exterior, glimmering softly in the twilight. Her attraction to the house had truly taken her by surprise, since she was not one to be bowled over by any building, and even Pennistone Royal, where she had grown up, had always seemed too big and sprawling, even intimidating to her.

But then again, Clos-Fleuri was *his*, and perhaps that explained her liking for it. Anything to do with him fascinated her.

A few minutes later Jean-Claude was parking at the front door, and this was opened immediately, almost before he'd pulled on the brake. A youngish man, in a white butler's jacket like Hakim's, came down the steps rapidly, greeting them all with enthusiasm, especially Jean-Claude. Once they had been introduced to the houseman, whose name was Gérard, Jean-Claude led them into the house and Gérard went to retrieve their luggage.

'Let me take you to your rooms,' Jean-Claude said, leading them both across the well-furnished hall and up the wide central staircase with highly polished mahogany banisters. 'I must then go to the kitchen and unpack the hamper so that we can decide what we are going to have for dinner.'

'Tessa's a great cook,' Lorne announced rather proudly as they went up the stairs. 'She'll cook dinner for us.'

Glancing at her swiftly, Jean-Claude seemed surprised to hear this, and said, 'I don't think there *is* anything to cook. Lurdes filled the hamper with a number of cold dishes she had prepared for this evening. And of course she'll be here tomorrow to cook for us.'

'But I'd like to make supper, I really would!' Tessa exclaimed. When he didn't answer she added, 'If that's all right with you.'

'*Mais oui* . . . what a nice idea.'

She glanced at him through the corner of her eye as they stepped onto the landing, and thought that he hadn't sounded at all enthusiastic, but she said nothing further, followed him along the carpeted corridor with Lorne.

Halfway down he opened a door, turned to Lorne and said, 'Here we are, *mon vieux*, I know you like this room,' and so saying he ushered her brother inside.

Tessa peered in, saw how charming it looked with a blue-and-white *toile de Jouy* documentary-print fabric on the walls, at the windows and on the bed, and there was a blue carpet on the floor.

'Thanks Jean-Claude, it is my favourite. See you downstairs in a few minutes.' Smiling at them both, Lorne closed the door.

When they came to the end of the corridor, Jean-Claude stopped. 'You're in here, Tessa, I hope you like it,' and he turned the knob, led her inside.

The entire room was covered in an unusual parchment-coloured print patterned with pink roses and green leaves, but it had long since faded, and there was an old-world feeling to it now, a hint of days long gone. Like Lorne's room, the fabric had been used everywhere. She turned around slowly, taking everything in, noting the large four-poster bed, the pretty dressing table, the chaise.

'Well, what do you have to say?' he asked, scrutinizing her intently.

'It's beautiful,' she murmured and gave him a smile, but it was a smile that quickly faltered. Studying her as he was he instantly saw the downcast expression on her face, and understood immediately what was amiss. Striding across the room, he opened a door and said, 'I am in here if you need me. This is my room, Tessa. Do you wish to come in?'

Instantly her spirits lifted and she flew across the floor, ran after him into his bedroom. He was standing waiting for her in the middle of the room, a faint smile flickering on his sensitive yet sensual mouth. He wrapped his arms around her, and against her hair he murmured, 'Does this make you feel better?'

'I thought you were banishing me,' she whispered.

'That is something never to be considered, *chérie, je suis là. Toujours.*'

'Am I going to sleep in here with you?' she asked, her voice still a whisper.

'You had better not think of sleeping anywhere else. But I think it's important to be discreet, for your sake rather than mine, that is why I gave you your own room. You'll use it as a dressing room, of course.' Moving her slightly away from him, he bent down, kissed the tip of her nose. 'My father taught me that discretion is the better part of valour.'

* * *

393

A short while later Tessa went down to the kitchen, and her face lit up when she walked in. It was spacious, built entirely of pale stone, with Provençal tiles and a beamed ceiling, truly country style. But as she glanced around she saw all of the latest modern appliances, and exclaimed, 'I'd love to cook in here, Jean-Claude!'

Turning around, he laughed, nodded. 'I know it is very conducive to creating a gourmet meal. However, I'm afraid that tonight we do have supper already prepared by Lourdes, as I mentioned earlier.'

'I know.' She joined him at the big oak table and looked down at the items he had unpacked from the hamper which Gérard had brought in from the car. Country pâté in a stone dish, cornichons, sliced country ham, a creamy potato salad, a tin of Beluga caviar, and a large glass bowl of luscious dark red cherries. 'It's quite a feast,' she murmured.

'And Gérard just told me there is a wheel of brie cheese in the pantry and fresh baguettes, so I don't think we're going to starve.'

'That's true,' she laughed, and then glanced at the door as Lorne strolled in looking rather debonair in a pair of white slacks and a black linen shirt. 'Gosh, you changed, and I didn't even think of it,' she muttered, shaking her head. 'Perhaps I should go –'

'It's not necessary, *chérie*,' Jean-Claude said, putting a hand on her arm lovingly. 'You look beautiful the way you are.'

She glanced at him and smiled, then said, 'I need a glass of iced water, I'm very thirsty.'

'I'll be bartender,' Lorne offered, walking over to the refrigerator, taking out a bottle of water. 'What about you, Jean-Claude? What would you like?'

'Pink champagne, I think.' Jean-Claude swung around to face Lorne. 'I believe you will find a bottle in there, Gérard usually has one cooling.'

Opening the refrigerator again, Lorne peered inside, took out the bottle of Billecart he found. 'Yep, here it is, and I think I'll join you. Now scoot the two of you, I'll bring the drinks out to the terrace.'

'That's a good idea.' Jean-Claude took hold of Tessa's hand and drew her across the kitchen floor. 'Don't worry about the food, Gérard will attend to it in a moment,' he said to her.

A side door led out to the terrace which ran along the back of the house, and Jean-Claude and Tessa walked over to a group of chairs casually arranged around an old wrought-iron coffee table painted white.

'What a truly beautiful evening it is tonight, Tess,' he murmured, as they sat down together. 'I am so glad we left Paris when we did; there's nothing like a summer evening in the country. I must admit, I do forget how lovely Clos-Fleuri is when I'm away from it.'

'It *is* lovely here, and I agree with you, it was a good idea to leave Paris tonight. It's a pretty name, Clos-Fleuri . . . it means field flower, doesn't it?'

'Exactly. When I found the house it was called that. It was terribly neglected, a broken-down old place, but my sister Marie-Laure helped me to bring it back to life. You will meet her tomorrow, she is coming to lunch with her husband.'

'I can't wait,' Tessa said, smiling inwardly. She wanted to know as much about him as she could, and his sister would certainly offer a few more clues.

Tessa settled back comfortably in the chair, looking up at the sky. It was a very deep blue now and a few stars had already come out. They were extremely clear and bright, seemed so close to the earth she felt as though she could reach up and pluck one down. The gardens surrounding the house were quiet; the only sounds she could hear were the rustling of the trees under the light breeze, and a strange noise she couldn't quite place.

Glancing at Jean-Claude she asked, 'What's that odd sound?'

'*Les grenouilles* . . . the frogs . . . in the pond at the edge of the lawn.'

'Of course, I knew it sounded familiar. There's a frog pond at my mother's house in Yorkshire.'

Gérard came out onto the terrace and said, '*Monsieur, s'il vous plaît, c'est le téléphone pour vous.*'

'Oh. Excuse me,' Jean-Claude murmured, and got up.

Tessa closed her eyes, let herself drift with her thoughts while he went inside. Had she ever felt so peaceful? So complete and content? She doubted it. There had never been much peace with Mark Longden. He was always rushing around like a whirling dervish, restless, forever in a panic. Nothing had ever pleased him. She could do no right. Nor did he ever stop to think . . . about anything; he had no idea what was going on in the world, so self-involved was he. She couldn't wait to be free, a divorced woman.

Lorne and Jean-Claude came walking along the terrace talking. She sat up, took the glass of water from Jean-Claude as he handed it to her.

The three of them clinked glasses and as he sat down Lorne said, 'You know, I've been meaning to ask you something, Jean-Claude. Why did you call your book *Warriors*, using the English word rather than the French?'

'It struck me that warriors sounded better and it has such a good ring to it . . . I think it is more descriptive, so does the publisher, and everyone does know what warrior means. Don't you think it is more international than *querrier*, the French word?'

'I do. And you're right, it works in any language.'

Jumping into the conversation, Tessa said, 'Earlier today I asked you why you cover wars, put yourself in danger, but you know you didn't really answer me. So . . . why do you, Jean-Claude?'

'Most probably because I like to be where the action is. Also I have been doing it for many years, since I was young. In a way I think of myself as a war reporter.'

'But those wars you covered were hellish,' she said softly.

'All war is hell, Tessa, and yet we keep going to war.' He shook his head and a small sigh escaped. For a split second he looked perturbed, but he threw it off, then continued, 'Will we never learn? I suppose not, unless man undergoes a radical change in his nature which I consider most unlikely. War seems to be . . . an integral part of this planet, and I never stop wondering why that is so. I have the need to understand this and understand myself and understand the human race, I think that is why I keep constantly testing myself.'

A small silence settled over the three of them and no one spoke.

Jean-Claude finally cleared his throat, forced a light laugh. 'Enough of war. Let us relax here and count our blessings.' He turned his head, looked at Tessa, and added, 'Unexpected blessings.'

She smiled at him.

Lorne thought: It has worked between them. I knew they were right for each other. And he smiled to himself in the twilight, knowing he had done the right thing in bringing them together.

Before she could stop herself, Tessa blurted out, 'I shall worry about you if you go off to cover another war.'

Jean-Claude did not respond. Instead he took her hand in his, brought it to his mouth, kissed it. And he continued to hold it as he launched into a discussion about the film Lorne would be starring in. He was still holding her hand when Gérard came to tell them supper was ready to be served.

Much later that night, as she lay asleep in his arms, Jean-Claude remained awake, staring up at the ceiling, innumerable thoughts crowding his mind, jostling for prominence. He understood himself very well, knew that he wanted her with him at all times.

He remembered how once, long ago, he had asked himself if anyone could ever know whether a happy marriage would follow love at first sight. A love affair was a risky business. And yet he was sure of the way he felt, and sure about her, and the two of them together. Yet, it was a frightening prospect . . . because it would have to be serious. He had no time to waste, not at this stage in his life. He was fifty-three after all.

She was too young for him, wasn't she? Of course she was. She was only a year older than his son. And yet she was mature for her age, intelligent, educated, cultured, civilized. These were all attributes which he found seductive in a woman.

They had seduced each other in a day . . . drawn together as one soul, as one entity. What did age matter?

Wasn't she his destiny?

CHAPTER TWENTY-TWO

Gideon Harte picked up his briefcase, slipped his mobile phone into his jacket pocket and walked across his office. As he reached the door the telephone on his desk began to ring.

Hurrying back to the desk, he leaned over and picked up the receiver. 'Gideon Harte.'

'It's Andy. Can I see you for a moment?'

'I was just leaving. Is there some kind of problem?'

'Maybe.'

'Okay, come on down to my office.'

'Righto. Be there in a minute.'

Gideon went over to the plate-glass window, put his briefcase on the floor near his desk, then turned, stood looking out at the rooftops of London. The sky had a peculiar look to it, pinkish along the edge of the horizon, a dull glow like a fire in the distance, except that he knew there was no fire. Gideon sighed under his breath. He was very tired; it was almost ten o'clock on this Monday night, and he had had a long day. He was glad his father was coming back from New York at the end of the week. In his absence he had had the entire newspaper chain to supervise, and it had been quite a job since he also ran the London *Evening Post*.

Now his mind zeroed in on Andy McHugh, and he hoped his top investigative reporter was not coming to give him news he had been half expecting for some time – and dreading.

A moment later Gideon swung around as Andy knocked, came barrelling in, exclaiming, 'Sorry about this, Gid, but I felt you had to know tonight.' Closing the door behind him, Andy strode across the floor, joined Gideon at the window.

'Okay, give it to me straight, no frills please,' Gideon said, looking Andy right in the eye.

'It's about Dusty Rhodes.'

'Oh shit, I knew this was going to come and hit us in the face sooner or later. What's happened? Who's got the story?'

'Look, it's not a breaking news story, thank God. As you well know, the Harrogate police and the hospital conveniently forgot that stabbing ever happened. But there's going to be a special piece in the *Daily Mail* tomorrow or Wednesday. An in-depth interview with Melinda Caldwell.'

'Well, thank God it's not about the stabbing. India's name would have been all over that story!'

'You're right, and she probably isn't mentioned in this one, although we don't know that for sure. But listen, Gideon, there's something else. This Caldwell girl has a child with Dusty. A little girl, Atlanta, three years old.'

Startled, Gideon gaped at the reporter. 'Oh God, and he never told India. That I know for sure. She would have confided in me or one of her other cousins, we're all very close. This is going to be a big shock to her. In a sense it changes the picture for India. He's lied.'

'Maybe not. I do believe that the relationship between Dusty Rhodes and the Caldwell girl is over, and has been for a long time. Harry Forster and I really did do a lot of digging into Dusty's past, into his background, and he'd definitely broken up with Melinda Caldwell by 1998, actually maybe just after the child's birth. He's been truthful with India about all that.'

'He just omitted to tell her he has a three-year-old child. Lying by omission, I would call it.'

'That's true.'

'How did you find out, Andy?'

'As you know, I have a contact at the detox clinic, well-paid by us, a male nurse I asked to keep me informed about Melinda. He just phoned tonight with some useful information. About two weeks ago, a friend of Melinda's, Carrie Vale, went down to see her, as she has over the past few months. But this time she brought another woman, who was passed off as also being a friend of Melinda. I say passed off because the other woman is a writer for the *Mail*. Obviously, the two of them induced Melinda to sell her story. "My Terrible Life with Britain's Greatest Living Artist", or something or other like that. My contact told me that unexpectedly Melinda opened up to him tonight, boasted that she'd been paid a lot of money to tell her side of the story, although Barry, my contact, believes she's been motivated by revenge, not money. Wants to get her own back on Dusty Rhodes for dumping her . . . you know how it goes . . . hell hath no fury . . .'

Gideon sat down at his desk, pondering for a moment, then said to the investigative reporter, 'Come and sit here for a minute, Andy,' indicating the chair at the other side of the desk. 'Let's try to assess the damage . . . to India.'

Andy nodded, lowered himself into the chair, also looking thoughtful. 'I don't think there'll be any real damage to her, Gid, I mean as far as the story goes. There's nothing wrong with her having a relationship with Dusty Rhodes. He's single, available. However, I'm fairly certain she herself won't be too favourably disposed towards him, *if* he hasn't told her about his child. And I do say *if*. He may well have explained the whole situation.'

'I doubt it! She'd have confided in one of us. But I agree with you, as far as the actual story's concerned.' Gideon blew out air, slumped down in the chair. 'I shall have to alert her, especially since you said it might appear tomorrow.'

'That's right, and one of the reasons I wanted to talk to you tonight is that there could be repercussions, as far as certain tabloids are concerned. Once the story appears, other papers may do follow-ups, write about Dusty and his kid. If India is with him at Willows Hall she'll be exposed to them, maybe even in the middle of the feeding frenzy. You know what they're like, some are real buggers if you ask me,' Andy finished.

'Damnation, that might easily happen!' Gideon exclaimed, sitting up. 'I can just imagine the headlines in some of the tabloids . . . playing up their different backgrounds. Anyway, it was smart of you to pay off that male nurse, at least we're not going to be taken completely by surprise.'

'I'll stay on top of it, Gideon, but there's not much we can do about other papers picking it up, rehashing, running with it.'

'I realize that. However, let's be thankful for small mercies. I shall call India to warn her, and if she's staying at Willows Hall with him I shall advise her to beat a hasty retreat at once.'

Linnet was sitting in the upstairs parlour at Pennistone Royal, studying the sketches for her wedding gown, as well as those for the bridesmaids' dresses. She had spread them out on the coffee table, and suddenly she glanced up at Evan, who sat at the other side of the room near the oriel window.

'I know you're going over the list of tomorrow's chores at the Leeds store, Evan, but can you spare me a couple of minutes?' Linnet asked.

'Of course. What do you need?'

'Your eyes. I just can't make up my mind about my wedding dress. Maybe you can help me, you've got such good taste.'

Evan put down her notebook and came to join Linnet on the sofa, picked up one of the sketches and gazed at it for a few minutes. She suddenly made a face. 'No, not this one. Far too modern.' Slowly, paying great attention to the details of the sketches, she went through all of them, discarding every one. Then she turned to Linnet and said, 'I'm not really crazy about any of these, Linny, to be really honest. This one isn't too bad.' As she spoke she selected a sketch, handed it to Linnet and added, 'Even so, it isn't the kind of wedding gown I picture you in, or how I see you in my mind's eye on that very special day.'

'How do you see me?' Linnet asked, sitting back against the cushions, staring at Evan with interest, valuing her opinion.

'I think you should look elegant yet romantic.' Evan lifted her hands, moved them around in front of her, as if trying to draw a shape in the air. 'I think you should wear a medieval dress, no, not that, but something that hints of . . . the Tudor period! Yes, that's it, and not white, it's too sharp for your pale skin and red hair. I think the gown should be cream-coloured, *rich*, like clotted cream, and made of satin. *Heavy* satin. There should be pearl embroidery on it, too. The style I envision is with a high bustline, *Empire*, perhaps even with a high neckline and long sleeves. A full skirt, almost a crinoline. Elizabeth Tudor style, I think. That's how *you* should look, like a young Tudor queen . . . and you are a queen that day, you know.'

Linnet was staring at her, her bright-green eyes sparkling. 'I love what you're describing, that dress sounds fabulous. Listen, you're a fashion designer, so design it for me! Oh, please say yes, Evan. There's just enough time, if you start immediately. Today is September the fourth, my wedding is on December the first, that's a good three months.'

'Do you really want me to design your wedding dress?' Evan asked, eyeing her warily. 'Are you sure you don't want a gown from Balmain or Yves Saint Laurent? A big-name designer?'

'No, I want Evan Hughes. Say you'll do it. *Please*.'

At this moment the phone on the desk began to ring, and Linnet got up, and went to answer it. 'Hello? Pennistone Royal.'

'It's Gideon,' he said.

'Hi, darling! Are you looking for Evan? She's right here.'

'I'll speak to her in a minute, Linny, but first I want to have a word with India.'

'Oh, Gid, India went over to Niddersley to have dinner with her grandmother. Great-Aunt Edwina's been wanting to meet Dusty Rhodes, so they drove over there at six-thirty. Have you tried her on her mobile?'

'It's off. Hmmmm. Is she staying with Dusty tonight? Or is she coming back to Pennistone Royal, do you know?'

'Oh, she's definitely coming back here. She told Evan they could drive to Leeds together tomorrow morning, since they're both in the middle of the renovations at the store. That's their baby.'

'I'm glad about that!' he said somewhat sharply. 'I mean that she will be with you.'

'Gideon, you sound ever so put out. Is there something the matter?'

'Sort of,' he responded, sighing heavily, and then repeated everything Andy McHugh had told him a short while before.

When he had finished, Linnet said, 'I doubt she knows Dusty has a child. She once made a reference to the fact that he hadn't been married, that he had no children. *Phew!* She's not going to like this, is she, Gid?'

'Not at all, she's so straight and open and she can't abide duplicity in others.'

'He may have just been embarrassed to say something,' Linnet pointed out, as usual trying to find the best in others.

'Perhaps you're right. On the other hand, don't you think he could have mentioned it after the stabbing? Let's face it, his affair with Melinda Caldwell had suddenly come to light – why not tell the whole truth? Shouldn't he have trusted India to understand?'

'I suppose so, but we don't know Dusty Rhodes, now do we?' At that moment India walked in, a look of puzzlement on her face. She stared at Linnet quizzically.

'Hi, India!' Evan exclaimed, smiling at her, then turned to look at Linnet, signalling with her eyes. 'Here's India!' she added, putting great emphasis on her name.

'I know that. Gideon, India just arrived. I'm going to put her on before you speak to Evan.'

India walked to the desk, frowned and muttered, 'Why were you talking about Dusty?'

Linnet remained silent, thrust the receiver at her, stepped away, went back to the sofa, grimacing to Evan as she did. She knew India was going to be upset . . . and why shouldn't she be?

The room was silent. The two other women said nothing as India stood at the desk, listening to Gideon, her face impassive. But Linnet and Evan both saw the little vein pulsing at one side of her temple, and her eyes had narrowed perceptibly. She was angry but the anger was contained.

At last Gideon finished and she replied, 'Yes, absolutely. Of course I'm not going to stay with him at Willows Hall, Gideon, that would be asking for trouble, since you believe that some of the tabloids might follow up. Anyway, it just so happens that I was planning to stay here at Pennistone Royal all week because of my work at the store. Evan and I are on a project together; oh, and here she is. Thanks, Gideon, for the warning and the advice.'

Evan rushed to take the phone. 'Gideon, how are you?'

'Worn out tonight, bloody knackered, actually. I can't tell you how happy I am that Dad's going to be back at his desk on Monday.'

'I know it's been rough, especially this month.' Turning around, facing the windows, Evan lowered her voice, and asked, 'You're not still angry with me, are you, honey?'

'No, that's all been blown away by hard work,' he laughed. 'I love you, Evan, you mustn't forget that. Just because we have a disagreement now and again doesn't mean I've fallen *out* of love. Just out of bed on the wrong side. Anyway, on some days, that's what's really making me irritable.'

She laughed with him, although she knew he didn't really mean this. He had been annoyed with her all last week. But now, tonight, he sounded more like his old self to a certain extent. 'By the way, I think I might have to stay up here this coming weekend, Gid.'

'Because of work?'

'Partially. I also promised Robin I'd go and see him. It's not a problem for you, is it?'

'No. As a matter of fact I think my parents will come straight up to Yorkshire, they usually do when they've been abroad. I'll be there, too. So, how do you like them apples?'

'I positively love them apples.' Stepping further away, she dropped her voice another octave, and whispered, 'From what I heard Linnet say to you, there's problems with Dusty.'

'Linnet will tell you all the gory details, but the bottom line is that Dusty has a child by the woman who stabbed him, and he never told India.'

'He's been a bit stupid, hasn't he?'

'Oh, yes. And I've got to go, darling, I'm beat. I'll ring you tomorrow. Big kiss.'

'Big kiss. I love you, Gideon.'

'Me too you.'

Evan put the phone down and went to join her cousins who were seated together on the sofa. She saw at once that India looked unusually pale and her face was strained.

'So, Evan, what do *you* think?' India asked softly, looking across at her, a silvery-blonde brow lifting.

Sitting down opposite Linnet and India, Evan answered, 'Well, I don't actually know the whole story. What's happened?'

Linnet explained everything, mentioned the feature which was about to appear in a national newspaper, probably the next day, and finished, 'Gideon's worried about the aftermath, the tabloids having a field day with it. You know they love scandals, and especially those involving well-known people.'

Evan looked at India sympathetically. 'And you never had an inkling?' she asked softly.

'No, I didn't. And after the stabbing I don't understand why he didn't explain. Gideon's right, he told me about Melinda, so why not mention his little girl?'

'He may very well have felt embarrassed,' Linnet murmured, reaching out, taking India's hand in hers, squeezing it reassuringly.

'I agree with Linny,' Evan remarked. 'I think that's the only possible explanation. And where is the little girl, by the way? Since her mother's in rehab who's looking after her?'

'Presumably the child's grandmother,' Linnet volunteered.

'I do wish he'd told me, I feel rather foolish.' India leaned back against the sofa, looking saddened. 'And he misjudged me.'

'How was Great-Aunt Edwina tonight?' Linnet

now asked, wanting to distract her for a moment. 'And how did the dinner go?'

'Fine. It went well.'

'Did she like him?' Linnet probed.

'Oh yes, very much. If you'll pardon the expression, he charmed the pants off her.'

Evan's mouth began to twitch, and she couldn't help it, she started to laugh. Linnet joined in, and after a moment India was laughing with them. For a few seconds they were hilarious.

Finally coming to a spluttering stop, wiping her eyes, Linnet cried, 'Oh, India, you do say the funniest things sometimes. I had this wonderful picture of Great-Aunt Edwina without her knickers. But seriously, what *are* you going to do?'

'I'm going to ask him about it. What else is there to do?'

'When are you going to do that?' Linnet asked, as usual like a dog with a bone.

'Tomorrow morning. On the way to Leeds. Evan and I are driving over very early, so we'll stop off at Follifoot to see him. Are you game, Evan?'

'Absolutely, India. You can throw down the gauntlet and I'll be right there at your side. Harte rule number one, isn't it?'

Dusty Rhodes was not fully awake, still half dozing on the edge of sleep. But as more daylight filtered into his bedroom he began to bestir himself, knowing he should get out of bed, go to his studio, attempt to paint. And so finally he sat up, and as

411

he did so he became conscious of another presence in the room.

Blinking in the dim light, peering, he now saw a figure standing at the bottom of the bed, although it took him a moment to determine who it was.

'India!' he suddenly exclaimed, bringing his long legs onto the floor, standing up, moving towards her rapidly. 'What are you doing here, sweetheart?'

For a moment she didn't answer, merely stared at him, until at last she said, 'I came to warn you.'

'Warn me? About what?'

'Melinda Caldwell has sold her story to the *Daily Mail*.' As she spoke she handed him the newspaper.

He felt as if his insides were going to drop out, even though he had known that inevitably, one day, something like this would happen. He took the paper, threw it on the bed, stood gaping at her speechlessly. He saw how cold her eyes were, noted the severity of her mouth, became aware of her contained demeanour, yet there was anger hovering below the surface.

Feeling suddenly vulnerable and stupid, standing there stark naked, when she was dressed for work, he snatched his robe from the bottom of the bed and pulled it on hastily.

'It's not in the paper today,' she continued in that icy voice of hers. 'But the feature is announced inside. It's going to run for two days, starting tomorrow. I thought you should know my cousin Gideon thinks that some of the tabloids will want to rehash it, try to interview you, and so I suggest you make a hasty retreat, go somewhere for a week until it dies down. The press are going to be on your tail, you know.'

'But there's a lot of security here now, thanks to you and Jack Figg,' he protested. 'I'm protected behind the gates.'

'I just wanted to alert you, it's up to you what you do. I'd also like to ask you a question.'

'Yes, ask me, sweetheart.' He stepped towards her but she immediately backed away, and he knew at once that winning her over wasn't going to be quite so easy. 'India, you know you can ask me anything,' he repeated.

'Why didn't you tell me you had a child with Melinda Caldwell?'

He stared at her blankly, at a loss for words; he had no excuse really, and he should have told her, explained. He felt suddenly embarrassed, didn't know what to say, and so he shrugged, looking help-less. 'I guess I thought it might come between us.'

'And it has, but only because you didn't trust me enough to confide in me. You've totally misjudged me, Dusty, and that makes me feel very sad. Because I realized last night that you don't really understand me or know who I am, where I'm coming from . . . emotionally and philosophically. You've just no idea about *me*, and I don't think it's possible for us to continue our relationship.'

'Don't say that!' he exclaimed. 'I do know you and understand you. And I care for you, India. You're very important to me, surely you realize that.'

She shook her head. 'I do know one thing . . .

you're totally wrong in your attitude towards my family. You've dismissed them as snobs whom you don't care to meet, when in actuality they're not. They're very nice, normal, hard-working people. But you never bothered to find that out. And that leads me to believe that you are arrogant, self-centred and a coward.'

'How can you say such things! I met your grandmother last night, didn't I?' he blustered.

'Oh, don't be so ridiculous! An old lady of ninety-five whom you had eating out of your hand in five seconds, because you flirted with her, charmed her. I'm talking mostly about my cousins, my closest friends. You don't want to meet them because they're more your size, and not so easily manipulated.'

'India, listen to me, you're going off at the deep end. I *was* going to tell you about Atlanta when I got out of the hospital, but to be honest I didn't want to spoil our little romantic interlude and —'

'It's certainly spoiled now,' she snapped and headed towards his bedroom door, opened it, stepped onto the landing.

'Hey, wait a minute! Are you breaking up with me because I have a child, for God's sake?' he exploded, suddenly irate.

'No, I'm not. I certainly have enough compassion to understand about your little girl, understand that she's part of your life, that you have a commitment to her. I am leaving you because you don't trust me, don't know me, and certainly you make no effort to see things from my point of view.'

414

'You're being very unfair, India,' he chastised, but his voice was lower.

'And so are you, Dusty. You know how much I love you, and actually I think you love me. Yet you don't want the relationship to move forward, certainly you don't want to make a commitment.' She shrugged. 'So what's the point? I think it's time for me to move on, frankly.'

She started down the staircase.

He ran after her. 'India, wait!' he begged from the top of the landing.

'It's over, Dusty.' She continued on down the stairs without looking back.

'But listen, what about your portrait?'

'Fuck my portrait,' she shot back, crossed the hall and went out of the front door. She slammed it so hard he thought the glass panes on either side would shatter, but they merely rattled.

Dusty was unable to move for a moment, stood staring down at the door. Finally he turned away, went back to the bedroom, filling with a sense of desolation now that he was alone. Could he win her back? He wasn't sure. She was furious with him and he understood the reasons why. He cursed himself under his breath for not trusting her more. But then he had never been able to trust those who truly loved him. Would he never learn from the mistakes of the past?

Once she was outside the house, India ran all the way to the Aston Martin, which she had parked near the big barns a short while before. She scrambled into the driver's seat and immediately turned to look at Evan.

'Are you all right?' Evan asked, touching her arm lightly, her face ringed with concern. 'You're awfully white, India dear.'

'I'm okay,' India replied, and promptly burst into tears.

Evan put her arm around her, and tried to soothe her, offering her tissues, murmuring kind words. And after a moment India, who was very strong, pulled herself together. She quickly recouped a little, blew her nose, and turned on the ignition. 'Let's get out of here,' she said, driving forward. 'I want to put some distance between myself and Mr Rhodes.'

'I understand,' Evan murmured, and decided not to ask any questions for the moment.

A little later, once they were on the road to Leeds, India told her what had happened, adding, 'I do love him, you know.' She was staring ahead, her eyes focused on the busy road as she explained, 'But I can't be with a man who doesn't know who I am. So that's it. I'll get over him. Eventually.'

'I'm sure you will,' Evan agreed, but she couldn't help wondering if India would.

CHAPTER TWENTY-THREE

Paula looked up as the door to the upstairs parlour opened, and her face broke into smiles at the sight of her eldest daughter. 'Good morning, Tessa darling,' she said. 'I see you're bringing me a very welcome pot of coffee. Don't stand there hesitating, come in. And you've brought a cup for yourself, that's good; we can have a little chat, catch up.'

'I know you've been up since the crack of dawn, working, and I didn't want to disturb you before. But it's almost eleven and I thought you could use some refreshment by now.' Tessa walked over to the coffee table standing between the two big plump sofas, and setting the tray down, lowered herself onto a sofa.

Pushing back her chair, Paula left the time-worn Georgian desk once her grandmother's, and joined Tessa, sat facing her, pouring the coffee. After putting milk and a sweetener in her cup she took a sip, then sat back, eyeing her daughter, affection written on her face. 'You look lovely, Tessa, very

417

well indeed. I thought so at dinner last night. Paris must have done you good, agreed with you.'

'It did, yes, and Lorne is always so kind, thoughtful. We had a nice time together.'

'So he told me,' Paula murmured, immediately thinking of Jonathan Ainsley and Mark Longden and their troubling presence in Paris together last weekend. First Linnet and then Lorne had filled her in separately, and Jack Figg had given her a full report yesterday. The information he had supplied had only made her more determined than ever to deal with Tessa's husband in the most appropriate and effective manner.

Leaning back against the cushions, Tessa said, 'Last night you told me you are having the meeting with Mark and all the lawyers on Monday afternoon. And that I have to be there. But do I really?'

'Yes, actually you do, Tessa,' Paula replied, leaning forward. 'I know you can't abide him, and neither can I, but it *is* necessary. Christopher Jolliet is rather insistent about that, and he's one of the best lawyers I've ever had. I do listen to his advice, you know, whatever you might think about me "running the show", as you call it.'

Tessa laughed. 'Then I'll be there, Mummy . . .' She did not finish her sentence, frowned, and hesitated before asking, 'Will I have to do anything? Say anything?'

'Not unless you're asked any questions by Christopher, or Mark's lawyers, then you will have to answer,' Paula explained.

'I see. A couple of weeks ago, when I spoke to

you in New York, you told me that you had a plan. What is it?'

'I'd prefer not to discuss it with you today, Tess, if you don't mind,' Paula answered swiftly. 'I still have a few things to iron out, talk over with Christopher this weekend, before it will be all settled in my mind. But please be assured I am certain my plan will work.'

'If you say so, Mummy, and really it's all right, we don't have to talk about it now. I trust your judgement: in my opinion there's nobody smarter than you.'

'Probably your father, I'm sure,' Paula laughed. 'But thank you for your confidence. By the way, I had a little visit with Adele early this morning, in the kitchen. And she's so adorable, perfectly fine, and as happy as a lark.' Paula paused, then added, 'Thank God she wasn't hurt in any way on that awful day. And I'm so sorry I wasn't here to share your burdens –'

'But Linnet was,' Tessa interrupted, 'and she handled things extremely well. Actually, I don't know what I would have done without her. It was so smart of her to bring in Jack, but I've told you that.'

'Yes, you did, and you're quite right. She used great judgement.'

'I've agreed to be Linnet's matron of honour, Mummy.'

'You changed your mind?' Paula was taken aback, and she looked at Tessa alertly.

'Well, yes I did, because I think she was a bit hurt when I refused originally.'

'So now it's going to be India, Evan and Emsie as bridesmaids, and you as matron of honour? Is that it?'

'Not exactly. I've changed my mind about Adele being part of the wedding. I told Linnet the other day that Adele can be a bridesmaid after all, just as she wanted her to be.'

Harmony at last between them, Paula thought. It's hardly believable. 'I think that's lovely of you, darling, and I'm so glad you decided to participate. I know Linny was truly disappointed when you said no.'

'Did she tell you that Evan's going to be designing her wedding gown?'

'No, she didn't, but it's only Saturday, I've hardly caught my breath since arriving in Yorkshire. Do tell me all about it, Tess.'

'Linnet didn't like any of the sketches she'd had from various designers, and she asked Evan's opinion the other evening. Evan came up with some superb ideas . . . like heavy cream satin, pearl embroidery, a style reminiscent of the Tudor period, and Linnet loved her suggestions. So Evan's been busy sketching, in between tearing down the Leeds store and rebuilding it with India.'

'You *are* joking? About the Leeds store?' Paula asked, looking askance at her daughter.

'Of course. But they are doing a lot of innovative things. You'll be surprised, Mummy. They've certainly been much more radical in the changes they're making there than I have at Harrogate.' Tessa drank some of her black coffee, and added,

'Much to the annoyance of that old harridan of a secretary of yours apparently.'

'Which secretary do you mean?'

'Eleanor. At the Leeds store.'

'She's not really an old harridan,' Paula answered. She knew Eleanor was not spying for Jonathan any more. There was nothing to find out.

'It's just a manner of speaking, Mums, but she is a grumpy, bad-tempered woman.'

'Now, you mentioned India,' Paula said. 'How is she? Linnet told me there's been a bit of trouble between her and the artist, Russell Rhodes.'

Tessa filled her mother in, and finished, 'I do feel sorry for her. India's so good, such a straight person, I suppose it's only natural she feels let down.'

Paula nodded, picked up the coffee pot, poured another cup for herself. As she put the pot down she gave Tessa a long, concentrated look, understanding as she had last night that there had been something of a change in Tessa's attitude, in her demeanour. A change so remarkable there was obviously more to it than met the eye. It was particularly pronounced at this moment.

Her daughter was not as prickly or sharp, intent or aggressive as she so often was. In fact there was a lovely new softness about her, something Paula had never seen in her before. Tessa appeared much more feminine, more relaxed. She had a wonderful glow about her, the kind of glow that usually emanated from a woman who had been well and truly loved, who was sexually satisfied – that was the only way Paula could describe it.

Oh, my God! Paula sat bolt upright on the sofa, instantly looking across at Tessa, scrutinizing her carefully. *There's a man in her life*. She's fallen in love. It's obviously reciprocated, so it's genuine. Yes, that was it. Undoubtedly. Love had caused this most extraordinary change in her daughter.

So startled was she by this sudden and unexpected knowledge, Paula instantly got up, walked over to the window, stood looking out at the moors, not wishing Tessa to see the expression on her face. That she was flabbergasted was an understatement. Who can it be? she asked herself, when did it happen? Paula had been absent for almost two months so she had no real answers for herself.

Only Tessa had the answers. If anyone else in the family had known they would have mentioned it to her on the phone, she was quite positive of that.

Tessa was in love but no one knew. Did that mean there was some kind of problem attached to the relationship? A married man perhaps? She hoped not.

'Mummy, I forgot to tell you about the dinner India and I had with Great-Aunt Edwina. Please come back to the sofa, I want you to hear all about it.'

Arranging a neutral expression on her face, Paula straightened her navy linen shirt and walked back to the sofa. 'I'm all ears,' she murmured, sitting down opposite her daughter.

Tessa told her mother the entire story of the evening with Edwina and the gift of the unique pieces of jewellery to herself and India.

Tessa went on, 'Great-Aunt Edwina told me that I shouldn't dwell on my marital problems, that I should get the divorce and move on to greener pastures. She said she hoped the débâcle with Mark wouldn't put me off men, that I had to get over that hurdle. And immediately.'

'Did she now.' Paula gazed at Tessa, her head on one side, and after a slight pause, she said, 'I'm making the assumption you took her advice to heart.'

'Yes, I did.' Jumping up, Tessa came and sat next to Paula on the sofa. 'The most wonderful thing has happened to me –'

'You've fallen in love,' Paula interrupted.

'How did you know?'

'It's written all over your face, darling. I noticed a great difference in you last night, and it's more marked than ever today. I'm assuming he's fallen in love with you?'

'Yes,' Tessa said, blushing. 'At first sight.'

'And who *is* this man who has wrought this change in you?'

'It's Jean-Claude Deléon, the French writer. You met him in Paris with Lorne . . . he's Lorne's friend. Do you remember him?'

Although she was rarely at a loss for words, Paula was speechless and she sat staring at Tessa, and then recovering, taking a deep breath, she said, 'Of course I remember him. He's an extraordinary person. Very attractive, very celebrated. And when did this happen?'

Before Tessa could respond Margaret appeared in the doorway of the upstairs parlour, clearing her throat, and murmuring, 'Excuse me, Mrs O'Neill, but I was wondering how many we'll be for lunch today?'

'Goodness, Margaret, I'm afraid I've no idea,' Paula answered, turning to Tessa. 'There's you and me, and Grandfather Bryan, right Tess? What about Linnet and Evan?'

'Oh, yes, Mums, they'll be here, because right now they're working downstairs on the designs for the wedding gown and bridesmaids' dresses. At least, Evan is, and Linnet's going over other details for the wedding.'

'Very well, Margaret, it looks as if we'll be five. Oh, and there's Emsie and Desmond. So we'll be seven.'

'No, no, wait a minute,' Tessa interjected. 'Linnet mentioned something about Julian coming for lunch with Uncle Ronnie.'

'Oh, that'll be lovely, I can't wait to see them. Why don't you think in terms of ten for lunch, Margaret. There's always the possibility that Gideon might end up here as well.'

The housekeeper nodded, and, glancing at the piece of paper in her hand and then at Paula, she said, 'I've made your favourite Mrs Beeton's Mulligatawny soup for the first course, and I'd planned to make a cottage pie. Mr O'Neill likes it so much, you know, and a steak-and-kidney pie as well. Plus steamed fresh vegetables, and I've also got a luverly Yorkshire ham baking in the oven, Mrs O'Neill. For dessert I'm going to make bread-and-butter pudding. And fresh fruit for those on a diet,' she thought to add, glancing at Tessa.

'It sounds like a delicious feast. I must admit, I've missed your wonderful cooking, Margaret.'

'Thank you, Mrs O'Neill, and I'm ever so glad you're back.'

Once they were alone again, Tessa hurriedly went on, 'Getting back to Jean-Claude. We met last week, Mummy, when I went to Paris with Lorne. It was one of those instantaneous things: we responded to each other immediately, and well, what can I say, we both feel as if we've been hit by a bus.'

Paula nodded. 'Is this a flash in the pan on your part, Tessa dear?'

'No, and it's not on his either. Jean-Claude wants a serious, long-term relationship?'

'Are we talking marriage here?'

'Well, he hasn't used that word, but yes, I think that's what he means when he says long-term relationship.' Noting the worried look settling on her mother's face, she asked quickly, 'Don't you approve of him?'

Paula was silent for a moment, and then she murmured, 'There's something of an age difference, isn't there, darling?'

'Yes. But it doesn't matter to me, nor does it matter to him.'

'How old is he?'

425

'He's fifty-three.'

'Really. He certainly doesn't look it, and I'm sure he's serious in his intentions, he's that kind of responsible, caring man, from what I've observed.'

'So it's all right then?'

Paula fixed her eyes on Tessa. 'Would it matter if I said it wasn't, that I objected to him?'

'Yes, it would, because I want you to approve. But it wouldn't make me change my mind . . . how can I change what I feel for him?'

'You can't, not if you really love him. And you are thirty-two, a mature adult, and therefore you can do anything you wish with your life. But it just so happens that I don't disapprove of Jean-Claude, no not at all. Quite the contrary, in fact. I always thought he was a charming man, and your father likes him, too.'

Tessa sat back, relaxing her taut muscles. 'That's a big relief, Mummy. After the horrible problems we've all had with Mark, it's important to me that you like the man I'm involved with now.'

'I do. And I just want to say this. I think you must be careful at the moment, while we are trying to settle the details of the divorce.'

'Do you mean I shouldn't see Jean-Claude?' Tessa asked, appalled at the thought.

'No, that'll be all right, providing you are discreet, don't flaunt yourselves.'

'We wouldn't do that, in fact we didn't in Paris. We ate at his apartment, and at the weekend Lorne and I went with Jean-Claude to his country house. We'll be circumspect.'

'There's another thing, Tessa.'

'Yes, Mummy?'

'You're looking exceptionally pretty and happy at the moment. But on Monday I'd prefer you to look sad, miserable, and a little bit plain, if you can manage that. For the meeting with the lawyers and Mark, I mean.'

'I'll make myself look drab, use hardly any make-up, that should do the trick.'

'It will. You must play the victim, which indeed you are. And that's the last thing you look at this moment.'

Tessa left the upstairs parlour, intent on playing with Adele before lunch, and Paula returned to the old Georgian desk near the window. She picked up her pen, thinking she would do some more work, but it instantly struck her that she was no longer in the mood. No, not this morning, she decided, I've become too distracted.

Putting the pen down, she sat back in the chair and gazed out of the window. Already the heather was blooming on the moors, and by the middle of September the rolling hills would be an undulating sea of purple as far as the eye could see. How beautiful it was out there today . . . the sky a soft light blue with puffy white clouds skimming towards the horizon. Paula loved the moors best at this time of year when the bees hovered in the sunlight where the heather bloomed; her daughter Linnet was addicted to them all year round, just as Emma had been.

Paula's thoughts shifted, and she suddenly

realized how truly happy she was to be back here at Pennistone Royal, the house she had grown up in and which she loved so much; she was glad to be sitting here at this window, at the desk where Grandy had worked for so many years, savouring the memories, thinking of her enduring love for Emma. But a moment later her thoughts veered away, went directly to her first-born child.

Smiling to herself, Paula understood how brainwashed she was; they all were because for years Tessa had drilled something into them: *She had been born five minutes before Lorne.* And so, Tessa pointed out to anyone who would listen, *she* was the eldest of Paula's children.

Tessa McGill Harte Fairley Longden. A rather special young woman.

Forget about the Longden, Paula reminded herself. Her daughter had already dropped *his* name, had gone back to her maiden name, one she had always been inordinately proud of.

How tragic it was that Tessa had been physically and mentally abused for years, and none of them had ever known because she was too ashamed and afraid to confide in them. Until the day had come when she couldn't take it any longer, and fearing for her very life she had fled the marital home. She had been a victim for such a long time, but eventually she had found the strength, courage, pride, determination and will to survive – all of which Tessa had inherited through her from Grandy. And so Tessa had saved herself and her child from a deadly fate.

And now a man called Jean-Claude Deléon had arrived on the scene. If he stayed, nothing would ever be the same again. And everyone's life would be changed, of that Paula was absolutely convinced. He was the catalyst to end all catalysts. In a sense, the family's future was in his hands. But this did not alarm Paula.

She sat pondering him . . . a man of such stature, intellect, ethics and vision. Most of France was at his feet. She knew full well of his prominence, his celebrity, not only through the media but from Lorne as well, who idolized him, and with good reason.

Jean-Claude had impressed her on numerous occasions when she had been in his company; she liked his humility, his lack of pomposity. He had a wonderful sense of humour, and he had frequently made her laugh uproariously; she had also been impressed by his wisdom and his kindness, and she knew very well the potency of his considerable charm.

He was twenty-one years older than her daughter, just three years younger than she was, but it struck Paula now that his age was an advantage. He was mature, serious-minded, responsible and trustworthy. Should their liaison last Tessa would be in safe hands for the rest of her life, and for that Paula was thankful.

Yes, the advent of Jean-Claude was a serious matter for the family, and for her especially to consider. She had already seen the effect he had had on Tessa, the startling change in her demeanour;

suddenly she was a much nicer person, or so it seemed to her. And if Tessa were with him on a permanent basis there might well be other changes in Tessa's personality and in her life.

Would her eldest child push her overweening ambition to one side? Could she give up her dream of running the Harte Stores to be the full-time wife of the writer–philosopher? Or would she remain determined to be the heir-apparent? The Dauphine, as she called herself?

Funny that she would choose a French name to describe herself, Paula now thought, gazing absently out of the window, but seeing nothing except Tessa's face . . . how softly beautiful she was today. If that was the effect this man had on her daughter then he would be welcomed joyfully with open arms by her.

If Tessa gave up her dreams of glory, of being the great merchant princess, then the way would be open for Linnet. She could run Harte's without fear of interference, couldn't she? Would Emsie want to join her sister one day? And where did India fit in, if Tessa was gone? And what about Evan? Paula was fully aware of Evan's enormous ambition, her desire to play a major role at Harte's. And if Evan married Gideon, would he object to a working wife?

No, not Gideon, Paula had a ready answer for that particular question. Gideon was a true Harte, since both of his parents were Hartes, and he had grown up understanding the female work ethic. His mother Emily ran Harte Enterprises and had since before he was born. Working women were the norm not the exception for him.

We're all women at Harte's . . . and it's the women Jean-Claude will affect the most, if he marries Tessa. Because so many things turn around her, Paula thought, her eyes narrowing. I have to meet him again, and soon. I need to see him through different eyes, a mother's eyes. And also through the eyes of the head of a major corporation . . . because he could so easily change the balance of power . . .

The door flew open, interrupting Paula's thoughts. Her granddaughter ran towards her, shouting, 'Gran, Gran, come and play with me.'

Paula rose, moved forward, caught the child in her arms, hugged her closely. Over her shining silver-gilt hair she looked at Tessa, who stood near the door. 'Is he all right with this one, do you think?' she asked. 'Does she present any problems?'

'None whatsoever,' Tessa answered with the utmost confidence. 'We discussed the whole subject at length. He's very happy about her. Very happy indeed.'

Paula nodded. Tessa might have her chance of happiness after all, provided that Paula could put Mark Longden in his place.

Chapter Twenty-Four

The conference room of the law firm of Crawford, Creighton, Phipps, Crawford and Jolliet had not changed over the years.

Paula had been coming here for most of her adult life, whenever it had been necessary to seek legal advice from John Crawford, senior partner of the firm and the family solicitor. And now on this Monday afternoon there was something reassuring about the familiar room with its dark wood panelled walls, long mahogany conference table surrounded by twenty-four chairs and the handsome bronze chandeliers which hung from the ceiling.

One of the secretaries had shown Paula into the conference room a moment ago, and she walked across to the window, looked down into the street, knowing Tessa was due to arrive at any moment. But there was no sign of her yet.

Moving away from the window, she strolled over to the large painting of John, stood gazing at it, thinking what a handsome and distinguished-looking man he was, a man whom she had relied on for so much diverse advice over the years. He was semi-retired these days, but readily available when his wisdom was required, or when some detail of the vast Harte family affairs was needed. He had a prodigious memory and a unique knowledge of the Hartes and their business empire stretching back to Emma's days.

In many ways John was like a member of the family, and he still had a meeting once a month with her mother, since he was a trustee of the Emma Harte Foundation, which Daisy ran. This rich organization regularly doled out large amounts of money to a variety of deserving charities carefully chosen by Daisy and John.

'Good afternoon, Paula,' Christopher Jolliet, John's nephew, exclaimed, hurrying into the room. 'I'm sorry to keep you waiting, I was just finishing a phone call with Uncle John when you arrived. He sends his love, by the way.'

Paula smiled, nodded, and clasped Christopher's hand as he kissed her cheek. 'Hello, Christopher.' Indicating the wall she added, 'I was just admiring his portrait. And you didn't keep me waiting, I was early.'

Glancing at her quickly, he took in the smart black suit and white silk blouse, the elegance of her overall appearance. But there was a severity about her, a grimness in her, and he knew better than anyone that she meant business. She was about to demolish a man today and he really couldn't blame her. Mark Longden had asked for what he was about to get. 'It's nice to see you, but

433

I must admit I'm sorry it's on such a miserable occasion,' Christopher went on as he led her over to the conference table. 'You're looking well, Paula, New York must have agreed with you.'

'It did. We were all rather busy, but I do love that city, and it was such a nice change.'

'When does Shane get back?'

'He's leaving Tuesday – tomorrow. He has a meeting in the morning at the World Trade Center, and then he'll be taking the night flight to London, arriving on Wednesday morning. He had to stay on in New York because he had business to deal with, and then this meeting came up all of a sudden. It's about building a new O'Neill hotel in Manhattan, and it was important enough for him to attend the meeting himself. Usually his sister deals with most of the American business, as you know, but Merry's on vacation with her family somewhere in the Canadian Rockies at the moment.'

'Shane's really made such a wonderful success of the hotel chain, it's understandable why Grandfather Bryan is so proud of him.'

Paula laughed. 'His father adores him, as you know, and adores all of us for that matter. He's a terrific old man.'

'It would be nice if we could have dinner when Shane gets back,' Christopher said, pulling out a chair for Paula, then sitting down next to her. He put the sheaf of manila folders he was holding down on the table, leaned back in the chair and asked her, 'Is there anything else we need to discuss before the others arrive?'

Paula shook her head. 'I don't think so. You clarified various points over the weekend, when we spoke on the phone. I'm fine with it. In fact, I've gone over everything so many times in my head, I know it off by heart.'

'I'm sure you do.' Christopher rose when the door opened and one of the secretaries brought Tessa into the conference room.

'Hello, Christopher,' she said, and went to take his hand, shook it.

'Good afternoon, Tessa,' he answered, smiling at her, kissing her cheek.

'Hello, Mummy,' Tessa murmured and went to embrace her before sitting down. 'I hope I'm not late.'

'No, you're on time. As you can see, we're waiting for the other side,' Paula replied, staring hard at her daughter.

'I look awful, don't I?' Tessa asserted and then began to giggle. 'You told me to make myself look plain and drab, and I did.'

Christopher burst out laughing. 'I'm afraid your beauty does come shining through, Tessa my dear, despite your obvious efforts to the contrary. And I have a feeling it always will, whatever lengths you go to in order to obscure it.'

'I've always hated you in brown. Where on earth did you find that dreadful, frumpy brown linen dress?' Paula demanded, her dark brows coming together in a frown.

'I have a whole department store at my disposal,' Tessa exclaimed. 'And that's when I spotted it. I know brown is not *my* colour, but it does have the desired effect, doesn't it? I think it sort of deadens me, drains the colour out of my face and kills my hair.'

'Well, yes, I suppose it does, but after today throw it away, and get rid of the ponytail as well. That's not your style, my darling.'

'I will, but Mummy, you *did* tell me I shouldn't look happy and well, more like a . . . sad sack, the victim . . . of the abusive husband.' Tessa paused, looked from her mother to Christopher and back at her mother, and shrugged. 'I was just following your instructions, Mums.'

'I know that, and it's all right, Tess, you did well.' Deeming an explanation to be necessary, Paula told Christopher, 'Tessa's been away with her brother, he took her for a rest, and she came back looking wonderful, so well rested and pretty I thought it might be better for her to play that down. I *know* Mark Longden and he's going to walk in here and say to his lawyers, "Look how well my wife is, I never abused her." He'll deny everything, Christopher, if he gets a chance.'

'I know that, Paula. But I saw Tessa's bruises, and the photographs. You were right to tell her to look like . . . a sad sack, wasn't that the expression? Fortunately, she's not become quite that. I suppose it would be impossible for her to completely extinguish her flame.'

Startled, Paula stared at him, thinking he was sounding quite poetic all of a sudden. But then men did rather go for Tessa; they always had, perhaps because there was such an ethereal quality to her, and it wasn't entirely dimmed today, he was correct about that.

At this moment the door opened and Geoffrey Creighton, one of Christopher's junior partners, came bustling in, also carrying a pile of manila folders. After greeting everyone, he took a seat on the other side of Tessa, and told them: 'Longden's solicitors are just arriving downstairs. But no sign of Longden yet.'

'It's typical, he's always been late for as long as I've known him,' Tessa muttered.

'I'd like to go over a couple of points with you, Tessa,' Christopher said, opening one of the folders. 'Let's endeavour to get it out of the way before we're surrounded.'

Mark Longden was the last to arrive.

From the moment he walked into the conference room Tessa was tense, on her guard, not knowing what to expect. His appearance was more or less the same, rather collegiate and youthful at first glance. But she noticed new lines around his mouth, and there was a strange bleakness in his eyes. As he moved across the conference room she saw that he was nervous, agitated underneath the surface. He was trying to control this, but she knew him so well she spotted all of the telltale signs, the odd quirks of his personality at once.

She could not help comparing him to Jean-Claude Deléon, even though she knew comparisons were odious. Jean-Claude was calm, purposeful, sure of himself in a quiet way, self-confident without being overbearing. Mark, who was spoilt, undisciplined and self-indulgent, showed how weak he was in everything he did. And he was avaricious beyond all reason.

When Mark smiled at her Tessa was startled. Her face was glacial. It remained stony and unforgiving.

Mark turned away at once, the smile still lingering, and then a smug look flashed across his face. He sat down with his solicitors and began to speak to them, appeared to be quite voluble.

After a few minutes, when greetings had been exchanged by all, Christopher Jolliet cleared his throat and looked across the table at Mark and his two representatives, Jonas Ladlow and Herbert Jennings.

He began: 'Gentlemen, as you know we are meeting today to work out the financial settlement between the two parties present, Tessa and Mark Longden, who are about to seek the dissolution of their marriage in the divorce courts. However, this –'

'I've made notes about what I want,' Mark interjected. 'Notes based on everything Tessa said to me several weeks ago, and what I want –'

'Please let me finish, Mr Longden,' Christopher said curtly, throwing Mark's solicitors a baleful look.

Mark displayed his annoyance, gesticulating, but Jonas Ladlow put a restraining hand on his arm, leaned closer, whispered a few words.

Christopher went on, 'I was about to explain that Mrs O'Neill is now going to take over. She wants her daughter and Mr Longden to understand the kind of settlement she is prepared to make to Mr Longden. However, there are several provisos –'

'No provisos!' Mark cried in a nasty voice.

'Mark, *please*,' Herbert Jennings said, taking over from his law partner. 'You must allow Mr Jolliet to say what he has to say without these interruptions.'

Mark threw him a dirty look, but sat back in his chair sulking, said nothing further.

Jonas Ladlow now spoke, addressing Christopher and Paula, who sat next to each other across the table. 'We are ready to hear the provisos, Mr Jolliet, and then perhaps we can discuss them.'

'*Proviso one*. After Mrs O'Neill has presented her proposed settlement, and providing Mr Longden accepts it, the contract between them must be signed today.'

'That is rather fast,' Jonas Ladlow exclaimed, frowning. 'I'm quite sure my colleague and I will have to study the contract at length.'

'I don't think you will, but do let me continue,' Christopher responded politely. 'If Mr Longden accepts the settlement and signs it, there is another condition. The *second proviso* is that certain aspects of the contract must go into operation as soon as possible.'

'What aspects?' Jonas Ladlow asked.

'Mrs O'Neill will – explain them to you,'

Christopher murmured, looking unexpectedly enigmatic.

'Perhaps I should now take over, Christopher,' Paula suggested, glancing at her solicitor.

He nodded. 'Of course. Do proceed, Paula.'

'I am prepared to make a financial settlement on you today, Mark, as long as the contract is signed today, as Mr Jolliet just mentioned. It must be signed in this office, witnessed by your solicitors and mine. Do you understand, Mark? Gentlemen?'

The three of them nodded, but Jonas asked, 'Are you saying that your offer will be withdrawn if the contract is not signed this afternoon?'

'I'm saying exactly that, Mr Ladlow.'

'What are you offering me?' Mark asked, much to the irritation of his solicitors, who gave him furious glances.

'Ten million pounds sterling,' Paula said evenly, 'a very generous sum in my opinion, under the circumstances.'

Mark smiled. 'Where's the pen? I accept. I'll sign at once.'

His two solicitors exchanged swift glances and Jonas said rapidly, 'We need to know all of the provisos and see the contract, study it.'

'Of course you need to see it, so that you can familiarize yourselves with all of the provisos, Mr Ladlow,' Paula said with a small smile. 'I doubt you need to study it, however, since it is couched in extremely simple terms and is very short. Let me just add this. If Mark does not accept my offer and does not sign the contract, he will obviously have to take his chances in a court of law. And, under the circumstances, I doubt very much that the judge will award him anything – no settlement, no alimony.'

Tessa leaned into her mother and exclaimed, 'Don't do this, Mummy. It's far too much money. Withdraw the offer, let's go to court, leave him to the mercy of the judge, as you just said.'

Hearing Tessa's words brought a look of concern to the lawyer's face. Jonas Ladlow said, 'What are the *other* provisos, Mrs O'Neill?' He was fully aware of Paula O'Neill's reputation as a business-woman and he knew she was a tough negotiator. He was certain the ten million came with strings and he needed to know what those strings were.

'I would prefer to discuss the ten million pound settlement and the terms of the payout first,' Paula replied. 'This is what I am offering you, Mark. One million pounds thirty days after the signature of the contract. One million pounds when the divorce is granted by the judge, and one million pounds per year for the coming five years, starting in 2002. That will make seven million pounds paid out over six years bringing us to 2007. The final payment of three million pounds will be paid to you three years after that, in 2010.'

No one spoke for a few moments.

The lawyers appeared perplexed.

Mark was looking pleased.

Tessa was angry and it showed on her face.

Jonas Ladlow and Herbert Jennings excused

themselves from the table, walked to one end of the conference room. They stood near the window, discussing the terms of the contract, and Jonas whispered, 'There's a catch, Herb. Somewhere there's a catch.'

'I agree, Jonas. She's far too smart to hand out ten million pounds just like that. It *is* over a nine-year period starting now, I realize that, nonetheless, it's still a lot of money.'

'Under the circumstances, yes, because he's no angel.'

'Say that again. But look, let's hear the provisos, see what else she has to say.'

The two solicitors came back to the table, and Jonas asked, 'What are the other provisos exactly, Mrs O'Neill?'

'If Mark signs the contract today he will also be agreeing to move to Australia.'

'That's fine by me,' Mark announced. 'I'm happy to sign. Oh, and what about my Hampstead house? Do I get that? Tessa promised it to me, you know.'

'It's *not* your house, Mark. Nor is it Tessa's, actually. I gave it to you both when you married, but I never actually *gifted* it to Tessa. I retained the deeds. So actually it's mine, and I don't propose to give it to *you*. Or to Tessa for that matter. We are talking here about a ten million pound *cash* settlement, Mark, very serious business indeed. The Hampstead house doesn't come into play.'

Mark opened his mouth to say something, but Jonas Ladlow cut across him, saying swiftly, 'So if Mark signs the contract today, the payout will begin in thirty days from today, with two million paid altogether. And after the divorce he must leave for Australia, to live there? Am I understanding you correctly, Mrs O'Neill?'

'You are indeed, Mr Ladlow. Mark will be able to leave for Sydney once the judge grants the divorce and when he is no longer required in court. That is when he receives the second payment of one million. He will remain in Sydney for the next five years without returning to England, or going anywhere else, actually.'

'*What?*' Mark cried vehemently. 'I can't live there for five years! You're *exiling* me!'

'Call it what you will,' Paula answered coldly. 'But you will agree to stay there for five years, to build your architectural firm into a viable entity. After five years you can return to England for a visit of one month.'

'One month!' he shrieked. 'No way will I agree to these terms, Paula.'

'Very well, I understand. But don't forget, there's ten million pounds at stake here. We are talking very serious business. Don't make any foolish or hasty decisions, Mark. Think about it.'

'What happens when the five-year period is up?' Jonas asked quietly, staring at Paula. He couldn't help admiring her, although he kept his face neutral. She was a shrewd adversary, he had to admit that, and she obviously understood Mark Longden very well.

Paula was silent for a moment, then responded softly, 'After the five-year period ends, Mark can return to England once every two years, and after the final payment of three million pounds, in 2010, he is free to come and go as he wishes.'

'Yes, and by that time Adele will be twelve years old!' Mark shouted. 'I will have missed all of her childhood, her years of growing up.'

'That is true, yes, but you should have thought of Adele right from the start, Mark, and then perhaps you would still have a marriage with Tessa. You are the author of your own life. You've written this script and played the part.' Paula shrugged lightly, and added, 'Very sadly.'

After a whispered conversation, the two solicitors and Mark Longden all rose and walked over to the window, where they stood discussing the settlement for ten minutes. When they finally returned and took their places at the conference table, Jonas Ladlow took charge.

Clearing his throat, he looked directly at Paula and said, 'Mark has decided that he prefers to pass on the settlement. He'll take his chances in the courts. Hopefully it will be a fair judge, one who will understand a father's right to have access to his child, if not, indeed, shared custody.'

'Very well, Mr Ladlow, I do understand. It is Mark's choice.' Turning to Christopher Jolliet, Paula said, 'May I please have the folder which was sent to you two weeks ago? Oh, and the other one from the previous month please. From July.'

Christopher handed them to her silently.

Paula opened the top one, glanced inside, then looked up, stared across at Ladlow and Jennings.

'Spousal abuse. Drug-addiction. Alcoholism. *Kidnapping*. All the details are here.'

'I didn't kidnap Adele!' Mark shouted, growing red in the face.

'Be quiet!' Paula stared at him furiously. 'You beat my daughter, pushed her down a flight of stairs, caused her to hurt herself. What you did could have killed her or done permanent damage. You raped her. You abducted Adele. Without telling her you took Adele for a whole day. You've used her money recklessly. The list is endless, Mark.' She took a deep breath. 'So go ahead. Do as you wish. Take your chances in a court of law and see what happens. In fact, be my guest. However, let me tell you this – with the dossier I have on you here –' She paused, patted the folder. 'You'll be lucky if you don't get a jail sentence.'

Jonas Ladlow and Herbert Jennings sat gaping at Paula. They were stunned and appalled by her words; Mark, who was seated between them, leaned back in his chair. He was suddenly grey-faced, appeared frightened.

'May I please see those documents in the folders?' Jonas Ladlow asked quietly, although he was almost fearful to open them, look inside. It struck him it would be like opening Pandora's Box, letting hundreds of secrets fly out. Secrets he didn't particularly want to know about.

Paula nodded. 'There is one other thing I must say to you, before I pass these over to you, Mr Ladlow.'

'Yes, Mrs O'Neill?' He gazed at her questioningly, the frown appearing between his eyebrows.

'Although I cannot actually prove it at this time, I do want you to be aware that I suspect your client of plotting with my cousin Jonathan Ainsley to do bodily harm to various members of my immediate family. As yet I haven't taken my concerns and the information I have to Scotland Yard. But there is a strong possibility that I shall be doing that soon. You see, I know for a fact that Mark Longden and Jonathan Ainsley were in Paris together last weekend, and spent most of the weekend together. I also know that Jonathan Ainsley wishes to harm Tessa and her brother Lorne, and my daughter Linnet as well.'

Jonas Ladlow was unable to utter a sound. He just sat there immobilized, staring at her, as did Herbert Jennings. Both were wondering why they had ever taken on Mark Longden as a client.

As for Mark, he was speechless for once. But under his breath he was cursing Jonathan Ainsley.

Paula smiled faintly at Jonas, and finished, 'I don't think your client would want to be named in a conspiracy charge, a charge of conspiracy to commit murder, would he?'

After a moment's consultation with Jonas, Herbert Jennings began to speak, looking over at Christopher, Geoffrey and Paula. 'Could we see the contract for the settlement, please? And may we use a private room here for a short time, in order to confer with our client?'

'It will be my pleasure, gentlemen,' Christopher answered.

When the three men had gone out of the conference room with Geoffrey Creighton, Tessa took hold of Paula's arm and asked in an urgent whisper, 'Is it true, Mummy? Was Mark in Paris last weekend? And does Jonathan want to harm us?'

'The answer is *yes* to both questions. But you were not in any danger, darling. Jack Figg knew of Jonathan's presence in Paris, and Mark's also. He was having them tailed, and he knew everything they did, all of their movements. He'd told Linnet, and she alerted Lorne. You and Lorne were protected, believe me.'

'Did Linnet phone Lorne on Friday morning, do you think?'

'She did, yes, following Jack's instructions. Once she'd told him you were there he thought it better Lorne was alerted. Your brother didn't tell you because he didn't want to alarm you.'

'I see. Perhaps that's why his friend invited us for the weekend?'

Paula shook her head. 'I don't think so. It's a coincidence, but one that turned out to be convenient,' Paula explained.

'Is Adele at risk, Mummy?' Tessa asked, concern ringing her face.

'I don't think she is, darling, but just to be sure Jack is hiring a bodyguard. However, the man will function as your driver, so as not to create undue alarm anywhere.'

'I understand.' Tessa sat back, staring off into space, and after a few moments she turned to her mother and said in a voice that was hardly audible, 'I don't think you should have offered Mark all that money. He doesn't deserve to get anything, not after what he did to me.'

'I agree with you,' Paula replied. 'But I like to be in control of certain situations, and if Mark signs the contract, accepts all the provisos, it's money well spent. Because he will be in my control. Absolutely in my control.'

Tessa nodded, biting her lip. 'I understand that, but even so it's an awful lot of money to give him.'

'Here's a point you ought to consider, Tess,' Paula told her. 'I own the Hampstead house, and I paid about a million and a half for it some years ago now. I was planning to have it done up for Lorne, but he never wanted it. So it was rented out, as you know. That's all of ten years ago now, and the house is worth much, much more. I spoke to Emily about it and she's going to have it sold through the real-estate division of Harte Enterprises. She thinks it will fetch about three and a half million, maybe even four million pounds. I'll be making a good profit. And if I invest the money from the sale of the house, it will go towards the ten million pounds I'm planning to give Mark.'

'I see what you mean, and thanks, Mother, for looking after me and Adele, for dealing with Mark. Do you think he'll accept your offer?'

'I have no doubt about it.' Paula began to laugh, and turning she looked at Christopher. 'What do you think?'

'I think you not only demolished him but put the fear of God into him, about the Ainsley business, I mean. I'm sure he feels decidedly lucky to be getting ten million pounds and a trip to Australia. Far away from any Scotland Yard detectives. Wouldn't you, under the circumstances?'

'I certainly would,' Paula murmured.

And Tessa said, 'So would I.'

At this moment Geoffrey Creighton returned, followed by one of the firm's secretaries carrying a tray loaded to overflowing with a teapot, cream jug, sugar basin and cups and saucers, all of the necessary items for afternoon tea.

'Only biscuits, no nursery sandwiches,' Geoffrey explained. 'But they *are* Cadbury's chocolate fingers.'

Tessa laughed for the first time that day. 'My daughter's favourites,' she explained to Geoffrey who was staring at her in surprise.

Paula poured the tea, and they all had a cup; it was about twenty minutes after this that Mark and his two solicitors returned to the conference room.

After sitting down, Herbert Jennings handed the two manila folders to Paula. 'These make interesting reading, very interesting indeed. I'm assuming you would call Mr Jack Figg and his operatives as witnesses, if this divorce case took the normal route? You would, wouldn't you?' He glanced away from Paula, looked at Christopher.

'Of course,' Paula replied.

'We would have no alternative,' Christopher said.

'Mark has taken our advice, Mrs O'Neill, Mr

449

Jolliet, and he is ready and willing to sign the contract now,' Jennings told them.

'The contract is perfectly clear,' Jonas Ladlow said to the room at large. 'It was as you said, Mr Jolliet. Precise and to the point, not to mention short.'

'It's the way I like to work.' Paula smiled at him. 'Short and sweet. And this is a sweet deal. The sweetest.'

The two solicitors nodded.

Mark signed all the copies of the contract first, then Tessa, and finally Paula. The copies were then witnessed by the legal representatives of both parties to the divorce.

As she put her pen back in her handbag Paula thought: Got you, you bastard. Now you're under my control. You're no longer Jonathan Ainsley's creature. You're mine.

CHAPTER TWENTY-FIVE

Evan Hughes was a very special woman. Gideon was well aware of that. And he knew that he was in love with her; she was the first women he had ever been serious about, had wanted to marry. But suddenly, unexpectedly, in the last few weeks things had been strained between them, and he was having second thoughts.

He sighed to himself. It was not like him to be indecisive, yet that was his state of mind at the moment. The problem was her recent behaviour with her parents, perhaps most importantly her attitude towards her father. It seemed utterly ridiculous to him that she was so intimidated by him, actually in awe of Owen Hughes. Her father was a nice enough man, pleasant but rather dull. An ordinary man, really. With extraordinary good looks. And that was about it. He liked Owen well enough; however, it was Evan's mother he was really taken with and liked more. Marietta was warm, loving, amusing, very intelligent, and what's more she seemed perfectly healthy. He had seen no signs of the depressive in her, quite the contrary. He wondered what all *that* was about . . . the terrible worry Evan had about her mother's health, the way she trembled at the thought that she herself might have inherited her mother's illness. Yet there was a normality to Marietta and it had initially startled him, because he had been led to believe otherwise, had been told she was a sick woman.

Obviously Marietta had been a manic depressive when Evan was growing up, she wouldn't have invented a thing like that about her mother. But wasn't there something decidedly odd about this miraculous recovery? Oh well, he muttered to himself, there are all kinds of new medicines available today, revolutionary medicines. That was the answer most likely, the reason for Marietta's radiant health. Because radiant she was. No question about that.

He knew deep down that he was still annoyed with Evan because she had not told her parents she was engaged to him, had not been wearing her ring the day they had all gone to lunch at the Dorchester. He was hurt about that, and disappointed that she was so . . . *cowardly*. She was also weak-kneed about telling her father the truth about his parentage, about his mother's affair with Robin Ainsley during the war. Originally it hadn't really mattered to Gideon, but somehow, now, it did. He wanted Owen Hughes to know who his biological father was, to understand that *he* was a Harte and therefore Evan was, too.

Pity she's not acting like a Harte, he thought. In a sense that was at the root of his discontent, wasn't it? Her timid attitude. It still rankled a bit. He wished he could get over it. Wasn't he being mean-spirited and juvenile? After all, if he –

Four phones rang at once. The mobile in his trousers' pocket; three of the four lines on the land-line unit sitting on his desk.

The shrilling brought him bolt upright in his desk chair, and he pulled out his cellular first. 'Gideon Harte.'

'Terrorists have attacked New York. The World Trade Center. Turn on your TV,' his brother Toby yelled.

'Jesus Christ! Hold on. My other lines are ringing.' Gideon grabbed the receiver of the land-line, jabbed the first button. 'Harte here.'

'It's Andy, do you –'

'I know. I'll get back to you.' He cut the reporter off, jabbed the second button. 'Harte here.'

'It's me, Gideon,' Winston Harte said, sounding extremely strange. 'The World Trade –'

'I know, Dad. Just hold on, let me get my other line.' As he finished speaking, Gideon punched the hold button, jabbed the third line. 'Gideon Harte.'

'It's Joel. I'm pulling everybody in for an early editorial meeting for tomorrow's *Gazette*. Okay?'

'Okay. I'll get back to you in a minute.' Gideon now punched the second line again. 'I've got Toby on my mobile, Dad.'

'All right, talk to him. I'm coming up to your office. Be there in two minutes.'

'Okay.' He hung up then, grabbing his cellular, he said, 'Are you still there, Tobe?'

'Just about, I've got to get over to the newsroom. Can't talk now. Turn on CNN. Call me at the network if you need me.'

'Thanks, Tobe.' Gideon ran across the room, switching off the mobile, pushing it in his pocket as he looked for the remote control. Usually it was on his desk but now he couldn't find the damn thing anywhere. He spotted it on the shelf above the television set, grabbed it and punched buttons until CNN breaking news flashed across the screen.

He gasped as he gazed at the scenes in front of him, horror washing over him as he saw one of the towers crumbling before his eyes. He glanced at the clock on the shelf above the set and saw that it was two twenty-five, nine twenty-five on Tuesday morning in New York.

Gideon stood there in shock, his alarm spiralling. He was mesmerized by the terrifying images on the screen. Flames rising sky high. Thick billowing smoke. Dust. Falling rubble. The sound of collapsing buildings.

His breath caught in his throat as he focused his eyes on people jumping out of windows. Escaping the fire; falling to their deaths. Oh God! People running in the streets . . . fleeing. Sirens blaring. Crashing sounds . . . cars ablaze . . . He closed his eyes for a moment, hardly able to believe what he was seeing, hardly able to take it in.

The shrilling phone forced him to turn away and hurry to his desk. Seizing the receiver, he said hoarsely, 'Yes?'

'Gideon? It's Andy again. I'm taking the editorial

454

meeting for the *Post*. Tony Wharley had to leave early today. He's gone already. Doctor's appointment.'

'Go ahead. I'm waiting for my father. I'll leave it to you.'

Striding back to the television he stood there watching the ongoing mayhem, myriad thoughts racing through his head. Was this an act of war? *Who* was responsible for this catastrophe?

A positive attitude about life and enormous optimism were Winston Harte's stock in trade . . . his glass was always half full, never half empty, anything was possible, maybe he *would* conquer the world one day, and tomorrow could only be better. That was the way he had thought since his earliest days.

Optimism was second nature to him, and it had seen him through some bad patches over the years. But this afternoon, for the very first time in his whole life, his optimism had fled.

Winston felt totally empty inside. He was extremely depressed. The latter was an emotion unknown to him until today, one that was entirely unfamiliar and which he found hard to deal with.

As the lift came to a stop, he stepped out onto the editorial floor of the London *Evening Post*; as usual he walked over to the bank of plate-glass windows that allowed passers-by to look into the newsroom from the corridor. He stood there for a moment or two, as he usually did.

The sight of any newsroom, anywhere in the world, gave him a thrill, and most especially his

455

own, but the thrill was not there today. He was chilled to the bone, filled with a sense of despair, an aching sadness in his gut. Yet he knew he had to shake off these feelings . . . He was chairman, the boss, the staff would inevitably turn to him at some point for guidance . . . He must be there for them today, and in the ensuing days.

He took a deep breath, stood a little taller, pushing his shoulders back, reminding himself he was a newspaperman through and through. And for a few minutes he stood watching the activity in the newsroom . . . trying to relish it, to feel proud of his team.

Winston Harte's love of journalism was inherited from his grandfather and namesake, the first Winston in the family, who had run this newspaper company for Emma; it had also come from his great-uncle Frank, Emma's younger brother, a renowned journalist in his day, a war correspondent and political columnist. Printer's ink was in Winston's blood, just as it was in Gideon's.

Winston's gaze was now fastened on the television set positioned straight ahead of him . . . The appalling images of the tragedy in New York were still unfolding . . . filling the screen. His heart tightened at the sight of the devastation, the panic and fear.

Turning away, suddenly more sorrowful and morose than ever, Winston headed down the corridor to Gideon's office, needing to unburden himself as well as discuss coverage of the attacks in Manhattan.

When he reached the door, he took several deep breaths, braced himself and walked in.

His son stood in front of the television set, and unable to tear his eyes away, even for a split second, Gideon cried, 'Come and look, Dad! It's John Bussey of the *Wall Street Journal*. Reporting everything he's seeing from his office on the ninth floor. It's opposite the World Trade Center. Oh my God, the tower's coming down! *Oh my God!* This is staggering, just unbelievable! *Catastrophic!*'

Winston joined his son but only for a moment. He now found it difficult to look at the TV screen, and abruptly moved away, went and sat down in a chair, shaking.

Swinging around Gideon said, 'We'll only be able to get a brief mention in the Stop Press. The late afternoon edition is already rolling, but –' Gideon stopped speaking, startled by the look of terrible anguish and despair spreading across his father's face.

'Dad, you look awful! *So white*. Aren't you feeling well?' Gideon asked, hurrying over, putting a hand on his father's shoulder affectionately, immediately concerned about him. They were very close, and Gideon was aware he had always been his father's favourite, although Winston had never actually *shown* favouritism.

Winston looked up at his son, opened his mouth to speak, to confide, but no words came out. He simply put his hand on Gideon's resting on his shoulder.

Gideon scanned his father's face, noted the

beads of sweat on his forehead, the chalkiness of his skin. He was now so unusually white the freckles, normally quite faint, seemed to stand out on the bridge of his nose and across his cheek-bones. And then with a small shock Gideon became aware of the pain in his father's light-green eyes, the unexpected glitter of tears.

What's wrong with him? Gideon wondered. He knew his father was too much of a dyed-in-the-wool newspaperman to show his emotions about the tragic events now unfolding in New York, however much he cared. In a sudden flash Gideon understood there was something else troubling his father, that it was serious. And very personal.

Trying to keep his voice even and calm, Gideon asked, 'Are you ill, Dad?' As he spoke he peered into his father's face yet again.

Swallowing several times, Winston endeavoured to steady himself, and slowly, in a voice that was gruff and thick with tears, he answered Gideon. 'He's in there. In that lot. He'll never get out alive.'

'Who, Dad? Who're you talking about?'

'Shane,' Winston told him in a voice that faltered slightly. 'He had a meeting at the World Trade Center this morning. That's why he didn't come back with us.' Winston was unable to finish. He shook his head and a sob broke free. Bringing one hand to his mouth, as though he wanted to push the sobs back inside himself, he went on shaking his head, finally mumbled, 'He's probably dead already.'

Stunned and horror-struck by what his father

458

had just said, Gideon bent over him, put his arms around him, holding him close to his chest. After a moment or two, he said in a low, very loving voice, 'Dad, please don't jump to conclusions. You can't be sure Shane didn't get out. At this moment we don't really know anything, except what we're seeing on television. I know this is a stupid question, but you have tried to reach him, haven't you?'

'I have, and of course I can't get through on his mobile. Not on any phone, actually. In fact, I can't get through to New York at all. Not to anyone. The lines are probably *totally* overloaded. Or down.'

Releasing his father, Gideon straightened, and asked quietly, 'Dad, what about Paula?'

'I phoned her as soon as I saw what was happening on TV. She was in a meeting. So I asked Emily to go over to the store, to be there for her.'

'Yes, Mum's the best person to be with her right now, at a time like this.'

'Our mothers were close friends, you know,' Winston volunteered, out of the blue. 'They used to take us out in our prams together when we were babies. That's how long I've known him. Sixty years.'

'I know. All your life.'

'We've never had a disagreement, a quarrel. *Never*. Never in all these years. He's my best friend, the brother I never had . . .' Winston stopped, unable to say another word.

'Let's try and be positive!' Gideon exclaimed. 'Maybe the office Shane went to for the meeting was on a lower floor. Perhaps he was able to walk down the stairs, get out. And listen, Dad, since you couldn't get through then maybe he couldn't either. It's more than likely that's why you haven't heard from him.'

'I pray to God that's so.'

The ringing phone forced Gideon to hurry to his desk. 'Gideon Harte here.'

'It's Paula,' she said in a faint voice that shook. 'Is your father there, Gideon?'

'Yes, Paula, he is, and –'

'Give me the phone!' Winston exclaimed before Gideon could say anything else, and jumped up, went to the desk, took the receiver from his son.

Gideon moved away, in order to give them privacy. But even if he had wanted to eavesdrop it wouldn't have been possible. After saying her name softly, very lovingly, his father had lapsed into silence, had become the listener, not the one doing the talking.

Moving closer to the television set, Gideon seated himself in a chair, continued to watch the never-ending disaster, knowing that very soon he would have to go, join Joel and later Andy at the editorial meetings. They had to plan tomorrow's first editions no matter what.

His heart ached when he thought of Shane O'Neill. How would any of them cope if he had been killed? He had no idea. He closed his eyes, visualizing Shane, and silently in his head he said: Please God, let Shane be alive. And he repeated this over and over again, as he waited for his father to get off the phone.

* * *

Tessa stood staring at the portrait of Emma Harte, which hung in an alcove in the main corridor of the management floor. Whenever she stopped to look at her great-grandmother she thought she was getting a glimpse of the woman Linnet would become when *she* was middle-aged like Emma was here.

Her sister truly did resemble their great-grandmother. It was actually more than that: Linnet looked more like Emma Harte than anyone else in the family; she was the spitting image of her. She was Emma's clone . . . the same clear, pink-and-white complexion, the large sparkling green eyes, the bright red-gold hair coming to a dramatic widow's peak. There were those in the family who said it wasn't only her looks Linnet had inherited from her famous predecessor but Emma's brains as well. And perhaps that was true. Maybe Linnet was the right one to run the department store chain, even though *she* thought of herself as the heiress, the Dauphine. Did she want to be top dog? The boss lady? The queen of the hill? She wasn't sure how to answer that anymore.

What did she want?

She had a ready answer. *Jean-Claude Deléon.* Lock, stock and barrel. All of him. For always.

Well, that might mean giving up her ambitions. Her career.

Could she do it?

Why not? She didn't want to sleep in a cold, lonely bed all night, every night, all by herself. As

Emma had done after Paul's death in 1939. They all knew the story of that great love, of his tragic accident and death. Actually, his suicide.

'You were a beautiful woman, Grandy,' Tessa whispered out loud. 'And you were right about everyone having their price. Mark Longden definitely had his price. But you'd say good riddance to bad rubbish, wouldn't you?'

Mark Longden was a rat. She couldn't change a thing now, but she still wished her mother had not given Mark all that money, such a big settlement. Ten million pounds. Her mother had told her again, yesterday on the way home from the solicitor's office, that the money from the sale of the house would be invested, and that it would all balance out in the end; she supposed it would. What an avaricious rat he was. All he wanted was money. He had protested about being banished, exiled as he called it, but in the end he had signed the contract. And willingly. The money was more important than his daughter. He preferred to take the money and run, rather than sweat it out in London so that he could visit Adele, have access to her.

Her mother had been smart, brilliant actually. She had judged him accurately, had bought Mark off. Banishing him to Sydney for five years meant he was off *her* back, and was no threat to Adele. And by the time he could return to England, permanently if he wanted, Adele would be twelve, going on thirteen.

She shivered involuntarily, remembering that he had been in Paris last weekend. How awful it would have been if she had run into him when she was with Jean-Claude.

Turning once again, Tessa walked towards the door which led to the business offices of the store. But before she reached it, the door flew open, and Linnet came rushing out. She was wearing pale blue and looked like a young Emma.

'Mummy wants you to come. *Now*, Tessa,' Linnet exclaimed, beckoning to her.

Frowning, Tessa said, 'What's the matter? You seem upset about something.'

'Where have you been, Tess?'

'In my storage room, going through the inventory. For over an hour and a half. Why?'

'You don't know, do you?'

'Know what?'

'Terrorists have attacked New York . . . they've flown planes into the World Trade Center. It's unbelievable –'

'Oh God, no! Linnet, how awful! *Frightening*'

'Come on, let's not waste time. Mummy's so upset. She needs us at a time like this.'

Shane, Tessa thought. Her father was still in New York. Oh God, no! Had something happened to him? She was unable to move, stood rooted to the spot, gaping at her sister, now seeing her clearly . . . the drawn face, the laughing mouth no longer laughing, stern, tight instead. Her dreadful paleness. The startled look in her green eyes . . . like a deer frightened by headlights.

'Is Dad all right? He hasn't been hurt, has he?' Tessa demanded.

Linnet stared back at her. 'We don't know anything. We haven't been able to reach him. Or anyone else for that matter. I think all the phone lines are down in Manhattan.' Reaching out, Linnet grabbed her arm. 'Come on, please, Tess. Let's go to our mother. She really does need us.'

Tessa allowed her younger sister to drag her through the door and into the foyer which led to the management offices. And she thought: It's taken me all these years to understand he truly *is* my father. It was Shane who brought me up, loved me all of my life. Helped to make me who I am. Not Jim Fairley. Jim was killed when I was just a toddler . . . killed in an avalanche. Now she prayed that Shane had not been killed in a terrorist attack . . . Her mother wouldn't be able to survive that. None of them would.

CHAPTER TWENTY-SIX

Linnet had only seen this look on her mother's face once before, years ago when her brother Patrick had died. *Devastation*. That was it, pure and simple.

She's shell-shocked, Linnet thought, as she followed Tessa into her mother's office; she thinks Dad is dead.

The mere idea of this brought a lump to Linnet's throat, and she blinked back the tears which had instantly sprung into her eyes. I don't believe it, I don't. And I won't. I would have known. Like Shane, Linnet thought of herself as a true Celt, and that meant she was different, more sensitive, spiritual, and intuitive than most other people. She and her father had a special bond, and if he were dead she would have known. *The moment he died.* Because he would have communicated with her in some way before his death

He's not dead. I know he isn't, she thought again; she also knew she must be strong for her mother. That was imperative.

Linnet hovered near her mother's desk, not far from the sofa where Paula sat with Emily Harte. These two were first cousins, had grown up together, and Linnet sometimes thought they seemed like sisters, so close were they to each other.

Her sister Tessa sat on the other side of Paula, saying similar things to their mother that Linnet had.

'Mummy, I don't believe Dad is dead, I honestly don't. You said he had an early appointment, around nine o'clock. If that's the case then Dad would have been arriving at the building just as the first plane was ploughing into it. Look, you can see the time frame there on the TV,' Tessa pointed out. 'He wouldn't have gone into a burning building, now would he?'

Passing a hand over her strained face, Paula tried to steady herself, to stay calm. Bleakly she stared at Tessa, and finally nodded. Gulping air, she said in a low voice, 'You're right, Tess. And your sister said the same thing. I just wish I could speak to him . . . be certain he's all right.'

Emily said, 'Darling, he's probably trying to get through right at this moment. Winston told me when he called a few minutes ago that nobody can get through to New York. It could be a dreadful overload, or it could be some sort of breakdown.'

'Have you tried to fax Daddy at his office?' Tessa asked, and then grimaced. 'Of course you have, I guess you've thought of everything.'

'More or less,' Linnet volunteered, walking to

the sofa, sitting down in a nearby chair. 'And Uncle Winston has tried to get through to our newspaper offices on Forty-Second Street, and he can't. I saw another timeline on TV, about ten minutes ago, and by nine twenty-one all of the bridges and tunnels leading into Manhattan had been closed down. The city's isolated from the rest of the world right now, and who knows what's happened to the telephone systems.'

'We just have to hope against hope he's safe,' Emily murmured. 'Look, maybe he never got to his appointment. If he realized something peculiar was going on he might have just turned around, gone back to the apartment or his office.'

Tessa exclaimed, 'He might not have even been able to turn around, or get to a side street. If there was a traffic problem. All sorts of things could have intervened, you know, Mummy.'

Paula took Tessa's hand in hers. 'I know you're right, but I am going to be on edge until I hear his voice.'

'Or get a sign,' Linnet suggested. Noting the odd look in her mother's eyes, she decided to play it very safe, and added, in a businesslike voice, 'Such as a fax.'

This comment startled Paula, and she said more energetically, 'We didn't try to fax *him*, Emily, maybe we should. Right now.'

'That's a great idea!' Linnet cried, jumping up, rushing to Paula's desk. She grabbed a piece of store stationery and after addressing the note to her father, she wrote, *Dearest Shane. We know you had an appointment at the World Trade Center this morning. Please let us know you are safe. Love, Paula, Tessa, Linnet and Emily.* Putting her pen down, she read it aloud to the others.

'Send it immediately,' Emily exclaimed.

'Yes, do that,' her mother added.

Paula had retreated to the dressing room which opened off her office some time ago, wanting to be alone, to pull herself together. She loved her daughters and Emily, knew how well-intentioned they were, trying to help her, but at this moment she needed space . . . peace and quiet.

It was unbearable for her to even consider that Shane might have been killed at the World Trade Center this morning, and yet there was that possibility. She shrank away from it yet again, curling up on the small loveseat, pressing her face into the cushion. Had he been in the wrong place at the wrong time?

Avalanche . . . the decades fell away. She remembered that awful day when her father and her first husband had been killed in an avalanche at Chamonix. *They* had definitely been in the wrong place at the wrong time. Everyone had called it an Act of God, or an Act of Mother Nature. The catastrophic event that had taken place this morning in New York was an Act of Terrorism . . . man-made.

She began to shake uncontrollably, feeling suddenly icy cold. And also frightened. She could not contemplate life without Shane. He had always been with her since they were children. They had grown up together, been best friends. And then they had gone their separate ways, in a certain sense, and she had eventually married Jim Fairley, the last of the Fairleys. But it was Shane she truly loved, with all her heart, and she had soon realized her terrible mistake as her marriage to Jim had begun to fall apart. Their separation had been very bitter. And then, so unexpectedly, he had been killed. She had never wanted that, only wanted a divorce . . .

Of course Shane could be alive. The girls and Emily were right. He might well have arrived late for his appointment, seen the disaster happening from the street and retreated. And even if he had been early for the appointment he may well have escaped; all of the things they had suggested *were* feasible. Think positive, she told herself sitting up on the loveseat, straightening her clothes. Think clearly.

After a moment or two Paula rose, went to the wash basin, cleaned her smudged eye make-up, put on fresh lipstick, and brushed her hair. And then she went back into her office knowing that she must be strong and brave for everyone in the family, that she must now take charge, hold everything together.

Three pairs of eyes turned to look at her as she walked into the room, and she saw the anxiety and worry on their faces. It was impossible for her to smile at them, but she knew she must reassure them, and so she said in a steady voice, 'I think we'd better start making phone calls to New York again.' Focusing on Linnet, she asked, 'Did that fax go through to your father?'

'No, it didn't. Look, fax machines are linked to phones, so . . .' Linnet shrugged, lifted her hands. 'Once that problem clears up the fax will automatically pass, Mummy.'

'I know. Please order some tea, Linnet dear. And Emily, would you give Winston a call, see if he knows anything we don't, which is more than likely. And Tessa, perhaps you can try to get through to the New York apartment.'

'Yes, of course,' Tessa answered, and walked over to the windows, took her mobile phone from her pocket and began to dial. Linnet hurried out to speak to Jonelle, one of her mother's secretaries, to ask for tea to be ordered. And Emily phoned her husband at the newspaper offices.

Paula sat down at her desk, wondering what their next options were. Not many. *Damnation*, she muttered under her breath. If only the phone system would spring back to life in Manhattan. Without phones and faxes they were isolated.

As if reading her mind, Tessa said in a low voice, 'No luck, Mums. Nothing happens. The number doesn't ring through to the apartment.'

Paula nodded, then looked at the clock. To her surprise it was almost four. Eleven in the morning in New York.

Emily said, 'I've just spoken to Winston, and he has the same problem as we do. They're not in communication with the New York offices, not even e-mails are going through.'

'Because everything is linked to the phone systems,' Linnet exclaimed, and went and sat on the sofa, her eyes glued to the television set once again, her horror intensifying at the scenes unfolding before her eyes.

After a short while Jonelle brought in a tray of tea, and they sat drinking it, saying very little to each other, all of them thrust down into their terrifying thoughts.

For the next hour the phones in Paula's office rang constantly, as various people checked in. Winston, Gideon and Toby called Emily to find out if Paula had heard anything from Shane; Julian called Linnet several times, and Lorne phoned his mother from Paris. When Grandfather Bryan came on the line later Paula lied and said Shane was nowhere near the World Trade Center.

At one moment Linnet said to the room at large, 'The airports are closed as well. So Manhattan is truly isolated now. Dad won't be able to get home for days.'

Paula threw Linnet a swift glance. 'You're convinced your father is all right, aren't you?'

'Yes, I am. We'll hear from him, you'll see. I just know it in my bones.'

The phone calls were never-ending. Grandfather Bryan rang again and so did India and Evan from the Leeds store. Shane's personal assistant Edgar Madsen rang up four times within the space of thirty minutes on some pretext or other.

Paula knew that Edgar was as frantic as they

all were, and kept calling her because hearing her voice reassured him. She almost told him to come over to the store at one moment, then changed her mind. It was far better he remained at Shane's office in Mayfair just in case Shane managed to get through.

From time to time she glanced at her watch, saw that the minutes were ticking away. She was relieved that Desmond had returned to boarding school on Sunday, and that Emsie was also back at school in Harrogate. Although they knew their father had remained in New York, neither of them had any idea that he had stayed behind to attend a meeting at the World Trade Center today.

Leaning back in her chair, taking a sip of the fresh tea Jonelle had just brought in, Paula's deep-blue eyes swept the room. Emily was near the windows again, talking on her mobile, either to her own office or to Winston.

Tessa had joined Linnet on the sofa, totally concentrating on the tragic events playing out in downtown Manhattan. Paula found she was mesmerized herself for a good fifteen minutes until there was a sudden lull in the coverage, and earlier film was played again, with a reporter giving a running commentary.

Linnet, who was holding the remote control, suddenly began to change stations in rapid succession, going from CNN to Sky News to the BBC, then zapping onto ITV. She zapped one more time and finally hit ITIN, their own Independent Television International Network. It was part of

Harte Media International, was run by Winston and Toby, had an affiliation with CNBC in New York. She watched closely, her eyes fixed on the TV set.

Her mother had jumped up, started to walk over to the TV set to join Linnet and Tessa when one of the phones on her desk shrilled. As she paused, reached to pick it up, she saw it was her private line, and her heart missed a beat. 'Paula O'Neill,' she said in a low voice.

'It's me, darling.'

'Oh *Shane!* Oh Shane darling! I've been frantic. Thank God you're all right! We've all been so terribly worried.' She burst into tears.

'I know you must've been. Don't cry, I'm all right. I couldn't get through, darling. Not to you, Dad, the office in London or Winston. I couldn't even get through to my office here in New York or the apartment. The phones are overloaded, probably down in some areas.'

'Shane darling, I'm here with Linnet and Tessa. Emily's here as well. We've been distraught. They're blowing kisses to you, and they'll come to the phone. But first tell me what happened? How did you manage to get out of the World Trade Center?'

'I never made it to the meeting, Paula,' Shane said, his voice sober. Then he went on to explain. 'Thomas Mercado, the chap I was having the meeting with, called me at home at eight this morning, asked me to come to his office at nine-thirty instead of nine. He had to take his son to school. By nine-twenty I was stuck in downtown traffic. I never got to the World Trade Center. But I saw it all happening, Paula: it was horrendous, so unbelievable I can hardly describe it. I realized after about ten minutes that there was nothing else to do but try to get back uptown. But we were in a gridlock. I finally had to abandon the car, and the driver came with me. I stood on the street trying to phone you and Winston with no success. And I also called everybody's mobiles as well.'

'You're so lucky, Shane,' Paula whispered, suddenly choked, her eyes filling with tears.

'I'm the luckiest man alive, darling,' he replied. 'I saw the South Tower collapse around ten o'clock and then the North Tower at about ten-twenty. A fireman nearby suddenly shouted at me, told me to run like hell. And I did. With my driver and everyone else, I ran through the streets of Lower Manhattan. The roar of the towers collapsing was like nothing I'd ever heard. Ever in my life. I'll never forget it.'

'Oh Shane, we're so lucky, you and I . . .' She was quiet for a moment, thanked God silently in her head. And then she said, 'Here's Linnet.'

Linnet, Tessa and Emily all spoke to Shane, and finally Paula came back to the phone. 'I suppose you're stuck there, darling?'

'I am, I'm afraid. All of the airports are closed. But I think they'll open up by the end of the week.'

'I've never even asked you where you are. So, where are you?'

'At home. At the apartment. As I said, I've been dialling numbers for several hours, and I couldn't believe it when I finally got through to you. Now I'll try to phone my father. But please call him in ten minutes to tell him I'm all right. Reaching you might have been a fluke.'

'That it might. I love you, Shane.'

'And I love you.'

CHAPTER TWENTY-SEVEN

From the moment she had met Robin Ainsley, Evan had felt perfectly at ease with him. She realized this was because he had treated her in such a warm and friendly way that all of her nervousness had instantly evaporated.

And he had continued to be natural, outgoing, and very open with her, spoke to her as if she were his only confidante. And perhaps she was. Certainly he unburdened himself to her from time to time, and she had understood for months how important she was in his life. She was his granddaughter and he treated her as such, and she did the same, having adjusted her thinking. He *was* her biological grandfather and she loved him, but it did not make her love Richard Hughes any the less. *He* had been her grandfather as well, and for her entire life until he died.

Now as she sat on the terrace at Lackland Priory, waiting for Robin to come back outside, she experienced a little rush of sadness that her parents had decided to go back to the States earlier than planned. She had hoped to inveigle them to Yorkshire, to stay at Pennistone Royal with Paula, and to meet Robin when they were here. But that idea would not work anymore.

The terrorist attacks on New York and Washington four days ago had made them realize how much they wanted to be at home, 'to help in any way we can', her mother had explained yesterday. And Evan understood their sense of patriotism, felt the same way they did. But she had responsibilities here, and crucial matters to deal with in the next few weeks. There was a lot at stake.

They'll meet Robin another time, she thought; they'll have to come back for my wedding, won't they? If it ever happens, she then added to herself glumly. Gideon had been difficult lately; they had not seen each other all week and so they had not been able to settle certain differences between them. She had been busy with the remodelling of the Leeds store, and he had had his hands full in London with the breaking news on the terrorist attacks.

Even though it was Saturday, he had chosen to stay in London for the weekend, and although she understood why, she was, nonetheless, disappointed not to be with him. But the newspapers came first, she had long known that. All of the Hartes put business first, for the most part anyway.

Lifting the silver coffee pot, Evan poured herself another cup, added milk and a sweetener, sat sipping it, enjoying the lovely September day. It was unusually warm, a pretty day with a blue sky and bright sunshine. A very clear day. No mists creeping down from the moors this morning.

She heard Robin's step and glanced over her shoulder, smiling at him.

He smiled in return, and came and sat down next to her. 'I'm sorry I was so long, but my sister Edwina needed to discuss a bit of business with me, and she doesn't take no for an answer.' He chuckled, added, 'She's in her nineties, as you know, but nobody would ever guess it.'

'So I've heard,' Evan replied. 'India and Tessa talk about her as if she's a bright young thing. Their age.'

Robin laughed again. '*She* thinks she is, I can tell you that.'

'Robin, there's something *I* want to tell you,' Evan said, leaning closer, looking at him squarely. 'I'm afraid I won't be able to bring my parents up to Yorkshire, as I'd planned. They're going back to America sometime next week. They feel they must, because of the terrorist attacks.'

Disappointment instantly flickered in his eyes, but he nodded, and told her, 'I do understand. I think I'd feel the way they do if this country were attacked like that. An act of war was perpetrated on the United States on Tuesday. Without a declaration of war being in effect. Thousands of innocent people have been killed in the most unconscionable way. Your mother and father have the genuine need to be at home, I realize that, and it's only natural.' He gave her a loving smile. 'But they'll come back to England, I'm sure, and anyway

478

hadn't we once decided that it might be better if your father didn't know who I am?'

She nodded. 'We did, but I'm ambivalent about it now. I know Gideon feels Dad ought to know the truth, and my mother, too, now that Gideon and I are engaged.'

'More than likely, but I can meet Owen another time. So don't fret yourself about it, Evan.'

'Thank you for being so understanding, always so kind to me, Robin.'

'I love you, my dear, and you are my only grandchild.' After refilling his cup with coffee, adding sugar, he continued carefully, 'Evan, I have something to explain to you but it must remain absolutely confidential . . . just between us.'

'I understand. You know I would never betray a confidence.'

'Of course I do. But what I am about to tell you *must* remain a secret, because I would not want Jonathan ever to find out about it. Do you understand?'

'Yes,' Evan said quietly, feeling suddenly cold as she always did when she heard that name.

Reaching into the pocket of his old tweed jacket, Robin took out a small white postcard and handed it to her. 'I have created a trust for you. All of the details are on the card. It's been handled in such a way that it can never be traced to me. But just to be certain, please don't discuss it with anyone, not even Gideon. All right?'

'I give you my promise,' she answered and went on quickly, 'But this wasn't necessary. I've told you before, I don't want anything from you, Robin. Only your affection.'

'I know, I know,' he said, sounding slightly impatient. 'However, I have a lot of investments and interests my son knows nothing about, and which cannot be traced back to me. I have transferred part of them to you.'

'But Robin –'

He shook a finger at her, looking stern. 'No buts, Evan. I don't want to hear another word about this. Put the card in your handbag, study it properly later, digest it, and then file it away somewhere safe.'

She did as he told her, then putting her bag on the flagstones again, she reached over and took hold of his hand. 'Thank you, Robin, you're very generous,' she said softly, genuinely touched by his gesture.

'It's my pleasure, my dear. Now, tell me, how's Paula? I know she's been upset about Shane getting caught up in the terrorist attacks in New York. Daisy told me.'

'She's feeling much better, I heard. She was exhausted on Wednesday, all that tension and anxiety got to her, Linnet told me. She and I had breakfast together this morning, before I drove over here, and Linnet sends her love, by the way. Anyway, JFK is open again, and Shane's coming back to London tomorrow morning. On Concorde, and the company plane will be waiting to fly him to the airport at Yeadon.' Evan gave him a shy smile, and finished, 'It must be wonderful to have their kind of marriage. Linnet says they're still in love after all these years.'

Robin looked at her keenly as he murmured, 'Indeed it must. But you sound wistful, Evan. Are things not going right with you and Gideon?'

'Yes, everything's fine . . .' Evan bit her lip, and then went on, 'It's just that . . . well, I think he's still miffed because I hadn't told my parents we'd got engaged.'

Robin sighed, and shook his head. 'Men are such fools at times. *I know*. I'm a man, and I've been a fool myself many times in my life. I wish Gideon would just move on from this situation. You're engaged, everyone knows it, including your parents. Now you and he should be planning your marriage, setting a date, not quarrelling.'

'We're not really quarrelling,' Evan explained. 'He's just . . . snippy with me. And remote sometimes, distant. And quiet.'

'Is he in Yorkshire this weekend?'

'No. He felt he had to stay in London with his father and Toby. He said there'd be a lot of news breaking.'

'Oh yes, he's a true Harte, Gideon is, totally dedicated to his work, and that's not a bad thing, I suppose. He's a newspaperman through and through, of course, like Winston and my uncles.'

The two of them sat talking for a short while longer, and then finally Evan said, 'I'm sorry about not being able to have lunch with you today, Robin, but Linnet and I are in the throes of planning her

481

wedding, and I promised I'd work with her this afternoon.'

He smiled, and they both stood up. Robin took her arm, and they walked around the terrace to the area at the back of the house where she had parked her car. 'I hope we can have lunch next weekend instead? When are you off to London?'

'On Tuesday morning. To be with my parents for a couple of days before they go home. I'm coming back to work with India early on Friday, and I'll be at the Leeds store on Saturday. How about lunch next Sunday?'

'That's splendid!' he exclaimed, instantly looking more cheerful.

When they came to her car, he hugged her and kissed her cheek. 'Perhaps Gideon can be induced to join us for lunch?'

'Absolutely. I'll make sure he comes.' Opening the car door, she got in, rolled down the window. 'Thank you,' she murmured softly. 'See you next weekend.'

'It's a date, my dear.'

Evan turned on the ignition and immediately frowned, puzzled, when the car did not start. She tried again with no success, and Robin looked in the car window and said, 'Do you think you've flooded it?'

Evan shook her head. 'No. It was flat.'

'It's more than likely the battery. This is one of Paula's old cars, isn't it? One of her ancient run-arounds she calls them.'

'Yes, she always lets me use it. But I think it needs to go in for an overhaul.'

'I tend to agree. Well, there's no problem. You can borrow my Rover. It's a perfectly good car.'

'But won't you need it?' Evan asked, getting out of Paula's slightly dilapidated Jaguar.

'I have my favourite jalopy in the garage.'

'Oh yes, your beautiful old Bentley Continental Drop Head Coupé. Circa 1960.'

'Ah, so you *do* remember what I told you,' he laughed, looking pleased.

'I do. And you told me it has a fluid fly wheel and that's why it has that special gearshift. I remember everything you tell me, Robin.'

'But it's not often girls commit to memory things about cars,' he shot back, laughing again as he led her towards the garage.

Within seconds she had driven the Rover out onto the gravel driveway. 'This is great, Robin!' she exclaimed, leaning out of the window. 'Thanks so much. I'll return it tomorrow. Linnet or India will come in another car to take me back.'

'There's no problem at all,' he called, waving as she slid forward towards the iron gates. ''Bye, my dear.'

Evan liked the feel of the Rover. It was solid, a substantial car and she found it easy to drive. It rolled along smoothly as she headed out of the tall gates of Lackland Priory and turned left on the road which led to the small hamlet of Lackland; beyond Lackland was the main road to Pennistone Royal.

She sat back, enjoying the car, deciding she really liked these old models. There was something about them that was different. Maybe it was the sense of luxury, of times long gone that appealed. She really wasn't sure what it was, but Paula felt the same way. They had once had a discussion about it, and Paula had told her that everyone in the family hung onto their old models. 'Maybe out of a sense of thrift,' Paula had said and had added, with a dry laugh, 'but I doubt that.' Even India drove an ancient Aston Martin that every male in the family drooled over and coveted. And Gideon had raved about Robin's forty-year-old Bentley Continental.

When she came to the rim of the hill, Evan automatically put her foot on the brake gently. The hill was steep and the car had weight, and she felt the instant pull of gravity as she began to roll down, pressed her foot harder on the brake.

Nothing happened. Immediately she knew there was something wrong with the car. The brakes didn't work! The car went hurtling down the hill, gathering speed, faster and faster; there was no way she could stop it.

Halfway to the bottom she saw the horse and cart come rumbling out of a side lane. Evan hit the horn hard.

The man sitting on the cart looked up the hill, saw her coming, but seemed unable to move. He was frozen in place in the middle of the hill.

Evan immediately understood that she had to swerve to avoid hitting the horse and cart, possibly even killing the man and the animal at the high speed she was going. Frantically, she pulled the wheel around with all of her strength, gritting her teeth, veering off to the right in a straight line. She saw the drystone wall too late. As it loomed up in front of her she knew she was doomed, that she would hurtle into the wall head-on. There was nothing she could do now to avert an accident.

Had somebody tampered with the brakes? she suddenly wondered. It was the last thing she thought.

Billy Ramsbotham sat on the cart, staring at the smashed-up car for only a split second, then he flicked the reins, made a clicking noise with his tongue, and went off down the rest of the hill hell for leather, heading for Lackland to get help.

But before he got there he saw Frazy Gilliger coming towards him on his bicycle and he flagged him down.

'What's up, Billy? You're going licketysplit! Summat wrong?' Frazy asked, noting the old man's agitation.

'Aye, there is. Up yonder, near bottom of t'hill, there's a lass in a smashed-up car. It b'aint hard ter see it's a Rover. Aye, it looks like Mr Ainsley's Rover she's gone and bunged up. And she's in a right bad way, she is, poor lass.'

'Oh my God, it must be Miss Evan!' Frazy cried, and without another word to Billy he began pedalling up the hill towards Lackland Priory as hard as he could.

He was out of breath and panting as he cycled through the gates and around the back of the house. He leapt off the bicycle, threw it down haphazardly, and burst into the kitchen loudly and unceremoniously.

Bolton, the butler, was standing talking to Mrs Pickering, the cook, and he swung around, looking startled at the noise. 'Good heavens, Frazy, what's wrong, bursting in like this?'

'It's Miss Evan. She's crashed the Rover. I saw it out of t'corner of me eye, but I didn't stop ter look. I knew I had ter get here as quick as I could. Billy Ramsbotham saw her hit yon drystone wall, he's sure she's in a right bad way. Best phone for t'ambulance, Percy.'

'Oh my God, yes!' He turned to the cook. 'Can you make the phone call, Maude? I'd best go and speak to Mr Ainsley. And ring the hospital in Ripon, not Harrogate. It's closer and they've got an ambulance and paramedics. They'll be able to treat her. If not, they'll move her to Harrogate.'

'I'll do that right away, Percy,' Cook said and hurried to the phone.

Bolton moved across the kitchen with great speed, and headed for the library. Within seconds he was relating Frazy's story to Robin Ainsley.

Robin was standing near the window, and he reached out, held onto the back of the wingchair as he listened to the butler. His heart was thudding hard in his chest, and he thought his legs might buckle under him. He needed the support of the chair to steady himself.

'Is she alive?' he finally managed to ask.

'I don't know, sir. I'm going to nip down there

right now. Cook is calling Ripon hospital for an ambulance.'

'I'll come with you, Bolton,' Robin said.

'Very well, sir.' Bolton turned around and rushed off, followed by Robin, who thought his world had just been torn asunder. To lose this girl now when he had just found her was inconceivable. And for her to lose her life would be a tragedy, she who was so young and lovely and vital. He prayed she was not dead, prayed she was not badly hurt. Evan had everything to live for, a whole future ahead of her: a life with Gideon, a career at Harte's, children . . .

As he followed his butler into the backyard Robin asked himself if someone had tampered with the car, the car he used more regularly than the Bentley. He knew Evan was an excellent driver and careful. So what had gone wrong? Why had she crashed on the hill?

It suddenly struck him that if the car had been tampered with, whoever had done it had been gunning for him, not her. He pushed these thoughts away, dreaded conjuring up the name that lingered at the back of his mind. No, he thought, he wouldn't do that, surely not. Why would he try to kill me?

It took Bolton only a couple of minutes to drive to the scene of the accident. He wouldn't allow Robin to alight, insisted he remained in the Bentley.

'Let me go, Mr Ainsley,' he said gently. '*Please*, sir.'

'All right then,' Robin reluctantly agreed.

Bolton hurried over to the mangled Rover and peered in through the open window. He saw at once that Evan lay across the steering wheel at a strange angle, but her seat-belt was on, and this brought him a little comfort. He couldn't tell if she was dead or alive, and then he heard her moaning, and his heart lifted. Turning, he ran back to give this news to Robin.

'Miss Evan's alive, sir!' Bolton exclaimed. 'I heard her moaning. I daren't touch her, Mr Ainsley. We'll just have to wait for the ambulance men to arrive to know more. They have the proper experience.'

'Thank God she's not dead,' Robin responded, a great weight lifting. 'And you're right, I know it's best not to move an injured person; damage can be done so easily by those who aren't trained medics.'

Robin sat back against the car seat and began to breathe more normally. He closed his eyes and offered up a silent prayer to the God he had long ago ceased to believe in, understanding, suddenly, how comforting this was in an overwhelming crisis. Believing in a higher omnipotent power could work miracles, somehow offered hope. He prayed for Evan's recovery.

Bolton had gone back to the crash site near the wall, and he hovered about on the hill, returning to the car several times to check on Evan. He didn't hear any more sounds from her and his belief that she was still alive began to waver. All was silent in the crashed Rover. He avoided Robin Ainsley, not wishing to be questioned by his employer. And then he suddenly heard sirens. He listened hard and his relief knew no bounds. A few minutes later the ambulance was speeding towards him.

Once the ambulance was parked, two ambulance men and a paramedic took over. After speaking to Bolton perfunctorily they began to study Evan and the car. Once they had discussed the problems, assessed the situation, she was lifted out carefully, put on a stretcher and taken to the ambulance.

'Who is she?' the driver who had remained behind now asked Bolton.

'Evan Hughes, Mr Robin Ainsley's granddaughter,' he explained.

'Of Lackland Priory?'

'Yes, that's correct. Is she alive?'

The driver nodded. 'Yes, she is. But we've got to get her to the hospital. At once. We can't tell what condition she's in.'

'Thank God she's not left us. We'll follow you to Ripon.'

'See you there,' the driver replied, and ran back to the ambulance.

It was Bolton who drove the Bentley to the hospital; once he had parked the car, he accompanied Robin into the waiting room, and refused to leave him alone. They sat together, not saying anything, waiting for the news from the doctor. After a few minutes had passed, Robin realized he must let Linnet know what had happened to Evan, since she had been expected back to lunch.

'Do you have the mobile phone, Bolton?' he asked, turning to the butler.

'I do, sir, yes. Here it is.'

Robin dialled Pennistone Royal, and it was Linnet herself who answered. After telling her what had transpired, he added swiftly, 'But Evan is alive, Linnet. However, we don't know the extent of her injuries at the moment.'

'I shall drive right over, Uncle Robin.'

'No, no, it's not necessary. You can't do anything, and I'll stay in touch with you, I promise.'

'I don't want you to be alone,' Linnet told him firmly. 'I'm coming, so don't try to stop me. I'll let Mummy know. She's at the Harrogate store. See you in about half an hour.'

'All right then,' he acquiesced, knowing it was futile to argue with her. If anyone was like his mother it was Linnet. She was another Emma, and once she'd made up her mind to do something there was no stopping her.

Half an hour after this conversation, Dr Gibson came out to see Robin, and much to his relief he noted a smile on the doctor's face.

'Good morning, Mr Ainsley,' the doctor said. 'I've examined Miss Hughes, and she's going to be all right. She's suffering from shock, of course, and she has a broken rib, a broken ankle, and a lot of bruising to her arms and legs. But as far as I can ascertain, there are no internal injuries. And I know you'll be relieved to hear she hasn't lost the baby. She's a very lucky young woman: her injuries could have been much worse. She could have so easily miscarried. It's a miracle she didn't.'

Robin was an old man now and hardly anything ever shocked him. But he had to admit to himself that he was surprised to hear Evan was pregnant. He had judged her as being practical and cautious, and he wondered how she had allowed this to happen before marriage to Gideon. And then, with a quick intake of breath, it struck him that she might have done it on purpose. To bring the situation with Gideon to a head? He just wasn't sure. He didn't think of her as devious, not at all. All he knew was that he loved this young woman and he was delighted she was pregnant, that she was carrying his great-grandchild.

The doctor opened the door, showed Robin into a small private room, and disappeared. Evan was lying propped up, wearing a white hospital gown. She looked pale, exhausted, and was still slightly dazed, coming out of shock. There was a large bruise on her cheek, and he realized she was in pain when she tried to move her body, and instantly winced.

As Robin walked over to her, she muttered in a faltering, strained voice, 'I'm sorry about the car.'

'That doesn't matter, Evan dear. All that matters is that you are alive. You could have been killed, you know.' Leaning over her he kissed her forehead, then took her hand in his. 'Are you able to tell me what happened? Or is that too much of an effort?'

'The brakes failed . . . on the hill. No control

of the car.' She took a breath and added weakly, 'The horse and cart appeared. Swerved to avoid them.'

Robin was silent for a moment, and then he gave her a questioning look, asked, 'Do you think the brakes simply failed because the car is old? Or because they'd been tampered with?'

'I don't know . . .'

He shook his head, a grim look tightening his mouth as he said in a low voice, 'The Rover is kept in good condition. I'll have my garage check the brakes, but perhaps the police might want to do that themselves.'

Evan sighed, looked at him, but remained silent, not wanting to mention the name hovering in the back of her mind.

'I telephoned Linnet,' Robin went on. 'She's driving over.' Pulling a chair over to the side of the bed, he explained, 'They're going to throw me out of here in a moment, they've got to put a cast on your leg. It must be painful, isn't it?'

She nodded, feeling suddenly weak.

He said quietly, 'Evan, the baby's perfectly all right. Dr Gibson told me.'

Taken aback, she gaped at him, and colour rose from her neck to fill her cheeks with a bright pink blush. She finally said in a low voice, 'Please don't tell anyone I'm pregnant.'

'Of course I won't. How does Gideon feel about the baby?'

'He doesn't know.'

'Why haven't you told him?'

'Don't want it to influence him . . . about our future.'

'I understand. Whether you two marry or not is your business, my dear, but I just want you to know that I will be there for you and my great-grandchild no matter what.'

Evan's eyes brightened and she gave him a faint smile. 'Thank you.'

There was a sudden loud knocking on the door, and Robin called 'Come in.'

A moment later Linnet was hurrying over to the bed, exclaiming, 'I've been scared to death all the way over here, Evan! Whatever happened?' She took Evan's hand in hers, staring at her in concern.

'The brakes failed,' Robin explained. 'It was nice of you to come, Linnet. Thank you.'

Linnet smiled at Robin, and turned back to Evan. Pushing back thoughts of Jonathan Ainsley and his dangerous vendetta against them all, she said, 'Are your injuries very bad?'

'Broken rib, broken ankle,' Evan whispered. 'Getting a cast.'

'Thank God it's nothing worse,' Linnet said.

Dusty Rhodes stepped out of the lift onto the fifth floor of Harte's department store in Leeds. He glanced around, understanding immediately why India Standish's secretary had told him to be careful, that the floor was undergoing remodelling. And indeed it was. The floor was roped off, and he had to walk around the roped-off area to find a way to get to India.

He could see her in the distance, in the middle of the floor, dressed in beige cotton trousers and a beige cotton blouse, clipboard in hand, tortoise-shell glasses pushed up on top of her bright blonde head. Normally casually chic in the latest styles, she was much more workmanlike this afternoon in her understated outfit. But he understood how practical it was, and she was nothing if not practical. There were piles of rubble everywhere and obviously a minor demolition job was in progress.

India was talking to two workmen, looking concerned, and for a split second he hesitated. He had not seen her for several weeks and he needed to speak to her. Having parted on a sour note he was certain she would not take his phone call, so he had come here instead.

After a moment he decided to brave it, to plunge ahead, and so he stepped over a pile of planks, avoided a wheelbarrow and buckets of plaster and moved towards her.

It was one of the workmen who spotted him first, and his face lit up. 'Hey, Dusty, how're yer?' the man asked, his smile wide, his light green eyes suddenly sparkling. 'Long time no see, mate.'

Before Dusty could answer, India swung around to face him, surprise flickering on her face, but only momentarily. She was good at hiding her feelings, and instantly became poker-faced again.

'Hello India,' he said.

'Dusty,' she answered, inclining her head.

Looking past her, he addressed the workman. 'It's Jackie Pickles, isn't it?'

The man grinned. 'Yer've got that right, Dusty. So yer remember our old school, do yer?'

Nodding, Dusty laughed. 'I do indeed. Christ Church C of E, in Theaker Lane, Upper Armley.'

'Lotta water under t'bridge since then,' Jackie said. And glancing at the man next to him, he added, 'I bet yer don't remember Harry Thwaites, do yer, Dusty?'

'I certainly do. Hello, Harry, last time I saw you was at West Leeds High School, right?'

Harry Thwaites smiled. 'Long time ago, Dusty. I'm a married man now. With a couple of kids.'

India, who had been paying great attention to this little exchange between the three men, now said, 'You wanted to talk to me, Dusty, didn't you?'

'Yes.' But again looking past her he said to Jackie, 'What's the problem here? Those steel girders, I'll bet.'

'Correct. Lady India's sketches for this area don't show them. Because we didn't know they were there. We found 'em when we knocked a wall down. It's a problem.'

'Show me the sketches, India, please,' Dusty said, glancing at her. 'I studied architecture.'

Handing him the sketches, she said, 'Yes, I know. I'd like them to be removed.'

Dusty stared at the sketches, walked over to the floor-to-ceiling beams, looked around the area, and then he said, 'I'll bet my bottom dollar these steel pillars are supporting the ceiling, which is also the floor above.'

Harry Thwaites said, 'That's what we thought . . . they can't be removed.'

Gazing at India, Dusty explained, 'Take these out, your ceiling will fall down and the floor above will be weakened. You'll have to incorporate them into your new scheme somehow. There's no other way.'

The two workmen were beaming at him.

India looked annoyed with him, and then suddenly a resigned expression settled on her face. 'Okay then, that's it.' Turning to the two men, she said, 'Please excuse me for a few minutes. I'll be back shortly. Maybe you want to take your tea break?'

'Thanks, Lady India,' they said in unison as they gave Dusty another grin and moved away.

'You're sure I can't move the beams?'

'Well, you can move them,' Dusty replied, 'but *I* wouldn't. It'll be a disaster.'

'I understand,' she replied, and glanced up at him, added, 'This is a surprise. Why did you come looking for me?'

Running into the two men he had gone to school with, having the discussion with them about the beams, had somehow broken the ice, and Dusty felt quite relaxed as he answered, 'First to apologize and secondly to try and explain . . . about Melinda and Atlanta.'

'Let's go up to my office, we can talk there for a while.'

'Thanks, India.'

They rode up to the seventh floor in silence.

When they came to her office, India opened the door, and said in a very brisk, cold tone, 'Well, come in. Let's talk. But I haven't got long.'

'This won't take long.' Dusty closed the door behind him, knowing she was not going to be very forgiving.

India went and stood behind her desk. His arrival had startled her, thrown her off balance, but the chit-chat between her carpenters and Dusty had given her time to recover her equilibrium. Much to her surprise she discovered she was now calm. And she had to admit to herself that she had missed him, had longed to go to him. She was still in love with him; he haunted her days.

Dusty looked well, she decided, but there were dark rings under his eyes. He was tired. She suddenly understood that he had more than likely buried himself in his painting to counterbalance his unhappiness about her, and her defection.

Hovering in front of her desk, Dusty exclaimed heatedly, 'Look, I admit I was pretty bloody stupid. I should have told you about my child when I came out of hospital, when I explained who Melinda was. I was embarrassed, though, and in a blue funk. Also, I'm not used to discussing my private life with anyone.'

'I know that,' India said. She sat down in the chair, motioning for him to be seated also.

He took the chair on the other side of her desk, and continued. 'I never confide in anyone. I'm a loner, independent, you know that. I've never ever made a commitment to anyone, I mean to a woman,

497

and I vowed long ago never to get married. To be honest, until you walked out on me that day, I actually didn't understand how I really felt about you.'

She gave him a long hard stare and snapped, 'At least you're honest. What you're saying, Dusty, is that I was just another woman passing through your life, that you saw no reason to share your past with me. Correct?'

'In a way, I suppose. But not quite . . . You see, I did *know* I was hooked on you, although perhaps I didn't understand how much. I respected you, India, and I looked up to you. I realized all those things that afternoon, but I was also confused, self-conscious and I didn't know how to explain that she and I had a child.'

'I would have understood, and that's why I was so upset. You underestimated me, and you didn't give me the benefit of the doubt.'

'I know, and I'm sorry for that. I'm an idiot.'

'Well, it was nice of you to come and apologize.' She stood up. 'I've got to get back to –'

'India, there's something else I need to tell you,' he said, cutting her off. 'I have always supported Melinda, her mother Mrs Caldwell, and Atlanta. And I pay Melinda's medical bills.'

She nodded, began to edge around the desk, anxious to return to work.

'I just wanted you to know this.'

'Why didn't you two get married?' India asked, suddenly wanting now to know more.

'I wasn't in love with her. Actually, we broke up before she knew she was pregnant.'

'I see.'

Dusty walked towards the door, realizing there was no point continuing the discussion. He felt depleted, worn out. He had told her the truth about Melinda, and there was nothing else to say. She was not in the mood to hear his pleas, his declarations of love.

India said, 'When did she get hooked on drugs?'

'Just after Atlanta was born. Thank God for that at least.' He opened the door, turned around, gave her a faint smile. 'Well, that's it, I guess –' His throat felt constricted, and he was amazed when he realized he was choked up, on the verge of tears. How stupid he was.

India felt herself growing panicky as Dusty walked out. She couldn't let him go. She loved him so much. Now was her chance to make everything right between them. Moving around the desk, she exclaimed, 'Dusty, wait! Please don't leave!'

He swung around, stood staring at her, his eyes widening when he saw the look on her face. It was one of absolute love.

He came into the office, closed the door, walked towards her, saying as he did, 'What is it, India?'

'I love you,' she said, 'I've always loved you. And I just wanted you to know that before you left.'

'Do you want me to stay?'

'Oh yes. *Yes.*'

He moved close, put his arms around her, held her tightly. 'I love you too. I want to spend the rest of my life with you, if you'll have me?'

She looked up at him, her silvery eyes glazed with tears. 'Is this a proposal of marriage, by any chance?'

'It is. I love you. I want you to be my wife.'

'And I want you to be my husband,' she whispered, and standing on tiptoe she kissed him on the mouth.

CHAPTER TWENTY-EIGHT

As it so often did in Yorkshire, the weather underwent a sudden change. After a warm and sunny weekend, it rained on Monday, and Tuesday dawned cool and overcast, the leaden sky threatening rain.

As she always did when the weather turned inclement and hinted at autumn, Margaret had gone around earlier lighting fires in the downstairs rooms which were used the most – the Stone Hall, the breakfast room and the library. The fires took the chill out of the air and were a welcome sight, a lovely antidote to the grey skies, the housekeeper thought.

Evan agreed with her, and after a light lunch, which Margaret had served her in the breakfast room, she thanked her and said, 'I think there's nothing nicer than a fire, Margaret, even on a summer's day. My grandmother often used to have them going in our Connecticut house, even when the weather was sunny and warm. She just loved fires.'

'My mother did, too,' Margaret remarked, and continued, 'Her name is Hilda, and she worked for Mrs Harte for years as housekeeper. Emma Harte, that is, and she told me Mrs Harte used to stoke the fires herself, always complained of feeling the cold. Anyway, the rooms in this great big house are always chilly, what with their wood floors, high ceilings and all. They need to be warmed up long before winter comes, at least I think so.'

'It's true. And a fire's so cosy and welcoming, Margaret.'

'It is indeed. Now, would you like some more coffee, Miss Evan?'

'No, thank you, and thanks for a lovely lunch.'

'It's my pleasure, miss. And what time can we expect your parents to arrive?'

'My father insisted on driving up from London. He said they'd be here in time for tea. So I suppose they'll arrive at – *tea-time*.' Evan started to laugh. 'Four o'clock, right?'

'That's correct.'

Pushing back the chair, Evan struggled to her feet, with Margaret's help, and after thanking the housekeeper she made her way across the Stone Hall to the library. She had been discharged from the hospital yesterday afternoon, but only after promising the doctor she would call him if she had any unusual pains, which might suggest problems with the baby. It had only taken her a couple of hours to get used to the cast on her right leg, but her broken rib was painful, especially when she tried to sit up. Yet all in all, she knew she had been lucky. She might easily have been killed. An involuntary shiver ran through her as she thought of the brakes failing the way they had, and she couldn't help wondering if Jonathan Ainsley had been behind it. Having resisted mentioning his name to Robin, she now decided to forget the vicious Jonathan, and so she put him out of her mind determinedly.

A few weeks ago she had discovered Emma's photograph albums, wonderful, giant-sized books which her great-grandmother had assiduously filled with snaps and pictures taken over the years.

Joe, the estate-manager and Margaret's husband, had taken them all out for her this morning, and she started perusing them again, tremendously interested in seeing her ancestors, mostly in black and white but sometimes in colour as well.

Fascinated by the earliest photographs, she opened the first album once more. It was of Victorian style, handsomely bound in crushed red velvet and enhanced with ornate silver corners and a silver clasp. It was filled with Emma's notations in her neat but flowing script.

The man who fascinated her the most was Emma's older brother, Winston. There was a picture of him in his Royal Navy uniform, taken when he was only seventeen during the First World War. He was Gideon's great-grandfather, and she saw the man she loved reflected in this ancient snap. Gideon had inherited the Harte good looks from Winston the first, it wasn't hard to spot that. A photograph next to it had been removed, but next to the gap Emma had written: *My father, Big*

Jack Harte. She couldn't help wondering who had taken the picture out of the album, and why. Further along there was another snapshot with the notation: *My father*, and it was in Emma's writing.

Evan sat staring at it, and she suddenly realized who the man in the picture reminded her of: Toby, Gideon's brother. That was it! And why not? Toby was also descended from Big Jack's son, Winston. Next to this Brownie snapshot of Big Jack was a faded picture of Elizabeth Harte, Big Jack's wife and Emma's mother. Goodness, Robin's twin sister Elizabeth looks just like her, Evan whispered to herself. *And so do I*. Robin was right when he said I was a true Harte, descended in a direct line from Emma's mother and father.

Carefully and slowly, she turned the pages, intrigued by pictures of Paul McGill in his army uniform; Robin and Elizabeth when they were small, with their father Arthur Ainsley; Kit, Emma's son by Joe Lowther, her first husband, with Edwina who was all dressed up in elegant clothes that smacked of the Roaring Twenties.

In the second album were pictures of Kit, Robin and Elizabeth during the Second World War. How glamorous her great-aunt Elizabeth looked, with her flowing black hair and dressed in her Red Cross uniform. And here was her great-grandmother standing outside the House of Commons with an elegantly-dressed couple. Emma had written: *My dear friend Jane Stuart Ogden and her husband Bill*.

The third album held photographs of Daisy,

Emma's daughter by Paul McGill. And there was a snap of Paul and Emma together, another with their only child, Daisy. And next to that there was a picture of Paula and Philip with their mother Daisy and their father David Amory.

Evan sat back, amazed at the hundreds of photographs which dated back to the beginning of the twentieth century. Why, the albums, twenty-one in all, covered almost a hundred years. If I were a writer, I could create a history of this family from these photographs, she thought. What a wonderful family saga.

And now *she* was carrying another Harte, the next generation. Evan sat back, placed her hands on her stomach, thinking of her baby. It had not been planned, it was all an accident, but she was glad she was pregnant. How lucky she had been not to lose the baby in the car crash. Again she shivered at the thought that she and the child could so easily be in the morgue.

Evan closed her eyes, drifting with her thoughts of the baby and the sudden change in her life that she or he would bring in the years to come. She hoped she would be married to Gideon. He was her true love, the love of her life, and she knew what she had to do now to make things right between them.

Robin stood in the doorway of the library studying Evan from the threshold, appreciating how lovely she looked this afternoon. So much better than yesterday: not so pale and wan, and the periwinkle-blue blouse she was wearing was the perfect colour for her.

She was a good person, he had known that from their first encounter. Ethical, sincere and straight as a die, that was Evan, and he knew she would come through this current crisis with flying colours. She was practical and down to earth, and he believed she would be able to settle the differences she had with Gideon.

Tapping on the open door, he walked in, exclaiming, 'There you are, Evan! I hope I'm not disturbing you.'

She looked up at once, her face changing, breaking into smiles. 'Robin, you're early!'

'Yes, I am, but I wanted a few moments alone with you before your parents arrive.' He walked over to the table where she was seated, his eyes on the piles of photograph albums. With a chuckle he said, 'Boning up on the family, are you?'

'Of course. And it's fascinating!'

Leaning over her, Robin kissed her cheek, sat down, and went on, 'I want to tell you again how thrilled I am about the baby, Evan. And although I said it was Gideon's business and yours the other day, I was just wondering whether you plan to tell him or not?'

'Yes, I will tell him, but I will have to choose the right time.' Leaning towards him, she gave him the benefit of a radiant smile. 'I'm going to call the baby Robin whether it's a girl or a boy. I hope that pleases you.'

He beamed, obviously delighted by her words.

'Of course it does, my dear. Now what do you have in mind for this afternoon? When you said I should come to tea with your parents I must admit I was somewhat startled . . . What are you actually planning?'

She laughed. 'I'm not too sure, to be honest. But I thought I'd get you all together and . . . let the chips fall where they may.'

'I see. And when do they plan to return to New York now?'

'I'm not sure. When I called them after the crash they were sort of hysterical at first, until I convinced them I was actually all in one piece except for a few broken bits. My mother insisted on coming up to see me when she understood I was going to stay here until I was a little bit more mobile. So they've postponed their flight home for the moment. Anyway, I do plan to go back to work at the Leeds store later this week.'

'Don't rush it, Evan, I'm sure Paula's not quite the slave-driver we sometimes all imagine,' he laughed. 'I suppose I'm the only person who knows you're pregnant?'

'Oh yes, and please keep it a secret, won't you?'

'I will. You *did* tell Gideon about the car crash though, didn't you?'

'Oh yes, and he was very upset. He said he'll get here to see me as soon as he can. But there's such a lot going on because of the terrorist attacks in America, and he does like to be at the centre of the action, at the papers.'

'I know.' Clearing his throat, reaching for her

hand, Robin said slowly, 'I don't want you to be upset or fearful, Evan, when I tell you that the police phoned me this morning. They did a thorough examination of the car, and looked at the brakes. The pipes had been cut.'

She was not surprised to hear this, and she nodded. 'You mean someone tampered with them?'

'I do. The brakes were gone when you started down the hill. But the police say they have no way to find the culprit. No fingerprints, you see.'

She felt chilled to the bone when she thought of what could have happened to her. Not only might she and the baby have been killed, but the old man on the cart and his horse as well. Staring at her grandfather she said softly, 'Nobody knew I would use the car . . .' Her voice trailed off and she stared at him worriedly, her large grey-blue eyes filling with concern for him.

'No, they didn't. I think I was the intended victim, my dear, which is why I don't want you to worry too much about yourself.'

'But I'll worry about you!' she cried. 'How could I not?'

'Please don't, I shall be fine. And certainly more on my toes than before! Very cautious and wary in the future, I promise.'

'Has . . . has *he* been here?'

'You mean Jonathan, of course. No, he hasn't, but you know as well as I do that doesn't mean a thing. He can get lots of people to do his dirty work for him, and I'm sure he's willing to pay well for such *favours*, shall we call them.'

Evan remained silent, sat back in the chair staring at Robin, thinking what a lovely, dignified old man he was. Her heart went out to him. How terrible to think that your own son had tried to do you harm, because that was exactly what the severed brakes of the Rover implied. Evan leaned forward again, squeezed his hand, and then glanced up as she heard a noise.

'I got here as soon as I could,' Gideon exclaimed, appearing in the doorway, hurrying into the library, looking anxious, his eyes fixed on her.

'Gideon! I didn't expect you until later in the week.'

Rushing over to her, he wrapped his arms around her and held her close, but gently so. 'I can't bear to think you might have been killed, darling.' Drawing away from her he looked into her face. 'Sorry if I held you too hard, Evan. How's the rib? I didn't hurt you just now, did I?'

'No, I'm fine. I *was* lucky, Gid, just a broken rib and a broken ankle, a lot of bruises. It could have been so much worse.'

'I realize that, darling.' Turning to Robin, Gideon greeted him, shook his outstretched hand, and said in a quiet voice echoing with gratitude, 'Thanks for looking after her for me, Uncle Robin. I really appreciate it.'

Robin merely smiled and nodded, pleased his great-nephew had arrived.

Evan said, 'Sit down. Gideon, there's something I want to tell you.' The moment he had walked in so unexpectedly she had made a snap decision to tell him about her condition. It was the right thing.

Staring at her questioningly, he did as she asked, took a chair next to Robin at the other side of the card table. Puzzled by her tone, he said, 'You sound odd . . . is there something wrong?'

'No. At least I don't think so . . . I'm pregnant. I'm carrying our child, Gid.'

Gideon was flabbergasted and he gaped at her for the longest moment. Then he pushed back the chair, jumped up and went to her. He stood over her, his hands on her shoulders. 'Oh my God! We're having a baby. This is wonderful news, Evan! Just wonderful!'

Turning her head, looking up at him she saw the genuine pleasure on his face, and those light green eyes, often so cold, critical and appraising, were filled with joy. There was no doubting his feelings, and relief flooded through her.

'Why didn't you tell me before?' he suddenly demanded.

'I didn't want it to influence you – about *us*, our *future*.'

'I understand. But you didn't think I'd be upset, did you?'

'I don't know what I thought . . . except that I was happy I had your child inside me, growing . . . part of you, Gid.'

He smiled at her, the joy bringing sudden laughter to his sparkling eyes, then he tilted her face to his, bent down and kissed her forehead. 'I'm *thrilled*, Evan. Thrilled and happy, and I feel . . . so blessed to have you, sweetheart.' He glanced at Robin. 'What do you say?'

'I'm as happy and as thrilled as you, Gideon. It's wonderful news, and I know your parents are going to be just as excited as I am.'

'That's right. They'll be over the moon, in fact.' Standing behind Evan, his hands resting on her shoulders again, Gideon gave Robin a very direct look, and asked in a low voice, 'What about the brakes in the Rover? Evan told me they failed.'

A long sigh escaped Robin, and his face changed, became serious, and Gideon saw the worry suddenly flickering in his blue eyes. 'Don't tell me they'd been tampered with?' Gideon said.

There was a short silence and Robin finally nodded. 'Yes. The police just told me this morning that the brake pipes had been severed.'

Worriedly, Gideon shook his head. '*Unbelievable*. Let's not go into the whys and wherefores right now, Uncle Robin, but you must be very careful, on your guard. You were the target here.'

'Oh yes, I realize that. I just told Evan I was going to be very, very wary in future. But let us move on, Gideon my boy. Evan's parents are due to arrive any moment. For tea.'

Startled yet again, Gideon exclaimed, 'Well, well, well, that's going to put the cat amongst the pigeons!'

There had been a change in her, Evan was well aware of that. It was a subtle change but, nonetheless, it was important. It had occurred because of the car crash, and if something good could come out of something bad, then it was this.

The day after the crash she had come to understand how vulnerable she was, how mortal, and she accepted that life as such was not in her control. Life was life. It happened. And you never knew what was going to come at you. Or how you would defend yourself. The only thing she was certain of was herself. And unexpectedly, she knew exactly *who* she was. Not her mother, not her father, not her grandmother Glynnis. *She was herself.* And she *knew* herself. And with this sudden knowledge came the understanding that no one could lead her life for her.

It was her life. And how she lived it was up to her. She knew deep in her bones that she must take charge of herself very firmly, no longer be influenced by her father, her image of him, or by the past. The past was always there, lived inside of you, and it helped to make you who you were. But it had to be placed in its own perspective. The past could not dominate the future.

And so Evan had made her mind up to be open and straightforward with her parents, her father in particular, and that was exactly what she intended to do.

In the same way, she had made up her mind to be absolutely honest with Gideon. The moment he had arrived she had told him about their baby. She hadn't expected him this afternoon, but she had taken it in her stride, taken a deep breath and plunged, in a way revelling in the truth. What a wonderful relief it was to be truthful.

Pushing herself up before either man could help

her, she steadied herself against the table, and then walked across the room, carefully manoeuvring her leg in the cast. It was good to be upright. Her ribcage hurt much less when she was standing. Sitting down wasn't too bad either. But when she lay down to sleep she felt discomfort, even a little pain. Despite this, she kept telling herself how fortunate she had been on Saturday.

Laughingly, Linnet had said yesterday that she had a guardian angel, and perhaps she did. All she knew was that her baby was safe inside her, and she herself was strong and vital and would soon be back to normal.

Deep inside she was thrilled that Gideon was thrilled. His response to the news had been genuine, and there was no question in her mind that they would now be able to work things out. Especially after today.

Her parents were due at any moment, and she had decided she was going to tell her father the truth about Robin. He would find out one day anyway, and in the not-too-distant future, and so she felt the necessity to explain everything to him in advance. Forewarned was forearmed, wasn't it?

'Are you all right, sweetheart?' Gideon called across the room, interrupting his conversation with Robin.

'I'm fine and dandy,' she shot back, smiling at him, 'I just needed to be upright, to stretch. My ribcage gets a bit . . . uppity.'

He laughed with her and turned back to Robin, delved back into their conversation about terrorism.

Robin had been talking about the attacks on New York and Washington. As a former Member of Parliament Robin knew what was what, still had a lot of important connections. Gideon always thought of his great-uncle's knowledge as being fine tuned, very much the truth. Having been an MP for most of his adult life, he certainly knew enough men of power in the government today to get some quick and honest answers.

Evan, standing near the window, watched them talking for a moment or two longer, smiling to herself. Gideon would be a father in seven months and Robin a great-grandfather. Her child was going to be well blessed. She wondered if she were carrying a girl or a boy? She would know the sex when she went for the amniocentesis test.

At this moment she heard a car in the driveway, and walking back to the card table she said, 'I think Mom and Dad are just arriving, I heard a car pulling up.'

'Did they drive?' Gideon asked, sounding surprised.

'Oh yes, Dad insisted. He said he knew the way. The night we had dinner, when they first arrived in London, he told me he'd been to Yorkshire as a child.'

Robin looked as if he was about to say something, and then obviously changed his mind. Rising, he walked over to the window, stood next to Evan, and putting his arm around her, he said, 'Let me second-guess you, my dear. You invited me because you're going to tell him who I am, aren't you?'

'Do you think I'll have to, Robin?'

'What do you mean?'

'You two look very much alike. Don't you agree, Gid?'

'Afraid so,' he laughed, and joined them; laughing again, he added, 'And we look like a very formal church welcoming committee, the way we're standing here looking so serious.'

'I'm just more comfortable standing at the moment,' Evan explained, leaning against Robin.

Margaret appeared in the doorway and said, 'Oh hello, Gideon, I didn't know you were here.'

'I just crept in like a little church mouse, Margaret,' he answered, his manner jovial, 'like I've done all of my life.'

'Aye, that you have,' she shot back, and then looking across at Evan she continued, 'Your parents have arrived, Miss Evan, I've shown them to their room. They'll be down in a moment or two, they're just freshening up. I told them where the library is. I'm going to bring the tea-tray in straight away. They must be parched. Not to mention famished.'

'Thank you,' Evan replied as Margaret disappeared.

'I'd better move those few things off the coffee table,' Gideon muttered almost to himself, hurrying over to the fireplace. He removed an ashtray, a bowl of flowers and a book, placed them on a side table, then pulled two chairs closer to the sofa. 'There, that's fine, we can now seat five. In a circle.'

Margaret returned with a large wooden tray

laden with the tea things. After placing it on the coffee table, she told them, 'Back in three shakes of a lamb's tail with the nursery sandwiches, scones and one of my cream sponge cakes.'

'My mouth's watering already,' Gideon told her, offering Margaret a winning smile. 'And your jam-and-cream sponge is the best in the world. None like it anywhere.'

'You've always been a flatterer, Mr Gideon,' she muttered and left the library again. Returning a few moments later the housekeeper came back with a second tray of food, which she placed on the desk. 'Do you want me to stay and pour, Miss Evan? Or can you manage?'

'I think we'll be all right, Margaret. Thanks anyway.'

'I'm a dab hand at pouring tea and passing cake,' Gideon reassured Margaret, who nodded and was off again, hurrying to the kitchen.

Gideon said, 'I'm glad I'm here to witness this, Evan. How're you going to do it?'

'I'm not sure . . . play it by ear, I guess.'

'It's up to you, my dear,' Robin ventured. 'Don't do it for *me* . . .'

'I want to do it for myself, for my child, for Gideon, and for *you*, Robin. The truth matters to us all, don't you think? Especially under the circumstances with my child on the way.'

'Indeed it does,' he responded, looking at Gideon. 'I'm sure you agree?'

'I certainly do. Are you going to tell them about the baby, Evan?'

516

'Maybe.'

'In which case, let me just say this . . . since we're engaged I am expecting you to marry me, and as soon as possible. Please say yes.'

'Yes!'

'Yippee! We're finally getting married!'

Listening to them both, Robin smiled to himself. They were going to be all right, these two, definitely all right. And very happy together, if he knew anything at all about human nature. They were well suited.

Suddenly Owen and Marietta were hovering uncertainly on the threshold of the library, staring into the cavernous room.

'Mom! Dad! Come in, come in,' Evan cried, hobbling forward, her face full of smiles. 'It's wonderful to see you both.'

Her mother rushed into the room but embraced her gingerly. 'I know all about broken ribs,' she whispered against her hair. 'Oh Evan, thank God you're all right. I've been so worried about you.'

'I'm great, Mom, really fine.'

A moment later her father was kissing her cheek, grabbing her hand. 'We're so glad to see you, honey,' he said, his bright blue eyes warm and loving as they searched her face. 'You're sure you're all right? No internal injuries?'

'Don't be silly, Dad! The doctor wouldn't have let me come out of the hospital if that were the case.'

Gideon was suddenly by their side, hugging her mother, shaking her father's hand. 'It's good to see you both, Mr and Mrs Hughes. Welcome to Pennistone Royal.'

'We're glad to be here,' Marietta answered, giving him a wide smile. 'We're only –' Marietta stopped speaking as she caught sight of Robin standing near the fireplace. She stared at him, then looked at Owen swiftly.

Not missing a thing, Evan saw her opportunity, took hold of her father's hand and said, 'I want you to meet someone, Dad. This is Robin Ainsley, Emma Harte's son.'

Leading Owen over to Robin, she went on, 'Grandfather, I want you to meet your son at long last. Dad, I hope this is not too much of a shock but this is your biological father . . . he and Glynnis were together during the war.'

Robin put out his hand.

Owen took it, staring at Robin, recognizing himself in the older man. For a long moment he was unable to speak.

It was Robin who spoke the first words. Releasing Owen's hand, he said, 'We met once before, so long ago I'm sure you've forgotten it. Here in this house with my mother, your grandmother, Emma Harte. Glynnis . . . your mother brought you to see Emma, and I stopped by, quite unexpectedly. Do you remember?'

'Vaguely,' Owen replied quietly, staring intently at Robin. 'We'd come up to Yorkshire because Mom loved it so much. We came here to tea. Yes, I do remember. But I didn't know . . . you were my father. I thought Richard Hughes was my father.'

'And he was, Owen, he was! He brought you up, loved you as his own. He *was* your father and a wonderful one,' Robin told him in all sincerity. 'You must understand that.'

Owen simply nodded.

Marietta came forward, edging closer to Owen, and he said quickly, 'This is my wife, Marietta.'

'I'm pleased to meet you.' Robin took her hand in his, smiled at her.

'My goodness, don't you look alike,' Marietta exclaimed after a moment. 'I always thought Owen resembled Richard. But he's the spitting image of you.'

She had been remarkable. So remarkable, in fact, she had startled him. And brave . . . to be as honest as she had been *had* taken bravery. She had spoken out, left nothing to chance, speculation or innuendo, and it had worked. Perhaps because of her genuineness and simplicity. And she had been so straightforward, had not dressed her words up, and that counted too.

Now she lay stretched out on the bed next to him, propped up by pillows for comfort, dozing in the dim light of early evening. She had been so tired all of a sudden, he had helped her upstairs to her bedroom, and stayed with her . . . because he didn't want her to be alone, and because he himself had felt so utterly alone of late, so lonely and solitary without her. Their differences had created distance between them . . . but now, thank God, that distance had closed, and no matter what happened in their life together, he would not let anything come between them ever again.

Gideon propped himself up on his elbow and looked down at Evan's face. Calm in repose, and lovely. How could he have ever doubted her? Through his own stupidity, of course.

He had known when he first met her nine months ago that she was different from the other women he had known, that she was as straight as an arrow, a young woman with moral fibre and ethics, and great intelligence. It had been her ambivalence of late that had put him off. That, and her attitude to her father. But her adoration of Owen was only natural – he felt the same way about his own father, didn't he?

He moved a strand of hair away from her face, and she opened her eyes and looked straight at him.

He stared back at her, a smile playing around his mouth, his clear green eyes filled with love, spilling that love for her.

'Penny for your thoughts, Gideon Harte.'

'That's simple. I was thinking how much I love you.' He placed his hand on her stomach gently. 'And how much I love this child of ours growing inside you.'

A smile brought a surge of happiness to her face, and her blue-grey eyes seemed light-filled and translucent at this moment. 'Me too.'

'Oh Evan, darling, I'm so sorry I was difficult these last few weeks. Forgive me?'

'There's nothing to forgive. I was being very difficult.'

'But today you were courageous, telling your father about Robin.'

She made a face. 'Telling the truth can be hard. But in the end it's worth it, because it's the right thing to do. How awful if someone in the family told my father about Robin before I did. Imagine how he would feel – *betrayed*, I'm certain of that.'

'He didn't bat an eyelash when you said *we* were pregnant and getting married in January. And you hoped he and your mother would come to the wedding, that it wouldn't be the same without them present. You were so matter of fact, even I was startled for a second.'

'I knew I had to get it out, *say it*, just tell them, in the most down-to-earth way. I didn't want a lot of free-floating emotion getting in the way.'

'He took it very well, Evan, I must say, and your mother was just over the moon about the baby. "My first grandchild" she kept saying, and in the end your father was smiling, too. And he didn't ask one question. But *I* have one, darling.'

'Yes, what is it?'

'Why January? Why can't we get married sooner?'

'In a way, I'd like to, Gid, but we can't upstage Linnet. We really can't, and even if we had a quickie wedding at a registry office, or eloped, it would still upstage her marriage to Julian, don't you think?'

'Yes, you're right. But you're going to look . . . very pregnant when we tie the knot.'

Evan began to chuckle, nodding her head. 'I am,

yes, but I don't care, and anyway, I want a small wedding. Just your family and mine.'

'Mine's quite large, and it's yours as well, come to think of it.'

'True. There's another thing, Gid. People are a little nervous about travelling right now, wouldn't you agree?'

'I know what you're getting at . . . your sisters might not want to fly the Atlantic with terrorists in the news, and perhaps in the air.'

'*Exactly*.'

'January it is then,' Gideon agreed, and glanced at his watch. 'I think I'd better go downstairs and see what's happening. Are you coming?'

'Yes, I think I'd better, I'd like to know what's transpired between Robin and my father.'

The three of them were sitting in front of the fire in the Stone Hall. Her mother, her father and her grandfather. She had called Robin *grandfather* to make a dramatic point earlier, but now she wondered if he would mind if she called him that all the time, instead of Robin. She would ask him later, when they were alone.

Three pairs of eyes gazed at them as Gideon helped Evan to the big armchair, but it was her mother who asked, 'That cast must be unwieldy to drag around, honey, isn't it?'

'It sure is, Mom. And tiring.' Looking from Robin to her father, she then said apologetically, 'I was rather blunt earlier, Dad, but I thought it was the only way to tell you about Robin and Glynnis.'

Owen hurried over to her, kissed the top of her head. 'You did the right thing, Evan. It was only a question of time before I discovered the truth. Better coming from you, honey. Your mother and Robin agree. And I'm a grown man, not a kid. I can handle the truth, however unexpected and startling it is.'

'I know that, Daddy.'

Aware of the time, Gideon said, 'I'm afraid I do have to leave, Evan.'

'Oh, but it's such a long drive!' she exclaimed. 'You're going to be tired.'

'No, I won't be, because I'm taking a helicopter from Yeadon Airport. I'll be in London before you can blink, almost.' Gideon kissed her on the cheek, telling her, 'Don't get up, sweetheart. I'll call you later.'

'All right, Gid,' she answered, smiling up at him. Kissing her fingertips, she then pressed them against his mouth. 'I love you.'

'And I love you.'

He took his leave of the others and was gone, and Evan leaned back in the chair, enjoying the comfort of its roominess and the cushions, the warmth of the fire, the lambent light. It was very cosy here in spite of the vastness, the high-flung ceiling, and she was relaxed and suddenly happy sitting here with her parents and Robin . . . her family.

The three of them had cocktails and chatted amicably as she sipped a glass of orange juice, thinking about the baby and Gideon and the future they had together . . . Her overwhelming joy and happiness seemed unreal for a while.

Later Margaret came in and announced that supper was served in the breakfast room, and her father helped Evan up out of the chair; it was Robin who led them out of the Stone Hall, chatting to her mother about horses, of all things. She had never known her mother liked horses and horse-racing. She wondered why not. But then there was so much she didn't know about her mother. And about her father. This afternoon it had come out that he had met Robin before, had been to this house . . . Why had he been so mysterious? Well, she knew the answer to that . . .

Evan was so bone-tired after dinner she asked her mother to help her upstairs, excusing herself to her father and Robin. Once she was undressed and in bed, Marietta sat down on the edge of the bed and took hold of her hand.

Clearing her throat, looking serious, her mother said, 'I'm glad you told your father about Robin, and about the baby, Evan, but most especially about Robin. He needed to know.'

Frowning, Evan looked at her mother alertly, and said slowly, 'You say that in the strangest way, Mom, almost as if *you* knew already.'

There was the merest hesitation on Marietta's part before she answered, 'I did, actually, although I never told your father.'

Evan's eyes opened wider, and she drew closer to her mother. 'Who told you? Why do I ask that: it must have been Gran, who else.'

'That's right. Your grandmother told me, but not in so many words.'

'I'm not following you.'

'I realize that. Give me a moment, I'll be right back.' As she spoke Marietta was heading for the door, and she went out without saying another word.

Evan had barely had time to ponder on her mother's sudden confidences when Marietta came back to the bedroom, closing the door behind her quietly. She was carrying a package, and, returning to the bedside, she sat down and put the package in Evan's lap.

Looking down at the brown paper parcel, Evan then glanced up at Marietta and asked, 'What's this?'

'Letters from Emma Harte to Glynnis, written over the years. Glynnis kept them all, and one of the last things your grandmother asked me to do was to retrieve them from her apartment. She told me I had to give them to you, not to your father, and *only* to you. She made me promise not to break faith with her, and of course I did.'

'You read them, though.' It came out sounding like a statement rather than a question, and Evan's brows lifted.

'Most of them, yes. The package wasn't sealed like this. I wrapped them up. I knew, deep within myself, that she wouldn't mind . . . We had a special relationship, and your grandmother loved me, trusted me.'

'I've always known that, Mom. So, you read the letters and discovered that Dad was Robin's son.'

Marietta sighed. 'Yes . . . and other things. But

she did insist I give them to you, and so here they are . . .'

Evan leaned back against the pillows. 'She wanted me to know everything, didn't she? But why?'

'I have always believed that the truth sets you free . . . and I think that was her reason . . . she wanted you to know the truth about her, about her life long ago, and your father's heritage.' Bending towards Evan, her mother lovingly and tenderly kissed her on the cheek. 'They're yours now, honey . . . to read whenever you feel like it. But remember, they're not for anyone else's eyes . . . *just yours*.'

'I understand, Mom, and thank you for bringing them to me. But are you sure Dad doesn't know anything about them, that he hasn't peeked whilst you've been here?'

'Oh no, I've kept them in my bank-deposit box,' Marietta reassured her.

Evan couldn't help laughing. 'Mom, you constantly surprise me!'

Once she was alone, Evan couldn't resist looking inside the parcel tonight, even though she was tired. After untying the string, she found a large cardboard box filled with letters. She pulled one out at random, and began to read; and slowly, for the next two hours, she continued to read the letters from Emma to her grandmother . . . reading and digesting until she could hardly keep her eyes open. And what she read startled and amazed her, sometimes made the tears well up.

Eventually she had no choice but to put them away, turn out the light and go to sleep. But it was not a restful sleep for her and her dreams were filled with Emma and Glynnis and everything that happened over fifty years ago . . .

PART TWO

Emma and Glynnis
Summer 1950

Love is a breach in the walls, a broken gate,
Where that comes in that shall not go again;
Love sells the proud heart's citadel to Fate.
'Love': RUPERT BROOKE (1913)

Chapter Twenty-Nine

A rush of warm memories flooded Emma when she saw the postmark on the letter. WALES. Instantly she knew who it was from, because she also recognized the handwriting. She opened it eagerly, filled with anticipation, and read it swiftly.

May 27th, 1950

Dear Mrs Harte,

I'm here in the Rhondda visiting my family in the Valleys. It's been wonderful seeing everyone, and now I'm planning to come up to London for a visit. I do hope you'll have time to have lunch with me, or a cup of tea. I will be staying at the Hyde Park Hotel and I expect to be there towards the end of next week.

Love from Glynnis.

Without hesitation, smiling, Emma slipped the letter back into its envelope, reached for a piece of her personal stationery and wrote back.

Dearest Glynnis,

*What a lovely surprise to hear from you.
I'm thrilled to know you're on our shores, and
it will be so nice to see you after all these
years. Actually, I can't wait. Please phone me
as soon as you arrive in London, and we'll
arrange to have lunch.*

With much affection, E.H.

After folding the letter in half, Emma put it in
an envelope, addressed it and added a postage
stamp. She propped the envelope against the lamp,
stared at it for a moment, another smile spreading
across her face. To see Glynnis again would be
such a treat; she'd missed her former secretary . . .
missed her beauty, her glamour, her lovely charm
and grace, her pretty, lilting Welsh voice. Emma
couldn't help wondering how Glynnis looked these
days. She hadn't sent any photographs lately.

Pushing back her chair, Emma rose, walked
across to the large window which faced the moorland, stood looking out. It was such a glorious day
today, sunny and warm, and the sky was as blue
as speedwells.

It was the first day of June. And if the weather
was anything to go by, they would be in for a
lovely summer. She hoped so. It had been quite
rainy last year, and she'd felt as though she was
living in the middle of a rain forest.

Emma was planning to spend as much time in
Yorkshire as she could this year, although she was

aware she had to go to the Villa Faviola in the south of France. It was a necessity.

Even though the war had been now over for the last five years, the villa still needed much work. Wartime neglect and its occupation by Nazi officers for quite a long period of time had created a great deal of damage. Some of it she had attended to last year, but there were a number of areas which still required her attention and much work.

Perhaps she could go over there in August or September; Blackie had promised to make the trip with her, and she knew full well that she needed the benefit of his good eyes, his expertise and skill. She often teased him, said he was still a bricklayer at heart, just as he had been when she had first met him over forty-five years ago. He always laughed with her, enjoyed her teasing; like her he remembered, with much nostalgia, their early days together: in those days they were both impoverished and eyeing their prospects in the world, wondering how to improve their lot in life.

Glancing at her watch, Emma saw that it was only eleven o'clock. There was time to go for a walk on the moors after all. Turning her back on the magnificent view, she walked across the upstairs parlour, sat down at her old Georgian desk once more, and finished going through her correspondence. After she had phoned the Leeds store and rung her secretary in London, she hurried into her bedroom and changed her shoes.

A short while later she was hurrying downstairs, crossing the Stone Hall and heading for the kitchen.

Hilda glanced around with a start when the door flew open, and she exclaimed, 'Oh goodness me! You did make me jump, Mrs H. Gave me a right start, that you did.'

'I'm sorry, Hilda. I just wanted to tell you I'm going for a walk. I need a bit of fresh air. I thought I'd have lunch around one-thirty. Is that all right with you?'

'It is, madame. I'd planned on making you some luverly plaice and chips, with fresh summer peas, and cauliflower from the garden, steamed that way you like it, and a right grand parsley sauce. Do you fancy that, Mrs Harte?'

'It sounds delicious, Hilda. And when I come back we can plan tomorrow's dinner if you like. Mr O'Neill's coming, as he always does on Fridays, and I think you should consider making a few of his favourites. Miss Daisy's going to be here with Mr Amory and little Paula.'

Hilda's entire face became one huge happy smile. 'Oooh, madame, she's a right bonny snippet, that she is. We all luv her, Mrs H.'

'Yes, there's no doubt she's the most adorable child, Hilda, I'll grant you that. But she knows it, you know.'

Hilda laughed, and turned back to her pots and pans, thinking about tomorrow's dinner and the menu.

As she walked towards her beloved moors, which she had claimed as her own when she was only a child of ten, Emma glanced around, taking in the cool, solitary beauty of this land. There were those who thought it bleak and unwelcoming, but she saw it through different eyes, found the solitariness consoling and restful. It was from the implacability of this land that she drew her strength and determination. She never felt lonely or alone up here, and she was always at peace amongst these rolling hills, for it was from here that she came.

She climbed steadily to the top, noticing how parched and dried-out patches of grass looked, but then it was always dun-coloured at this time of year. By late August the heather would be blooming, and even though it was only the plain ling, it nonetheless covered the hills like mantles of purple, was a sea of undulating brilliant colour under the late-summer breeze.

Finally, she came to her favourite spot at the top, and sat down on the big stone wedged into the niche created by two giant boulders. Above her soared great monoliths from the Ice Age which she had always marvelled at. Dropped here by nature millions of years ago, they resembled massive sculptures carved by some mighty omnipotent hand. And out in front of her stretched the breathtaking and familiar panorama she knew so well . . . the encircling moors and below them the green and verdant valley where the flowing river was a thin sliver of silver in the bright June sunlight.

Glancing around, Emma suddenly sniffed, caught the scent of the moorland flora . . . it filled her nostrils, carried her back to her childhood, and she closed her eyes, for a moment thinking of her mother who had also loved these moors. Most especially the Top of the World. One day she would go there again . . . where she had gone so many times with her mother, and with Edwin Fairley. So long ago . . . when she had been only a very young girl, inexperienced and far too trusting. She heard the faint buzzing of the bees as they danced around in the air above the yellow gorse and tiny moorland flowers, and when she glanced up she saw the linnets and larks wheeling and turning against the sun. It was a gorgeous balmy day, soft, enfolding.

Closing her eyes, she drifted, lost in her thoughts, thinking of Paul as she always did up here on the moors. But then she thought of him every day at some moment or other. He was in her heart forever. How much she missed him, missed his irreverent humour, his love and understanding, his charm, his devilishness . . . There never had been a man like him, and there never would be. He had been unique, and she missed him so much . . . more, sometimes, than she could bear.

And yet she was so lucky in her life. She had her devoted brothers Winston and Frank, and her beloved friend, Blackie O'Neill. And her children and grandchildren . . . even another grandchild now, her darling Paula. Named for Paul McGill, she was *his* granddaughter, and so like him in looks: dark, exotic, with those wonderful blue-violet eyes.

Emma's mind suddenly went to her son Robin, and she felt a little flash of dismay when she considered his old romance with Glynnis. She must be very careful not to let him know Glynnis was in London. He might want to see her.

But then there was no problem, Emma reassured herself; Glynnis had told her long ago that she never wanted to see Robin Ainsley again. He had treated her so badly, and had broken her heart. Well, broken hearts did mend, in her opinion; but Glynnis obviously had no interest in Robin. She had married her GI – Richard Hughes – and he was bringing up Robin's child as his own, and what more could a woman want than a good man, a loving husband who accepted her as she was, and adored her in the process. Glynnis was lucky, too.

'You've never looked better, Blackie,' Emma said, staring him fully in the face. 'You're quite . . . splendid. Yes, that's exactly the right word to describe you. Or perhaps *magnificent*. That's a beautiful suit you're wearing.'

He threw back his head and laughed. After he recovered from his mirth, he peered at her and said, 'Flattery will get you everywhere, mavourneen, and if I didn't know you better, after all these long years, I'd be saying you were after something.'

'Don't be silly, of course I'm not.'

'That's what I just said, Emma, my sweet. But just so you know, you can have anything of mine that I have. Anything at all. You know how much I love you, Emm.'

'And I love you, too, Blackie. Goodness, all these years we've been friends. All of my life, actually.'

'Aye, and what a funny little snippet of a lass you were, all skin and bone, but so beautiful, even then, me darlin'. Like a precious flower growing among the weeds of Fairley Hall.' He let out a sigh. 'Aye, that was long ago now, almost fifty years.' He eyed her carefully. 'And I might say you're looking pretty nifty yourself, Emma Harte. All dolled up for a party, eh?'

She smiled at him indulgently. 'No, not a party. However, when you said you wanted to come early, I thought I'd better be dressed and ready for the rest of the day.'

'You look as elegant as you always do, Emma. Now, I understand from Winston that congratulations are in order.'

She stared at him blandly, and her green eyes narrowed.

'I was told by your brother that the Yorkshire Consolidated Newspaper Company has taken control of the *Yorkshire Morning Gazette*. It's yours now, Emma. You've finally bested Edwin Fairley. You've won, me darlin'.'

'You always knew I would, didn't you, Blackie O'Neill?' she answered, sounding challenging, and there was an undercurrent of defiance in her tone. She sat up straighter in the chair.

'I did. It seems to me you had set your mind to getting that paper, come hell or high water. So tell me . . .'

'I've been very patient, and I had a weak adversary. My newspapers are the most successful in the north, and they've eaten up a lot of the *Gazette*'s circulation, as well as the circulation of a few other newspapers. To be honest, Blackie, the *Gazette*'s been losing money since the end of the war, and anyway, I ran the *Gazette* into the ground.'

'Deliberately?' Blackie took a puff on his cigar, sat studying her thoughtfully.

'But of course. And without compunction. Edwin Fairley's never been a good businessman. He's a much better lawyer. He should have stuck to the law, in my considered opinion.'

'Winston told me Edwin sold off a lot of his shares. That was obviously a foolish move. He weakened his position, didn't he?'

Emma nodded. 'He's not been dealing from strength for a long time. But he stayed on as chairman, and that was *really* a mistake.'

'Why?'

'Because his situation was very tenuous, and the other shareholders were upset with him, but he paid no mind to them. He thought he was in the right. He didn't understand and they weren't loyal to *him*, only to their own bank balances. I made them a huge offer, volunteered to put new management in, but it was the money that did it. Naturally. *Money talks*, Blackie. You taught me that when I was still a bairn.'

He smiled at her, rose and walked over to the balustrade of the terrace, looking down the long stretch of lawn, his eyes reflective. Suddenly he turned and nodded, saying swiftly, 'Winston said Edwin finally sold his shares to Harte Enterprises.'

'He did. He had no alternative.'

'Winston calls it a coup for you, and I agree with him. But I'm surprised you didn't go to that board meeting.'

'Why would I go? Winston was representing me.'

'To witness Edwin's defeat, Emm.'

Those beautiful green eyes turned flinty and cold, and there was a sudden iciness about Emma. She drew herself up in the chair, her head held proudly, and said in a voice that was glacial, 'Forty-five years ago I told Edwin Fairley I never wanted to see him again as long as I lived, and I haven't. You surely can't think that I want to set eyes on him now, do you? Not you, Blackie? My one true friend.'

'I don't suppose you would,' he murmured in a quiet tone, memories rushing at him. Once he'd been ready to horsewhip Edwin Fairley, because of his treatment of Emma. And for a long time, many years in fact, he had regretted that he hadn't done so. Edwin had deserved it.

Emma said, 'But all that's water under the bridge. However, Winston told me something odd, that he thought Edwin looked gratified at the meeting. I thought that was a strange thing to say, and I told him that more than likely it was *relief* he saw on Edwin's face.'

'I can't imagine he'd be gratified, Emma. The *Gazette*'s been in the Fairley family for three generations. Now he's lost it to you.'

She began to laugh. '*Relief*, Blackie, I've lifted a burden from Edwin's shoulders. For a second time.'

'True, mavourneen,' Blackie replied softly, his face bland. And then he thought that perhaps Edwin had indeed been relieved, but not for any reason Emma could conjure up.

'Grandy, Grandy, Grandy! Here I am!' Paula cried, the five-year-old child running along the terrace on her fat little legs, her summer frock billowing around her, her face full of smiles.

Emma jumped up, rushed forward to meet her granddaughter, exclaiming, 'Not so fast, darling, I don't want you to fall!'

Bending down, Emma caught hold of Paula, and hugged her to her. 'You mustn't run so fast, lovey.'

The child looked at her solemnly, and then she struggled free and ran to Blackie at the end of the terrace. 'Uncle Blackie, hello, hello!'

Smiling in delight, Blackie bent over her, smoothing her dark curls gently with the palm of his hand. 'And aren't you just the most beautiful girl, mavourneen,' he said softly, his black eyes full of love for this child.

'Shane, I want Shane, Uncle Blackie. *Where's Shane?*' she demanded.

'He's at school, me darlin'.'

'Can he come and play tomorrow?'

'I'm sure he can, Paula.'

She clapped her hands. 'Oh *good*.'

As Emma came towards them, Blackie looked up and his breath caught in his throat. From even this short distance she looked for a moment as she had when she was a girl . . . her red-gold hair shimmering in the sunlight. She was as beautiful to him now as she had been then . . . so many years ago when he had met his little starveling girl on those mist-filled moors, and followed her to that wretched house, Fairley Hall. An involuntary shiver ran through him as he thought of that time.

When Emma came to a stop she looked up into his face and said, with a frown, 'You look so sorrowful, Blackie. Is something wrong?'

'No, not anymore, mavourneen. Not anymore.' He gave her a bright smile, leaned over the child and kissed Emma's cheek. 'But I just want you to know you're still my young colleen of the moors. And you always will be 'til the day I die.'

CHAPTER THIRTY

The moment Glynnis walked into the office Emma felt as though she had never left. In an instant, a decade fell away, and for a moment Emma was back in the past, in the war years. Memories came at her in full flood, bringing a lump to her throat.

Rising, she hurried across the floor of her office, and the two women embraced affectionately. Standing away from her former secretary, Emma looked into her face, and smiled. 'Glynnis, you've hardly changed!' she exclaimed. 'You look just the same, perhaps a tiny bit thinner, but as lovely as you always were.'

'I'm a few years older now, Mrs Harte, but thank you. And you never get a day older, I must say.'

Emma chuckled as the two of them walked over to the seating arrangement at one end of her office in the London store. 'I'll let you into a secret,' Emma confided as they sat down opposite each other. 'I was sixty this past April, not that I feel it, mind you. Actually, I still feel like a young woman inside.'

'And that's how you look,' Glynnis answered, meaning it.

'I did want to take you to lunch, Glynnis dear, but you said you preferred to have tea, and you mentioned a problem when we spoke on the phone. Is there something the matter?'

'Oh no, Mrs Harte. It's just that . . . well, you see, I brought Owen with me to England. My parents haven't seen him since he was a baby, and he's with me now, in London. He does like his lunch, it's his favourite meal. That's the only reason I suggested tea.'

Emma shook her head, suddenly laughing. 'He could have come to lunch with us, you know. And let's not forget, he's *my* grandson, too. I'm so glad he's here, I haven't seen him since he was a toddler.'

'He's a nice boy, I'm proud of him.' Glynnis hesitated, then went on in a lowered voice, 'He looks like Robin.'

'Does he really?' Emma responded, her vivid green eyes lighting up with interest. Leaning forward, she asked, 'And where is Owen now?'

'With my cousin Gwyneth. She's taken him to the zoo. She's married now and lives in Hampstead, but it's only a small flat, so I decided it was better for us to go to a hotel. That's why we're at the Hyde Park.'

'I understand. And she's well, is she? Your cousin, I mean.'

'Oh yes. No children yet, but she's very happily married . . .' Glynnis let her sentence trail off.

There was a little silence.

Emma sat back on the sofa, scrutinizing Glynnis Hughes intently, her mind full of questions, some of which she decided not to ask. But she couldn't help wondering if Glynnis were happy in her marriage to Richard Hughes, if it had worked, still was working. Although Glynnis continued to write to her on a regular basis she never said much about Richard or referred to her domestic life.

Becoming aware of Emma's fixed gaze, Glynnis cleared her throat. 'You're staring at me, Mrs Harte. Now it's my turn to ask if something's wrong.'

'Not at all, Glynnis. I was just wondering if *your* marriage had worked out all right? You never really reveal anything in your letters. At least about Richard. But I always thought he was such a nice young man.'

'He is, and it's fine, I mean everything's good. The marriage is sound, and he does love Owen so very much. Richard's treated him like his own child since the day he was born, but then you know that. And he's never asked me who the father was. He's a good man, and kind.'

'Then my judgement of him was correct. I never doubted him, Glynnis, and I'm glad you have him. By the way, why didn't he come with you?'

'To tell you the truth he didn't want to come. You see, in the past year his business has grown in leaps and bounds. He's doing really well with his antique shop in Manhattan, and he's even done some interior design for a couple of clients who collect English Georgian furniture. He's an expert in that field. Anyway, he has a couple of big jobs at the moment and nothing ever interferes with *his* business.' A smile suddenly played around Glynnis's mouth. 'He's like you in that way, Mrs Harte. I'm sure that's why I understand him so well, because I worked for you.'

They both laughed in a conspiratorial way, and then a moment later there was a sudden knock on the door and it opened. Alice, Emma's secretary, popped her head around it, and asked, 'Shall I bring the tea in now, Mrs Harte?'

'Yes, thank you, Alice.' Looking across at Glynnis, Emma asked, 'What are your plans for the weekend?'

Glynnis gave a little shrug. 'I don't really have any. I thought I'd take Owen to Hampton Court, do a few jaunts like that. I want him to know his other country . . . my country.'

'How about showing him Yorkshire?' Emma suggested, raising an auburn brow. Seeing the surprise crossing Glynnis's face, she continued, 'I think you ought to bring Owen to Yorkshire, to stay at Pennistone Royal with me. For the weekend. I'm leaving tonight, and if you travel up tomorrow you can spend Friday night, Saturday and Sunday. I'm sure he'd enjoy it, my dear.'

'Oh Mrs Harte, that would be lovely, but are you sure?' Glynnis's blue eyes sparkled.

'Absolutely positive, and I would love to get to know Owen. In a way, I feel as if I do already, because your letters are very enlightening, but having the boy around me in the flesh, so to speak, would be . . . well, it would make me very happy.'

'There's just one thing.' Glynnis paused, her face changing. She gave Emma a worried look. '*He* won't be around, will he? I wouldn't want to run into him.'

'No, no. Robin always calls if he's going to pop in to see me, but usually he stays in London all the time these days. He's made a success of being a Member of Parliament, made a success of politics.'

Glynnis merely nodded, not trusting herself to say his name or ask any questions.

Alice came in with the tea tray and put it down on the coffee table between them, then smiling at Emma, she hurried out.

After pouring the tea and passing a cup to Glynnis, Emma said, 'Tomkins is driving me to Yorkshire later, but I'll arrange a car and driver for you, Glynnis. For tomorrow morning.'

'No, no, I don't want you to do that, Mrs Harte! It's kind of you, but we can come on the train to Harrogate. Really, that'll be –'

'I think you'd better come by car,' Emma cut in. 'The trains can be slow, and often late. However, if you prefer to drive yourself, then you can borrow my Riley, that's no problem at all.'

'If you're sure, Mrs Harte,' Glynnis began, nodding. 'I think I'd like that, and certainly it's a chance for Owen to see the English countryside.'

'So it's settled then,' Emma said, beaming at her former secretary. 'I'm looking forward to our weekend. The three of us will have fun.'

* * *

'We've now become the biggest newspaper propri-etors in the north,' Emma said, gazing at her brother Winston across the desk. 'But I want to expand further, I want to own . . . a *national*.'

Winston stared back at her, as usual taking everything in his stride. Long ago he had ceased to be surprised by Emma. She was a wonder to him, a wonder to them all, and she had expanded her business empire enormously since the end of the war. And he knew she had done it all by using a combination of determination, sheer nerve and hard work. She was a genuine tycoon now.

'You're not saying anything, Winston.'

'I was just thinking . . . thinking that there're no newspapers for sale at the moment, our Emm, as far as *I* know, anyway. National *dailies* I'm talking about.'

'I know that. And I've been thinking too . . . perhaps we ought to start one of our own. From scratch.'

'Good God, Emma, that'll cost a fortune!'

'And buying one wouldn't? Come on, you know I'd have to pay through the nose if I attempted to buy an existing newspaper. It might even be cheaper, starting one.'

'Well, let's not rush in. Remember what Henry Rossiter always says. Fools –'

'Rush in where angels fear to tread,' Emma inter-rupted him, 'but I've always done that all my life. So I guess I'm a fool,' she laughed, her eyes full of spirit.

'Nobody could call you that. Many other things, but not a fool,' Winston declared.

'Let's at least think about it, Winston,' she said, her tone a shade lighter. 'Also, when I saw Blackie last Friday I asked him about the land which we looked at last week, that bombed-out building site. He thinks we should buy it, since it *is* a commercial property site, and it could become very valuable.'

Winston nodded. 'To tell you the truth, it is already, Emma. Very valuable, in fact, and I was going to suggest we put in a bid for it on Monday.'

'Yes, do it, Winston, because Blackie said we can't go wrong.'

Emma stood up, walked over to the big window in the upstairs parlour, glancing out. The weather was still very sunny and warm, as it had been for the past week. Her gardens were beginning to look truly beautiful, and she made a mental note to tell Mr Ramsbotham, the head gardener, how pleased she was. And she would also give a word of praise to Wiggs, his nephew, who would take over from him one day. They had done a wonderful job with the parterres which looked better than they ever had.

Finally swinging around to face Winston again, she said, 'You'll never guess who I had tea with in London yesterday.'

'I'm sure I won't, you know so many people. So why don't you tell me?'

'Glynnis . . . the lovely Glynnis Jenkins from Wales.'

'Good Lord, is she here from New York?' He grinned. 'Well, of course she is, that's a daft question. How long is she staying? I'd like to see her again.'

'Several weeks I think. I invited her up to Yorkshire for a couple of days, with her little boy, Owen.'

'How old is he now?' Winston asked.

'He's six, and apparently quite a smart little lad, from what she's said. Anyway, she was thrilled to be invited, and she's arriving today. I was always very fond of Glynnis.'

'Weren't we all,' Winston murmured, and looked off into the distance.

'What do you mean?' she asked swiftly, detecting a strange note in her brother's voice.

'I didn't mean anything, actually, except that she was always tremendously popular, and she was such a lovely person I think we were all a little bit infatuated with her. Not only the men but you too, our Emma, and some of the other women at Harte's. Glynnis had the knack of making everyone love her, and she was very beautiful.'

'She still is,' Emma remarked. 'A little thinner, but there's an aura of glamour to her that will never fade, I don't suppose. It comes from inside, glamour, although not everyone understands that. It's nothing to do with the length of one's hair or the colour of one's eyes.'

Hovering near the fireplace, Emma continued after a moment, 'I thought you and Charlotte might like to come to lunch tomorrow, or on Sunday. Or perhaps supper tomorrow evening. If you're free, that is. It's up to you. I can ask Blackie, too, he's always at a loose end.'

'We'd enjoy that. Charlotte likes Glynnis, she always thought she was the best secretary I'd ever had. I'll ask her when we can come over for a meal. Anyway, I thought Blackie always came on Fridays for supper.'

'He does, but he can come on Saturday as well, can't he?'

Winston chuckled. 'You and Blackie might as well tie the knot, you're always together.'

Emma gaped at him, her surprise apparent.

'Don't look like that, lass. Blackie adores you, he always has. You just went off and married other men, that's what *you* did.'

'I love Blackie. I always have, for as long as I've known him; he's my best friend. But I don't want to get married again.'

'Not even to that handsome American major?' Winston teased, his eyes full of mischief.

Emma gave him a long, blank stare, and asked haughtily, 'Which American major?'

'Don't pretend you don't know who I mean . . . the one you met at our brother's house,' Winston shot back.

'Oh *him* . . . I thought you were referring to *my* American major, my nice pilot whom I used to entertain here during the war.'

'I never knew about that,' Winston replied, looking at her in astonishment.

'Well, I don't have to tell you everything, you know.'

'Who was he?'

'He still is, Winston, he didn't get killed or die.

551

His name's James Thompson, and he's been to see me several times since the end of the war. He's a good friend.'

'How did you meet him?'

'He was stationed at Topcliffe. I used to give Fourth of July parties, and I had them over often . . . James and the whole crew.'

'I see.' Winston looked at her carefully, and wondered, suddenly, about Emma. He'd never known her to be secretive, but certainly she had been about this major. Was she involved with him in a romantic way? 'Don't you ever feel lonely, our Emm?' he blurted out before he could stop himself.

'How could I ever feel lonely, Winston dear, with you lot always running in and out and looking over my shoulder? And Blackie, too. I'm always surrounded.'

Emma knew exactly what Glynnis had meant when she had said Owen looked like Robin. The six-year-old boy was a small replica of her favourite son, with the same dark hair and those beautiful vivid blue eyes that were one of Robin's best features. Even the shape of the child's face was the same, and when he grew up he would be tall and slender, as was Robin.

As he stood in front of her the boy gave her a tentative smile and put out his hand. 'I'm Owen Hughes,' he said, scrupulously polite.

Emma gave him a wide smile and took his small hand in hers. 'My name's Emma Harte. Welcome to Pennistone Royal.'

'Thank you, and I'm pleased to meet you.'

'We actually know each other, Owen. We met long ago, but I'm afraid you won't remember. You were just a little baby and then later a toddler.'

He frowned and looked up at Glynnis, his vivid, intelligent eyes full of questions.

Bending over him, Glynnis explained, 'It's true, Owen. Mrs Harte did know you when you were a baby, but we left England when you were quite small, and we haven't seen Mrs Harte since then.'

'And more's the pity,' Emma murmured, moving across the terrace, sitting down. 'I've missed watching you grow up, Owen, and I'm sorry about that. You're quite a tall boy for six, aren't you?'

'Like my father,' he explained solemnly. 'Dad's tall. And dark and handsome, Mom says. And it's true.'

Emma chuckled, and even Glynnis smiled, and said, 'It's so nice of you to have us for the weekend. I've always loved this house, it's so beautiful, so tranquil. It's such a treat to be here.'

'I'm glad you could come. It is indeed quiet but I get a great deal of joy out of it, Glynnis. Now, Owen, come and sit next to me on this little seat. We can have a chat until Hilda brings the tea. Do you like strawberries and cream?'

He nodded, his eyes focused entirely on her, as he decided he liked her. His mother had told him she had once worked for Mrs Harte.

'Good. Because that's what we're going to have. There's nothing like strawberries and cream on a warm June day in Yorkshire. Now tell me about your journey.'

'Mom drove here, and I saw a lot of sheep and cows in the fields. Do you have any cows?'

'Certainly,' Emma replied. 'And later you can go with Tommy, the farm lad, he'll take you to see them. Do you like animals?'

'Yes, but I don't want to be a farmer. I'm going to be the President of the United States.'

'Are you now, Owen? Well, that's a truly wonderful ambition!'

'Dad says anybody can be President if they're clever, and work hard. And if they're good. I can work and Dad says I'm clever.' Owen nodded his head, looked across at Glynnis and asked, 'I am good, aren't I, Mom?'

'You're the best boy in the whole world, and –' Glynnis stopped speaking and she felt all of the strength draining out of her, as she stared at the man walking along the terrace towards them. She couldn't take her eyes off him and she felt her chest tightening. It was Robin Ainsley. The last person in the world she wanted to see. She was gripped by an internal shaking and her mouth was dry.

Robin lost all of his colour when he saw Glynnis, and then the child. *His child*. Oh my God, he thought, wondering why he had come here to see his mother, today of all days. He should have phoned first, he usually did. There was no way he could retreat. How could he turn and run like a scared rabbit? But he *was* frightened . . . of her, and of himself most of all. He had never stopped loving her or thinking about her or dreaming about holding her in his arms and making love to her. Theirs had

554

been such an all-consuming passion: together they had soared . . .

And oh how lovely and desirable she looked this afternoon. She was wearing a blue silk frock, the exact colour of the sky, the exact colour of her eyes. And her face was ravishing in its beauty and voluptuousness. She was around thirty now, just as he was, and these few additional years truly became her. Her hair was worn in the same soft pageboy he remembered, and it was luxuriant, a deep chestnut colour touched with natural streaks of gold. God, how he wanted her again. But he couldn't have her. He had renounced her and he knew within himself how much he had hurt her. She could never want him, not ever again. And she was forbidden to him anyway, he understood that. But he could dream, couldn't he?

As Robin came to a stop, he looked across at his mother. Emma's face was inscrutable. He hurried over to her and kissed her on the cheek. 'Hello, Ma.'

'Hello, Robin, darling,' she murmured, and then hissed against his ear, 'Why didn't you phone?' Drawing herself up, Emma then added in a normal voice, 'You remember Glynnis, don't you?'

'Yes,' he managed, and had no option but to walk across to the only woman he had ever truly loved. His legs felt unexpectedly weak and he was startled. 'Hello, Glynnis,' he said and was relieved his voice sounded so normal. Robin offered her his hand.

'Robin,' she answered in a low throaty voice and reluctantly took his outstretched hand.

He discovered her hand was icy in his, and he wanted to hold onto it, to warm it, but he realized he could not. He let it go. Reluctantly. Turning around, he looked down at her little boy, *his* little boy, and said, 'I'm Robin . . . *hello.*'

'I'm Owen, and I'm pleased to meet you.' He was very solemn.

'Mind if I join you all, old chap?' Robin asked, smiling warmly.

'Oh no. That's all right. Isn't it, Mom?'

All Glynnis could do was nod.

Emma explained, 'Robin is my son, Owen, just as you are your mother's son.'

And mine, Robin thought, as he sat down in one of the wrought-iron garden chairs. He had an overwhelming need to hug this boy, hold him close. This was their love child. His and Glynnis's.

Suddenly Emma said, 'Oh Robin, I'm sorry to disturb you, but would you please go and ask Hilda to bring another cup and saucer for you?'

Robin stood up, excused himself, and went through the French windows into the library.

Glynnis looked across at Emma mutely, unable to speak and especially in Owen's presence.

At once Emma recognized the look in her eyes. It was one of pure terror. Leaning closer to Owen, Emma said to him, 'Do me a little favour, run after Robin. He's gone to the kitchen. You'll find it, just through those doors and across the big Stone Hall. Ask him to please bring me a glass of water.'

'Will I find the kitchen?' Owen asked, a bit nervously, staring at her.

'You're a clever boy, of course you will,' she reassured him.

Once they were alone, Emma explained in a quick low voice, 'This is all an accident, Glynnis, truly it is, my dear. Robin always telephones me if he's coming, to make sure I'm here. For some reason he didn't today.'

Glynnis could not speak. Tears filled her eyes. All she could do was nod. Oh how she loved him. She had never stopped loving him. *Robin*. The name she could barely say . . . except when she was alone and wept into her pillow and said his name over and over and over again. *Robin Ainsley*. Her one true love. The only man she had ever loved . . . would ever love. Oh, to have him hold her in his arms once more; what she would give to have that. Nothing else. Just that. To be in his arms for a few brief moments.

As if from a distance she heard Emma saying, 'You mustn't see him, Glynnis. You mustn't see him alone.'

CHAPTER THIRTY-ONE

It was seven years since he had seen her. Seven long years. But he knew he was already entrapped again . . . longing to be with her, to hold her in his arms, if only for a moment. He would settle for that, or less: a few minutes talking to her, just holding her hand.

He had been married for six years, had a small child, a son. His name was Jonathan. But little Johnny was very much his mother's child, a lot more like Valerie in appearance than him. A handsome, fair-haired boy, but there was not much Harte in him, at least so it seemed to Robin.

It was the other son, *her* child Owen, who was so obviously out of his loins. The boy was his spitting image, even down to his hands. He had noticed the boy's long tapering fingers on Friday afternoon. Had his mother seen the likeness? Perhaps. And did it matter? Of course not. He had been quite certain for some years now that his mother had known of his love affair with Glynnis. She was shrewd, and understood the human heart.

Furthermore Glynnis had worked for her for several years and they had become close. Perhaps Glynnis had even confided in his mother at some time or another, but *he* would never know the truth about that because Emma would never betray a confidence.

As he drove at a steady speed along the main Harrogate road on the Saturday night, heading from Leeds to Pennistone Royal, he thought of his mother's reaction yesterday. She had been perturbed by his unexpected arrival, had hissed in his car that he should have phoned. And yet she had hidden her irritation behind her famous inscrutable mask. She was good at that, disguising her real feelings, dissembling.

A smile struck his face as he thought of Emma. They locked horns at times, and could often quarrel. On the other hand, he really loved his mother, respected her, and he knew he was her favourite son. Still, he didn't think she would approve of what he was about to do. Neither did he. Put simply he couldn't help himself. He had to speak to Glynnis in private.

Now he asked himself if she would listen. Or would he get the door slammed in his face? He wasn't sure. All he knew was that he had to see her.

As Robin drove up to the back of Pennistone Royal he saw that the house was dark, except for a couple of upstairs rooms: his mother's and Glynnis's. He had spoken to his mother earlier that day and she had told him she was dining alone with Glynnis, that Winston and Charlotte were coming over for lunch on Sunday. He had thought of cajoling an invitation out of her for the lunch, but decided not to put her on the spot in that way. It wasn't fair.

Parking near a copse of trees, Robin got out of the Humber and closed the car door gently. Then he walked quickly towards the service entrance of the house.

He glanced up. It was a beautiful June night, the sky a very deep blue, so deep it was almost black, was filled with a generous abundance of shining stars. There was a gorgeous full moon, perfectly spherical and brilliant, and it lit his way.

Fumbling in his jacket pocket, Robin pulled out the key to the kitchen door, which he had owned since he was a teenager, and let himself in, careful to lock the door behind him. Moving quietly across the floor, he pushed open the door which led to the back service corridor.

Within seconds he was climbing a steep staircase; this led up to the first and second floors. Bypassing the first floor, his mother's domain, he went on, climbing further still, and finally opened the door to the bedroom floor. He stepped into the corridor and made his way to the Blue Room, knowing *she* was the occupant of that suite.

Owen had told him yesterday, when he had taken the child to see the cows. He had confided proudly that he was in the Gold Room, all alone. The boy had also explained that they were staying at the Hyde Park Hotel in London. It had only taken a little prompting from him and Owen had innocently revealed quite a lot. What pleased Robin was that the child appeared to like him.

The corridor was dimly lit by the moon shining in through the tall window at the far end. Robin tiptoed down the long carpeted hallway until he came to the door with the brass plaque engraved: *Blue Room.* Tapping lightly, he stood waiting.

Several seconds passed before the door was opened a crack.

When Glynnis saw him her eyes widened in astonishment. He brought a finger up to his lips, making a shushing sound. Pushing against the door, he slipped into the room before she could stop him.

Glynnis stepped back swiftly, glaring at him.

Robin closed the door, leaned against it, and said in a whisper, 'I have to talk to you.'

She backed away and, balking at his presence, she moved across the sitting-room floor quickly, stood leaning against the desk in front of the window. And then obviously realizing, all of a sudden, that she was dressed only in a flimsy silk nightgown she flew into the bedroom.

He did not move, remained standing where he was, leaning nonchalantly against the door, although he didn't feel at all nonchalant. As tense and anxious as he was, he was telling himself not to follow her into the other room. Aware of her modesty, from their earlier days together, he was quite certain she had simply gone to get a robe. And a moment later she reappeared wearing a blue silk kimono over the nightdress.

Robin locked the door and walked towards her.

'Why have you locked the door?' she hissed, her blue eyes angry, her face strained, even fearful.

'For no other reason than our son, Owen. If he wakes up he might be afraid in a strange room, and come looking for you. This way, if he does knock on the door, he won't be able to open it. And I can go into the bedroom until you've taken him back to his own room.'

Glynnis said nothing.

Robin said, 'He shouldn't see me in here, especially late at night.'

'Nobody should.'

'I know.'

'What actually *do* you want?' she demanded in a curt whisper, her eyes growing icier by the minute. But he noticed that she was trembling uncontrollably.

'To talk to you, Glynnis.'

'I've nothing to say to *you*.'

'But I do, to you. I realize this is not the time and place, and I came to ask you to meet me when you come back to town.'

'I won't!' she snapped.

'In case you change your mind –' He searched around in his pocket, took out an envelope. 'In here there's an address and a latchkey. I want you to have them.'

'Why?'

'I want you to meet me there next week. Just to talk. I need to talk to you.'

'I told you I don't want to listen to *you* about anything.'

'The address – it's for Edwina's mews house in Belgravia. Her bolt-hole when she comes over from Ireland to do her shopping, or for business. There's a phone number as well. Please, Glynnis, come and meet me. On Wednesday.' He offered her the envelope but she crossed her arms tightly and pursed her lips, the eyes suddenly flinty as she stepped to one side.

Placing the envelope on the desk, Robin continued, 'I just want to tell you why things happened the way they did, that's it, really.'

'Oh Robin, please,' she muttered, 'you must go. *Now*.'

He didn't move. He gave her a small smile. 'The boy is so handsome, Glynnis, and bright, and very well mannered.'

She was totally silent.

Suddenly, he made a move towards her, so quickly she was taken unawares and caught offguard. Before she could utter a word of protest, or run, his arms were around her and he was pressing her tightly against his tall, lean body. 'Oh Glynnis, Glynnis,' he whispered hoarsely, and then kissed the hollow of her neck, her cheeks, and finally his mouth found hers.

Against her will she responded ardently; she kissed him back and clung to him, murmured his name, and she suddenly felt him harden against her thigh. He wanted her. She wanted him And for a moment she nearly gave in, gave way, almost pulled him into the bedroom, to her bed.

But she did not. With enormous resolve she

pushed him away gently, and a sob caught in her throat.

'Oh darling, please,' he begged, his eyes riveted on hers; they were twin reflections of his own, not only in their colour but the overwhelming desire raging there.

'No, Robin, no.'

'Yes, Glynnis, yes.'

Shaking her head, walking to the door on trembling legs, she turned and looked at him intently. 'Please, you must go.'

'There's a phone number for Edwina's mews,' he reminded her. 'Please phone me between twelve and twelve-thirty if you're not coming.'

She was silent.

When he stopped at the door, he added softly, 'You must let me know if you're not coming. *Promise*?'

All she had the strength to do was nod.

After he left she lay on the bed in the dark, thinking about him, thinking what a narrow escape she had had. She had almost succumbed to his charms, and where would she have been then? Not only hating herself for running back to him the moment he beckoned, but guilt-ridden as well for sleeping with him. Richard was a good man, and he had been good to Owen; she knew he loved her, with great devotion. She loved him back, in her own way, and she had tried to be a good wife, was as devoted as he was as a husband. She had been a good mother to Owen, perhaps that most of all.

*Robin, oh Robin . . . how I love you . . . how
I want you. Close in my arms . . .* She began to
cry, the tears running down her cheeks and she
wept and wept until she thought there were no
tears left.

The weekend passed without any further incident.
Robin didn't drop in to see his mother again, and
Glynnis was shocked at herself when she realized
she was disappointed.

After chastising herself quietly, and muttering
under her breath that she was a grown woman,
not a silly teenager, Glynnis did manage to shake
that feeling off. She made a supreme effort to be
her normal, cheerful self and eventually she
succeeded.

She had always got on well with Emma: they
were extremely compatible, both being positive by
nature, and optimistic. Glynnis had never had any
difficulties communicating with her and she was
able to chat to her about anything in the world,
as was Emma to her.

They talked about many things over breakfast
together on Sunday morning, and also when they
took Owen for a walk before lunch. He ran ahead
of them to the pond, shouting that he was going
to feed the ducks, and they both smiled indulgently.
Owen was in his element, that was obvious. All
morning he ran and jumped, laughed and chatted
to them both, and Glynnis was gratified to see the
look of approval in Emma's eyes.

At one moment her former employer turned to

her and exclaimed, 'He's such a lovely little boy, Glynnis, you've done a good job with him. I hope you'll bring him to England next year, and spend a little time with me, as well as going to see your family in Wales.'

'I hope I can come, Mrs Harte. I know my mother's anxious I bring Owen to the Rhondda next year . . . We'll see.'

Emma sighed, and unexpectedly said in a wistful tone, 'I do miss you, Glynnis. You were my friend you know, not only my secretary, when you worked for me during the war. I've always been so very fond of you, and now . . . well, he *is* my grandson . . . If things had worked out differently, you would have been my daughter-in-law.'

Glynnis merely nodded, and looked off into the distance; after a moment, she said, 'I know what you mean, but I've believed in destiny all of my life. It was *Fate* . . . that's why things are the way they are. Most of the time matters are out of our hands. They're in the hands of . . . Fate.'

She forced a smile and then went on swiftly, 'Mrs Harte, there's something else I need to talk to you about . . . *the money*. You really don't have to send the allowance every month. It's far too much, and besides that, Richard can support us. I don't *need* the money.'

'Oh goodness, Glynnis, I know Richard is doing well! And I certainly never meant the money to *undermine* him in any way. However, I do want to send it to you. Remember, you refused Robin's help during the war, and this is my way of . . .

well, ensuring Owen's future, in a certain sense. Save the money, put it away in the bank and let it earn interest. Later, when he's ready for college, you'll have quite a little nest egg for the boy. I am going to continue sending it, my dear, it's the least I can do. And that's that. No more arguing.'

Once again Glynnis tried to protest, without success. She knew from her experience that once Emma's mind was made up she wouldn't budge. Apparently that was the case now. Eventually she nodded, and thanked Emma . . . it was all she could do.

Winston and Charlotte came for lunch several hours later, and it was a lovely reunion between the three of them. It soon became apparent that Emma's brother was impressed with Owen, and if he noticed a family resemblance he didn't let on, simply remained quiet. Winston had a reputation for being the family diplomat: he behaved in the most normal way with Owen, talking to him naturally, as if he were an adult.

All too soon the lunch was over, Winston and Charlotte left, and Glynnis went upstairs to pack. They were leaving for London very early the following morning, and she always liked to plan ahead, be ready to leave on time.

As she folded Owen's clothes and laid them in his suitcase, she found herself sighing with relief that the day had passed so calmly. There had been no further hiccups. All had been tranquil, without event.

Suddenly, Owen's voice piped up, startling her for a split second. 'Mom, why didn't Robin come back to see me? When he took me to visit the cows, he said he'd see me later.' Putting his book down on the table, the child ran over to the bed where she was packing and tugged at her sleeve.

Glynnis looked down at him, and forced a smile. 'He's a busy man, darling. Maybe he just got caught up in work.'

'Oh. I see.' The child's disappointment was apparent, and he muttered, 'I liked him a lot. He was nice to me.'

When Glynnis made no response, Owen went on, 'He's a politician, Mom. He's going to take me to the House of Commons.'

'Oh I don't know about that –' she began.

'He is!' Owen cried passionately, interrupting her. 'He *promised*. And I *know* he'll keep his promise.'

Seeing that her little boy was really upset, she hugged him to her, and said soothingly, 'I know he'll keep his promise, Owen. I'm sure of it.'

CHAPTER THIRTY-TWO

Glynnis had never meant to go.

All of her instincts had told her to stay away from him, but in the end she had given in to her tumultuous emotions.

On Wednesday morning she had awakened with a feeling of tension in her body, a dull, nagging ache in the pit of her stomach, and unable to control herself she had phoned her cousin Gwyneth at seven o'clock, before taking Owen down for breakfast.

Immediately plunging in, before she changed her mind, she told Gwyneth that she could 'borrow' Owen for the day. This made her cousin exceedingly happy; childless, she longed to have a baby, and loving Owen the way she did she took great pleasure from taking him sightseeing. 'He's wanted to go to the Tower of London for ages,' Gwyneth said enthusiastically. 'I'll come and collect him at eleven, if that's all right?'

Glynnis had told her it was, relieved that Gwyneth was free, and that she hadn't suggested later in the afternoon for the jaunt to the Tower.

But Glynnis became furious with herself when, after breakfast, she did her hair and make-up so carefully, sprayed herself with scent, and chose her clothes for the day with such precision, picking out the blue silk dress with the flared skirt because he had said he loved her in blue years ago.

After Owen had left with Gwyneth, happily laughing and excited to be going on this unexpected treat, she had finally begun to dress. Pulling on sheer silk stockings and a blue garter belt, she then put on blue satin cami-knickers trimmed with blue lace, and finally stepped into a pair of high-heeled shoes. They showed off her legs to great advantage – Robin had always complimented her, told her that she had the loveliest legs in the world. Finally, she slipped into the dress, and gazed at herself in the mirror, suddenly quite pleased by her appearance.

And then a second later she felt wretched, hollow inside, and disgusted. Because she was going to *him*. It wasn't right, it just wasn't. She knew that only too well. But she also knew she couldn't stop herself.

Now, getting out of the cab in Belgrave Square, she hesitated, losing her nerve. It would be best not to go, she told herself firmly. She did not trust Robin. Nor did she trust herself, and being alone with him could only spell trouble. Even Emma had warned her of *that*.

Walking slowly around the square, wondering what to do, wavering, she found herself growing more nervous than ever. When she glanced at her watch she sucked in her breath. It was already twelve-fifteen. When he had come to her room at Pennistone Royal, he had told her to phone by twelve-thirty. Looking around frantically, her eyes sought out a phone-box. There wasn't one in sight.

She stood perfectly still for a moment, panic rushing through her. *What to do? What to do?* And then taking a deep breath, making a decision, she crossed the square purposefully, hurried to the mews located in one of the side streets just off the square.

Several seconds later Glynnis was ringing the bell of Edwina's house.

He opened the door immediately. Although he didn't smile or betray any emotion on his face, she saw the sudden intense flash of happiness in his blue eyes the moment he saw her.

He was unable to speak.

And so was she.

Silently, he opened the door a little wider; she stepped inside, hurried forward into a large rather charming living room. As she moved past him she was careful not to brush against him; being in his presence was bad enough, so unnerving was it. If she touched him she would fall apart.

After closing the door, Robin walked into the middle of the room, stood staring at her. They were just a few feet apart.

Swallowing hard, he said at last, 'I was waiting for you to phone.'

She simply stared back, speechlessly, her legs shaking.

'Why did you come – just like this?' he asked softly.

'I c-c-c-couldn't h-h-help myself,' she stuttered, her voice sounding hoarse, gruff, to her.

He gazed at her unblinkingly, wanting to hold her, yet feeling nervous, taut inside. He was afraid to say the wrong thing, or to approach her in any way, for fear she might bolt.

Glynnis gazed back, mesmerized by him. She thought she was going to burst into tears, and instantly stifled the sob rising in her throat.

Unexpectedly, as he continued to look at her, Robin noted the look of longing on her face. It reflected how he was feeling, and without another thought, unable to hold back any longer, he took a step forward. They moved at exactly the same moment, came together in a rush, fell into each other's arms as if in desperation.

He held her against him tightly, whispering her name over and over again, smoothing his hand down her back. He was filled with the most extraordinary sense of relief to be holding her like this at long last. After all these long years, there was a sudden absence of pain.

Glynnis held onto him tightly. Her legs had gone weak and she thought that if he let go of her she would fall. Strange though it was, she could not keep a limb still.

'Glynnis darling, you're shaking. Don't be afraid . . . afraid of me. I won't do anything . . . anything you don't want me to do. I just need to hold you like this,' Robin reassured her.

She moved slightly so that she could look up into his face.

Blue eyes locked with blue eyes.

She parted her lips as if to express a thought but no words came out. After a moment, she finally whispered, 'I'm not afraid . . . just nervous.'

'So am I.' Robin bent his head, kissed her fully on the mouth, and Glynnis kissed him back, felt as though she were slowly dissolving into him.

Without letting go of each other they stumbled towards the sofa near the fireplace, fell onto it, lay entwined in each other's arms. Pushing himself up, Robin studied her face, hardly daring to believe she was actually here with him like this, so intimate. He began to kiss her forehead, her cheeks, the hollow of her neck. Moving a strand of dark hair away from her face, he said gently, 'I just need to be near you . . . all these years I've ached for you, Glynnis. If you don't want to –'

Glynnis brought a finger to his lips. 'I do want to . . . make love,' she responded, her voice low. 'I want *you*, Robin . . . it's been so long since we've been together. Seven years.'

He touched her face, let his hand trail down across her breast, and then slowly he began to unbutton her dress. But within a moment or two she stopped him and said quietly, 'Take your jacket off, Robin, please.'

Standing up, he did so, threw it on a chair, went to the door, slid the bolt, then closed the curtains. As he came back to her he pulled off his tie, began to unbutton his shirt.

She rose from the sofa, stood in front of him, slipped out of her dress, let it fall in a pool at her feet as he took off his shirt. Robin came towards her, wrapping his arms around her once again. And he led her to the sofa, and lay down next to her.

And very slowly he began to make love to her, touching her neck, her breasts, sliding his hand inside the satin underwear. He touched it lightly with his fingertips, bent his head to kiss the nipple. Then he looked up, stared into her eyes. There was enormous intensity in his voice as he said, 'I love you, Glynnis, I've never stopped loving you . . . Tell me you feel the same.'

'You know I do, oh you do know that, Robin. There's only ever been you. Only you can make me feel this way.'

'It's the same for me,' he said, a catch in his voice. 'I belong to you, Glynnis. For always. I will always be yours as long as I live. And you will always be mine, no matter what you think.'

'Robin, oh Robin,' she whispered.

'Take this off, darling,' he said suddenly, touching her satin underwear. Then he unfastened the suspenders of her garter belt, and slowly rolled down her stockings one at a time. Once she was completely naked on the sofa, he swiftly finished undressing and rejoined her.

Stretched out next to each other, lost in each other, they stroked and touched and explored; after seven years apart they craved each other desperately, longed to be joined together as one; they were both on the verge of explosion.

Within moments, Robin was bending over her, kissing her breasts and her thighs. And as his tongue slid down her stomach, went directly to the core of her, she let out a long sigh of pleasure. Slowly, he began to kiss her where no other man ever had.

In a moment she was shuddering with pleasure and crying his name, telling him how much she wanted him, and swiftly he positioned himself over her, slid inside her, took her to him exultantly, repeating her name over and over as he pushed his hands under her buttocks and brought her closer to him. She felt the heat flowing through her as she grew more excited; she matched his passion and his ardour, and it was as if they had never been parted. Together they finally crested on a wave of love and emotion, and Robin called her name as he possessed her completely.

They lay together on the sofa for a long time, holding each other tightly as if they were genuinely afraid to let go.

After a short while, Robin said, 'I *did* want to talk to you. I wasn't setting out to seduce you.'

'I know that. And you didn't seduce me. It was a great example of the most splendid cooperation, wasn't it?'

'No better description! But just listen a moment, Glynnis, please. Look, I'm sorry I abandoned you when I did. But you and I had broken up when you came to tell me you were pregnant. And I –'

'Robin, this is not at all necessary,' she cut in.

'I *do* know all this, and what you say is absolutely true. And you'd become involved with Valerie by the time I appeared again to inform you that you were about to be a father. I truly understand your position, especially now. Also, I *was* difficult in those days, so volatile, so anxiety-ridden, and –'

'You were young, and so was I. It was wartime, and I was in the air in a Spitfire most of the time, dropping bombs on Germany and risking my life every day. I was as volatile as you were, in my own way. We were all under massive strain. It was war, for God's sake.'

'That's quite true, yes,' Glynnis agreed. 'I'm much calmer now. After all, I'm thirty, like you, a mature woman, a mother, a wife . . .'

There was a slight hesitation before Robin asked quietly, in a subdued voice, 'Is it happy . . . your marriage?'

'In its own way, yes. You see, it does work, Robin. Richard loves me and he adores Owen. He takes care of us very well. He's a good man.'

'Do you love him?' He hated himself for asking this question, but he had to know how she felt. He could hardly bear to think of her with Richard Hughes. Or any other man, for that matter. What a terrible fool he'd been, letting her go.

She took a while to answer. Eventually she said, 'Yes, I do. In a different way from . . . *us*. Let me put it this way: I do love Richard, but I'm not *in love* with him.' She looked straight at Robin. 'And your marriage?'

'I suspect it's pretty much like yours,' he replied.

'It works, Glynnis. There's stability there, and Valerie's very steady, practical, rather placid. Doesn't rock boats. And she's a good mother to Jonathan. Furthermore, she lets me have my life.'

Glynnis stiffened next to him. 'What life? What do you mean?'

He recognized that flash of jealousy he had been so familiar with in the past. 'Oh God, *no*, Glynnis! I didn't mean what you think! Not that kind of life, not other women. There are no women . . . just you. My one true love.' He looked down at Glynnis. 'She never interferes, gives me the freedom to pursue my politics.'

'I'm glad she does. Because that's what you always wanted. To be a politician, a Member of Parliament. I think you might even want to be Prime Minister one day.'

'I want *you*, Glynnis,' he shot back.

'Oh Robin, darling, *don't*. We're both settled, married.'

'I know.' He sighed. 'I want you always in my arms. It's such a relief to be with you. I can say anything I want to you, anything at all, and I can be myself. No pretence. I don't feel that with anyone else but you.'

'I feel the same. I know whatever I say, you won't be shocked.'

There was a pause.

'Are you hungry?' he suddenly asked.

'No. You?'

He shook his head. 'Where's . . . *our* son?'

'My cousin Gwyneth took him to the Tower of

577

London. He's been longing to go, and thankfully she was free to take him . . . so I could come to you.'

'I'm glad you did . . . come to me,' he murmured. 'I can hardly bear the thought that you have to leave, go back to the States.'

There was no response from her.

Robin said, 'I want to see Owen again . . . can I, darling?'

'I don't think you should, Robin. But only because he's such a little chatterbox. He might say something to Richard, mention your name. He's sort of fallen for you.'

This brought a smile to his face. He said, 'But Richard knows you know me, we all knew each other when we used to go to my mother's canteen for the troops. I know the boy's my look-alike, but Richard might not put two and two together.'

'He just might.'

Robin smiled at her. 'Yes, you're right. I think it's best to be careful. I want to see you tomorrow. And the day after, and the day after that. Every day whilst you're here.'

Glynnis looked stunned. 'Robin, I don't know – there's Owen.'

'Try to arrange it, my darling. Please. How long do we have today?'

He sounded unexpectedly desperate, and she glanced at him. 'Until six. I must get back by six-thirty. Gwyneth and her husband are coming to dinner with me tonight. She'll go back to the hotel around five to wait for me. She has my room key.'

'Talking of keys, please keep that latchkey for this house. It'll make me feel better, knowing you have it.'

'If you're sure . . . I mean what –'

'Oh I'm sure all right,' he exclaimed. 'Come to me. Let me hold you the way I used to.' Robin wrapped his body around hers. 'This is what I've missed all these years, being entwined with the only woman I've ever loved.'

She smiled against his arm. 'I love you so much.'

'And I you, Glynnis.' He touched her mouth with his fingertips, kissed her, closing his eyes as he did. A moment later he was fondling her breasts, and their lovemaking started all over again; and so it went for most of the afternoon.

It was one of those lovely balmy evenings in the middle of June. The sky was a soft pale blue, filled with puffy white clouds scudding along the horizon. Although the sun had set some time ago the evening sky had a wonderful shimmering clarity, and the Thames reflected that light, had a glassy sheen to it as it flowed along.

Robin Ainsley took in all this as he stood on the terrace of the House of Commons, staring down the river towards Big Ben. He often came to the terrace in the summer for tea with a colleague or special guests. But he loved it most at this time of day in the summer months. There was a feeling of tranquillity and peace out here. It was a view that he treasured, the ancient river going down to the sea. Seen from this great seat of power, it seemed so very special.

Robin leaned against the balustrade, his mind awash with so many diverse thoughts: *Glynnis*. The woman he loved and wanted to keep forever in his life. Their son: *Owen*. A most blessed little boy, so very much like him, and even more so than his other son, Jonathan.

More than anything else Robin wanted to spend time with Owen, a miniature replica of himself, but he could not. Glynnis would not permit it. There was nothing he could do: he knew he had relinquished any rights he had to the boy before he was even born.

In his mind's eye he saw them both . . .

Glynnis, lithe, beautiful, the epitome of glamour, but without any personal vanity, soft and gentle. There was not one ounce of hardness in her. A warm and loving woman who loved him as much as he loved her. How easy it was to picture her in the blue dress, walking towards him, holding Owen's hand, the boy in his short, grey trousers and white summer shirt, both of them smiling, so happy to see him.

Oh God, what was he going to do about her? How could he ever let her go?

And then there was Valerie: his wife. So devoted to him, a calm, caring woman who loved him, but was not in love with him, just as he was not in love with her. And yet she would be devastated if he left her and their small son, because her life revolved around him and his political career.

Robin was riddled with guilt about Valerie: yet, oddly enough, not at all about his involvement with Glynnis. What Valerie didn't know couldn't hurt her, that was what he believed. His guilt sprang from the plans he was formulating in his head. Plans for a divorce. But then there was Richard Hughes. Would Glynnis agree to divorce Richard in order to come to him? He didn't know the answer to that; he was on the horns of a dilemma.

Who could he talk to? No one. Not his siblings, not even Edwina, to whom he was especially close. His mother? She would listen attentively and be sympathetic, but inevitably Emma would disapprove. Although she had lived with Paul McGill for sixteen years until his death, and he a married man, Paul had been separated from his wife long before he had ever met Emma. And there had been no divorce from Constance McGill because she was Roman Catholic. She had always refused to give Paul his freedom.

Robin knew Emma so well, and he could hear her telling him that it was not possible to build one's happiness on the unhappiness of another. That would be her attitude, and he knew she was right.

Suddenly tears welled, and Robin brushed his eyes quickly, glanced around, relieved to see the terrace was empty but for himself. Quite suddenly, anger rushed through him. Here he was, a grown man of thirty, weeping about a woman! Here on the terrace of the House of Commons, the place of his dreams, the place where he belonged, the place that was his whole life.

How ridiculous he was being. Grow up, he chastised himself, anger still flaring inside. You let her go in 1943. You should have married her then.

Big Ben struck six, and he turned away, left the terrace, hurried to his office in the House.

In an hour he would go to Edwina's mews cottage in Belgravia, and wait for Glynnis. She had taken Owen to Wales for the past weekend, and was leaving him there so he could spend a few days with his grandparents . . . before they left for the States.

His heart lifted. She would come to him soon, straight from the railway station. They had the whole evening ahead of them. They would be alone.

Robin was in the kitchen making himself a drink when he heard the door close, and he hurried out, rushed to Glynnis. She stood in the doorway, her suitcase at her feet, a wide smile on her lovely face.

'Darling,' he exclaimed, his face lighting up. 'You got here sooner than I expected.'

'I took an earlier train,' Glynnis replied, her smile widening. 'I just had to get back to you, Robin.'

'I'm irresistible, I'm fully aware of that,' he laughed.

'And so *modest*,' she quipped, walking into his arms, holding onto him tightly, filled with such overwhelming happiness she thought she would burst.

After a moment locked in their embrace, they stood apart, linked arms and went into the kitchen. Robin fixed her a gin and tonic, and they returned to the living room, sat down on the sofa together.

'Cheers, my sweet,' he murmured, clinking his glass against hers, relieved she was here with him. He was brimming with love for her.

'Cheers,' she answered, and took a sip of her drink.

'Tell me about your weekend in the Rhondda.' Robin's eyes were fixed on her face. 'Did Owen enjoy himself?'

Glynnis laughed, her bright blue eyes sparkling. 'Yes, with his cousins, my brothers' children. As I told you, Dylan has two sons, and Emlyn a girl. They're all a bit rambunctious, I'm afraid, but a good time was had by all, to quote Tiny Tim.'

Robin smiled, touched her arm lightly, lovingly. 'That makes me happy, knowing he's having a good time. And what did my darling girl do?' he asked.

'Nothing much. Visited family, helped my mother with her chores, did the shopping for her, and thought about you. Constantly.'

'Likewise. You're rarely out of my thoughts.'

She nodded. 'Did you go to Yorkshire?'

'Yes, I went to Leeds. It's important to get back to my constituency whenever I can.' Putting his glass of scotch on the coffee table, he turned to her, took her drink from her, stood it next to his. And then he leaned closer, put his arms around her, kissed her passionately. She responded with equal passion, and after a moment, when they pulled away, he touched her face gently. He said in a low voice, 'Let's go upstairs. I want you so much.'

'I know, and I want you, Robin. I feel exactly the same.' She gave him a very direct look. 'But I want to talk to you for a moment. Let's talk first.'

Her seriousness, the sudden severe expression striking her mouth, brought him up short. 'This sounds like bad news . . .'

'Not bad news, Robin. Just a little bit of reality.' Taking his hand in hers, she said slowly, 'I know that you know how much I love you, more than anyone else in the world except for our child. I've always loved you, and marrying Richard didn't change that. You *do* know this, don't you?'

'Of course I do, and for the last few weeks I've been telling you the same thing.' His face changed, became sad. 'I made the worst mistake of my life when I let you go . . . and now I want you back. For always.'

'*Listen to me.* Because I do love you as much as I do, with all my heart, I'm not going to let you ruin your political career because of me.'

'Getting a divorce is not going to ruin it. This is 1950, don't forget that.'

'I know what year it is, and perhaps you're right. But what if there's a scandal? What if I get dragged into it . . . by Valerie? I think she'd fight you, if you attempted to divorce her. I'm a woman, so I know women, and we can fight dirty if there's a lot at stake. And what's at stake for her is you, your lifestyle, and your money.'

'How could you be brought into it?' he protested instantly, fearful of where this conversation was leading. He couldn't bear to lose her and he was determined to keep her. No matter at what cost.

Glynnis was silent for a moment or two, and then she said softly, speaking with great care, 'I know what being a Member of Parliament means to you. I've always known. And actually you married Valerie because you thought she would make a better political wife than me, a better wife for an ambitious politician like you.'

'I won't deny that entirely,' Robin answered quickly. 'But it's not *all* true. Let's not forget that we *agreed* to split up. We were both crazy, not only crazy in love, but crazy kids. We were too volatile together, Glynnis. Please don't deny that.'

'I don't. You're right. We would have been disaster together in those days.'

'And now we're older. We're thirty years old. We've matured. We were stupid kids then, living through a world war. It could work now.'

Ignoring his last comment, she said, 'I know all this, we keep repeating it. Please let's not quarrel about what happened when we were in our early twenties. That's long gone, and –'

'I can't stand not being with you. I can't face that, Glynnis. I simply cannot.' An ineffable sorrow struck his handsome face, and his blue eyes turned bleak.

'Neither can I. But I will not permit you to ruin your career for me. You're a young, very go-ahead

MP . . . Your constituents love you, you're highly popular and successful. There's serious talk that you could be Prime Minister one day. You have an important life ahead, a big life to live. I won't let you change your life, Robin. I will not have that on my conscience.'

'Glynnis, honestly –'

She interrupted him. 'I have an idea, a plan . . .'

'Tell me.'

She did.

He listened, let her say everything that was on her mind, and when she had finally finished, he shook his head. 'I don't know . . . I don't know if it could work . . . Anyway, that's not what I want, darling, not what I want at all.'

'Neither do I. It's a compromise. But I haven't been able to think of anything better. Not yet.'

He did not answer her.

She stood up, offered him her hand. 'Come upstairs, Robin, let's go and make love. Let's seal our bargain with a kiss.'

It seemed to Glynnis that tonight their lovemaking was not only more passionate than usual, but that it had a certain frenzy about it. And she knew that this was because she was leaving at the end of the week. Since they were both extremely conscious of her imminent departure, they were desperate to be together, and they clutched at each other more fervently than ever, devoured each other with a sexual need that was voracious.

She clung to him tightly, her hands moving down

his back, up into his thick dark hair and the nape of his neck as she murmured his name, her voice urgent with her desire and her need for him. And she moved with him rhythmically, her legs high around him, her head thrown back in pleasure, and when he convulsed, coming to a climax, so did she.

As if never to let him go she held him in her arms until the light in the room dimmed and all went black.

Much later, as they lay together, their urgent need for each other slaked for the present, Glynnis flung one arm over his body and lay her head on his chest. His hand moved into her hair, but they said nothing, just lay there together, lost in their own myriad thoughts.

She contemplated their conversation of a short while before, and she was aware she had averted disaster, stopped him in his tracks, had at least delayed the idea of him leaving his wife, getting a divorce.

Sudden tears slid down her cheeks, fell onto his chest, and he moved at once, sat up, filled with alarm.

'Darling, what is it? What's wrong?' Worry ringed his face.

'Nothing,' she said, smiling at him through her tears.

'Why are you crying then?'

'I'm missing you already,' she whispered.

'But it's just *au revoir*.'

She was silent.

'You *are* coming back to me, aren't you?' Robin asked in a low, concerned voice. 'Promise me, Glynnis.'

'I promise,' she answered, wondering if she would have to break it.

PART THREE

Angels Singing
Winter 2001

The world in solemn stillness lay
To hear the angels sing.
   'That Glorious Song of Old':
   EDMUND HAMILTON SEARS
              (1850)

CHAPTER THIRTY-THREE

It was Saturday, December the first, and in a short while Linnet O'Neill would go to the church in the village of Pennistone Royal, on the arm of her father Shane. And it was there she would marry her childhood sweetheart, Julian Kallinski. And with their nuptials the three clans of the Hartes, the O'Neills and the Kallinskis would finally be fully united in marriage.

Now, Linnet stood in the middle of her bedroom at Pennistone Royal, wearing her wedding gown. She thought it was the most wonderful creation, made of cream-coloured heavy Duchesse satin, cream-coloured Guipure lace, and thousands and thousands of tiny pearls and crystal beads.

Evan had designed the gown, and she stood staring at Linnet. Her head was on one side, and she was studying the gown intently, her eyes taking in every detail, looking for last-minute flaws, tiny things she might have missed earlier in the week, when the dress had finally arrived from the seamstresses. But she could find nothing amiss, and after a few more seconds of intensive scrutiny she finally announced: 'There's not a thing wrong! It's just perfection on you, Linnet, even though I do say so myself. You look like a dream in it.'

Linnet's sister, Emsie, who was also in the bedroom, exclaimed, 'Evan's right, Linny. I've never seen you look like this. Not ever. Julian's going to fall in love with you all over again.'

'He'd better,' Linnet said with a chuckle. 'Thank you both for your compliments. And Evan, thanks for designing my gown. And the bridesmaids' dresses, and for everything else you've created for the wedding. I don't know what we'd have done without you.'

'You're welcome, it's been my pleasure,' Evan replied. Moving across the floor, she took hold of Linnet's hand, and carefully led her over to the cheval mirror in the corner near the window. 'There! Just look at yourself.'

Linnet stepped in front of the mirror and caught her breath. She'd never seen herself looking so . . . *fantastic*. It was the gown, of course. Evan had adapted the Tudor style to suit her, and how well it worked. Although Linnet was of medium height, the gown made her look taller, and very elegant. Yet there was a youthfulness to it, because of the cut, the tight bodice, the sheer romance of it.

The dress had a square medieval neckline that cleverly came right to the middle of her shoulders, so that they were shown to advantage. The sleeves started narrow but became very wide bells, almost like kimono sleeves, while the skirt was also bell-shaped and fell into a longish train at the back. The bodice above was extremely tight, moulded to Linnet's slender figure, so that it gave her a very narrow waist.

The front of the skirt was cut away to reveal a panel made of the cream Guipure lace, and the same lace lined the inside of the bell-shaped sleeves. The final and most extraordinary touch was the embroidery. The front panel was covered in pearls and crystal beads, as was the Guipure lace lining the sleeves. Bands of tiny crystals and pearls outlined the square neckline, and the outer edges of the sleeves, and the billowing skirt made of the cream Duchesse satin had scatterings of tiny crystal beads all over it.

A single short strand of South Sea pearls encircled her long neck, and there were pearl clusters on her ears. The set was a gift from her parents. The only other piece of jewellery Linnet wore was her engagement ring.

Staring at herself, she shook her head. 'Evan, it's just the most gorgeous dress . . .' Her voice trailed off; words failed her.

'On you, yes, Linnet, because it suits you so well. I told you I was going to turn you into a young Tudor Queen for your wedding, and I have.'

Emsie, twirling around, asked, 'How do *I* look then?'

Linnet smiled indulgently, and was glad she was actually able to say, in all sincerity, 'Beautiful, Emsie, *beautiful*.' Usually Emsie looked somewhat bedraggled and untidy, was careless about her clothes. But this afternoon she did look lovely in the silvery grey-blue watered-taffeta gown all of the attendants were going to wear.

Touching her red-gold hair, Linnet now asked Evan, 'Are you sure my hair's all right, going back like this? Will the headdress sit well?'

'It will, trust me,' Evan replied. 'But don't put it on just yet, I'll do that. *And don't sit down.*'

Linnet laughed. 'Gosh no, I mustn't get all rumpled.' Glancing across at the eighteen-year-old Emsie, she sternly cautioned, 'You'd better not sit down either, my girl.'

There was a sudden loud knock on the door. 'Who is it?' Linnet called.

'Linnet dear, it's Uncle Robin.'

'Oh, don't come in, I don't want you to see me!'

'I'm looking for Evan. I got a message from her.'

'I'm here, Robin. I'm coming.' Hurrying towards the door, Evan said to Linnet, as an afterthought, 'You didn't forget, did you? Something *old*, something *new*, something *borrowed*, something *blue*.'

Linnet nodded. 'I've got all that . . . Emsie remembered, actually.'

'Good for you,' Evan remarked, glancing at the younger girl and went gliding out into the corridor, looking exquisite in her silvery-grey taffeta.

Robin Ainsley was standing waiting near her bedroom door, and she hurried along the corridor, smiling affectionately.

'Hello, Robin, thanks for coming. How did you know I was now ensconced in the Blue Room?'

Bending towards her, he gave her a kiss on the cheek. 'Hello, darling girl,' he said, added, 'Margaret told me you were moved earlier this week, in order to accommodate your parents. But the Blue Room's much nicer than the Yellow Suite, don't you think?' His eyes roamed over her, and he said in a loving voice, 'Oh Evan, how truly lovely you are today. The dress is superb. I do think you've done yourself proud with the design.'

'Thank you.' She gave him a knowing glance and asked, 'I don't look too pregnant, do I?'

'Not really.' His mouth suddenly began to twitch with silent laughter, and he added, 'Only to those of us who know you well and know your condition.'

'Oh God, how awful!'

'Don't say that, it's my great-grandchild you're carrying. However, quite seriously, my dear, your version of the Tudor style helps greatly. Actually, it's rather deceptive; yes, very deceptive indeed.'

'I hoped it would help,' she answered, and couldn't help laughing herself when she remarked, 'What a bride I'm going to make in January. I'll be very big then. Anyway, don't let's stand out here in the corridor. Come on in.'

Moving forward, Evan opened the door of the Blue Room and Robin followed her into the sitting room. Immediately, she hurried over to a chest of drawers, took something out of the top drawer and holding it tightly in her palm came back to Robin, who waited in the middle of the floor.

Evan stood only a few feet away, staring up at him.

'That's a rather appraising look you're giving me.' He regarded her thoughtfully, suddenly frowning. 'Is there something on your mind, Evan?'

'My look was one of admiration, not appraisal. I was thinking how handsome you look in your morning suit, Robin.' She nodded to herself. 'You know something else: you've looked so much better lately, especially since Dad's arrival in Yorkshire in September. Don't *you* think you look better?'

'Yes I do. I feel very fit these days.'

'Certainly you seem less frail,' she added quietly.

'Now Evan, earlier you left a message that you needed to speak to me about something before the wedding. About something very important,' he said urgently, and his eyes went to the clock on the mantelpiece as he explained, 'I'll have to be going quite soon, you know. Your parents and I must arrive at the church well before the bridal party, because of the special seating for the family, and all that security Jack Figg's put in place.'

Evan nodded. 'This won't take too long, but won't you sit down, Robin? *I* can't, because of my dress. I don't want to crush it. But there's no reason for you to stand.'

'I'm perfectly all right, my dear,' he reassured her.

Leaning against the desk in front of the window, Evan said slowly, 'Listen, I've got something interesting to tell you.'

'About what? Or should I say whom?'

'I've unravelled the mystery of Glynnis. Or perhaps I should say I've solved the puzzle . . . I

596

now know *exactly* why Glynnis sent me to London.'

'You do?' Robin Ainsley sounded taken aback and a silver brow shot up quizzically. His clear blue eyes focused on her keenly as he continued, 'Why don't you tell me . . . I would like to hear what's on your mind, Evan dear.'

'Okay, here goes,' she responded. 'Last year, when Gran told me to go to London to find Emma Harte, telling me that Emma was the key to my future, she had only one motive really.'

'And what was that?' he asked.

'I'll get to her motive in a second. Let's first examine Glynnis's method. When she told me to go to London to look for Emma she was absolutely certain I would do so. You might wonder why, so let me explain. I had always done everything she told me from my childhood; she knew she was the biggest influence on my life. Then again, she was well aware I was bored with my job in New York, that I wanted a change. A chance *to fly*, she called it. In other words, she didn't doubt that I would go, especially since she had left me money. However, when she sent me here Glynnis *knew* Emma Harte was dead.' Evan paused, stared hard at Robin, waited for a reaction.

His face revealed nothing; his expression was inscrutable, just like his mother's had frequently been. There was a lot of Emma in Robin.

Taking a deep breath, Evan continued, 'Consider this . . . there was no way Glynnis could have foreseen that I would actually end up getting a job at

Harte's that first day. Or that I would meet Gideon in the corridor and that we would fall in love. Am I right?'

'Yes, you are.'

'Basically, Glynnis had no *guarantee* that any of those things would happen. *None at all.* So her method of getting me to the Hartes, which was important to her, was somewhat convoluted, wouldn't you say?'

'I suppose it was,' Robin agreed, frowning again, looking baffled. Then he suddenly asked, 'So what are you actually getting at?'

'Glynnis, our very clever Glynnis Hughes, apparently wanted to heave *me* into the orbit of the Harte family, as we both know, and before she died she told my mother I would be *irresistible* to them. And by the way, that's something I only recently found out. Still, there wasn't any guarantee I would ever meet a Harte, was there, Robin?'

'No. In fact the way you're putting it now, it was quite unlikely. You could have gone to the store, discovered my mother was dead, and gone away. But you fell in love with the store, at least so you told me.' He paused, nodded his head. 'And so you decided your grandmother had been wandering in her mind that day, dismissed her words about Emma as unimportant, and got yourself a job. All very admirable on your part, but Glynnis didn't know this would happen. Of course you're correct about that, Evan.'

'But she knew that, too, and our very smart Glynnis covered her back, so to speak.'

'How?' he asked, his eyes narrowing keenly, wondering what was coming next.

'When my grandmother was in hospital in New York, last November a year ago, she told my mother to go to her apartment and remove a suitcase of letters. They were letters from your mother, as it turned out. Emma had consistently written to Glynnis over the years, and Glynnis kept the letters . . . just as Emma had kept hers.'

'I see.' Robin walked over to the window and sat down in a wingchair, his eyes thoughtful.

'Glynnis told Mom to give the letters to me, and she impressed upon Mom that I should read them all. She was very insistent about that apparently, and just as insistent that my mother did not show them to my father, or even tell him about them.'

'Really,' Robin muttered. Throwing her a direct look, he asked, 'And did Marietta give you the letters?'

'She did, Robin, but not for a long time. She says her reason for holding onto them was because she wished to give them to me in person, and to relate face to face what Gran had told her when she was in hospital. But, in fact, Mom kept them for a whole year. She says that was because I started working at Harte's in Knightsbridge and got involved with Gideon. She saw no urgency, she says, and decided the letters could wait. After all, I'd done what Glynnis had planned, had hoped would happen . . . I'd fallen right into the middle of the Harte family, and, let's face it, in a very big way.'

'Yes, that's true. But when did your mother actually give you Emma's letters to Glynnis?'

'Last September, after the car crash. She brought them with her when she came up to see me, before she and Dad went back to New York. I read most of them while I was recovering from my broken ankle and rib.'

'I see. And I suppose my mother's letters were revealing perhaps?'

'Oh yes. And I suddenly realized something crucial as I read the letters. It was this . . . if I hadn't met any of you, and if Paula hadn't found out the truth about Glynnis's past, I would still have discovered that you were my father's biological father. *Because of those letters.* That's why Glynnis wanted me to have them. She protected her back, as I said earlier. She wanted me to know the truth about my heritage no matter what.'

'I think you're correct,' Robin admitted, leaning back against the cushions, letting out a small sigh. Somehow he knew now that there was much more coming and he steeled himself.

'That's why she wanted me to go to London . . . to find my heritage.'

'But we've always known that, haven't we?' he answered. 'Or rather, assumed it. However, you are right about your grandmother's method.' Robin shook his head. 'Wouldn't it have been easier to simply tell your father and you the truth when she became so ill? After all, Richard Hughes was already dead. What harm could be done?'

'Glynnis was not from my generation, or my

mother's . . . she came from the old school. She was *afraid* to tell us, most especially Dad. That's what I believe, anyway. She didn't want to disillusion him, to be diminished in his eyes. She was proud, and she loved Dad very much. I guess she was scared – in the way I even was – about revealing the truth to Dad.'

'I understand what you're saying, I do, Evan. And you're right. Your grandmother and I grew up in a different world. A very strictured world where illegitimate children were frowned on.'

'And so Glynnis *set me up*. And left it to Fate with a capital F. Gran was always talking about Fate and Destiny, she believed in those things. Yet she only left it to Fate *partially* . . . because she made sure I would get my hands on those extremely revealing letters from Emma Harte.'

Robin closed his eyes, his silver head resting against the back of the wingchair. In his repose she saw his age more fully. He was, after all, eighty years old, and at this moment he looked it. Her heart went out to him. But after a moment, clearing her throat, Evan said softly, '*Robin.*'

He opened his eyes and promptly sat up. 'I wasn't asleep,' he said with a slight laugh. 'I was just pondering your words.'

She nodded, took a step closer to the chair. 'I worked it all out, you know.' There was a pause, and then Evan finished, 'She was sending me to you, Robin.'

Not a word left his mouth, but his blue eyes turned flinty, and the look he gave her was shrewd.

'Glynnis was so worried about you when she was ill, she needed *me* to come to *you*, and possibly my father, too. But it was mostly me she wanted in London with you.'

'Why do you say all this?' Robin asked, his voice rising slightly.

'Because it's true! Glynnis wanted you to have the grandchild you'd never had, and she didn't want you to be alone either. When she was gone, I mean.'

Robin let out a long sigh. 'Continue,' he said in a low voice.

'You never gave each other up, did you?'

There was a silence. The only sound was the clock ticking.

'No,' he admitted at last. 'No, we didn't.' His voice was resigned.

'You and Glynnis got back together when you were both thirty!' Evan exclaimed. 'And you were together for almost *fifty* years, weren't you?'

'Yes,' Robin answered softly, 'we were, thank God.'

'In your own way you were like a married couple,' Evan went on. 'Glynnis came to London whenever she could, at least several times a year, using any excuse she could think of, and you came to New York and Connecticut. You spent all of your vacations with Glynnis, never with your wife. You came to New York when the House of Commons was in recess, and as often as you could. You were so madly in love with her you would have done anything to get her. Divorced Valerie, given up your political career, anything to be with my grandmother *always*.' Evan gazed at him, her eyes warm.

'But Glynnis loved you so much, Robin, she wouldn't let you do that, ruin yourself in politics. It *was* different in those days, the fifties, and there could have been a scandal about her. And so you . . . *compromised*. That's what she called it . . . *The Compromise*. You stayed in your marriages, so as not to hurt Richard or Valerie. But you loved only each other and you spent as much time together as you could.'

After a few minutes, Robin murmured, 'This is too much –'

'Robin, Robin, *don't!* It's me, your grandchild, out of your loins through my father. I'm not angry or upset, and you mustn't be upset either.'

Drawing closer to him, Evan put her hand on his shoulder, and looked down into his upturned face. 'Glynnis did something else. She left me *your* letters to *her*. Hundreds and hundreds of letters, which you wrote to her for fifty years. She kept them. In fact, she kept everything . . . your Christmas cards, birthday cards, the cards which came with your many gifts to her . . .' Evan broke off, suddenly noticing how stricken he looked.

Bending over him, she murmured in a gentle tone, 'Please don't think I'm criticizing you, or Glynnis. Because I'm not. I'm happy you had each other, that you gave each other so much joy. She loved you with all of her heart, and she was loyal to you all of her life.' Evan's eyes were suddenly very moist and she brushed them with her hand.

When she looked at Robin she saw that tears were rolling down his face and his mouth trembled. After a split second, he said in a slightly quavering voice, 'It's been so hard without her. I wanted to die too . . . until you came to me.'

'I know, I know,' she soothed, her hand on his shoulder. 'I really do understand . . . very few people have a love like yours.'

'Have you read my letters to Glynnis?' he asked, his eyes fastened intently on hers.

'Yes, but not all of them. Mom only gave them to me the other day, when she arrived here from New York for Linnet's wedding. There's a huge suitcase in that cupboard over there, and it's *full* of your letters. There are hundreds and hundreds of them.'

'Did I write so many?' he asked, and unexpectedly smiled at Evan.

She smiled back. 'Oh yes, you did! But I only read some of the recent ones. You saw her a few days before she died, didn't you?'

He nodded. 'How do you know?'

'I found the letter you sent to her in early November last year. You were coming to her. You wanted to bring her back to England. After all, you were both widowed, you could actually be together, could be married –'

'We were married,' he cut in, 'but without the benefit of a piece of paper. I consider Glynnis to be the only wife I ever had.'

604

'I understand,' Evan replied softly. 'But she was suddenly and unexpectedly so ill, wasn't she? And she couldn't travel . . . The last time you saw her was in the hospital in Manhattan.'

Robin could not speak. His grief was palpable. He took out a handkerchief, wiped his eyes, blew his nose, and tried to compose himself, trying hard to bring his swimming senses under control.

When he had recovered himself sufficiently, Evan opened her hand, showed him her palm. 'This is for you, Grandfather.'

She rarely ever called him that, and his eyes widened as he stared up at her.

'It was in a small envelope with your writing on it, Robin. You wrote out an address and a phone number.'

The sight of the latchkey brought a sparkle to his eyes, and the tiredness seemed to slip from his face.

'It's for Edwina's house,' Evan remarked.

'No. Ours. Glynnis's and mine. A lovely old mews in London. I used to borrow it from Edwina, and one day she finally agreed to sell it to me.'

'And you bought it?'

'Yes. For Glynnis. But the deeds have always remained in Edwina's name. If she dies before me, it comes to you through her son Anthony, India's father. If I die first, then it's the same process. The house will be yours, Evan.'

Evan stood looking at him, totally silent, unable to say anything so touched was she.

He said, with a little smile, 'That's where I still

live when I go up to London. It's full of memories
. . . of Glynnis . . . of our years together.' The tears
came again, and he searched for his handkerchief,
wiped his eyes. 'Do forgive a foolish old man, my
dear.'

'There's nothing to forgive,' Evan reassured him,
and began to laugh. 'Look at me, I'm crying too,
and ruining all my make-up. And it's Linnet's
wedding in an hour.'

'I'm very aware of that. I must go and find your
father.'

'Your son, Robin, your son by Glynnis.'

Nodding, he gave her the benefit of a huge smile.
'We loved each other so much, and we pulled it
off, you know. All those years we pulled it off,
Evan, and we never hurt anybody.'

I wonder about that, Evan thought, then pushed
the thought away.

He handed her the latchkey. 'It was Glynnis's. I
gave it to her. And now it's yours, Evan. Take it.'

She did, and then walked with him to the door.
'I'll drive over next week with the suitcase of your
letters,' she told him. 'But I wonder . . . could I
keep some of the photographs? The two of you
were so gorgeous when you were young, you
looked like movie stars.'

'*Glynnis*. Not I,' he protested.

'Yes, you too. Anyway, I'll bring your letters
over to Lackland Priory.'

'*No*. Glynnis wanted you to have them, and you
should.' Robin stared into her blue-grey eyes, and
added, 'If you wish, I will give you Glynnis's letters

to me. She wrote to me every week from 1950 until her last year.' He paused, and the look he gave her was odd, even worried, before he added softly, 'But I think they might be a little . . . *hot*, shall we say.'

Evan burst out laughing. 'I'll bet! Because some of yours certainly are! *Red hot*.' Her eyes were sparkling as she went on, 'And why not? Yours was quite a love story, incredible really, Robin.'

Now she came into his outstretched arms and he held her close to him, thinking how like his Glynnis she was sometimes. 'Glynnis was so worried about dying on me, leaving me on my own. We weren't together all the time, but what we had over all those years was something really quite . . . *magnificent*. Magnificent.'

CHAPTER THIRTY-FOUR

T he lovely little stone church in the village of Pennistone Royal was ancient, dating back over nine hundred years to the time of the first Norman kings of England.

Its square Norman tower was original, but the glorious stained-glass windows were later, having been put in only two hundred years ago.

For the entire time she had lived at Pennistone Royal, Emma Harte had paid for all of the restoration work the church required, and Paula was now following in her grandmother's footsteps. In consequence, the church was beautifully kept both inside and out, and was a local treasure.

On this Saturday afternoon, the first day of December, the weather was cold. But there was no wind and the sky was ice-blue and cloudless. The orb of the sun was pale, but it *was* shining, and the day was pristine, bright with that clarity of light so peculiar to these Northern climes.

Robin alighted from one of the first wedding cars to arrive at the church, and he helped

Marietta out, looking extremely smart in a dark-red silk outfit of a long, slender skirt to her ankles and a trim, fitted jacket embroidered with jet beads. Once Owen joined them they walked up to the church.

The entire village had turned out for Linnet's marriage to Julian, despite the coldness of the day; bundled up in warm clothes, they stood around in groups; hands waved enthusiastically, familiar faces broke into smiles as Robin was instantly recognized.

He had grown up in Pennistone Royal and was very popular. He waved back, smiled, and escorted Marietta and Owen along the church path.

Continuing to glance around, he spotted a number of faces he did not know: men in dark suits with earpieces and small microphones in their lapels. He knew at once they were Jack Figg's men, his operatives. *Security*.

As they drew closer to the porch, Robin suddenly noticed Jack hovering on the steps, dressed in a grey top hat and morning suit. He was a guest at the wedding, since he was like a member of the family, but he *was* head of security again, took his job seriously. Now he was scanning the crowds intently, his eyes everywhere.

Jack's face broke into smiles when he saw Robin. The two men shook hands warmly, and Jack greeted Marietta and Owen, whom he had met the night before at the dinner given by Paula and Shane.

Robin drew much closer to Jack, and said in a low voice, 'I see you've got good security in place.'

Jack murmured, 'I've got more men here than there are barnacles clinging to the hull of a ship. But Paula wanted it, and I aim to please, old chap.'

'Jonathan wouldn't dare attempt anything,' Robin said, the spectre of his other son rising up. He clamped down on it.

'I agree, but Paula's fearful of him, and especially today of all days. It's better to go overboard,' Jack explained, 'than to have too few men on hand. But they'll be invisible for the most part, especially in church and at the reception later. Don't worry, nothing's going to happen,' he finished in a reassuring voice, and then added, 'I'll join you inside shortly.'

Jack Figg stepped away from the porch, moved onto the grass, headed towards the graveyard. As he did so there was a tiny crackle of noise in his earpiece and Chris Light's voice came in. 'Jack, there's a white van coming down the hill from Lackland village. It's got to be the yobbos we were warned about.'

'Right, Chris. Move in. *Now*. Block the road with our cars and bring in the cavalry. Block the other roads leading into Pennistone village. I don't want any slip-ups. Keep them out of the village and alert the police. If they won't leave we'll have them arrested.'

'You've got it, Jack,' Chris exclaimed.

Standing alone in the middle of the graveyard, Jack Figg thanked God that Mark Longden had a streak of humanity in him. If Longden had not had the good sense to alert him about Jonathan Ainsley's wild talk in Paris in September, they might have had a tragedy on their hands today. A church burning to the ground and killing everyone inside. Including Longden's child, Adele. Obviously aware of possible danger to the little girl, Longden had made that crucial phone call and Jack was fully prepared. For anything. And anybody. Security was in place everywhere.

Lorne Fairley and Desmond O'Neill, Linnet's brothers, were two of the ushers who greeted Robin, Marietta and Owen when they finally entered the church. They showed them to the pew on the bride's family side of the aisle, and after a few words the two young men departed to take care of other guests now walking in.

'It's breathtaking,' Marietta whispered to Robin and Owen as she glanced around the charming little church. 'Just extraordinary.'

'It's Evan's floral design,' Robin whispered back. 'She's very talented, don't you think?'

'I'll say she is,' Owen murmured, taking everything in, a proud look crossing his face as he thought of his daughter's creative gifts.

There were great banks of white orchids everywhere, and in various areas and corners of the church small leafless trees stood in smart white tubs. The trees had been painted white, and from their branches hung nosegays of delicate white flowers held in small silver-lace ruffs, following through the Elizabethan theme. Throughout the church were huge vases of white tulips, carnations and jonquils, as well as hundreds of white candles, from tall, slender tapers to votives in little glass pots. Like every other person in the church, Robin was struck by the beauty of the flowers set amidst the flickering candlelight . . . it harked back to medieval times.

Suddenly a burst of sunlight flooded in through the stained-glass windows, and he thought they looked like shimmering jewelled panels set high in the ancient stone walls. This little church, which he had known since he was a boy, was the most beautiful setting for a wedding, and he silently vowed that his only grandchild Evan would be married to Gideon here next month. And it would be a wedding as breathtakingly beautiful as this. She deserved no less.

More of his family began to arrive, and went into the pew in front of him. Edwina, his favourite, was regal as always in an outfit of royal purple, a colour she always seemed to choose for special events. She glanced at him, smiled, then winked, and nodded at her escort. It was Russell Rhodes, the artist, looking handsome, if a little pugnacious, in his morning suit.

Robin was delighted that he was present this afternoon; he had warmed to Dusty last night when he had met him for the first time. Evan had confided that India had made up with him and that all was well between them. Dusty had obviously been welcomed into the family with open arms; he was seated next to India's mother Sally, who was looking elegant in deep blue. Anthony Standish,

India's father, turned around, smiled at Robin, nodded to Owen and Marietta, then said something to Edwina, his mother.

Robin saw Sir Ronald Kallinski, Julian's grandfather, coming up the aisle, accompanied by his son Michael, and Michael's ex-wife Valentine, Julian's parents.

A moment or two later, Robin's twin sister Elizabeth walked in on the arm of her husband of many years, Marc Deboyne. Although she was the same age as Robin, she looked much younger than eighty, and he noticed how chic she was in a tailored midnight-blue silk dress and coat.

She whispered her greetings to Robin as she hurried to her pew, followed by her daughter Emily, granddaughter Natalie and Winston. Emily was in a plum-coloured floor-length suit, her daughter in amethyst silk, and both of them gave him a small wave when they spotted him.

Within fifteen minutes the church had begun to fill up, and as he saw Paula walking up the aisle to the front pew, accompanied by her mother Daisy and Grandfather Bryan O'Neill, he knew the bride could not be far behind.

Robin had always admired Paula's ability to be a businesswoman, a wife and mother, and to somehow manage to look like a world-class model at the same time. Fifty-six years old, she seemed more like forty, and she was elegance personified in a dark fir-green velvet sleeveless coat, which came to her ankles, and was worn over a matching fir-green dress with lace sleeves. His mother's famous emeralds blazed on Paula's ears, and she wore Blackie's emerald bow pinned on the shoulder of the coat.

Daisy, his youngest sister, was dressed in gold lace, and her face broke into a smile when she glanced at Robin before walking to the first pew with her daughter.

'So many people, so many friends,' Marietta whispered to Robin. 'Heavens to Betsy, it's some crowd! Well, at least Evan's wedding won't be the same – much smaller, I guess.'

Robin chuckled quietly, shook his head. 'There aren't that many friends here . . . what I mean is, not too many outsiders. Almost everyone here is called Harte, O'Neill or Kallinski. It'll be the same group at Evan's marriage to Gideon, I can assure you of that.' As he spoke he looked around, saw so many Hartes he hadn't set eyes on for years, he was quite surprised. Wasn't that Amanda with her twin Francesca? And surely that was Sarah Lowther with Yves, her French husband, and their daughter Chloe. Goodness me, what a family, he thought. My mother and her brothers spawned quite a troop.

There was a sudden little flurry of activity, and peering ahead Robin realized that the choirboys were now filing in, and ten minutes after this he saw Julian arriving with his best man, Gideon. The two of them stood near the altar, the bridegroom waiting for his bride.

Robin thought that both young men looked composed, ready for anything. And next month

Gideon would be standing in the same spot waiting at the altar for Evan to arrive on the arm of Owen. His son. His granddaughter.

Then all of a sudden, before Robin could blink, the organist began to play the wedding march from Wagner's *Lohengrin*, and it rang out gloriously, rising to the rafters.

Everyone turned around. Here she came, the bride . . . In her cream gown in the Tudor style, Linnet looked beautiful and regal as she slowly walked up the aisle, holding onto the arm of her father Shane.

'Her gown's magnificent,' Marietta whispered to Robin, and he nodded in agreement. There was no other word to describe it, Marietta was right.

On her burnished red hair Linnet wore a simple diamond tiara to hold her delicate tulle veil in place, and Robin recognized it as his mother's. His eyes were riveted to her face . . . she resembled Emma so much, looked the way she must have when she was the same age.

Behind the bride followed her attendants in their billowing taffeta gowns: Linnet's sisters, Tessa and Emsie; then came India and Evan, and finally, all alone and walking as sedately as she could manage, came little Adele. She was a miniature version of the older bridesmaids and her mother Tessa, the matron of honour.

Robin smiled, and he felt everyone else smile when they saw this most beautiful blonde child, carrying her nosegay of flowers in the silver ruff so carefully. Her pretty face was solemn, her steps dainty, as the occasion merited. A Fairley, he thought. She looks like a Fairley; no doubt about where *she* sprang from.

For Robin Ainsley the ceremony passed as if he were in a dream, memories of long ago crowding his mind, thoughts of his wonderful Glynnis uppermost. How he missed her, still longed for her. And yet they had been so lucky; they had had so much, more than most. His thoughts turned to Evan. How clever she was, the way she had fathomed out everything for herself, although she'd had a great deal of help from Glynnis. He smiled to himself. Glynnis had wanted him to have Owen and Evan in the end, when she was gone. She had always felt guilty about keeping him away from his son. But Robin knew this was because she had not wanted to ruin the relationship Owen had with Richard Hughes. She had been right, as she usually was.

Yet he knew there was another reason. Glynnis had needed their grandchild to know who she was, what her heritage was, and that was why she had made sure Evan would receive all those letters. Letters that told their own story. And that was all right, too. Whatever Glynnis did had always been all right with him.

Robin's head came up suddenly as the music intruded. His heart squeezed and squeezed as the choirboys began to sing *O Perfect Love*, such a favourite of Glynnis's, and an anthem he loved himself. He thought the choirboys had wondrous voices, and drawing closer to Marietta he said softly, 'They sound like angels singing, don't you think? So pure.'

She touched his arm, nodded, loving this man for his great sensitivity and kindness, and his enormous generosity of spirit. No wonder her mother-in-law had been so very much in love with him for all those years.

When the bride and groom returned from signing the register they came walking down the aisle arm in arm, smiling and joyous, stepping out to the strains of Mendelssohn's Wedding March.

Slowly all of the guests left the church, following behind the loving couple, and when Robin stepped outside the church he couldn't help smiling at the scene. It was matchless. Snowflakes and flower petals blowing in the breeze. A radiant Linnet clinging to Julian's arm. The two of them laughing as they were driven off. Sitting in the wedding car beribboned in white silk bows. Old boots and cans tied to the boot, rattling loudly, making everyone chuckle at the incongruity.

The three of them stood in a corner of the big library: Tessa, India and Evan. All around them swirled the guests, drinking champagne, eating canapés, and having a wonderful time. A small trio played background music, and guests waved and smiled at them, but although they waved back the three young women remained aloof, waiting for their beaus to join them.

Tessa said, 'Come on, tell us about it, Evan. What was the big secret you discovered about Robin and your Granny?'

'She was never a *granny*,' Evan laughed, and took a glass of orange juice from a passing waiter. 'But let's wait until our men get here.'

'I've got something to tell you in the meantime,' India murmured softly, 'but we must keep it a secret between the three of us. I don't want Linnet to know, because she'll make a fuss about it tonight, and that wouldn't be right.'

'So tell us quickly, whilst she and Julian are having their photographs taken,' Tessa instructed, taking a swallow of champagne.

India smiled. 'Dusty and I are going to get engaged next week, whilst my parents are still here from Ireland. They think he's fabulous, and he's very taken with them. So there's no problem.'

'Congratulations,' Evan said. 'I know you don't want to steal any of Linnet's thunder today; that's so nice of you.'

India gave a little shrug. 'I never thought we would get it together, but he's been so abject and unhappy and apologetic about the Melinda mess. Edwina told me to stop squawking, grow up and marry him.'

Tessa grinned. 'She's such a card! And congratulations, India darling.'

Evan looked over at Tessa intently, and announced, 'I like your Jean-Claude. He's fascinating, and Gideon was very taken with him last night at the dinner. So tell us quickly, before they arrive, is he going to become a member of the family, too?'

Tessa blushed. 'I hope so. Actually, he's proposed. But I have to get the divorce yet. When Great-Aunt Edwina met him earlier this week she actually told me, in front of him no less, to grab him fast before another woman did. Can you believe that!'

'She's incorrigible, that granny of mine,' India exclaimed and began to laugh.

Tessa also laughed. '*She's* no granny either! Oh look, our chaps are heading this way.' Tessa moved her head slightly, began to wave.

Gideon, Dusty, Jean-Claude and Lorne strolled over, each nursing a glass of champagne. It was Lorne who said, 'Why are the three beauties huddled in the corner? Are you in hiding? Gosh, the three of you should be circulating, shouldn't you?'

'Oh phooey,' Tessa answered. 'Anyway, we were waiting for you to get here. Evan discovered something about her grandmother and Uncle Robin, and –'

'But we all know that story!' Lorne interrupted. 'It's been circulating in the family ever since Ma found out about their love affair during the war.'

'Oh, but there's something else, isn't there, Evan?' India said.

Evan nodded. 'Yes, there is. I'll try and make this short. I'll cut to the chase as fast as I can. My mother brought me a package of letters from Emma Harte to my grandmother, and also letters from Robin to Glynnis, and you'll never guess –'

'Oh do tell us, darling,' Gideon interrupted. 'It sounds very romantic.'

'I will, if you'll stop interrupting me,' Evan responded. Leaning against the window frame she told them about Glynnis and Robin and the years they had spent together.

Everyone listened attentively, but Jean-Claude was the first one to make a remark. 'But what a *magnificent* love story. Unbelievable!' Tessa put her arm through his, and responded, 'Yes, it is, and certainly a story a Frenchman like you would appreciate.'

They all laughed, and then Gideon, frowning, asked Evan, 'How the hell did they manage it? I mean manage not to get caught?'

'They were careful,' Evan told him, 'and they lived in different countries part of the year. I guess that helped and they made it work.'

'I bet they had an accomplice,' Dusty pointed out softly. 'They had to have had help at some time or another. Nobody can do that, not without a third person to give them cover.'

'Emma!' Gideon said, looking at Evan, his eyes fixed on hers. 'Did *Emma* know? Was *she* their accomplice?'

'I wouldn't exactly call her that, Gid. But our great-grandmother did know they'd started their affair again. Eventually. After it had been going on for a couple of years, in fact. Since she knew she was unable to stop it, I guess she decided to help them.'

'I'll be damned,' Lorne said, astonishment crossing his face.

Gideon also looked surprised. 'How old were they when they started up again?'

'They were both thirty. And they hadn't seen each other for seven years. Imagine that. But they were hot stuff,' she said, shaking her head, laughing.

'How long were they together?' Jean-Claude asked, intrigued.

'Fifty years, just about,' Evan told them all.

'*Mon Dieu*!' Jean-Claude looked at Tessa, and added, 'That was some love affair. I'd like to meet that gentleman again. Come, Tessa, let us seek out your Great-Uncle Robin. He must be . . . rather unique.'

'Oh he is! He sure is,' Gideon called after them.

'It's so sad she died,' India said, 'especially since they were both widowed ultimately. They could have been married.'

Dusty said, 'Isn't that your mother, isn't she beckoning to us?'

India followed his gaze. 'Oh yes, I suppose Grandmother wants us to join her. She's fallen for you, Dusty.'

'And I'm crazy about her,' he replied, leading India across the library.

Lorne bent over, gave Evan a kiss on her cheek. 'It's an extraordinary story, it truly is . . . remarkable. I wish I could find someone to love like that. Oh well, I'll go and look around. Maybe one of Linnet's girlfriends might strike my fancy.'

Evan and Gideon laughed, and Evan linked her arm through Gideon's as they watched the handsome young actor saunter off. And then Gideon stared down at her and asked softly, 'Do *you* guarantee *me* fifty years, Evan?'

Gazing up into his face, that face she had come to love so much in the past year, she nodded. 'I guarantee you *forever*, Gideon Harte. I promise I'll be with you all the days of my life.'

The Woman of Substance:

The Life and Work of Barbara Taylor Bradford

Piers Dudgeon with Barbara Taylor Bradford

For the first time ever, a fascinating look at the remarkable life of Barbara Taylor Bradford. From the cobbled streets of Yorkshire to the sweeping avenues of Manhattan, Barbara's own story is as dramatic a tale as any one of her bestsellers.

From humble beginnings, the only daughter of a labourer and a domestic servant, success was something that had to be grafted for. From an early age, however, her mother Freda had marked her daughter out for glory – at any cost.

This drive, ambition and desire to triumph instilled in her was to reap huge dividends when she took first the *Yorkshire Post* and then Fleet Street by storm. But her biggest achievement was undeniably *A Woman of Substance* which was to transform her life beyond measure.

Here, for the first time, Piers Dudgeon unearths amazing parallels in the lives of Barbara's fictional characters and her real-life family. More remarkable still is that he has discovered astonishing family secrets which Barbara herself was previously completely unaware of yet which still managed to make their way into her novels. In this incredible story, fact and fiction exist side by side and art unwittingly imitates life.

The Woman of Substance is a unique collaboration, the first time that Barbara Taylor Bradford has participated in a memoir of any kind, and one that has turned out to be as much of a shock to her as it will certainly be to her many fans.

ISBN 0-00-716568-4

Emma's Secret

Barbara Taylor Bradford

The legendary Emma Harte, heroine of *A Woman of Substance*, returns . . .

At the centre of this sweeping family saga stands Paula O'Neill, beloved granddaughter of Emma and the guardian of her vast business empire. Paula believes all that Emma left to the family is secure. However, beneath the surface sibling rivalry and discontent flare.

Into this volatile mix walks Evan Hughes, a young American fashion designer. She is looking for Emma Harte. But Emma has been dead for thirty years. And Evan bears an uncanny resemblance to Paula O'Neill.

Troubled by Evan's presence, Paula turns to Emma's recently discovered wartime diaries to find the truth . . .

The decades fall away. It is London in the Blitz. Emma Harte comes vividly back to life, accompanied by Blackie O'Neill and David Kallinski. Emma is holding her family together as bombs drop, sirens wail and her sons go off to war. As she struggles with her grief, her indomitability, willpower and strength come to the fore.

As the pages unfurl, Paula discovers the secret Emma Harte took to the grave to protect others. Its repercussions irrevocably change lives.

Emma's Secret is vintage Barbara Taylor Bradford. Emotion, drama, suspense, intrigue and passion fill the pages in a spellbinding novel which only she could write.

ISBN 0 00 226135 9